POKÉMON™ ADVENTURES

GOLD & SILVER

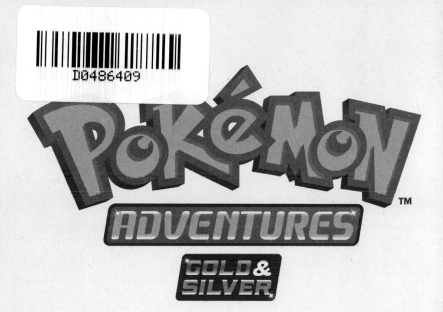

Pokémon ADVENTURES
Volume 13
Perfect Square Edition

Story by HIDENORI KUSAKA
Art by SATOSHI YAMAMOTO

© 2011 The Pokémon Company International.
© 1995-2011 Nintendo/Creatures Inc./GAME FREAK inc.
TM, ®, and character names are trademarks of Nintendo.
POCKET MONSTERS SPECIAL Vol. 13
by Hidenori KUSAKA, Satoshi YAMAMOTO
© 1997 Hidenori KUSAKA, Satoshi YAMAMOTO
All rights reserved.
Original Japanese edition published by SHOGAKUKAN.
English translation rights in the United States of America, Canada, the
United Kingdom, Ireland, Australia and New Zealand arranged with SHOGAKUKAN.

English Adaptation/Gerard Jones
Translation/HC Language Solutions
Touch-up & Lettering/Annaliese Christman
Design/Sam Elzway
Editor/Annette Roman

Printed in the U.S.A.

Published by VIZ Media, LLC
P.O. Box 77010
San Francisco, CA 94107

10
First printing, June 2011
Tenth printing, December 2016

PARENTAL ADVISORY
POKÉMON ADVENTURES
is rated A and is suitable
for readers of all ages.
ratings.viz.com

PERFECT SQUARE

www.perfectsquare.com   www.viz.com

Pokémon™ Adventures

Gold & Silver

13 Volume Thirteen

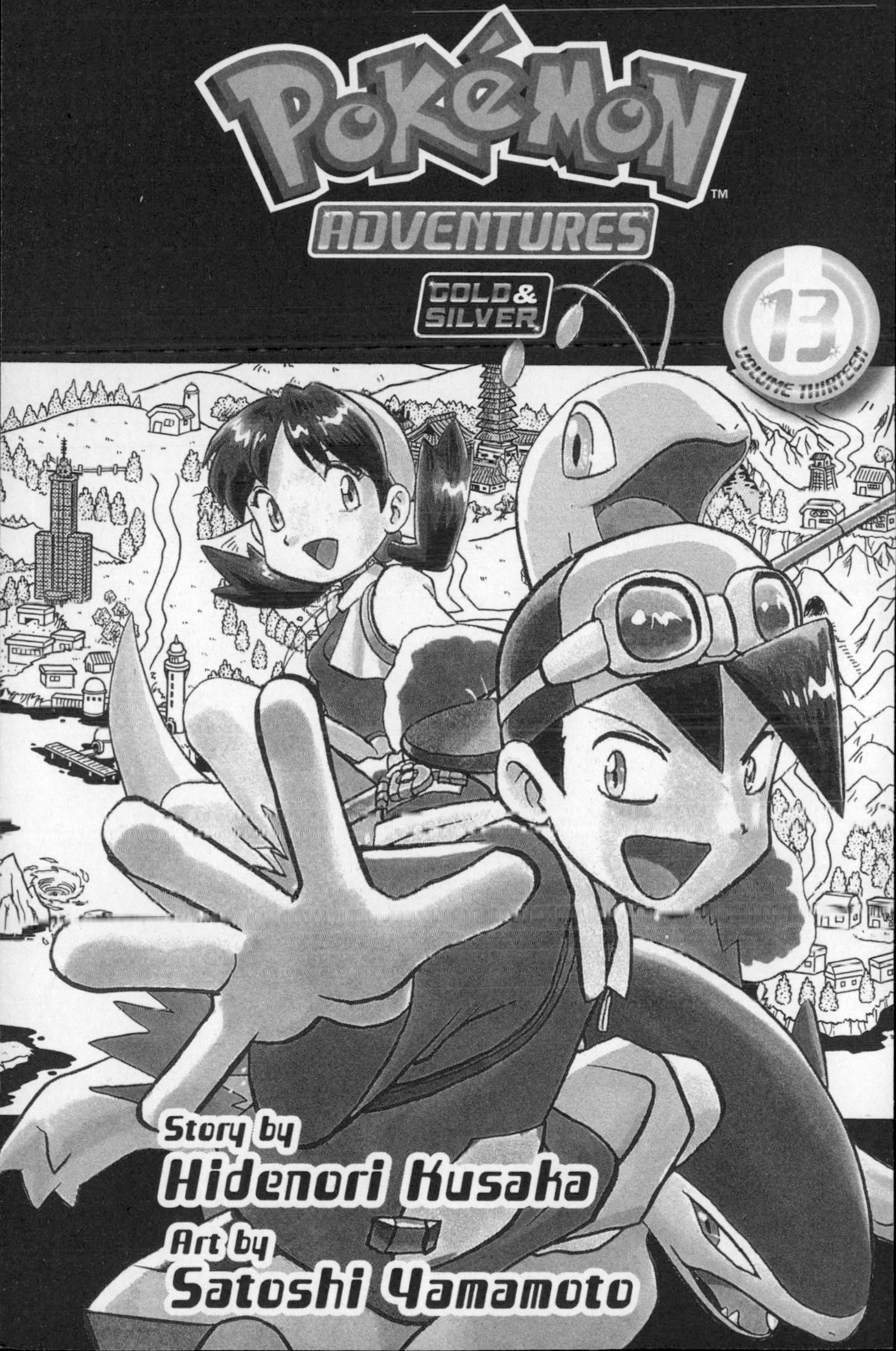

Story by
Hidenori Kusaka
Art by
Satoshi Yamamoto

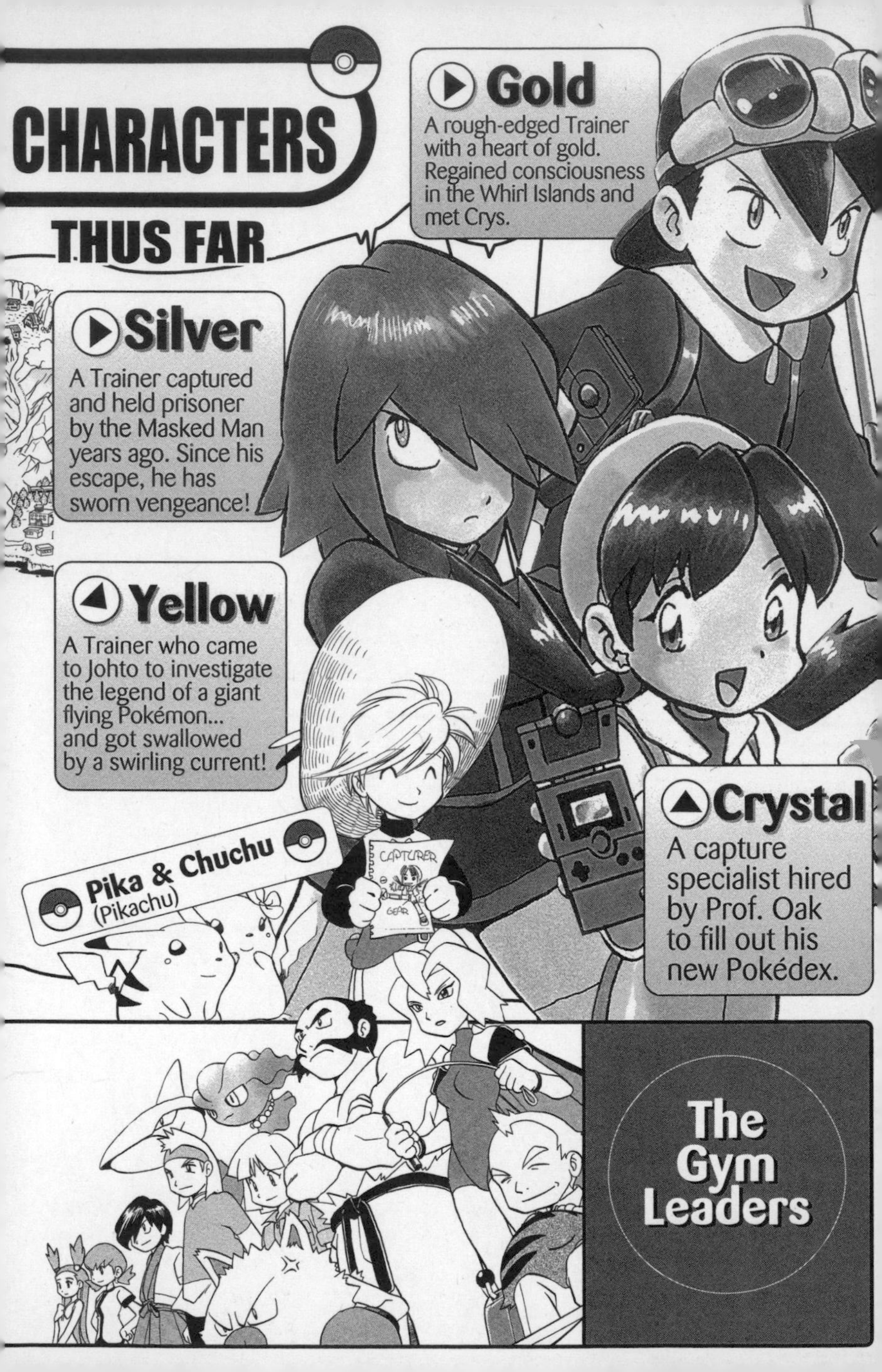
CHARACTERS
THUS FAR
Gold
A rough-edged Trainer with a heart of gold. Regained consciousness in the Whirl Islands and met Crys.
Silver
A Trainer captured and held prisoner by the Masked Man years ago. Since his escape, he has sworn vengeance!
Yellow
A Trainer who came to Johto to investigate the legend of a giant flying Pokémon... and got swallowed by a swirling current!
Pika & Chuchu
(Pikachu)
CAPTURER GEAR
Crystal
A capture specialist hired by Prof. Oak to fill out his new Pokédex.
The Gym Leaders

MAIN

THE JOURNEY

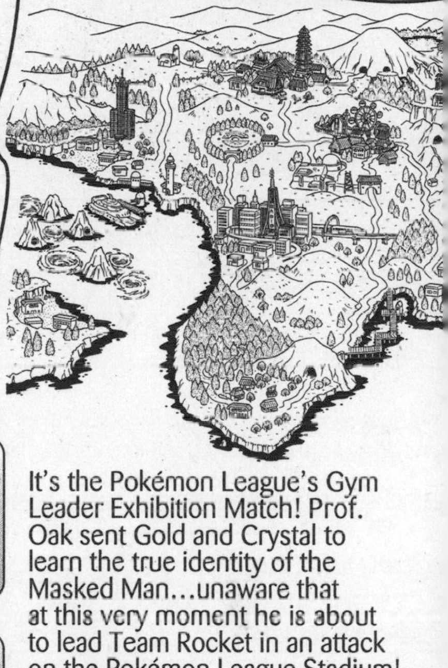

It's the Pokémon League's Gym Leader Exhibition Match! Prof. Oak sent Gold and Crystal to learn the true identity of the Masked Man…unaware that at this very moment he is about to lead Team Rocket in an attack on the Pokémon League Stadium!

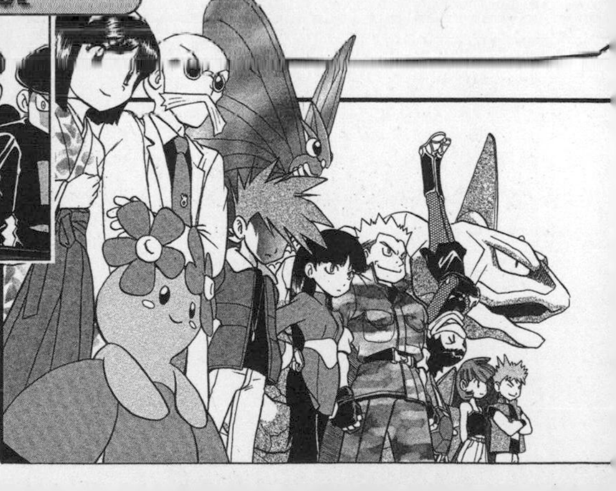

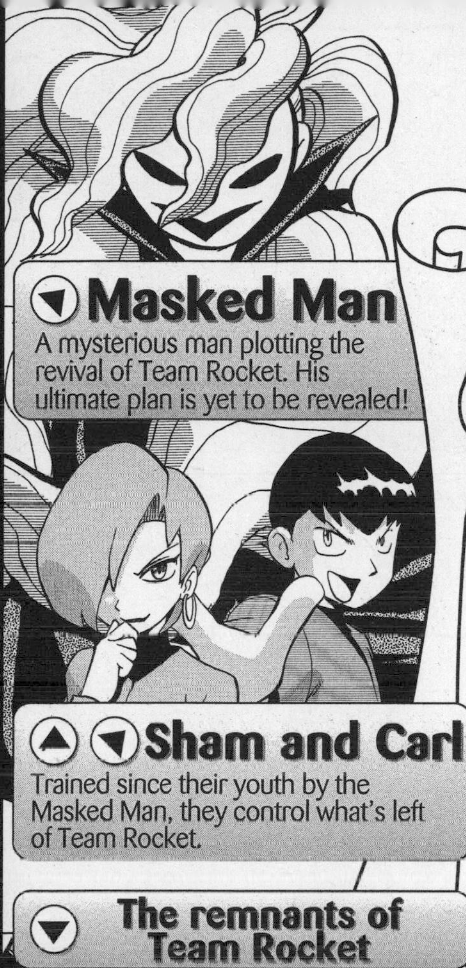

Masked Man

A mysterious man plotting the revival of Team Rocket. His ultimate plan is yet to be revealed!

Sham and Carl

Trained since their youth by the Masked Man, they control what's left of Team Rocket.

The remnants of Team Rocket

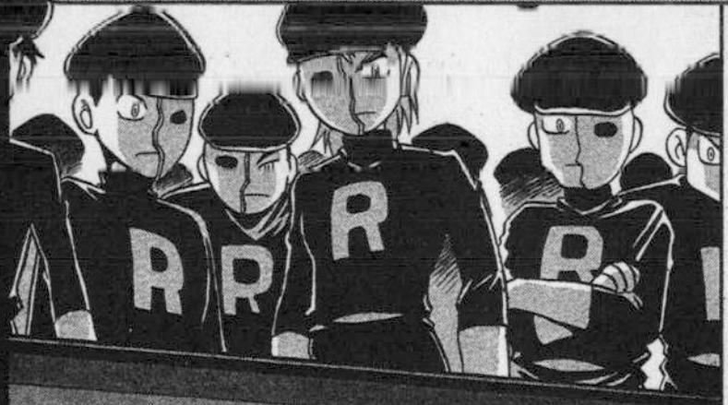
R
R
R
R

CONTENTS

RAIKOU

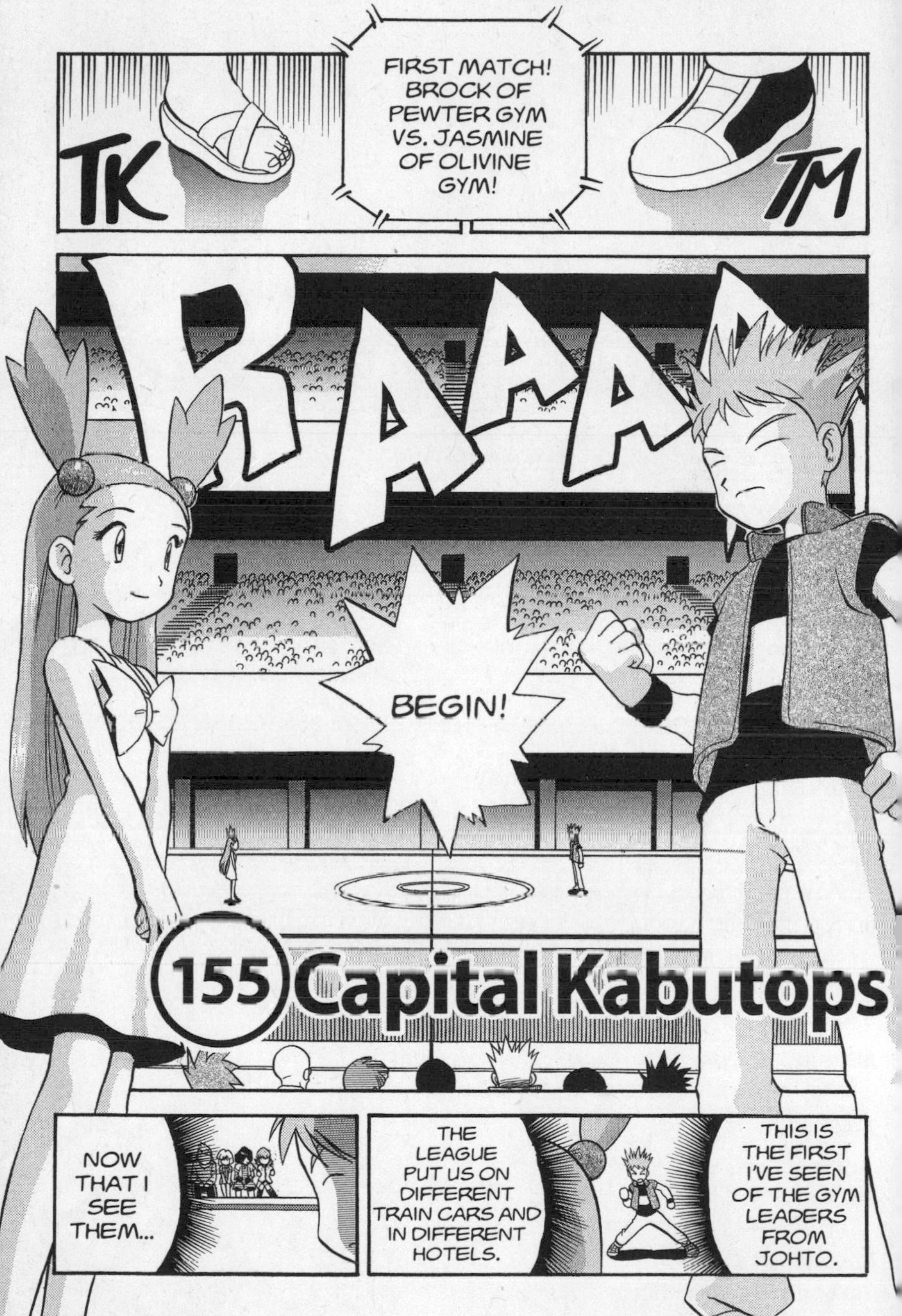
TM
FIRST MATCH! BROCK OF PEWTER GYM VS. JASMINE OF OLIVINE GYM!
TK
RAAA
BEGIN!
155 Capital Kabutops
THIS IS THE FIRST I'VE SEEN OF THE GYM LEADERS FROM JOHTO.
THE LEAGUE PUT US ON DIFFERENT TRAIN CARS AND IN DIFFERENT HOTELS.
NOW THAT I SEE THEM...

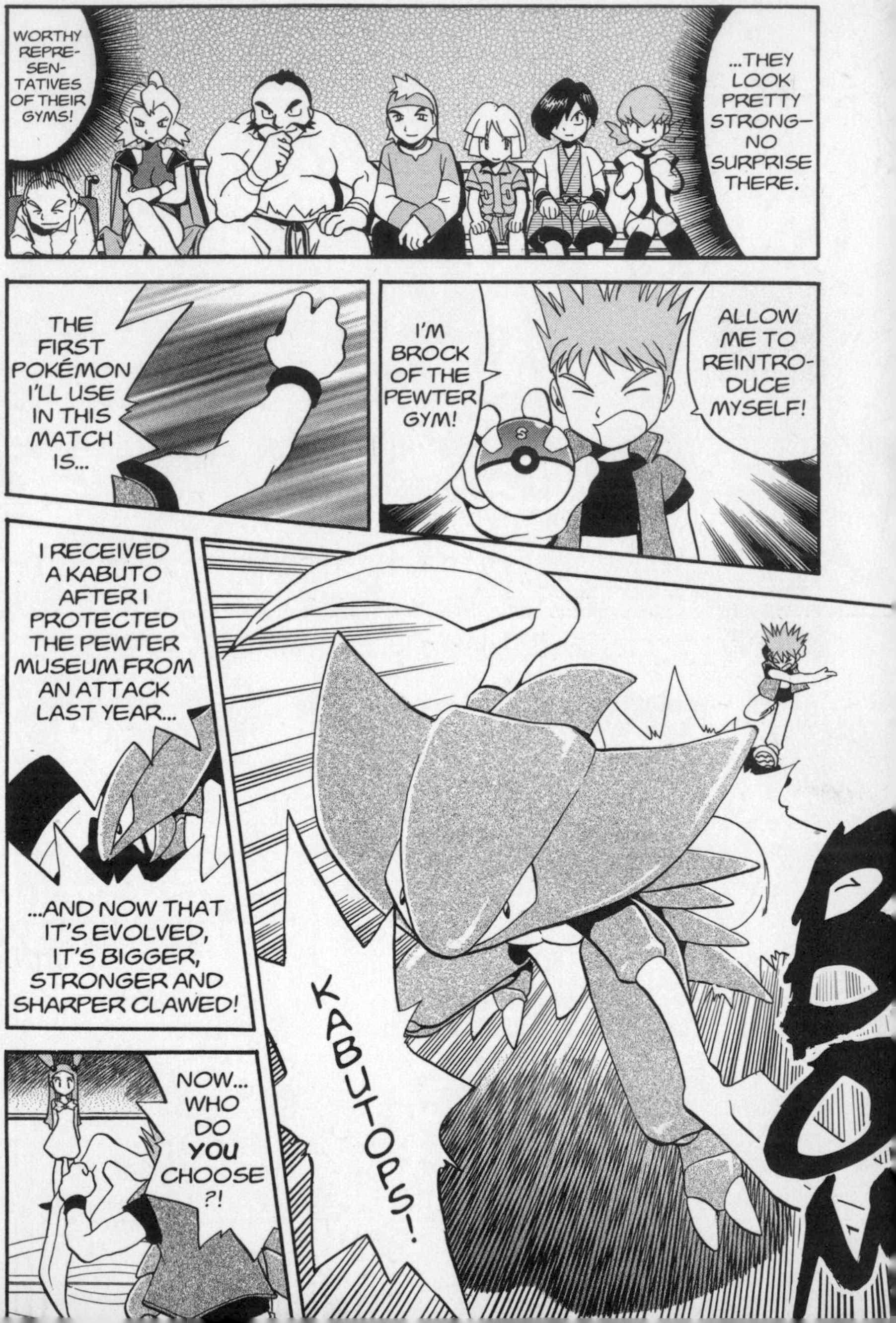
...THEY LOOK PRETTY STRONG—NO SURPRISE THERE.
WORTHY REPRESENTATIVES OF THEIR GYMS!
ALLOW ME TO REINTRODUCE MYSELF!
I'M BROCK OF THE PEWTER GYM!
THE FIRST POKÉMON I'LL USE IN THIS MATCH IS...
KABUTOPS!
I RECEIVED A KABUTO AFTER I PROTECTED THE PEWTER MUSEUM FROM AN ATTACK LAST YEAR...
...AND NOW THAT IT'S EVOLVED, IT'S BIGGER, STRONGER AND SHARPER CLAWED!
NOW... WHO DO YOU CHOOSE?!

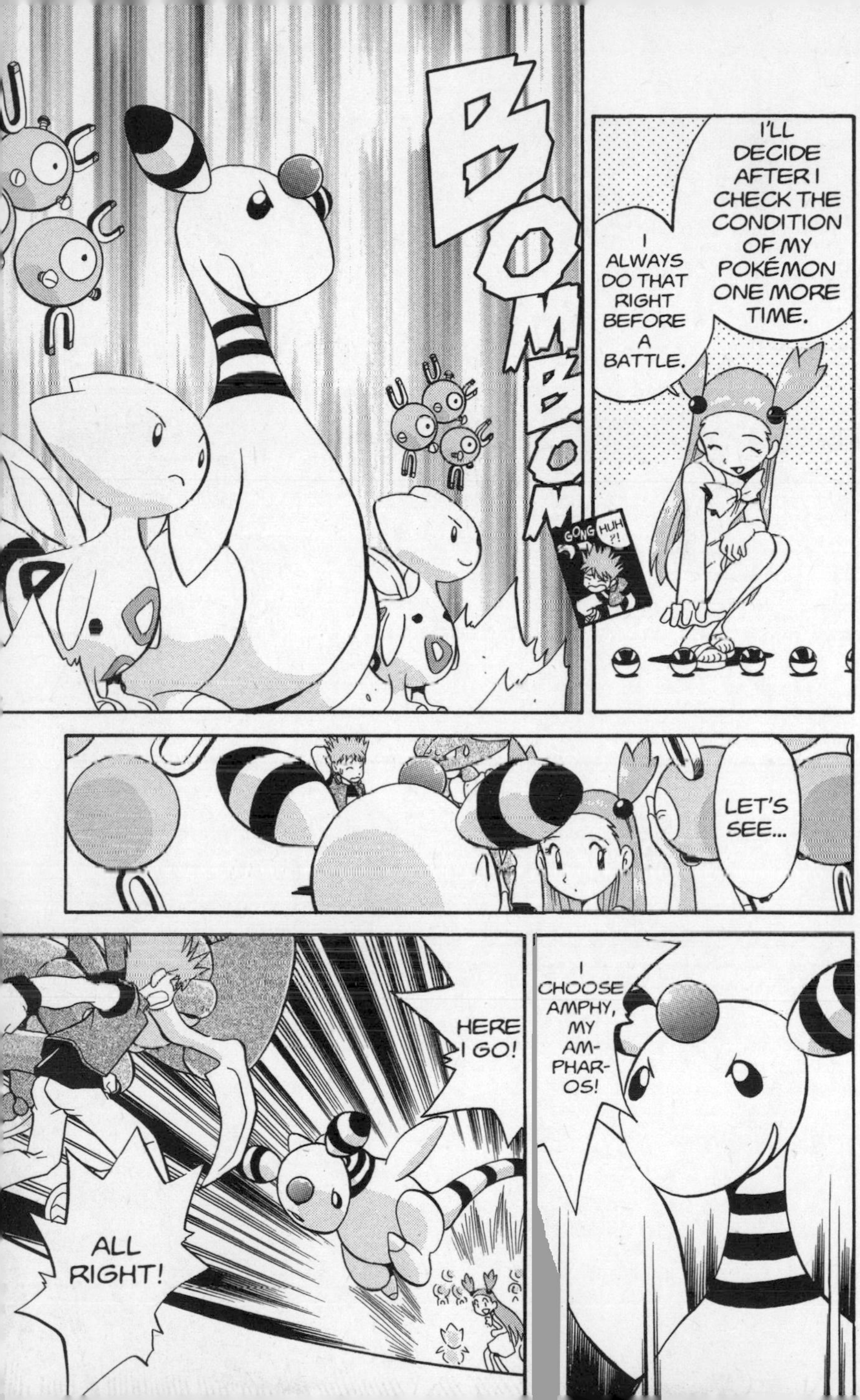
I'LL DECIDE AFTER I CHECK THE CONDITION OF MY POKÉMON ONE MORE TIME.
I ALWAYS DO THAT RIGHT BEFORE A BATTLE.
GONG
HUH ?!
BOMBOM
LET'S SEE...
I CHOOSE AMPHY, MY AMPHAR-OS!
HERE I GO!
ALL RIGHT!

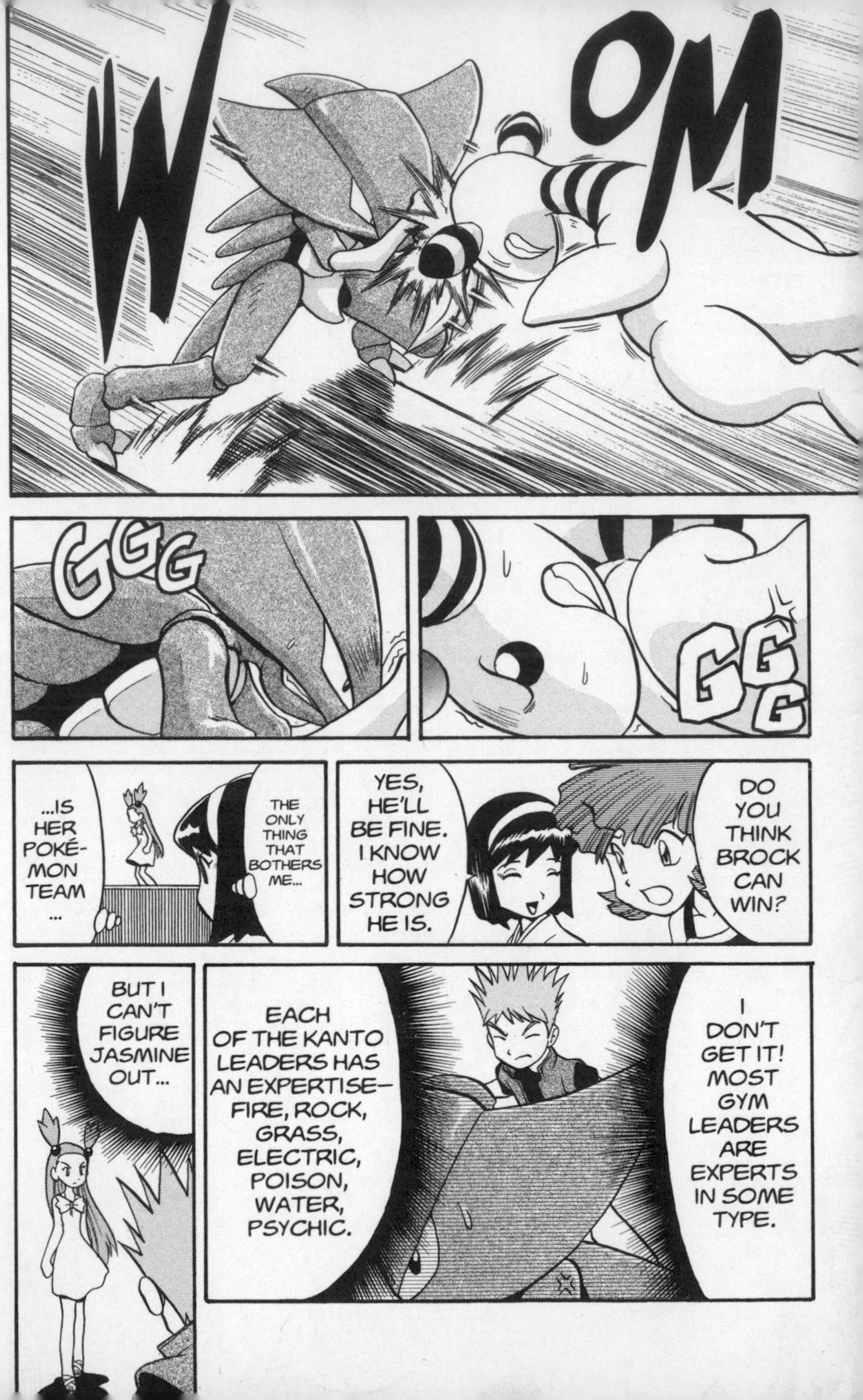
WOM
GGG
GGG
DO YOU THINK BROCK CAN WIN?
YES, HE'LL BE FINE. I KNOW HOW STRONG HE IS.
THE ONLY THING THAT BOTHERS ME...
...IS HER POKÉMON TEAM...
I DON'T GET IT! MOST GYM LEADERS ARE EXPERTS IN SOME TYPE.
EACH OF THE KANTO LEADERS HAS AN EXPERTISE—FIRE, ROCK, GRASS, ELECTRIC, POISON, WATER, PSYCHIC.
BUT I CAN'T FIGURE JASMINE OUT...

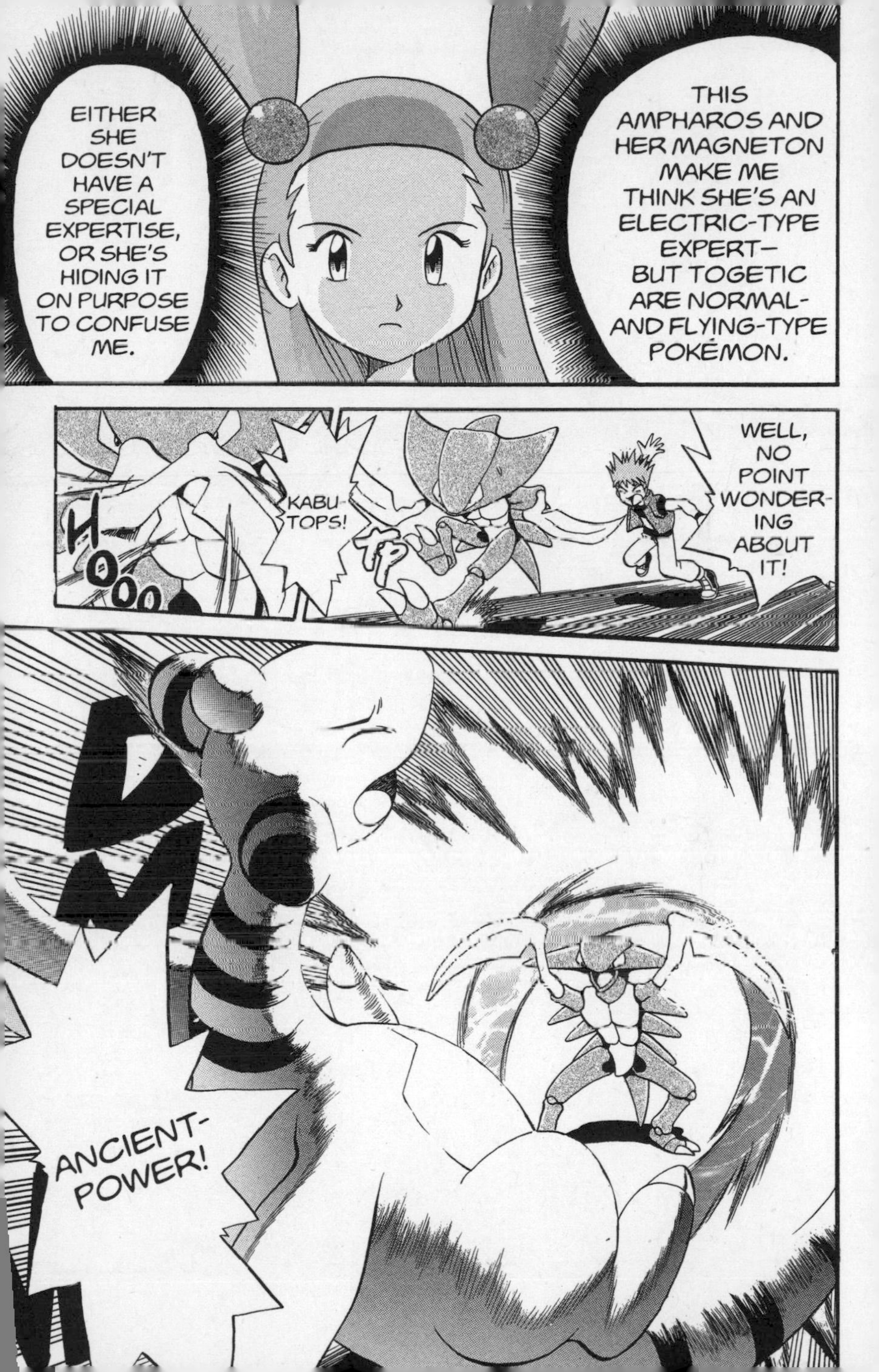
THIS AMPHAROS AND HER MAGNETON MAKE ME THINK SHE'S AN ELECTRIC-TYPE EXPERT—BUT TOGETIC ARE NORMAL- AND FLYING-TYPE POKÉMON.
EITHER SHE DOESN'T HAVE A SPECIAL EXPERTISE, OR SHE'S HIDING IT ON PURPOSE TO CONFUSE ME.
WELL, NO POINT WONDER-ING ABOUT IT!
KABU-TOPS!
ANCIENT-POWER!

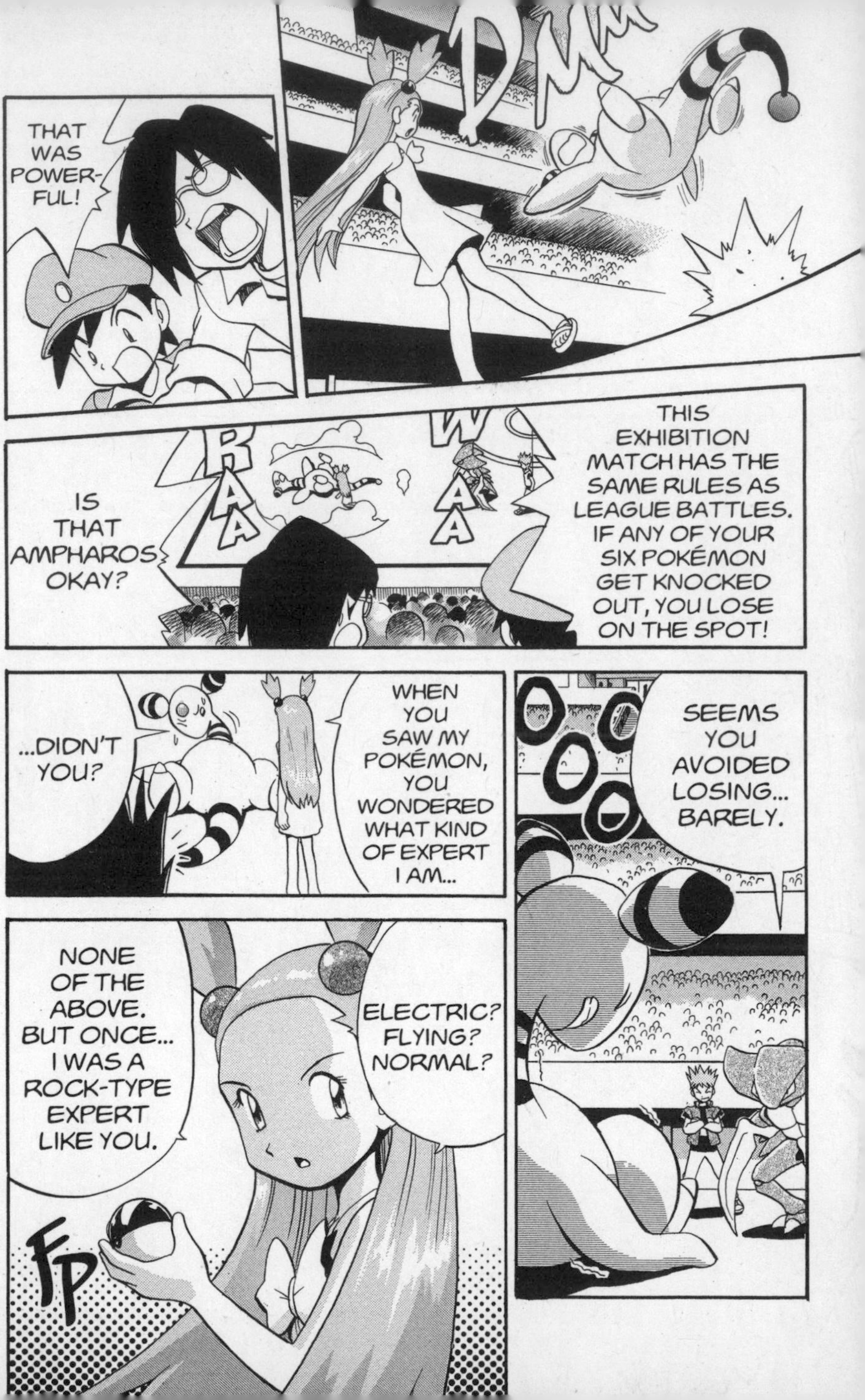
DM
THAT WAS POWER-FUL!
THIS EXHIBITION MATCH HAS THE SAME RULES AS LEAGUE BATTLES. IF ANY OF YOUR SIX POKÉMON GET KNOCKED OUT, YOU LOSE ON THE SPOT!
WAAA
RAAA
IS THAT AMPHAROS OKAY?
SEEMS YOU AVOIDED LOSING... BARELY.
WHEN YOU SAW MY POKÉMON, YOU WONDERED WHAT KIND OF EXPERT I AM...
...DIDN'T YOU?
ELECTRIC? FLYING? NORMAL?
NONE OF THE ABOVE. BUT ONCE... I WAS A ROCK-TYPE EXPERT LIKE YOU.
FP

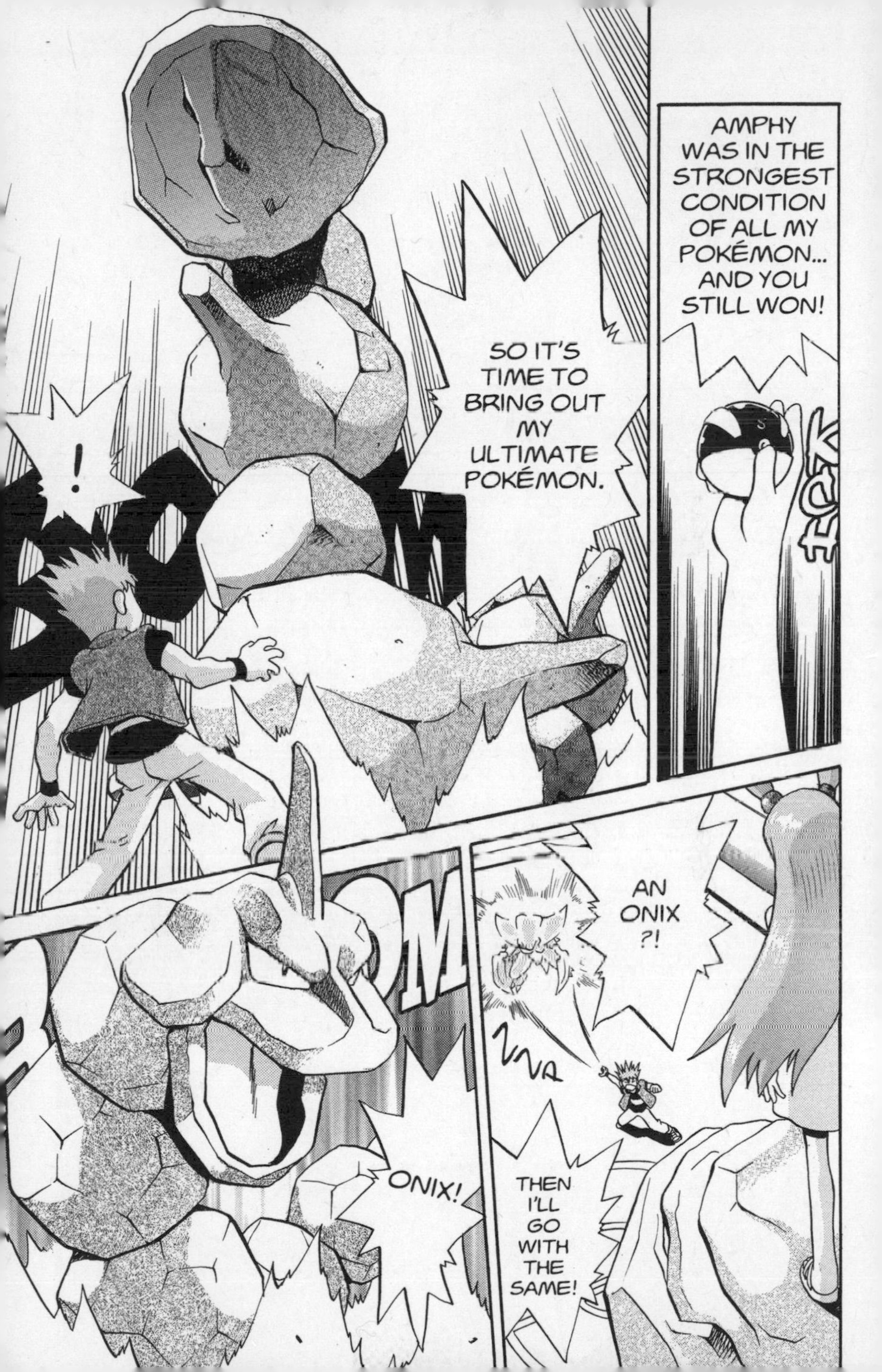
AMPHY WAS IN THE STRONGEST CONDITION OF ALL MY POKÉMON... AND YOU STILL WON!
SO IT'S TIME TO BRING OUT MY ULTIMATE POKÉMON.
!
AN ONIX ?!
THEN I'LL GO WITH THE SAME!
ONIX!

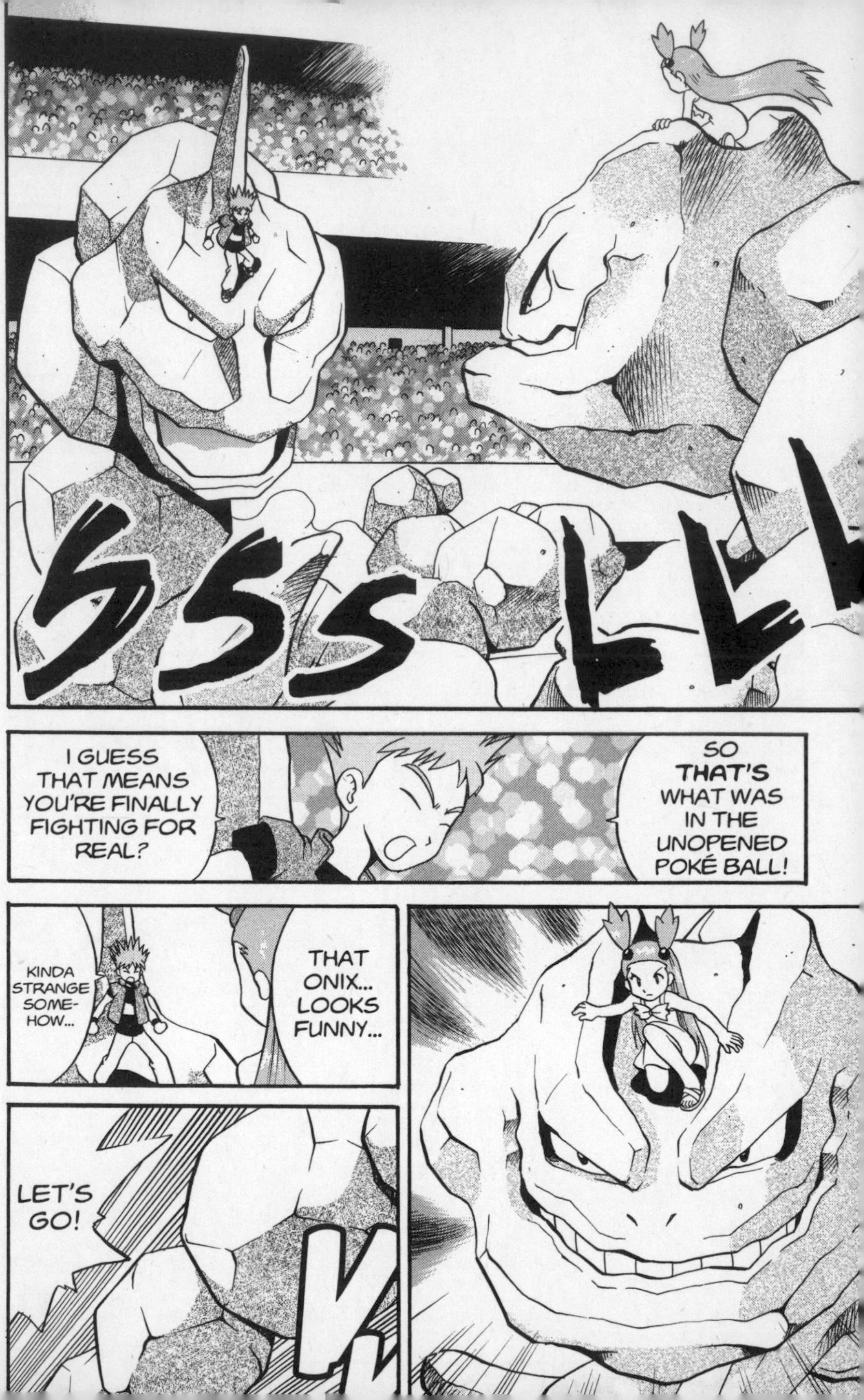
SO THAT'S WHAT WAS IN THE UNOPENED POKÉ BALL!
I GUESS THAT MEANS YOU'RE FINALLY FIGHTING FOR REAL?
THAT ONIX... LOOKS FUNNY...
KINDA STRANGE SOME-HOW...
LET'S GO!

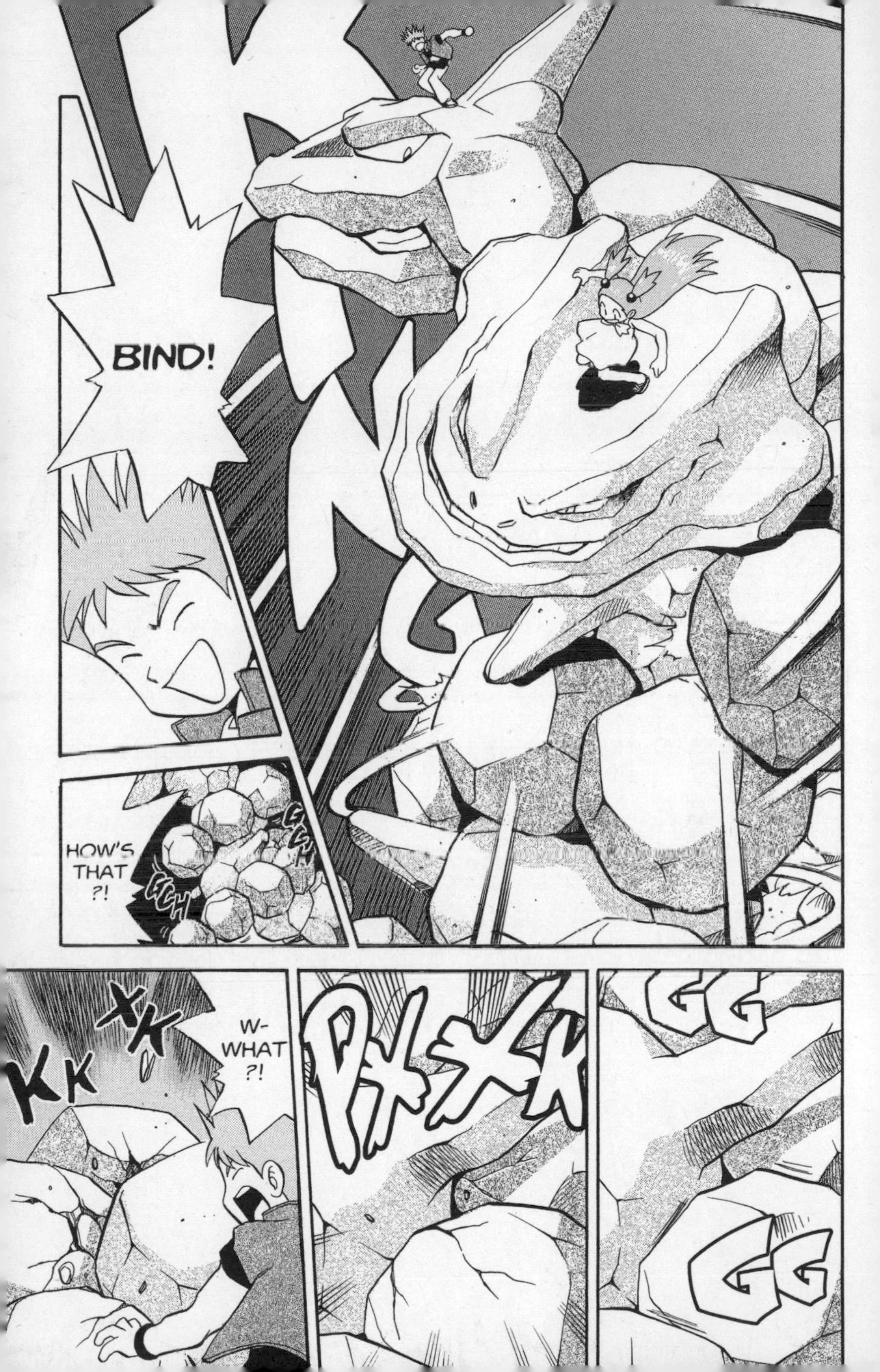
BIND!
HOW'S THAT ?!
GG
GG
W- WHAT ?!

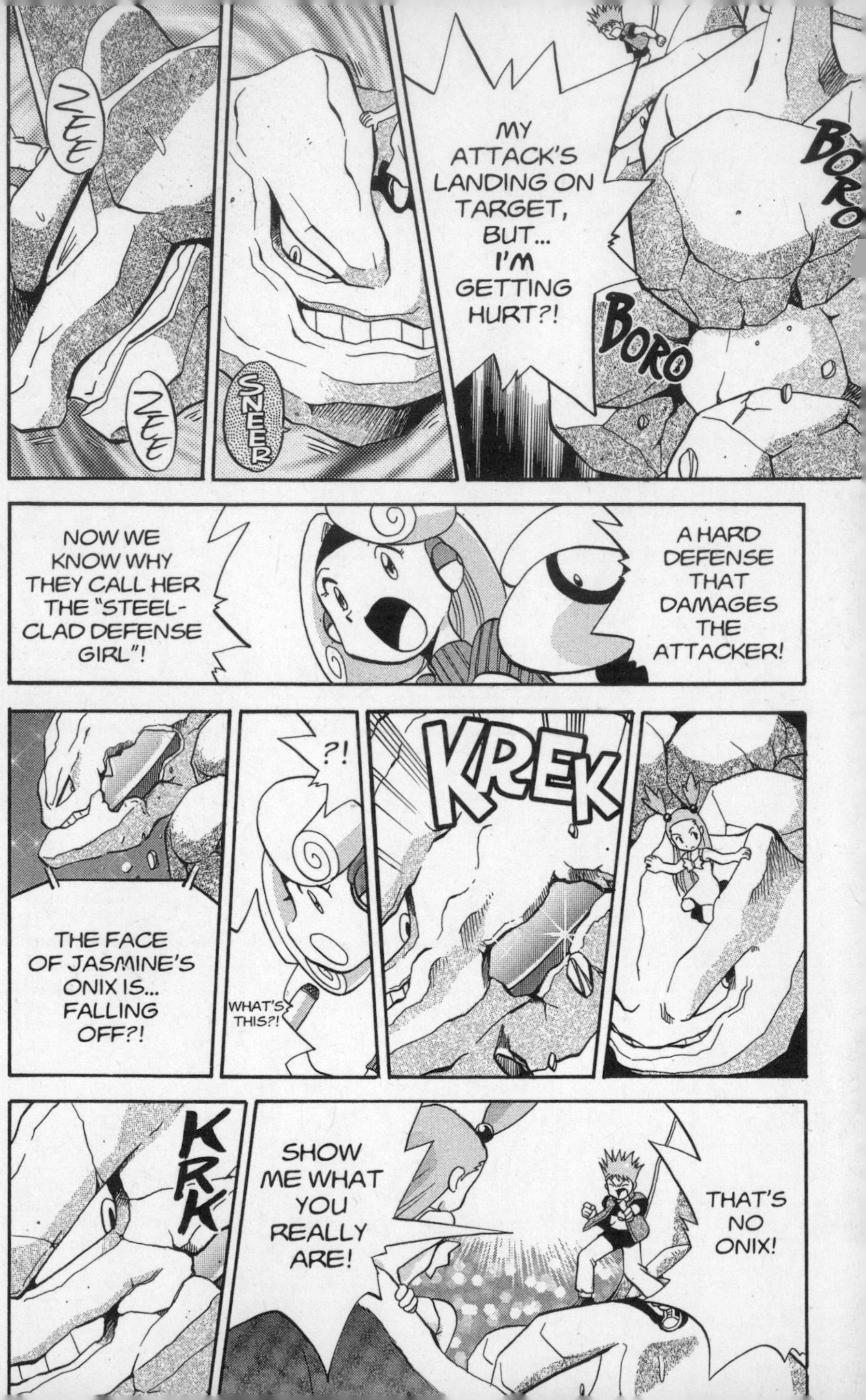
BORO
MY ATTACK'S LANDING ON TARGET, BUT... I'M GETTING HURT?!
BORO
SNEER
ZEE
ZEE
A HARD DEFENSE THAT DAMAGES THE ATTACKER!
NOW WE KNOW WHY THEY CALL HER THE "STEEL-CLAD DEFENSE GIRL"!
KREK
?!
WHAT'S THIS?!
THE FACE OF JASMINE'S ONIX IS... FALLING OFF?!
THAT'S NO ONIX!
SHOW ME WHAT YOU REALLY ARE!
KRK

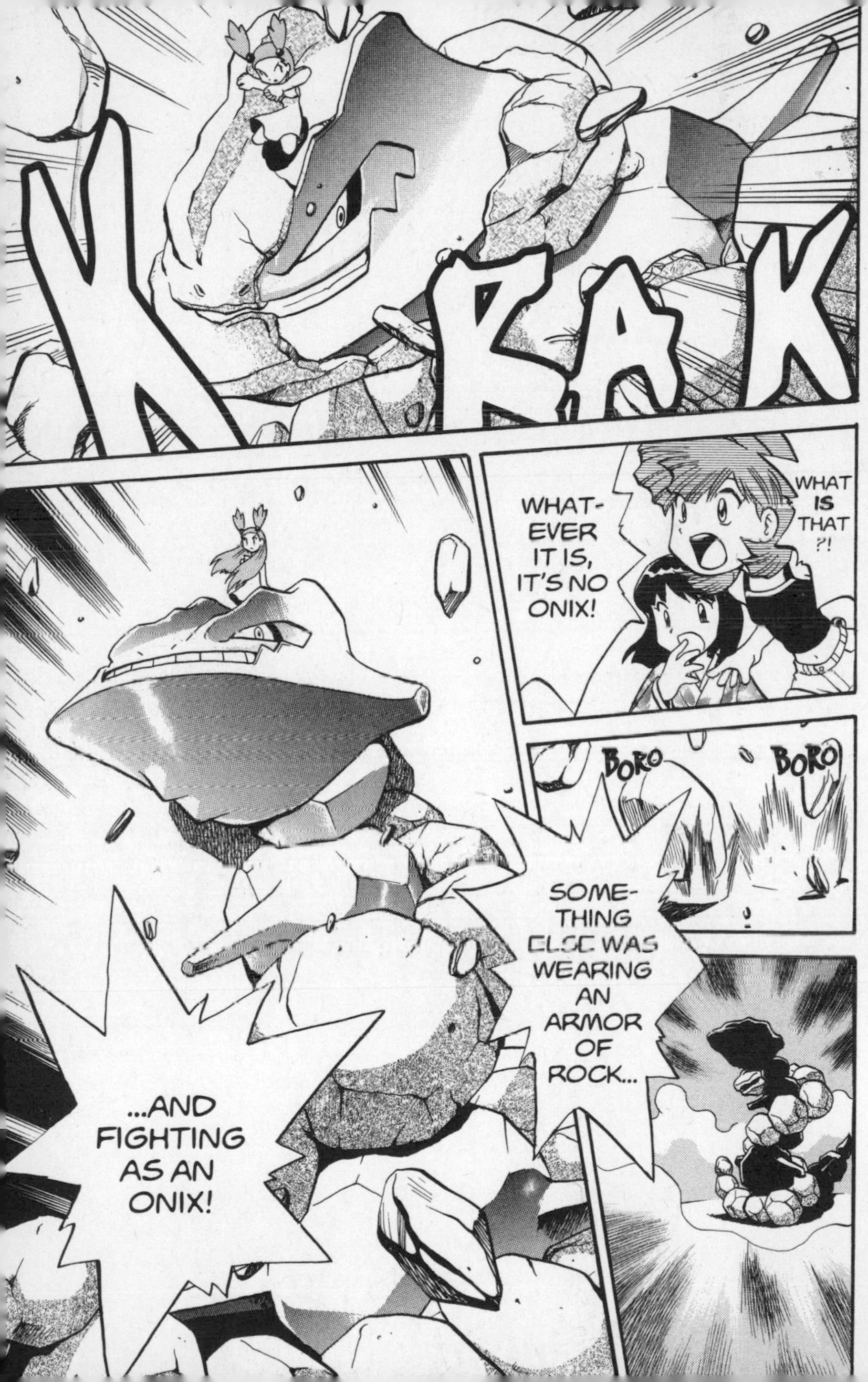
KRAK
WHAT IS THAT?!
WHAT-EVER IT IS, IT'S NO ONIX!
BORO
BORO
SOME-THING ELSE WAS WEARING AN ARMOR OF ROCK...
...AND FIGHTING AS AN ONIX!

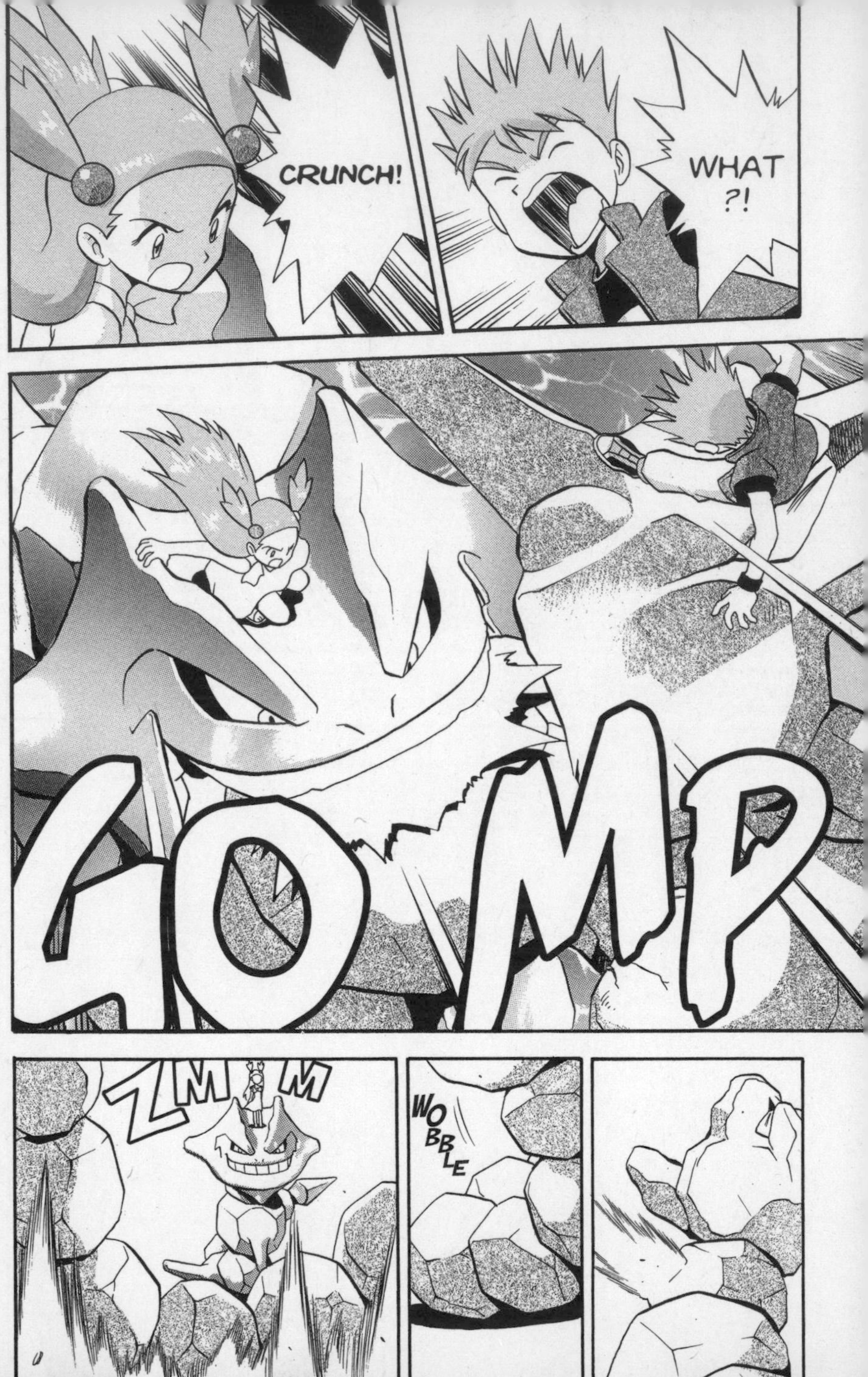
WHAT ?!
CRUNCH!
COMP
WOBBLE
ZM M

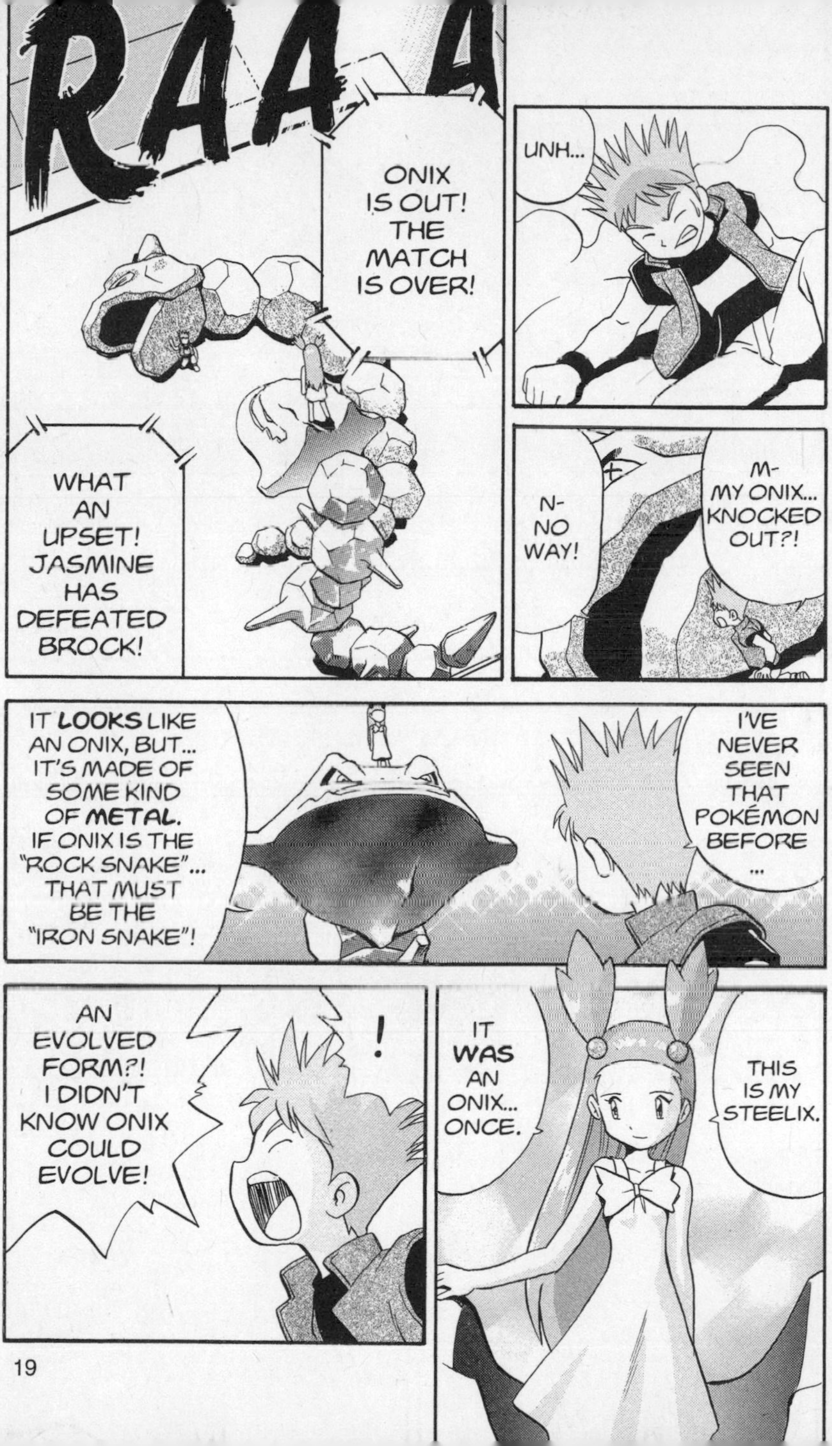
UNH...
M-MY ONIX... KNOCKED OUT?!
N-NO WAY!
RAA A
ONIX IS OUT! THE MATCH IS OVER!
WHAT AN UPSET! JASMINE HAS DEFEATED BROCK!
I'VE NEVER SEEN THAT POKÉMON BEFORE ...
IT **LOOKS** LIKE AN ONIX, BUT... IT'S MADE OF SOME KIND OF **METAL**. IF ONIX IS THE "ROCK SNAKE"... THAT MUST BE THE "IRON SNAKE"!
THIS IS MY STEELIX.
IT **WAS** AN ONIX... ONCE.
!
AN EVOLVED FORM?! I DIDN'T KNOW ONIX COULD EVOLVE!

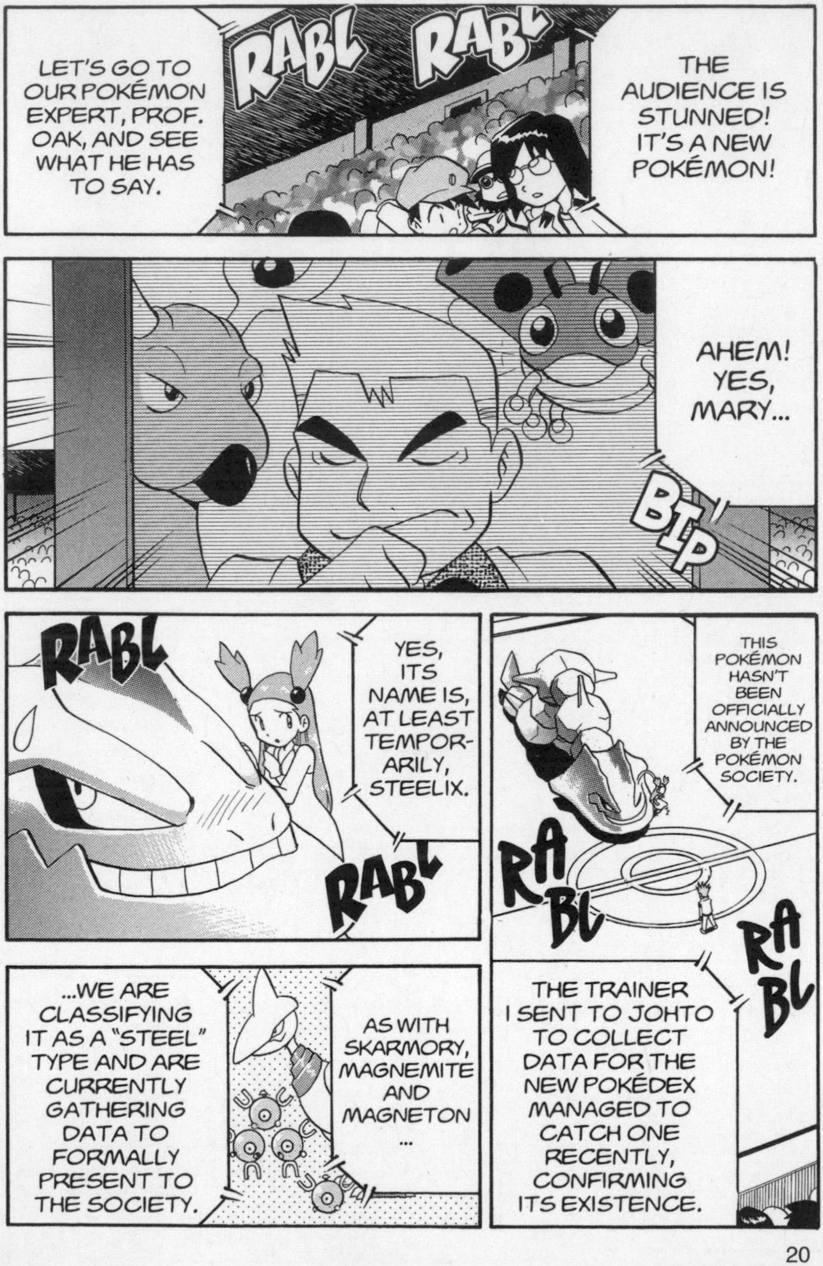

THE AUDIENCE IS STUNNED! IT'S A NEW POKÉMON!
RABL RABL
LET'S GO TO OUR POKÉMON EXPERT, PROF. OAK, AND SEE WHAT HE HAS TO SAY.
AHEM! YES, MARY...
BIP
THIS POKÉMON HASN'T BEEN OFFICIALLY ANNOUNCED BY THE POKÉMON SOCIETY.
RA BL
RA BL
RABL
YES, ITS NAME IS, AT LEAST TEMPOR-ARILY, STEELIX.
RABL
THE TRAINER I SENT TO JOHTO TO COLLECT DATA FOR THE NEW POKÉDEX MANAGED TO CATCH ONE RECENTLY, CONFIRMING ITS EXISTENCE.
AS WITH SKARMORY, MAGNEMITE AND MAGNETON ...
...WE ARE CLASSIFYING IT AS A "STEEL" TYPE AND ARE CURRENTLY GATHERING DATA TO FORMALLY PRESENT TO THE SOCIETY.

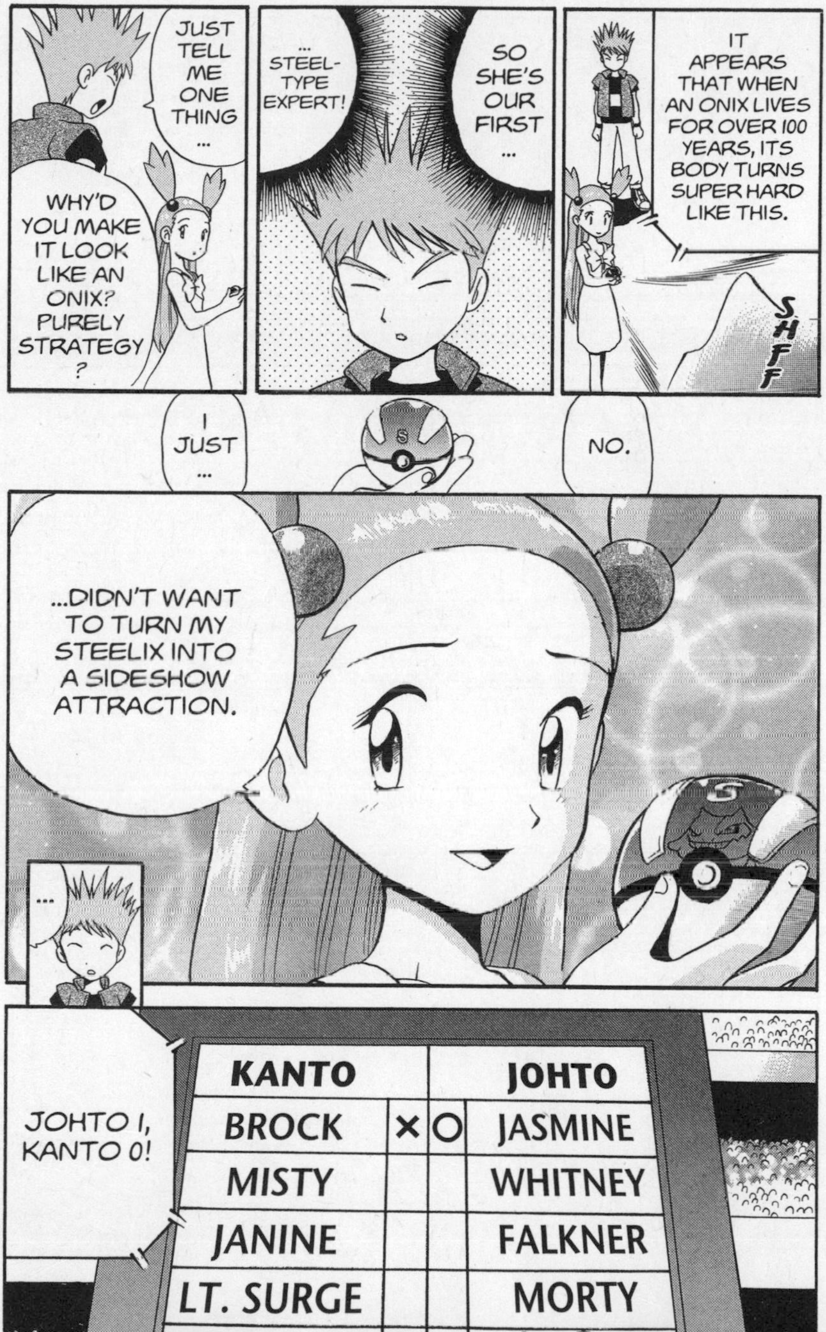
IT APPEARS THAT WHEN AN ONIX LIVES FOR OVER 100 YEARS, ITS BODY TURNS SUPER HARD LIKE THIS.
SHFF
SO SHE'S OUR FIRST ...
... STEEL-TYPE EXPERT!
JUST TELL ME ONE THING ...
WHY'D YOU MAKE IT LOOK LIKE AN ONIX? PURELY STRATEGY ?
NO.
I JUST ...
...DIDN'T WANT TO TURN MY STEELIX INTO A SIDESHOW ATTRACTION.
...
KANTO
JOHTO
BROCK × ○ JASMINE
MISTY
WHITNEY
JANINE
FALKNER
LT. SURGE
MORTY
JOHTO 1, KANTO 0!

156 Notorious Noctowl

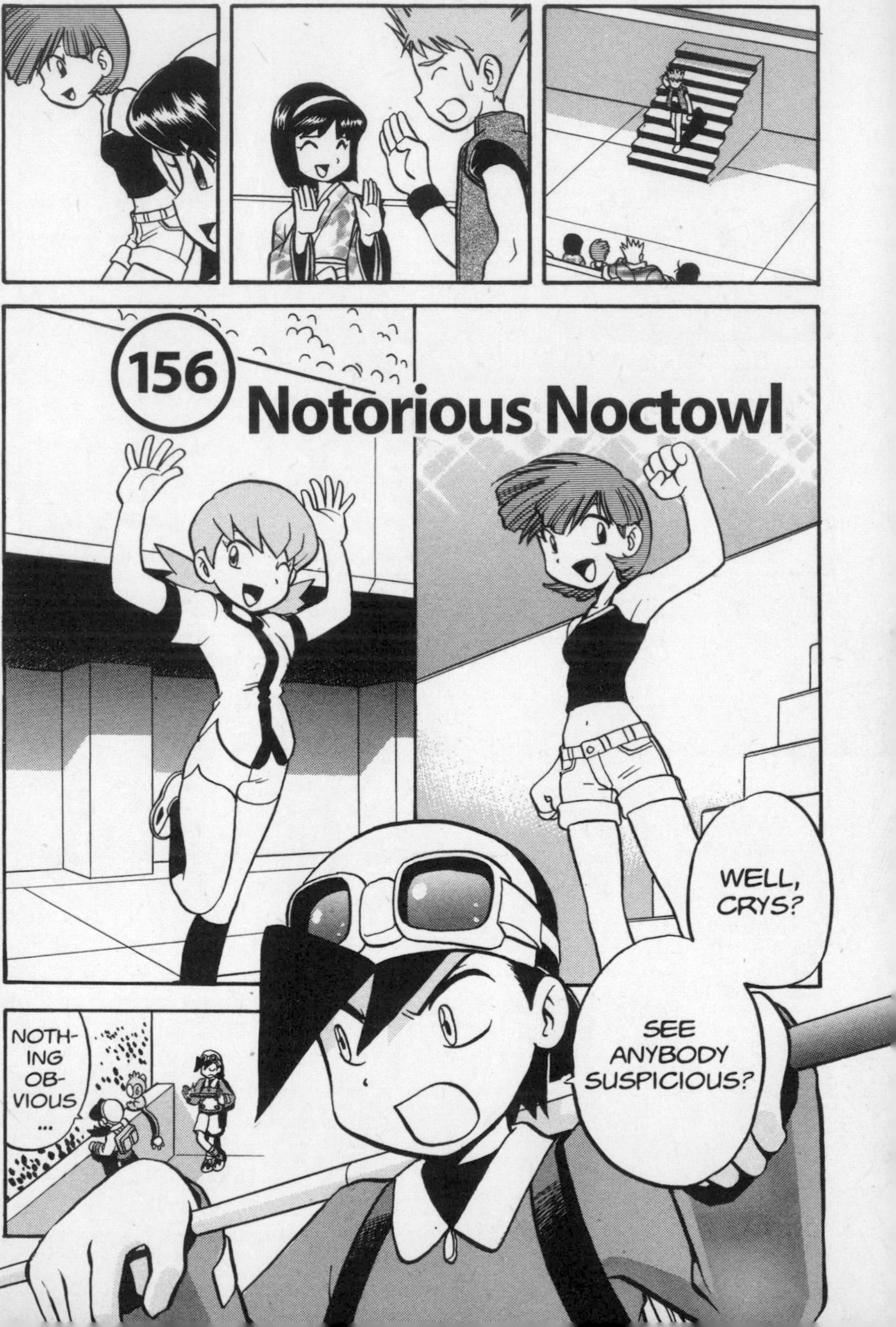
WELL, CRYS?
SEE ANYBODY SUSPICIOUS?
NOTH-ING OB-VIOUS ...

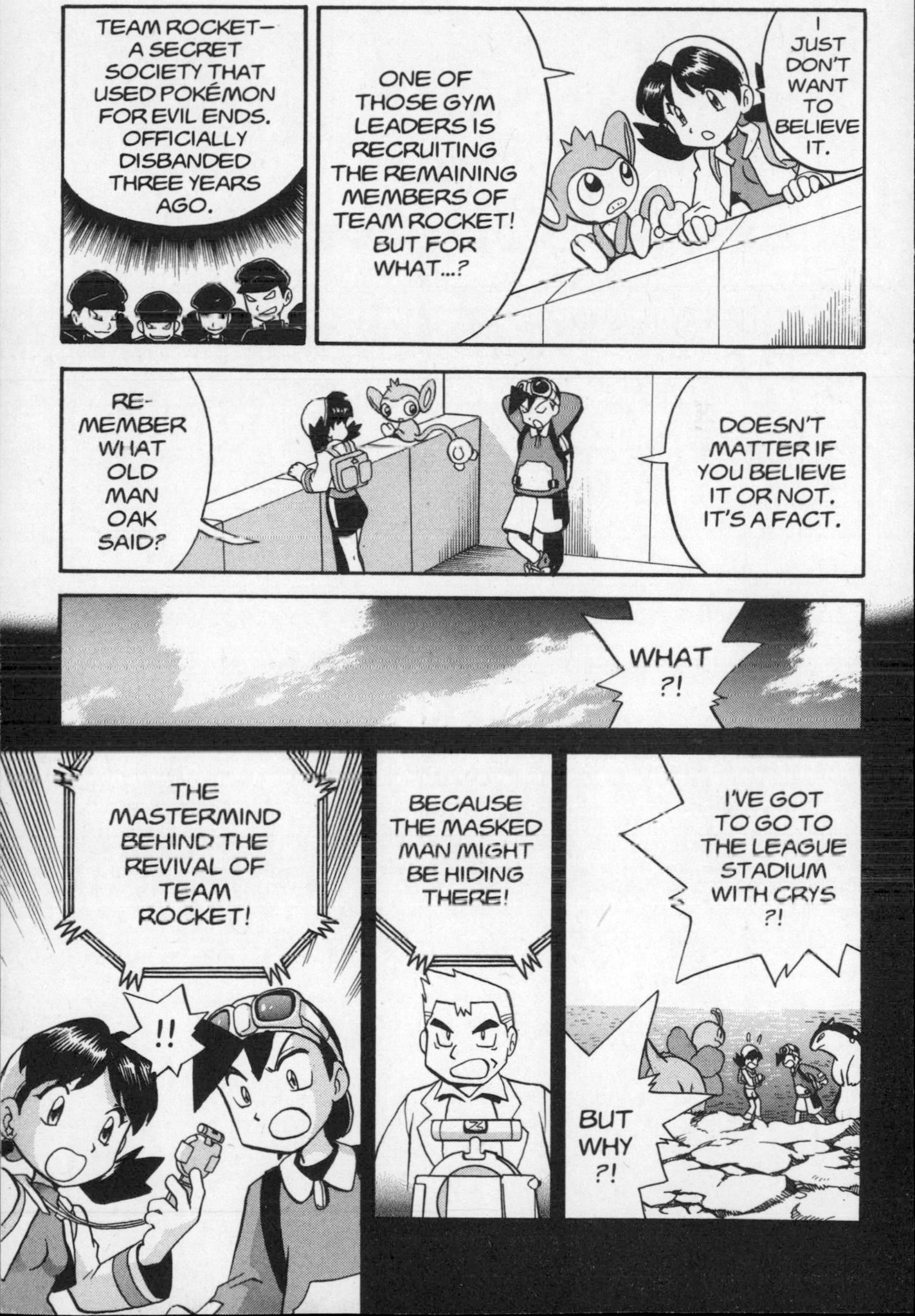
I JUST DON'T WANT TO BELIEVE IT.
ONE OF THOSE GYM LEADERS IS RECRUITING THE REMAINING MEMBERS OF TEAM ROCKET! BUT FOR WHAT...?
TEAM ROCKET— A SECRET SOCIETY THAT USED POKÉMON FOR EVIL ENDS. OFFICIALLY DISBANDED THREE YEARS AGO.
DOESN'T MATTER IF YOU BELIEVE IT OR NOT. IT'S A FACT.
RE-MEMBER WHAT OLD MAN OAK SAID?
WHAT ?!
I'VE GOT TO GO TO THE LEAGUE STADIUM WITH CRYS ?!
BUT WHY ?!
BECAUSE THE MASKED MAN MIGHT BE HIDING THERE!
THE MASTERMIND BEHIND THE REVIVAL OF TEAM ROCKET!
!!

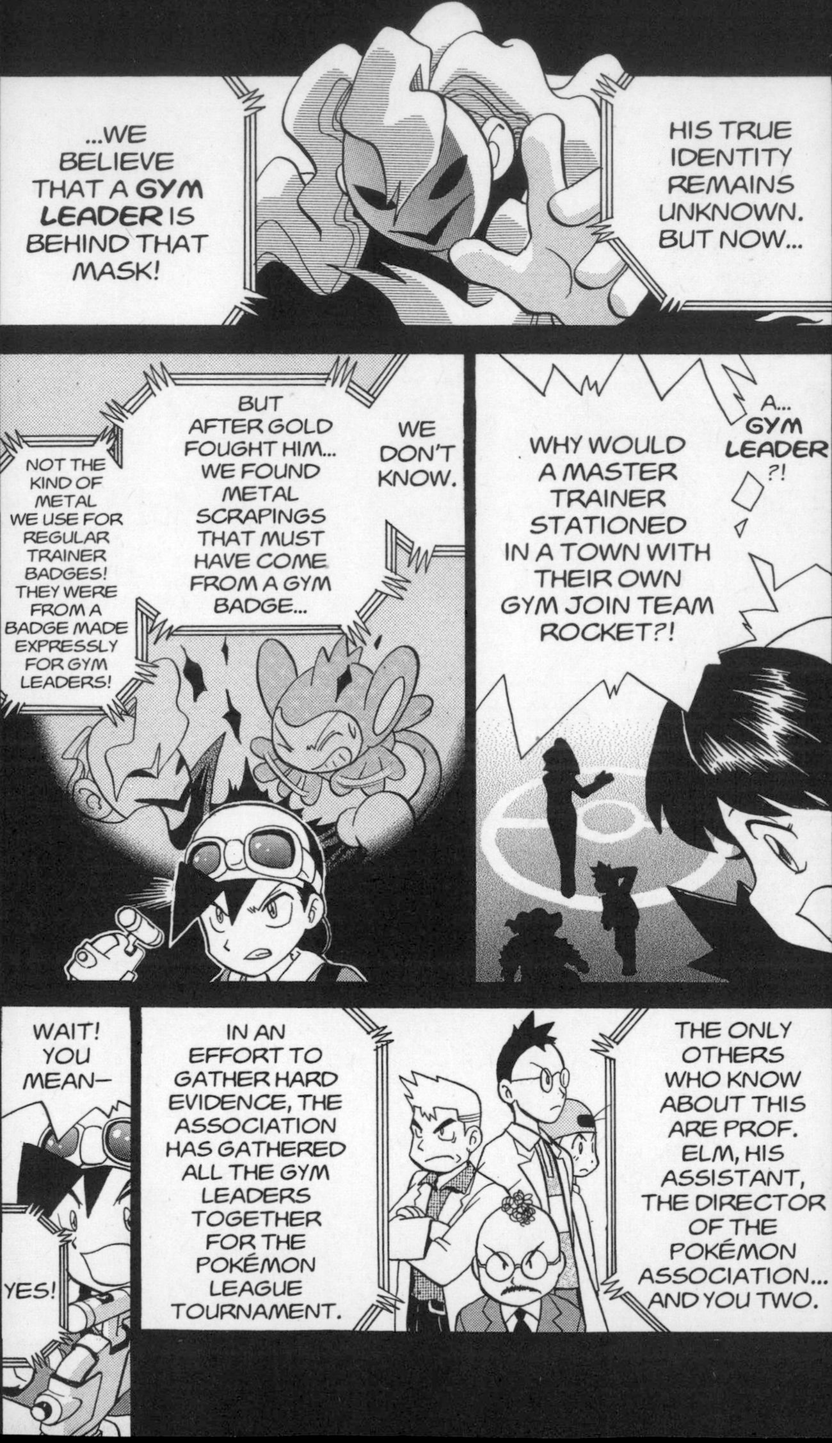
HIS TRUE IDENTITY REMAINS UNKNOWN. BUT NOW...
...WE BELIEVE THAT A **GYM LEADER** IS BEHIND THAT MASK!
A... **GYM LEADER** ?!
WHY WOULD A MASTER TRAINER STATIONED IN A TOWN WITH THEIR OWN GYM JOIN TEAM ROCKET?!
WE DON'T KNOW.
BUT AFTER GOLD FOUGHT HIM... WE FOUND METAL SCRAPINGS THAT MUST HAVE COME FROM A GYM BADGE...
NOT THE KIND OF METAL WE USE FOR REGULAR TRAINER BADGES! THEY WERE FROM A BADGE MADE EXPRESSLY FOR GYM LEADERS!
THE ONLY OTHERS WHO KNOW ABOUT THIS ARE PROF. ELM, HIS ASSISTANT, THE DIRECTOR OF THE POKÉMON ASSOCIATION... AND YOU TWO.
IN AN EFFORT TO GATHER HARD EVIDENCE, THE ASSOCIATION HAS GATHERED ALL THE GYM LEADERS TOGETHER FOR THE POKÉMON LEAGUE TOURNAMENT.
WAIT! YOU MEAN—
YES!

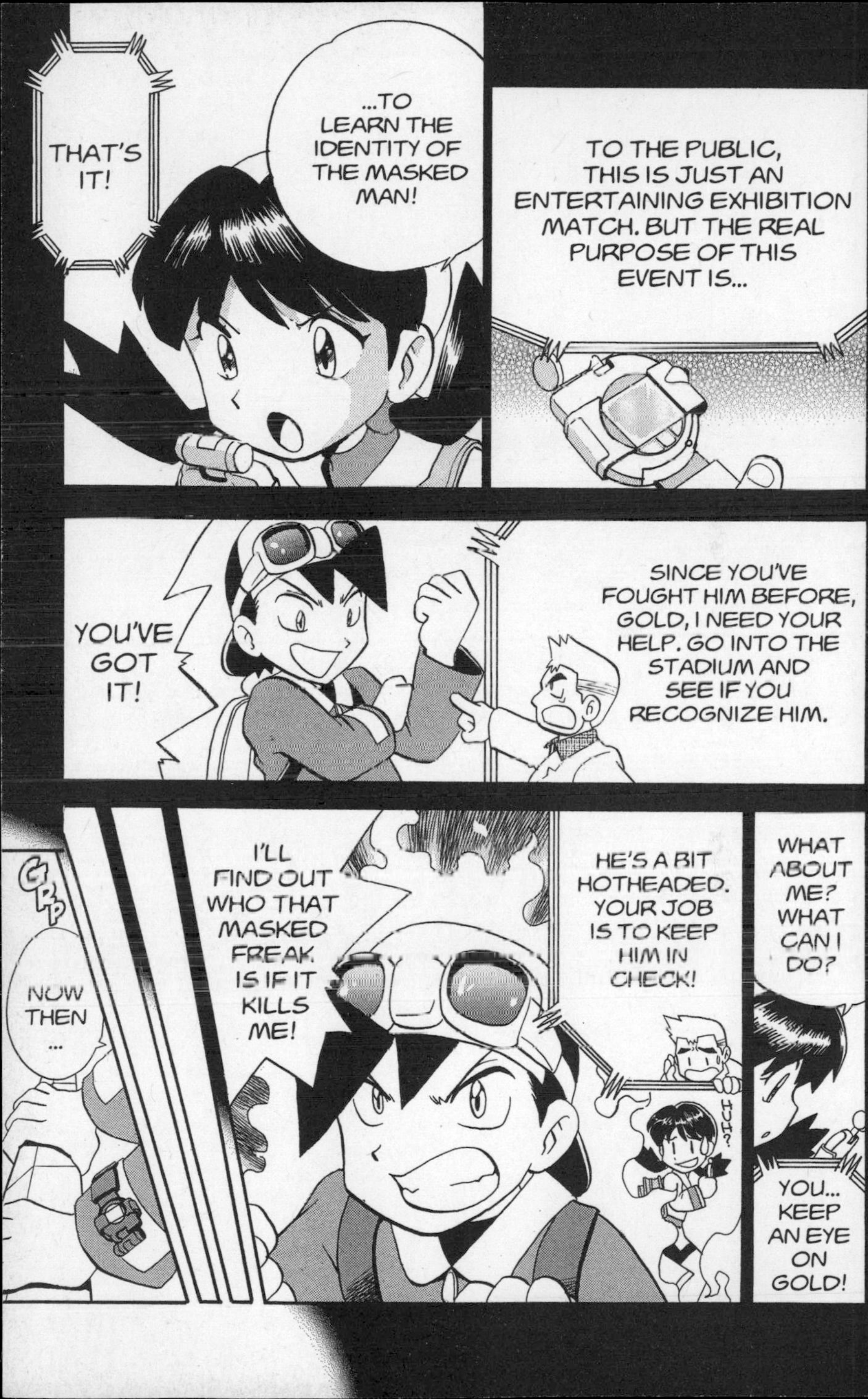
TO THE PUBLIC, THIS IS JUST AN ENTERTAINING EXHIBITION MATCH. BUT THE REAL PURPOSE OF THIS EVENT IS...
...TO LEARN THE IDENTITY OF THE MASKED MAN!
THAT'S IT!
SINCE YOU'VE FOUGHT HIM BEFORE, GOLD, I NEED YOUR HELP. GO INTO THE STADIUM AND SEE IF YOU RECOGNIZE HIM.
YOU'VE GOT IT!
WHAT ABOUT ME? WHAT CAN I DO?
YOU... KEEP AN EYE ON GOLD!
HE'S A BIT HOTHEADED. YOUR JOB IS TO KEEP HIM IN CHECK!
HUH?
I'LL FIND OUT WHO THAT MASKED FREAK IS IF IT KILLS ME!
GRP
NOW THEN ...

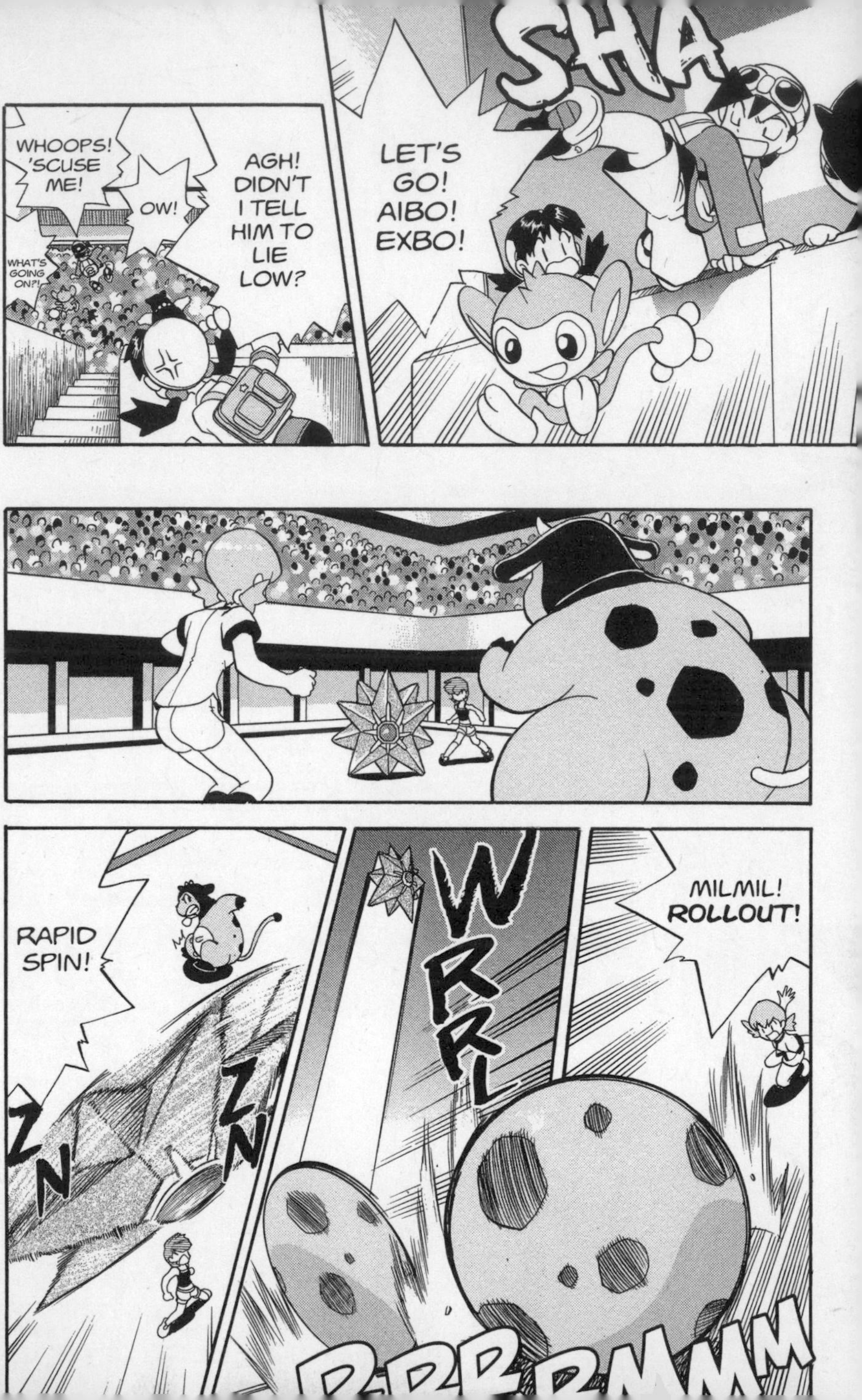
SHA
LET'S GO! AIBO! EXBO!
AGH! DIDN'T I TELL HIM TO LIE LOW?
OW!
WHOOPS! 'SCUSE ME!
WHAT'S GOING ON?!
MILMIL! ROLLOUT!
WRRL
RAPID SPIN!
ZN
ZN

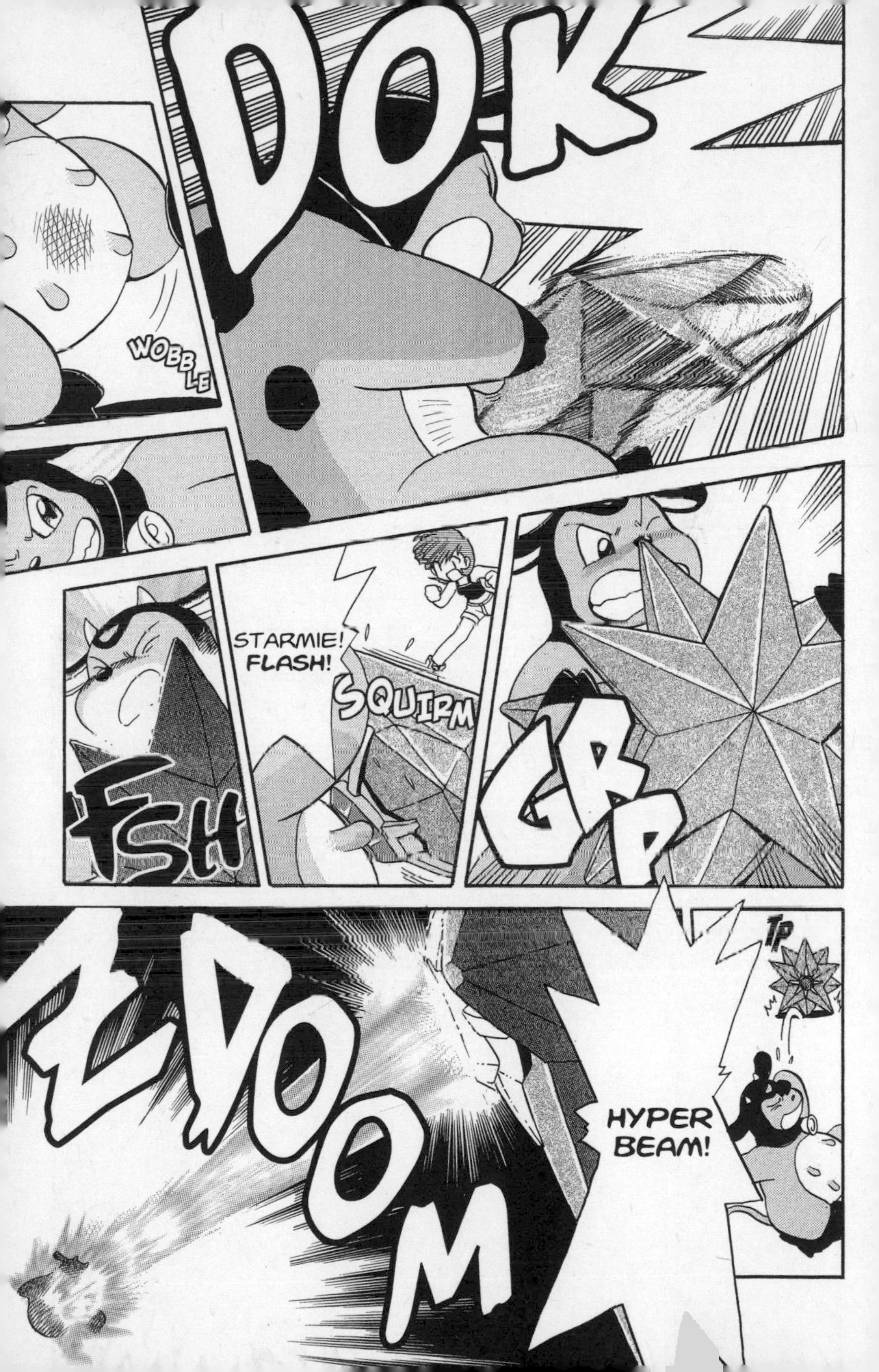
DOK
WOBBLE
GRP
STARMIE! FLASH!
SQUIRM
FSH
TP
HYPER BEAM!
ZDOOM

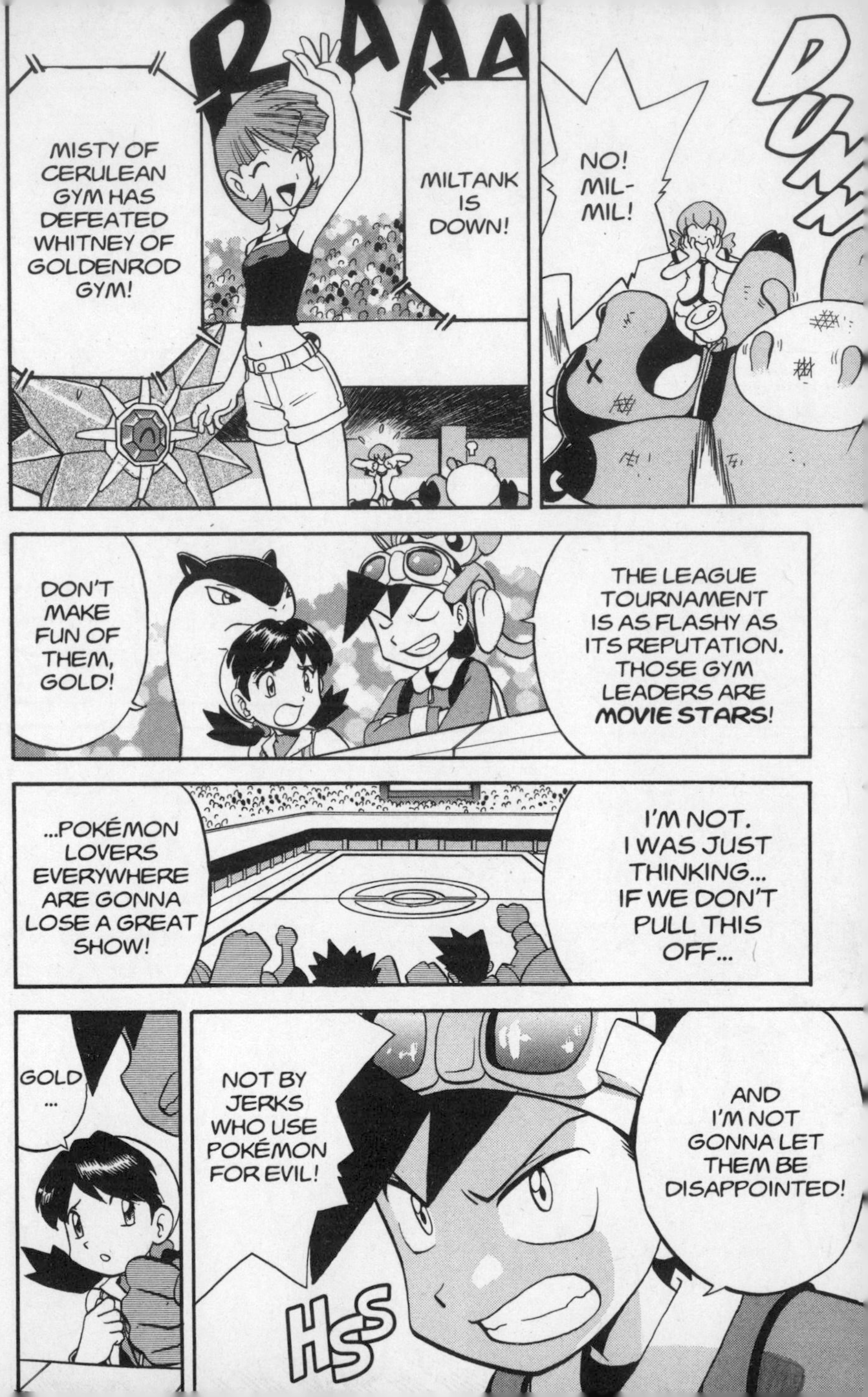
DUNN
NO! MIL-MIL!
RAAA
MILTANK IS DOWN!
MISTY OF CERULEAN GYM HAS DEFEATED WHITNEY OF GOLDENROD GYM!
THE LEAGUE TOURNAMENT IS AS FLASHY AS ITS REPUTATION. THOSE GYM LEADERS ARE **MOVIE STARS**!
DON'T MAKE FUN OF THEM, GOLD!
I'M NOT. I WAS JUST THINKING... IF WE DON'T PULL THIS OFF...
...POKÉMON LOVERS EVERYWHERE ARE GONNA LOSE A GREAT SHOW!
AND I'M NOT GONNA LET THEM BE DISAPPOINTED!
NOT BY JERKS WHO USE POKÉMON FOR EVIL!
HSS
GOLD...

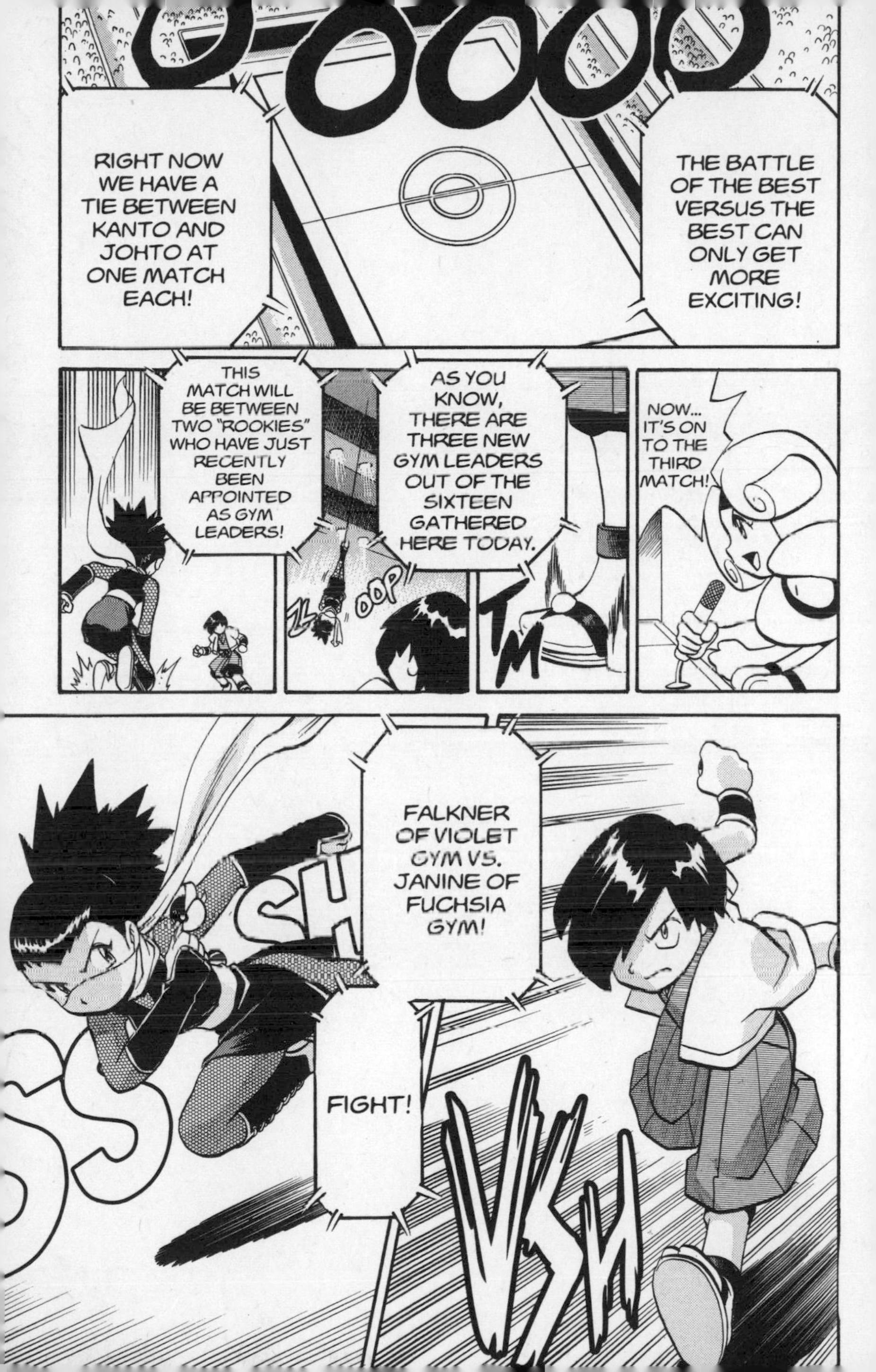
O-OOOO
THE BATTLE OF THE BEST VERSUS THE BEST CAN ONLY GET MORE EXCITING!
RIGHT NOW WE HAVE A TIE BETWEEN KANTO AND JOHTO AT ONE MATCH EACH!
NOW... IT'S ON TO THE THIRD MATCH!
TM
AS YOU KNOW, THERE ARE THREE NEW GYM LEADERS OUT OF THE SIXTEEN GATHERED HERE TODAY.
ZOOP
THIS MATCH WILL BE BETWEEN TWO "ROOKIES" WHO HAVE JUST RECENTLY BEEN APPOINTED AS GYM LEADERS!
FALKNER OF VIOLET GYM VS. JANINE OF FUCHSIA GYM!
FIGHT!
VSH
SH
SS

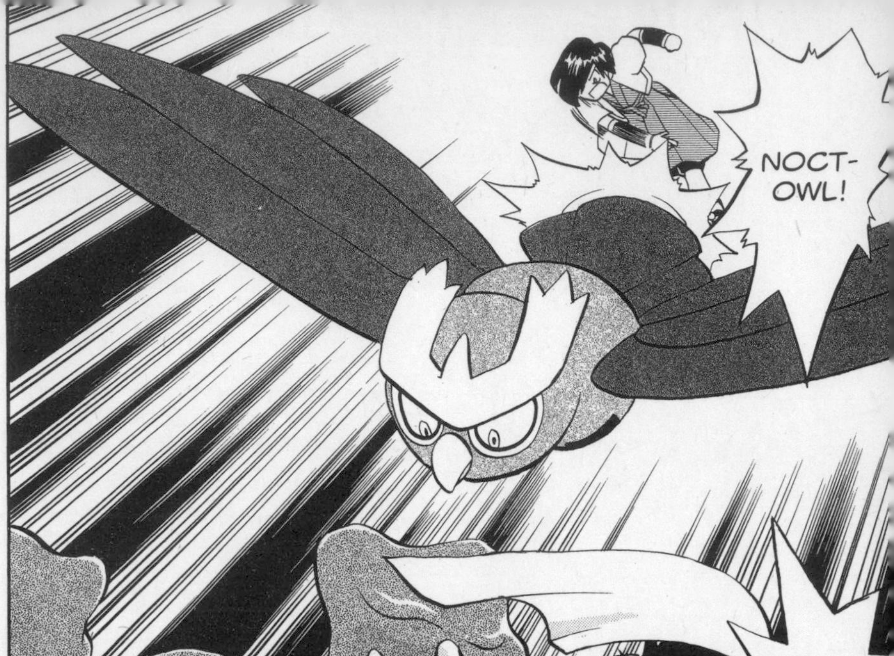
NOCTOWL!
GRIMER!

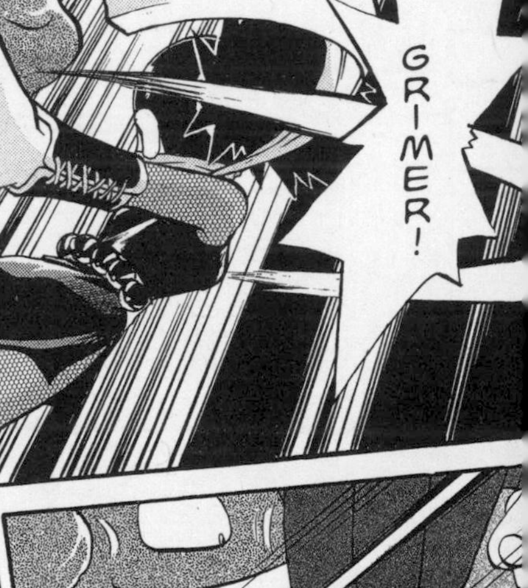
BOING

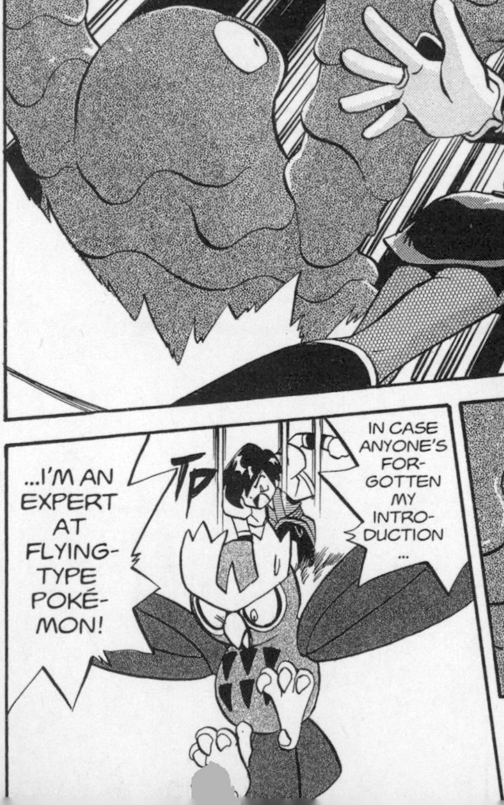
IN CASE ANYONE'S FORGOTTEN MY INTRODUCTION ...
TP
...I'M AN EXPERT AT FLYING-TYPE POKÉMON!

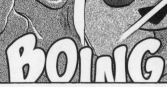

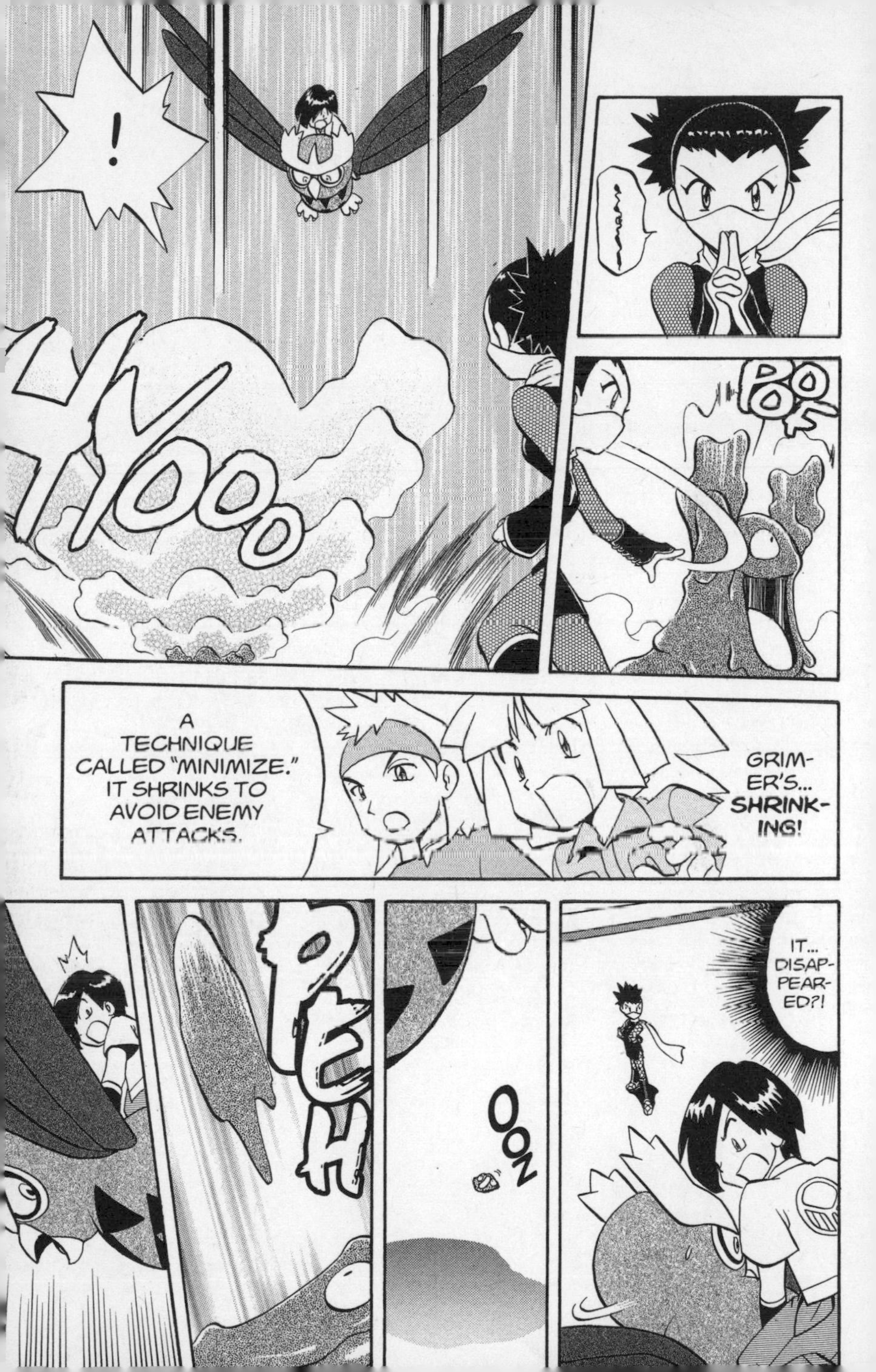
......
POOF
!
GRIMER'S... SHRINKING!
A TECHNIQUE CALLED "MINIMIZE." IT SHRINKS TO AVOID ENEMY ATTACKS.
IT... DISAPPEARED?!

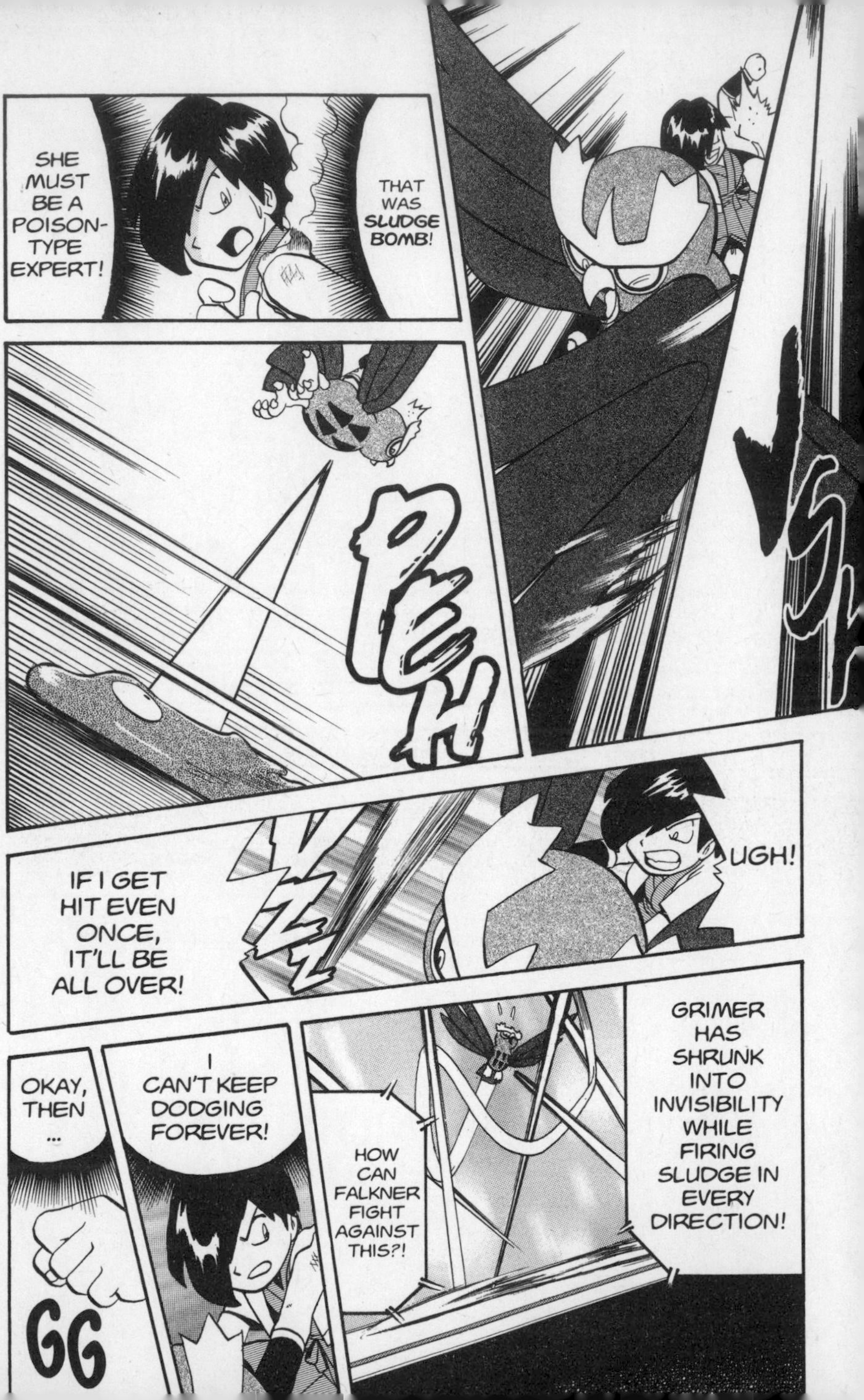
THAT WAS SLUDGE BOMB!
SHE MUST BE A POISON-TYPE EXPERT!
UGH!
IF I GET HIT EVEN ONCE, IT'LL BE ALL OVER!
GRIMER HAS SHRUNK INTO INVISIBILITY WHILE FIRING SLUDGE IN EVERY DIRECTION!
HOW CAN FALKNER FIGHT AGAINST THIS?!
I CAN'T KEEP DODGING FOREVER!
OKAY, THEN ...
GG

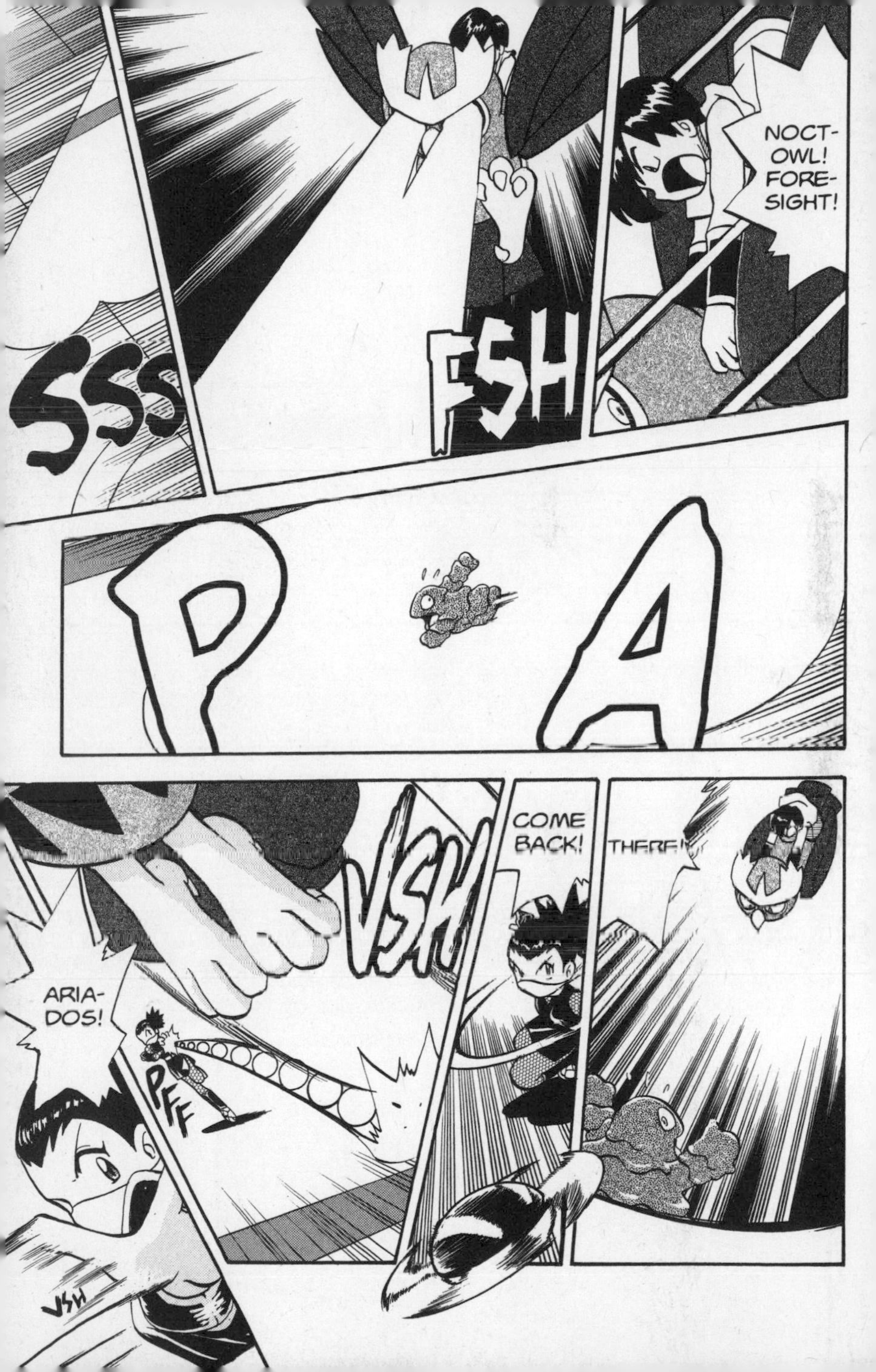
NOCT-
OWL!
FORE-
SIGHT!
FSH
SSS
PA
THERE!
COME BACK!
VSH
ARIA-
DOS!
PFF
VSH

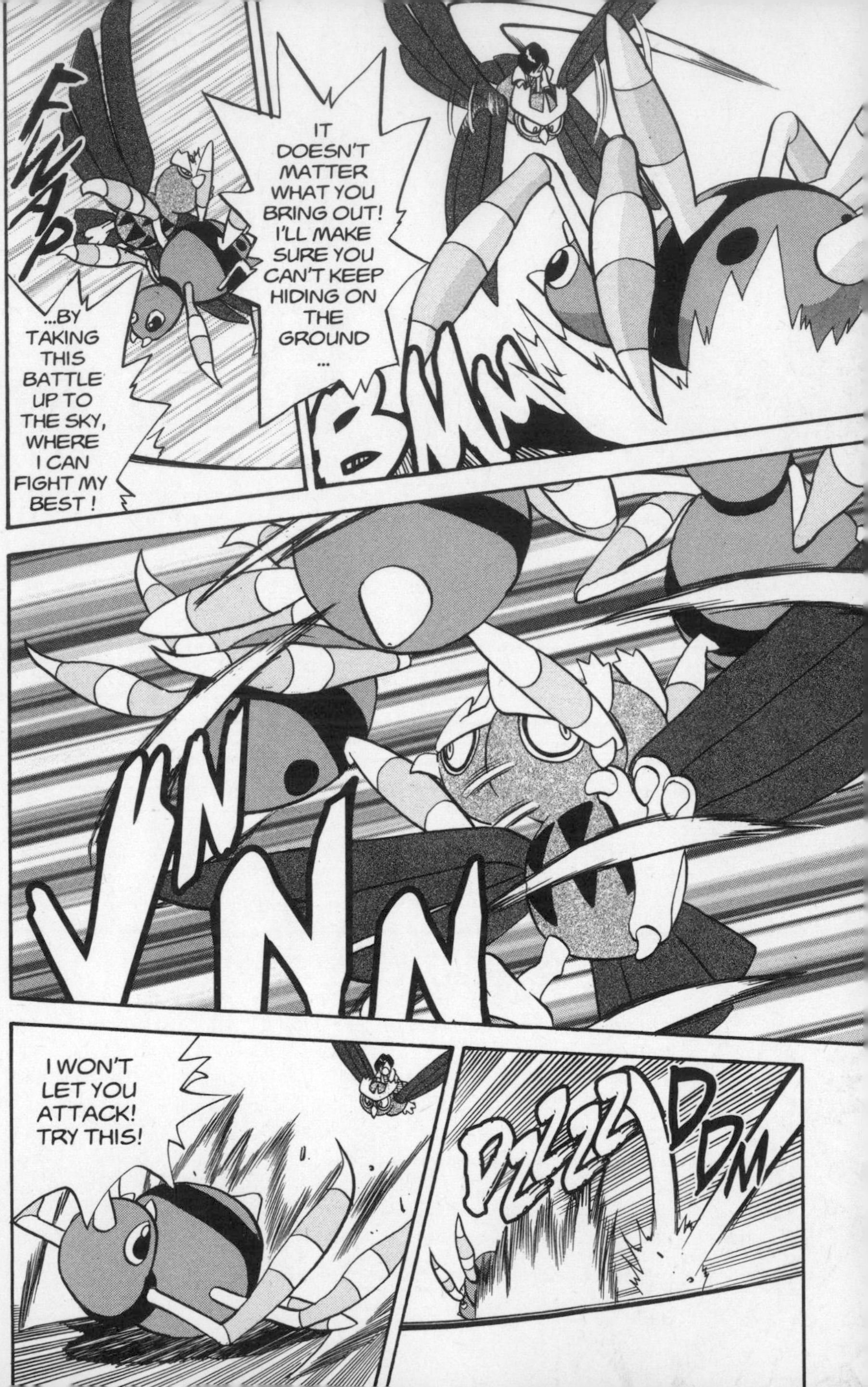
IT DOESN'T MATTER WHAT YOU BRING OUT! I'LL MAKE SURE YOU CAN'T KEEP HIDING ON THE GROUND ...
FWAP
...BY TAKING THIS BATTLE UP TO THE SKY, WHERE I CAN FIGHT MY BEST!
BMM
VN
VNN
DZZZZ
DDM
I WON'T LET YOU ATTACK! TRY THIS!

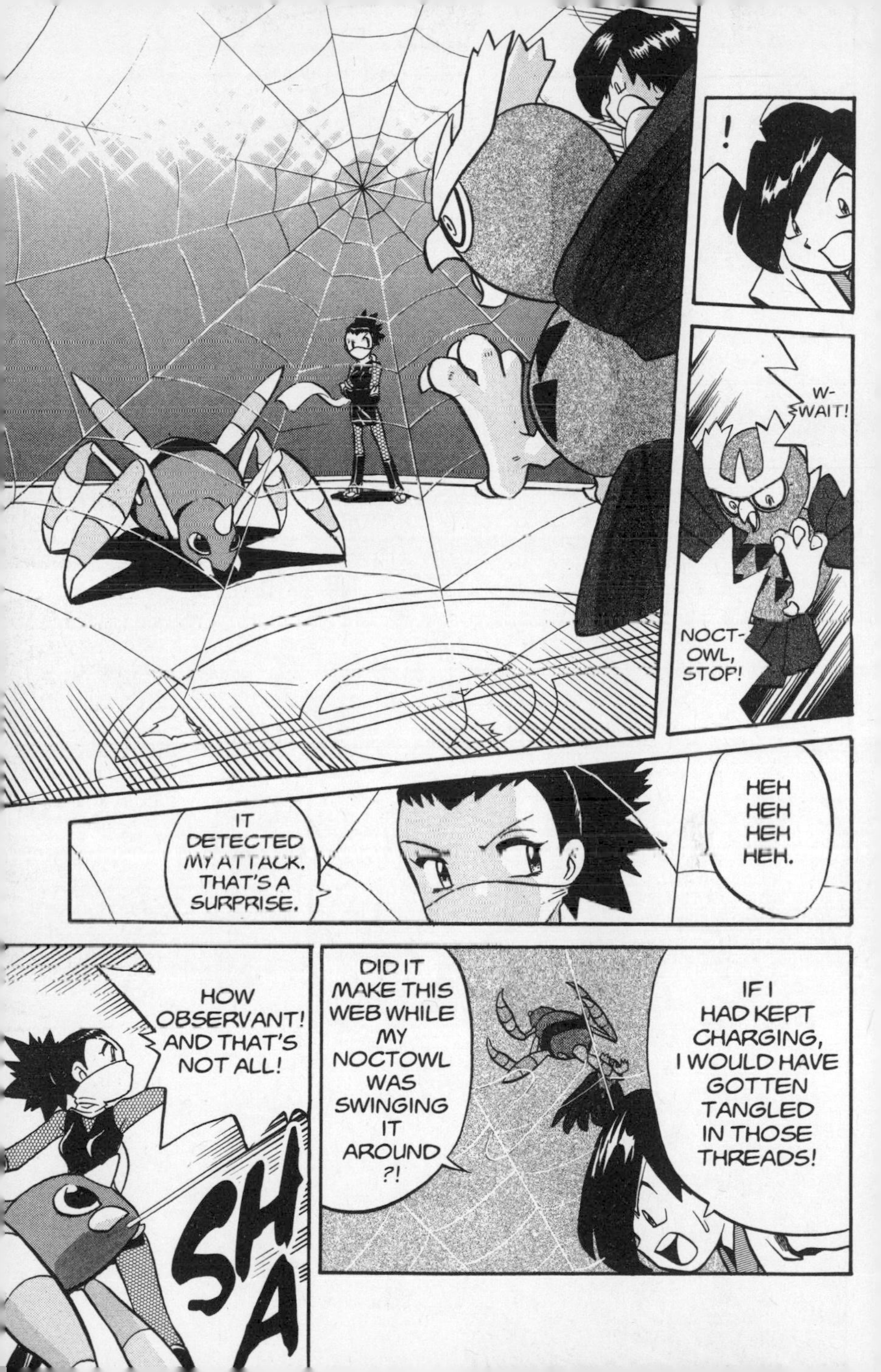
!
W-WAIT!
NOCTOWL, STOP!
HEH HEH HEH HEH.
IT DETECTED MY ATTACK. THAT'S A SURPRISE.
IF I HAD KEPT CHARGING, I WOULD HAVE GOTTEN TANGLED IN THOSE THREADS!
DID IT MAKE THIS WEB WHILE MY NOCTOWL WAS SWINGING IT AROUND?!
HOW OBSERVANT! AND THAT'S NOT ALL!
SHA

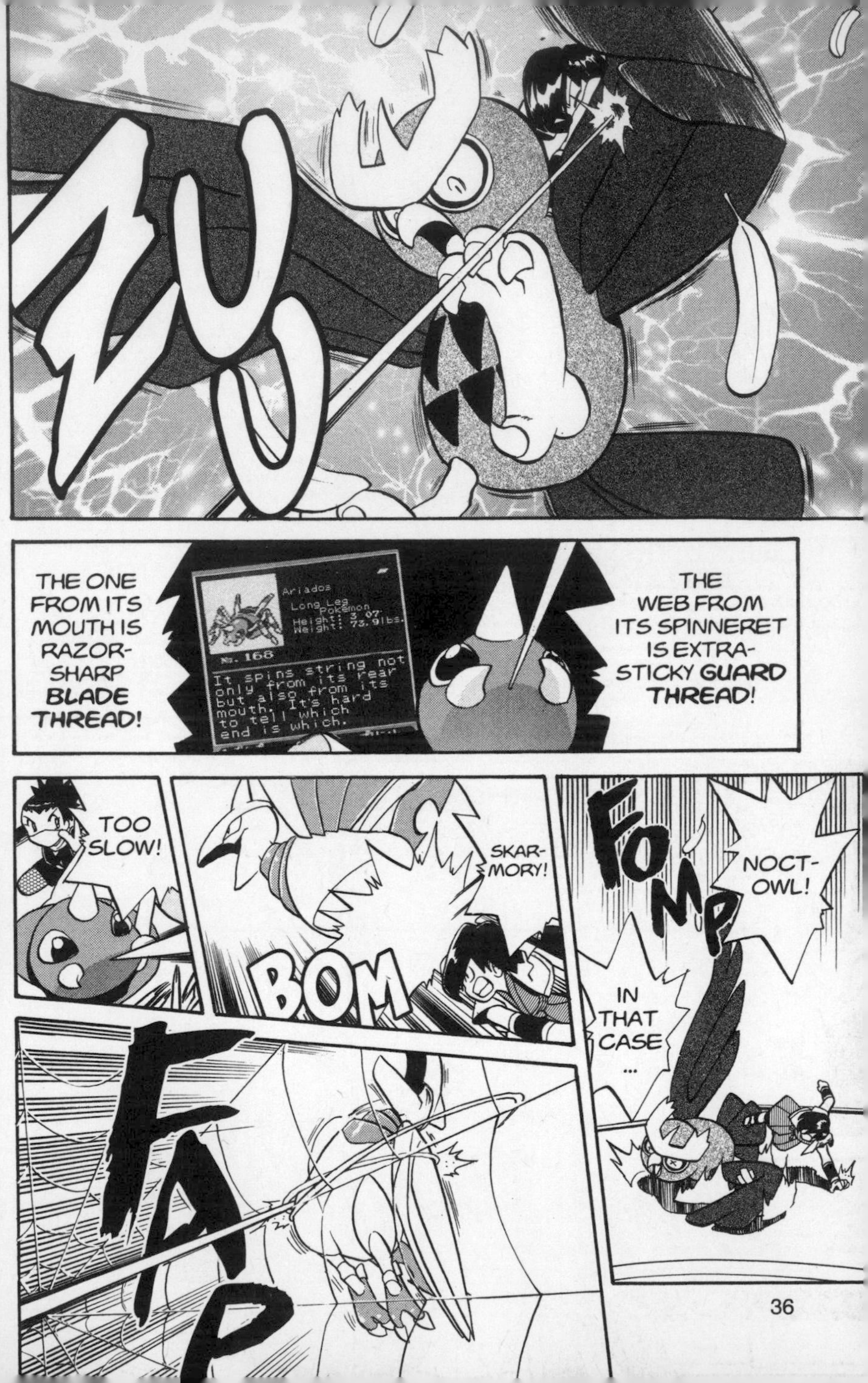
ZU
THE WEB FROM ITS SPINNERET IS EXTRA-STICKY GUARD THREAD!
Ariados
Long Leg Pokemon
Height: 3'07"
Weight: 73.9lbs.
No. 168
It spins string not only from its rear but also from its mouth. It's hard to tell which end is which.
THE ONE FROM ITS MOUTH IS RAZOR-SHARP BLADE THREAD!
FOMP
NOCT-OWL!
IN THAT CASE ...
SKAR-MORY!
BOM
TOO SLOW!
TAP

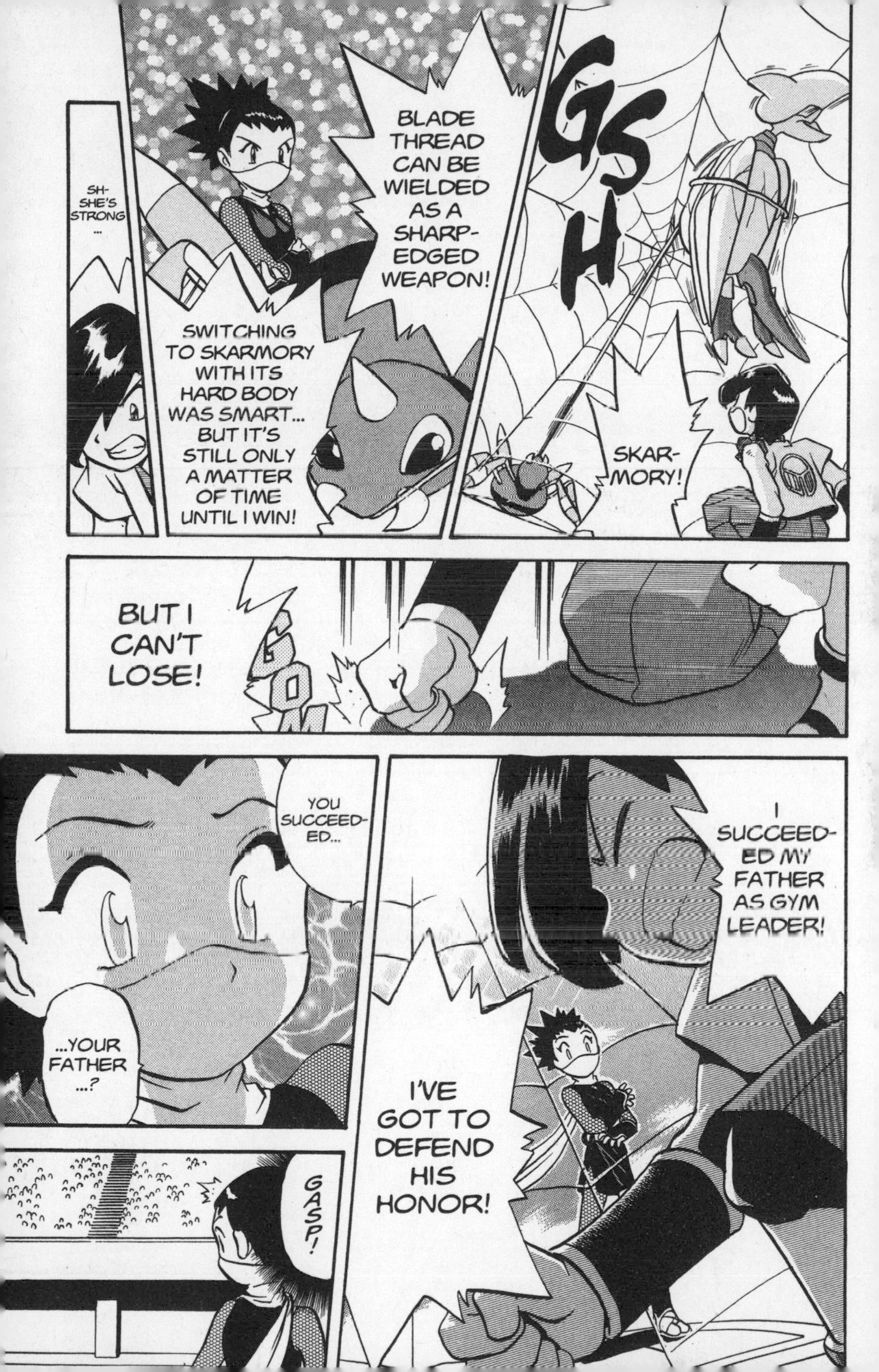
GSH
SKAR-MORY!
BLADE THREAD CAN BE WIELDED AS A SHARP-EDGED WEAPON!
SWITCHING TO SKARMORY WITH ITS HARD BODY WAS SMART... BUT IT'S STILL ONLY A MATTER OF TIME UNTIL I WIN!
SH-SHE'S STRONG ...
BUT I CAN'T LOSE!
GOM
I SUCCEED-ED MY FATHER AS GYM LEADER!
I'VE GOT TO DEFEND HIS HONOR!
YOU SUCCEED-ED...
...YOUR FATHER ...?
GASP!

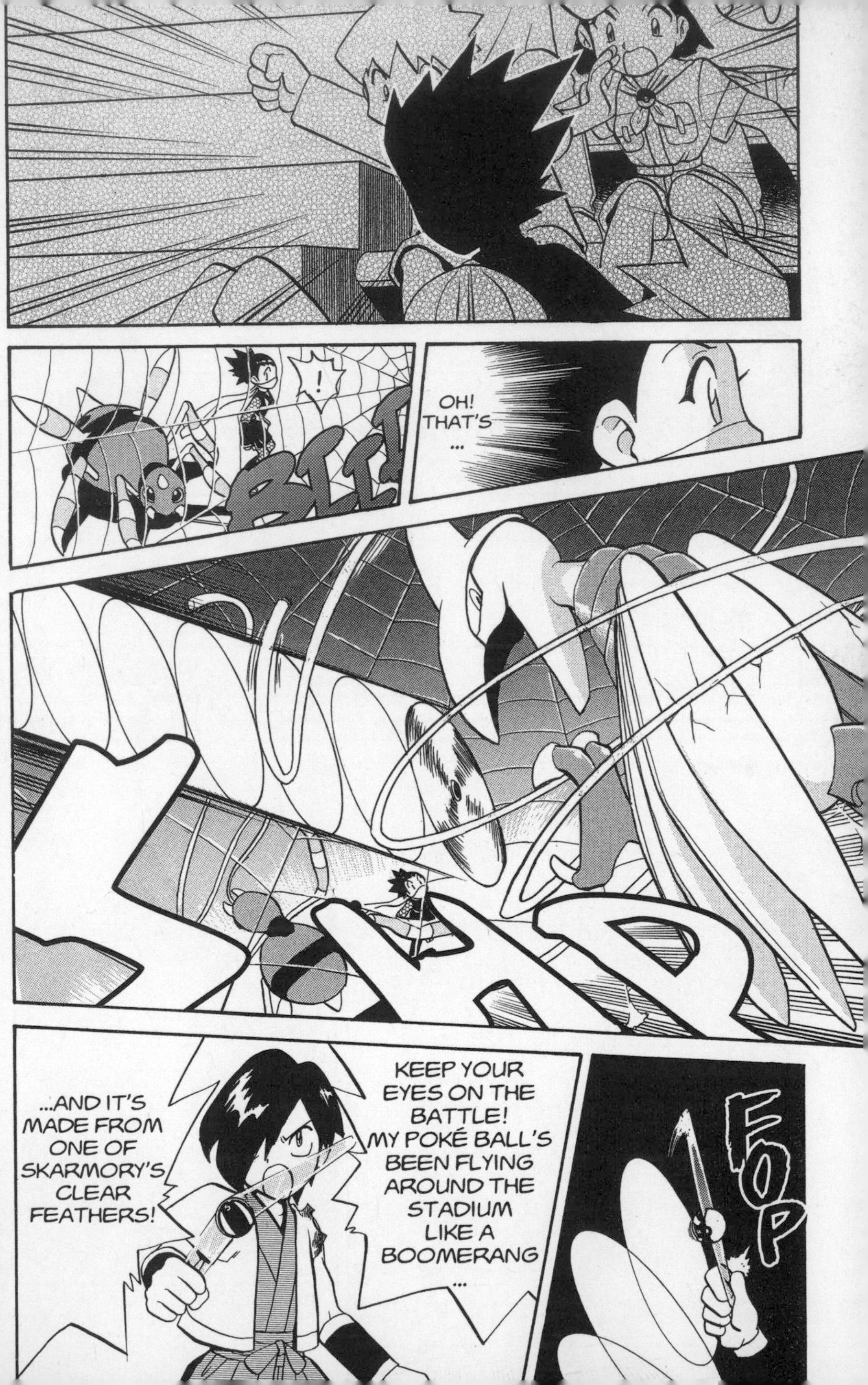
OH! THAT'S ...
!
FOOP
KEEP YOUR EYES ON THE BATTLE! MY POKÉ BALL'S BEEN FLYING AROUND THE STADIUM LIKE A BOOMERANG ...
...AND IT'S MADE FROM ONE OF SKARMORY'S CLEAR FEATHERS!

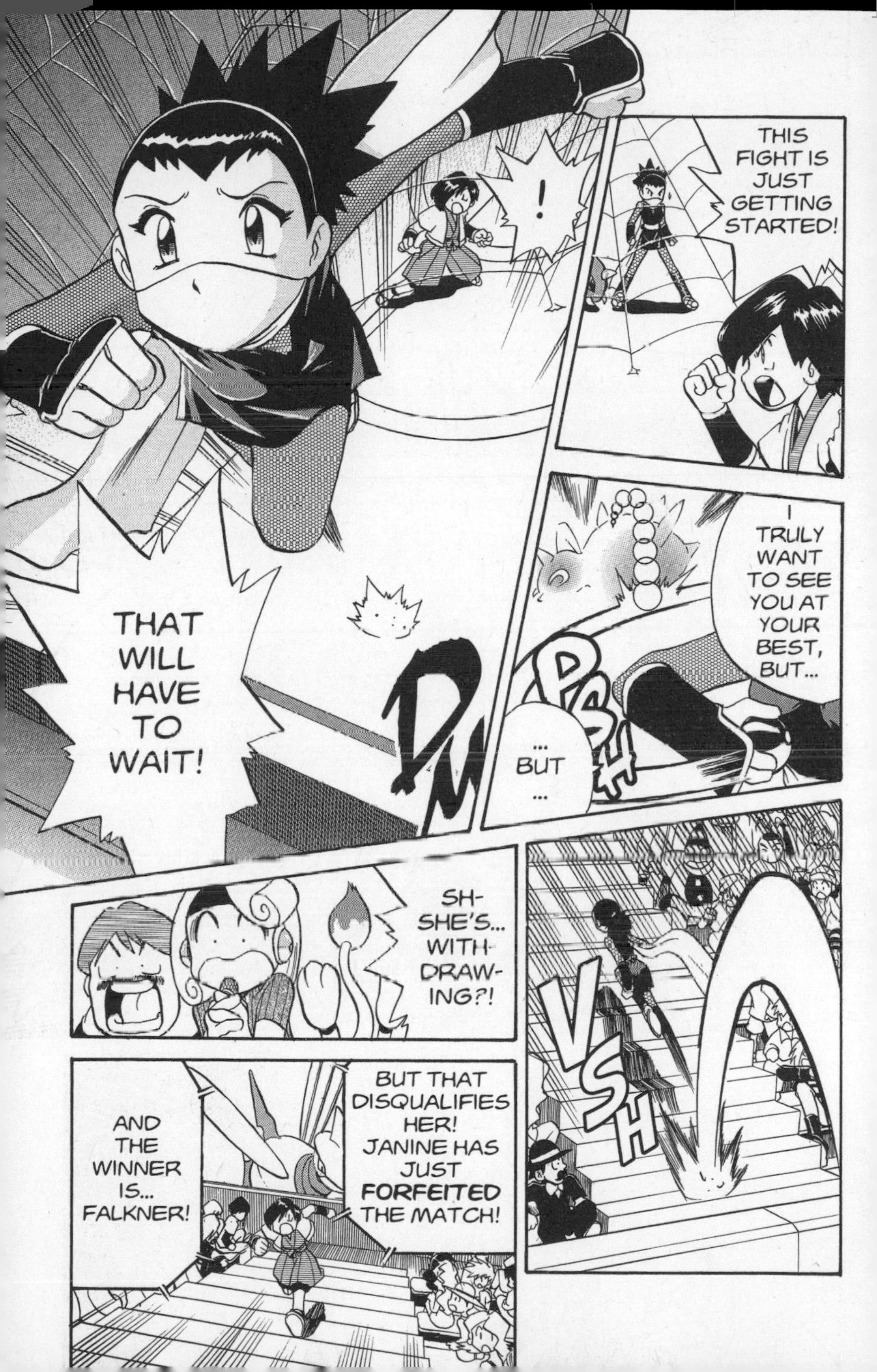
THIS FIGHT IS JUST GETTING STARTED!
!
I TRULY WANT TO SEE YOU AT YOUR BEST, BUT...
PSSH
...BUT...
THAT WILL HAVE TO WAIT!
VSH
SH-SHE'S... WITH-DRAW-ING?!
BUT THAT DISQUALIFIES HER! JANINE HAS JUST **FORFEITED** THE MATCH!
AND THE WINNER IS... FALKNER!

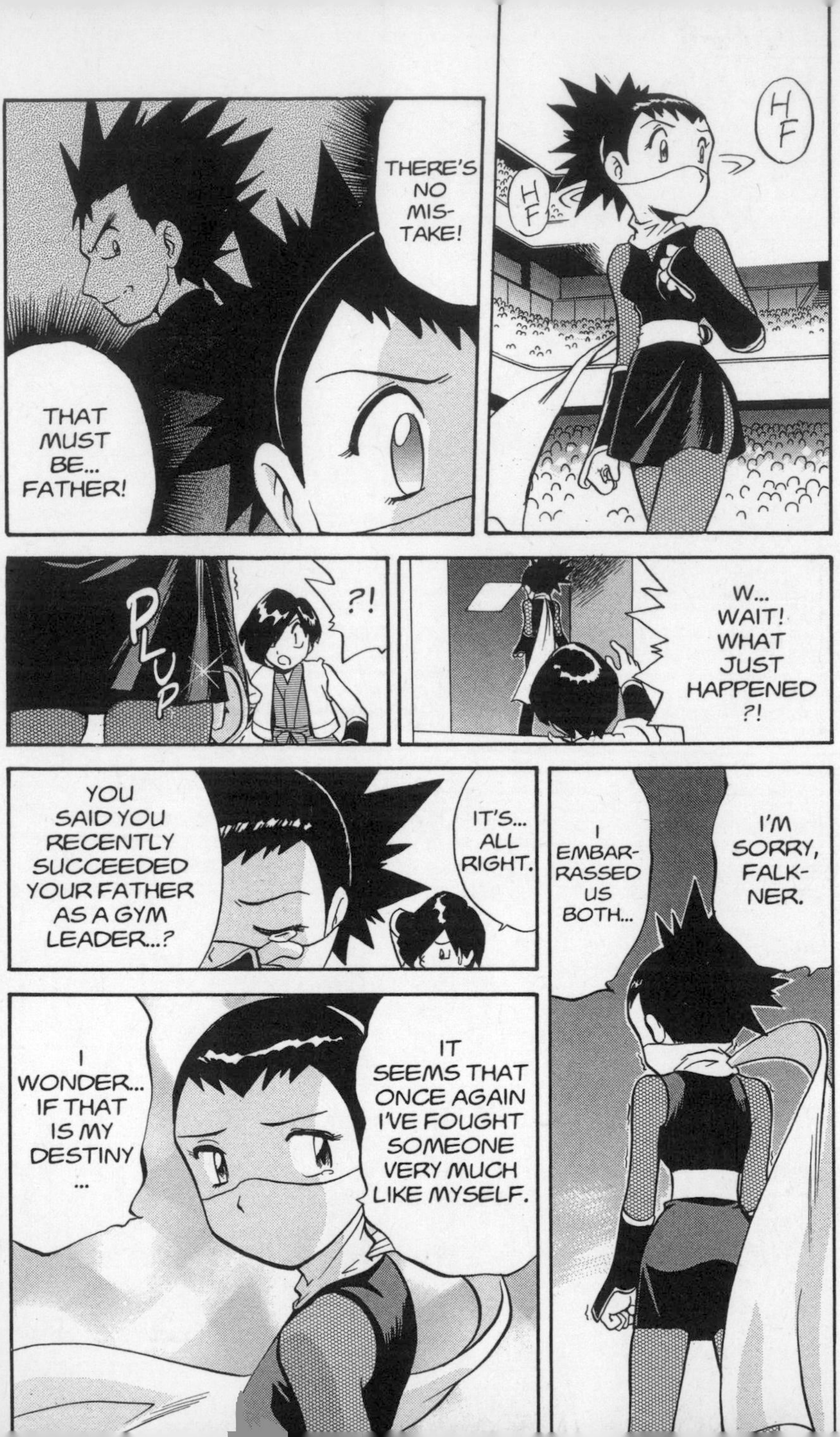
HF
HF
THERE'S NO MIS-TAKE!
THAT MUST BE... FATHER!
W... WAIT! WHAT JUST HAPPENED ?!
?!
PLUP
I'M SORRY, FALK-NER.
I EMBAR-RASSED US BOTH...
IT'S... ALL RIGHT.
YOU SAID YOU RECENTLY SUCCEEDED YOUR FATHER AS A GYM LEADER...?
IT SEEMS THAT ONCE AGAIN I'VE FOUGHT SOMEONE VERY MUCH LIKE MYSELF.
I WONDER... IF THAT IS MY DESTINY ...

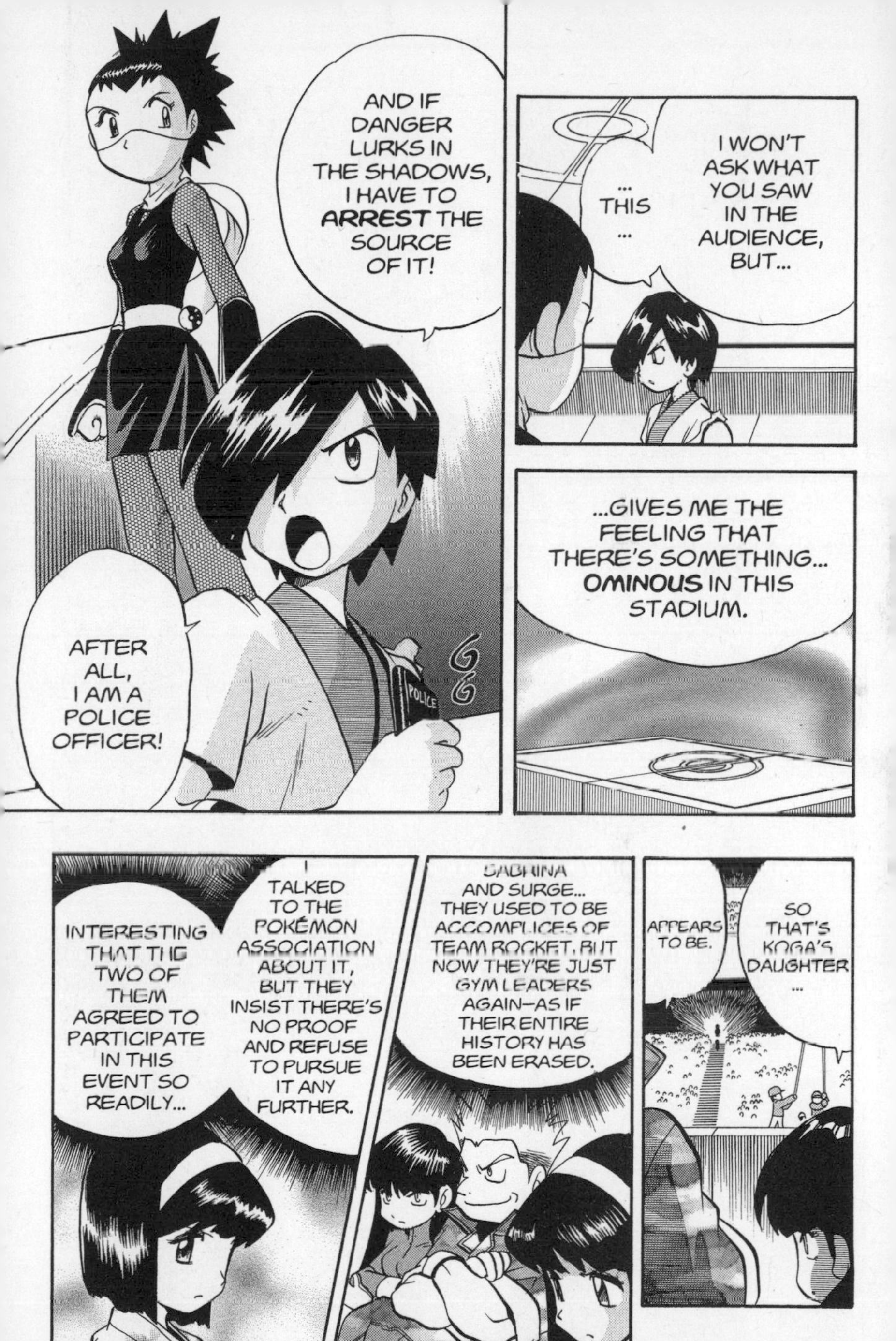
I WON'T ASK WHAT YOU SAW IN THE AUDIENCE, BUT...
... THIS ...
...GIVES ME THE FEELING THAT THERE'S SOMETHING... OMINOUS IN THIS STADIUM.
AND IF DANGER LURKS IN THE SHADOWS, I HAVE TO ARREST THE SOURCE OF IT!
AFTER ALL, I AM A POLICE OFFICER!
POLICE
SO THAT'S KOGA'S DAUGHTER...
APPEARS TO BE.
SABRINA AND SURGE... THEY USED TO BE ACCOMPLICES OF TEAM ROCKET, BUT NOW THEY'RE JUST GYM LEADERS AGAIN—AS IF THEIR ENTIRE HISTORY HAS BEEN ERASED.
I TALKED TO THE POKÉMON ASSOCIATION ABOUT IT, BUT THEY INSIST THERE'S NO PROOF AND REFUSE TO PURSUE IT ANY FURTHER.
INTERESTING THAT THE TWO OF THEM AGREED TO PARTICIPATE IN THIS EVENT SO READILY...

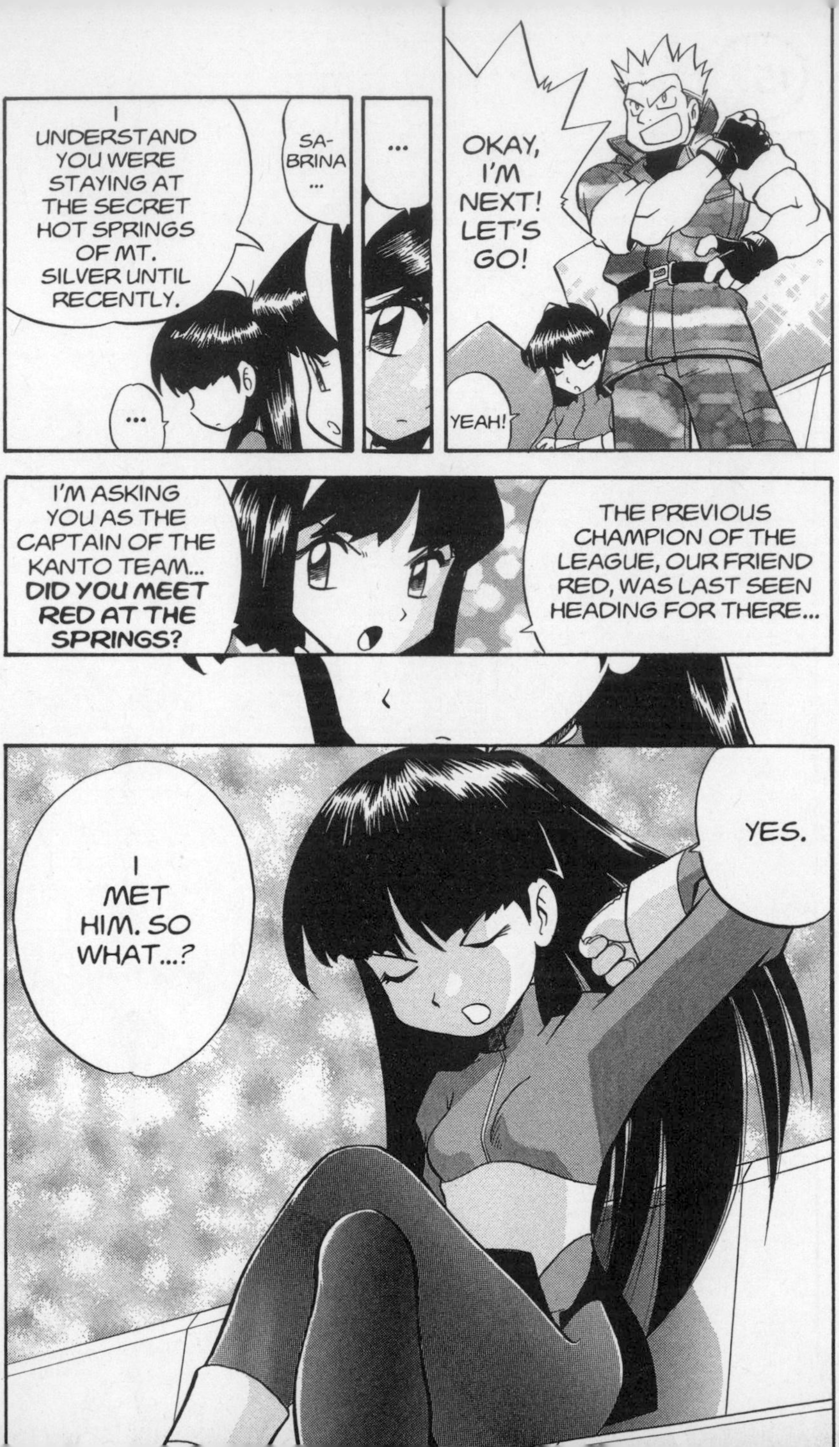
OKAY, I'M NEXT! LET'S GO!
YEAH!
...
SA-BRINA...
I UNDERSTAND YOU WERE STAYING AT THE SECRET HOT SPRINGS OF MT. SILVER UNTIL RECENTLY.
...
THE PREVIOUS CHAMPION OF THE LEAGUE, OUR FRIEND RED, WAS LAST SEEN HEADING FOR THERE...
I'M ASKING YOU AS THE CAPTAIN OF THE KANTO TEAM... **DID YOU MEET RED AT THE SPRINGS?**
YES.
I MET HIM. SO WHAT...?

157 Magnificent Magnemite

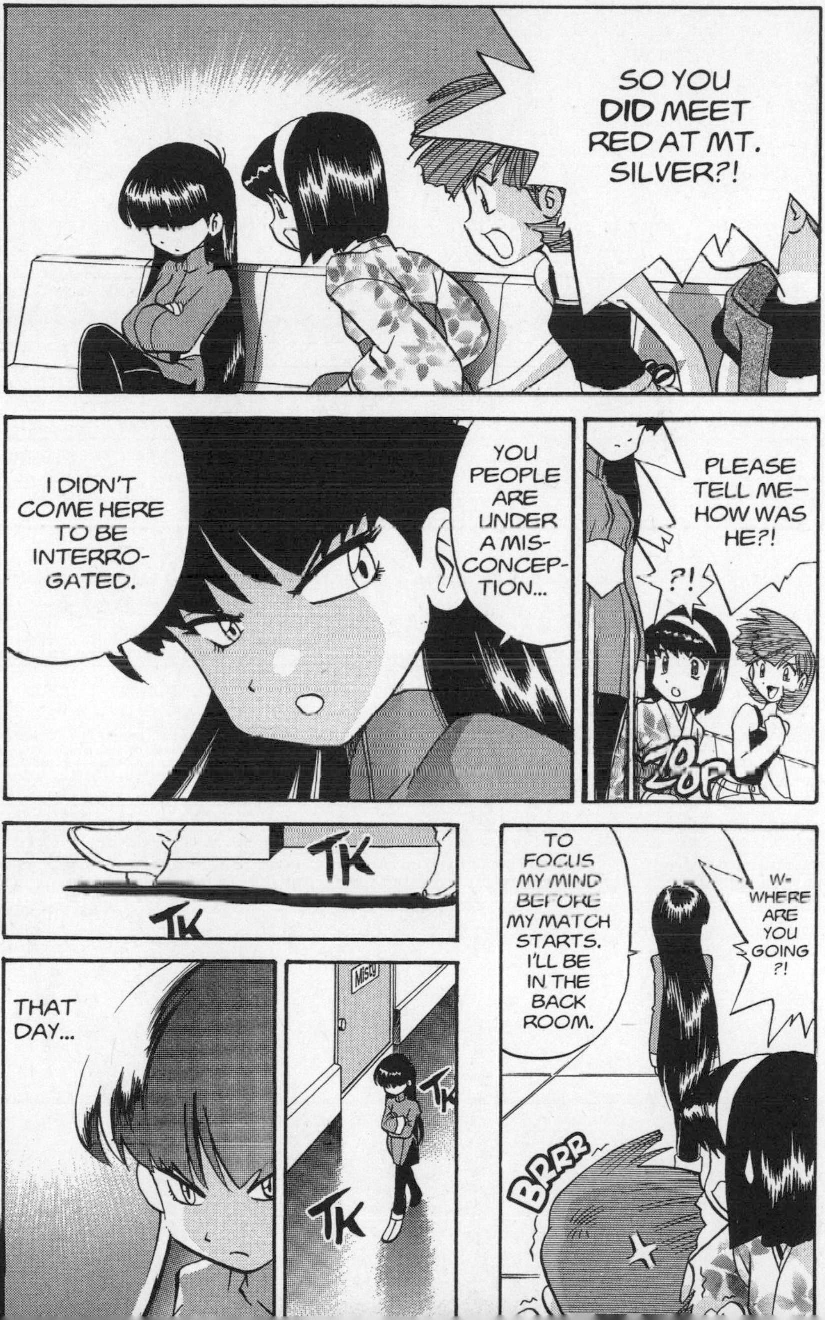
SO YOU DID MEET RED AT MT. SILVER?!
PLEASE TELL ME— HOW WAS HE?!
?!
ZOOP
YOU PEOPLE ARE UNDER A MIS-CONCEP-TION...
I DIDN'T COME HERE TO BE INTERRO-GATED.
W-WHERE ARE YOU GOING ?!
TO FOCUS MY MIND BEFORE MY MATCH STARTS. I'LL BE IN THE BACK ROOM.
BRRR
TK
TK
TK
TK
Misty
THAT DAY...

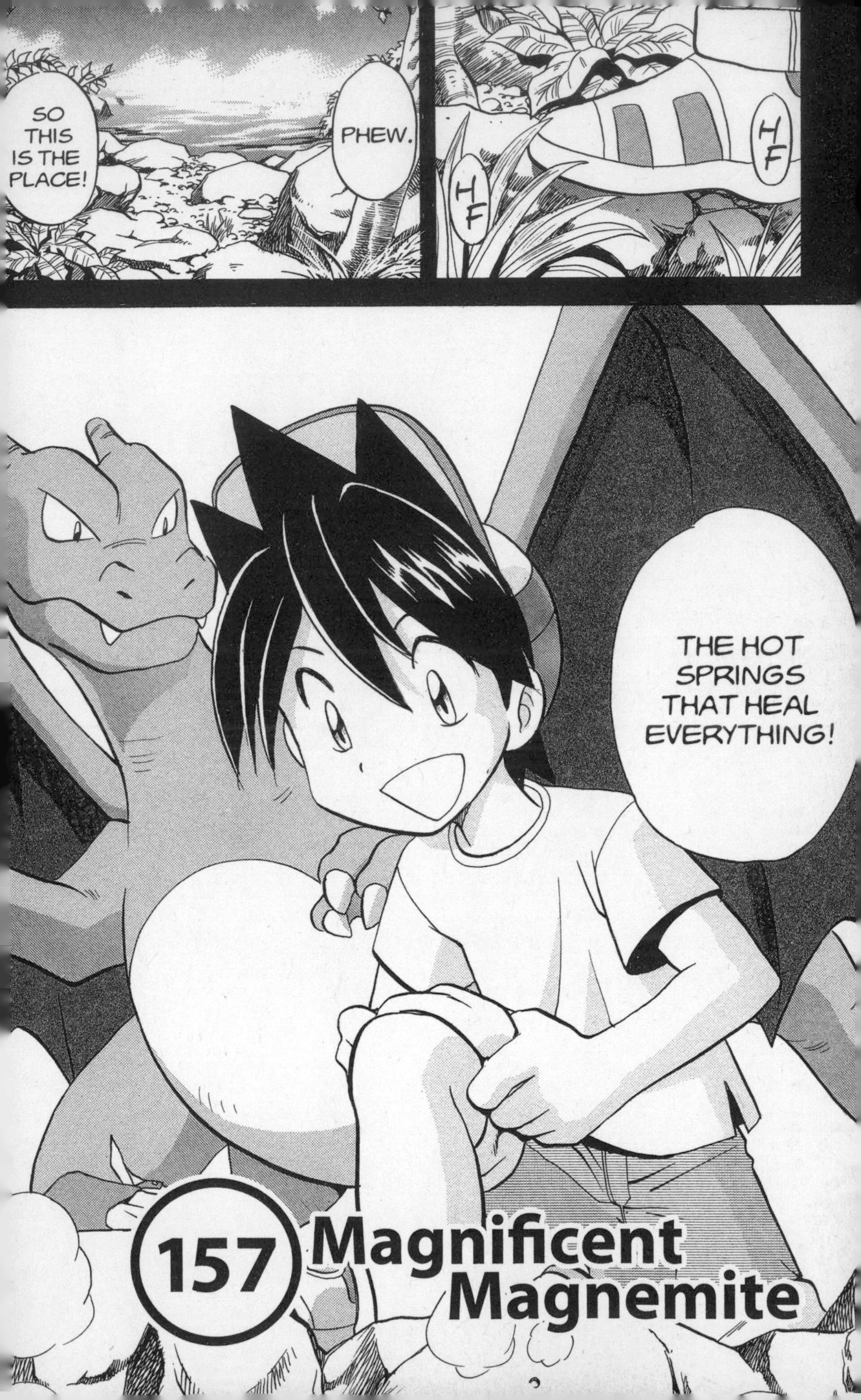
H F
H F
PHEW.
SO THIS IS THE PLACE!
THE HOT SPRINGS THAT HEAL EVERYTHING!
157 Magnificent Magnemite

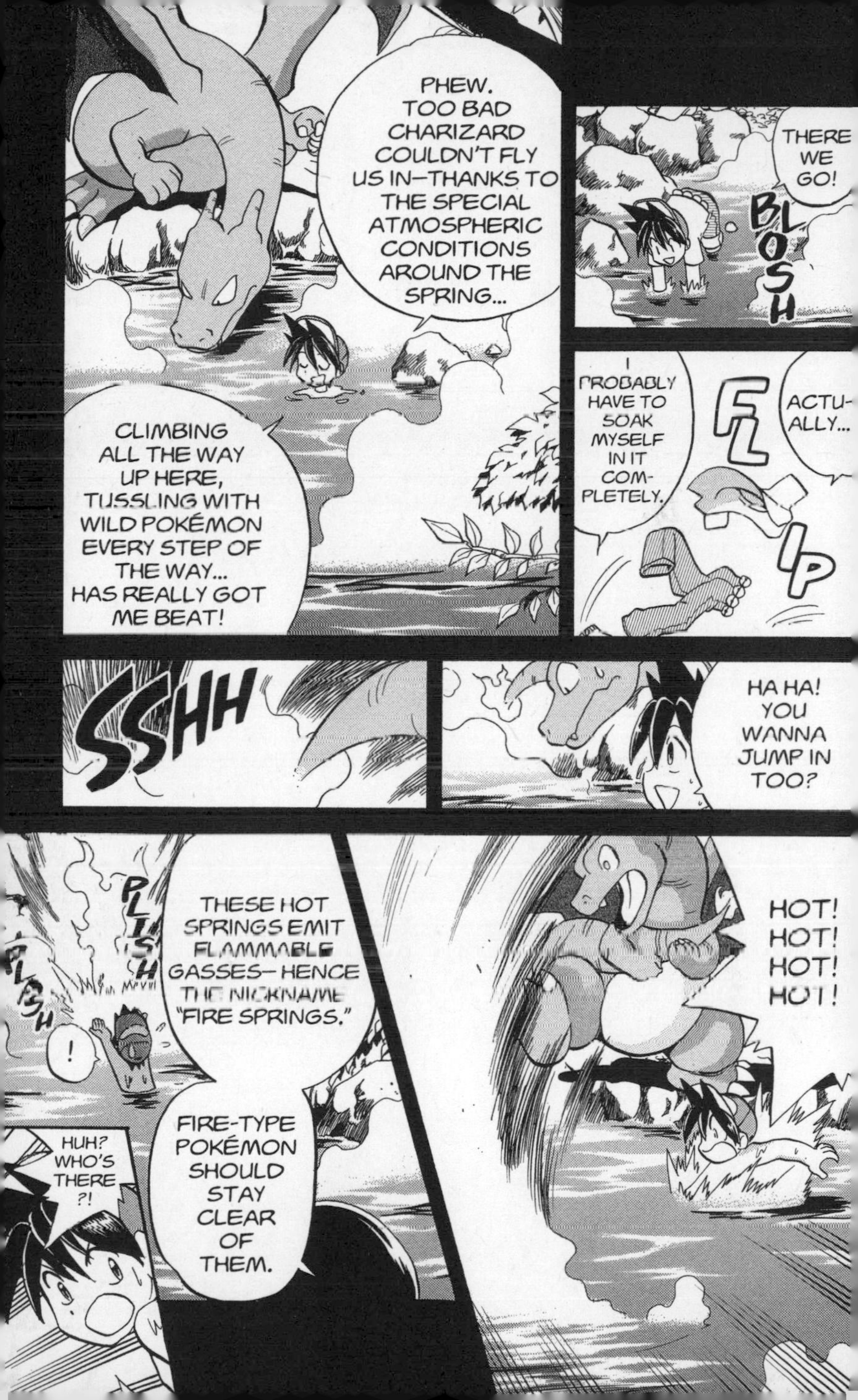
THERE WE GO!
BLOSH
ACTUALLY...
I PROBABLY HAVE TO SOAK MYSELF IN IT COMPLETELY.
FLIP
PHEW. TOO BAD CHARIZARD COULDN'T FLY US IN—THANKS TO THE SPECIAL ATMOSPHERIC CONDITIONS AROUND THE SPRING...
CLIMBING ALL THE WAY UP HERE, TUSSLING WITH WILD POKÉMON EVERY STEP OF THE WAY... HAS REALLY GOT ME BEAT!
HA HA! YOU WANNA JUMP IN TOO?
SSHH
HOT! HOT! HOT! HOT!
THESE HOT SPRINGS EMIT FLAMMABLE GASSES—HENCE THE NICKNAME "FIRE SPRINGS."
FIRE-TYPE POKÉMON SHOULD STAY CLEAR OF THEM.
PLISH
!
HUH? WHO'S THERE?!

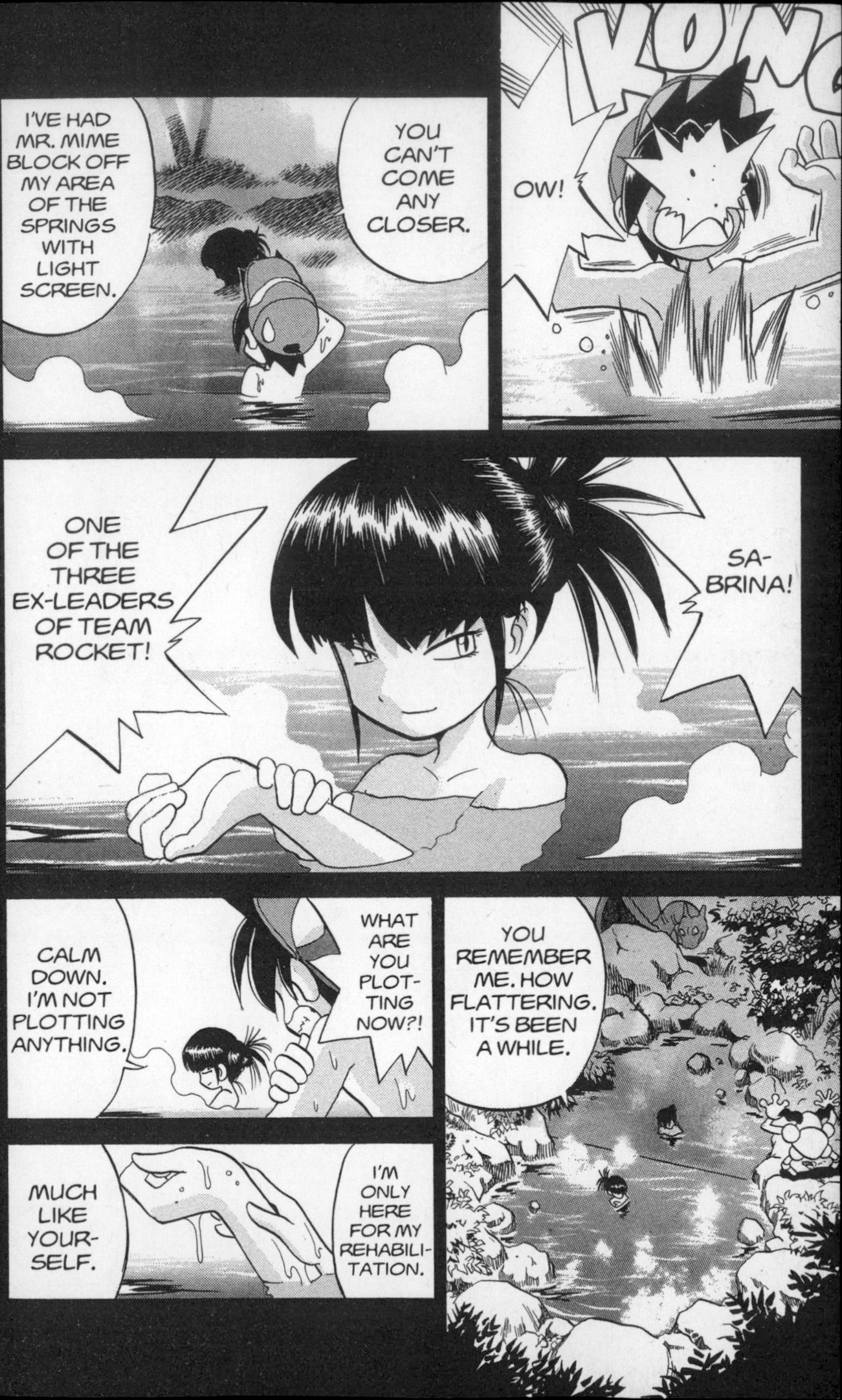
KONG
OW!
YOU CAN'T COME ANY CLOSER.
I'VE HAD MR. MIME BLOCK OFF MY AREA OF THE SPRINGS WITH LIGHT SCREEN.
SA-BRINA!
ONE OF THE THREE EX-LEADERS OF TEAM ROCKET!
YOU REMEMBER ME. HOW FLATTERING. IT'S BEEN A WHILE.
WHAT ARE YOU PLOT-TING NOW?!
CALM DOWN. I'M NOT PLOTTING ANYTHING.
I'M ONLY HERE FOR MY REHABILI-TATION.
MUCH LIKE YOUR-SELF.

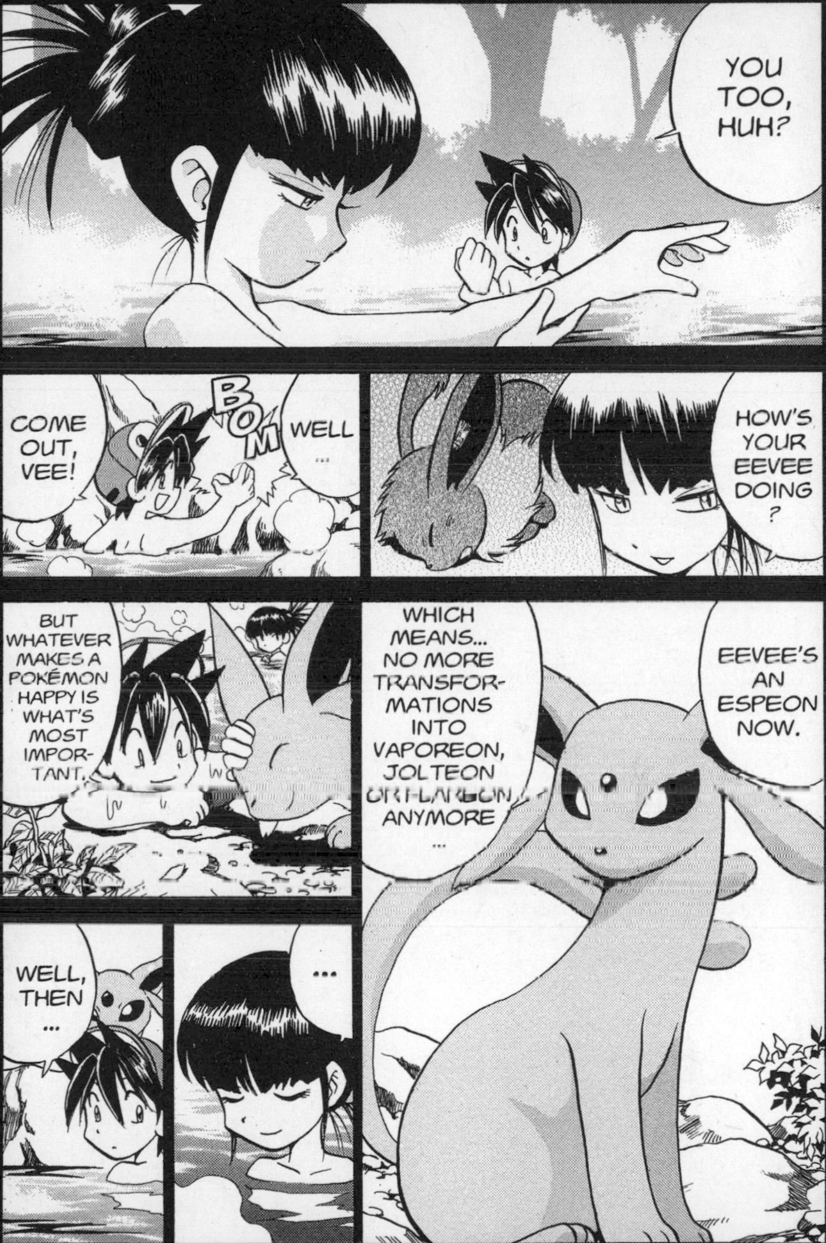
YOU TOO, HUH?
HOW'S YOUR EEVEE DOING?
WELL ...
BOM
COME OUT, VEE!
EEVEE'S AN ESPEON NOW.
WHICH MEANS... NO MORE TRANSFORMATIONS INTO VAPOREON, JOLTEON OR FLAREON ANYMORE ...
BUT WHATEVER MAKES A POKÉMON HAPPY IS WHAT'S MOST IMPORTANT.
...
WELL, THEN ...

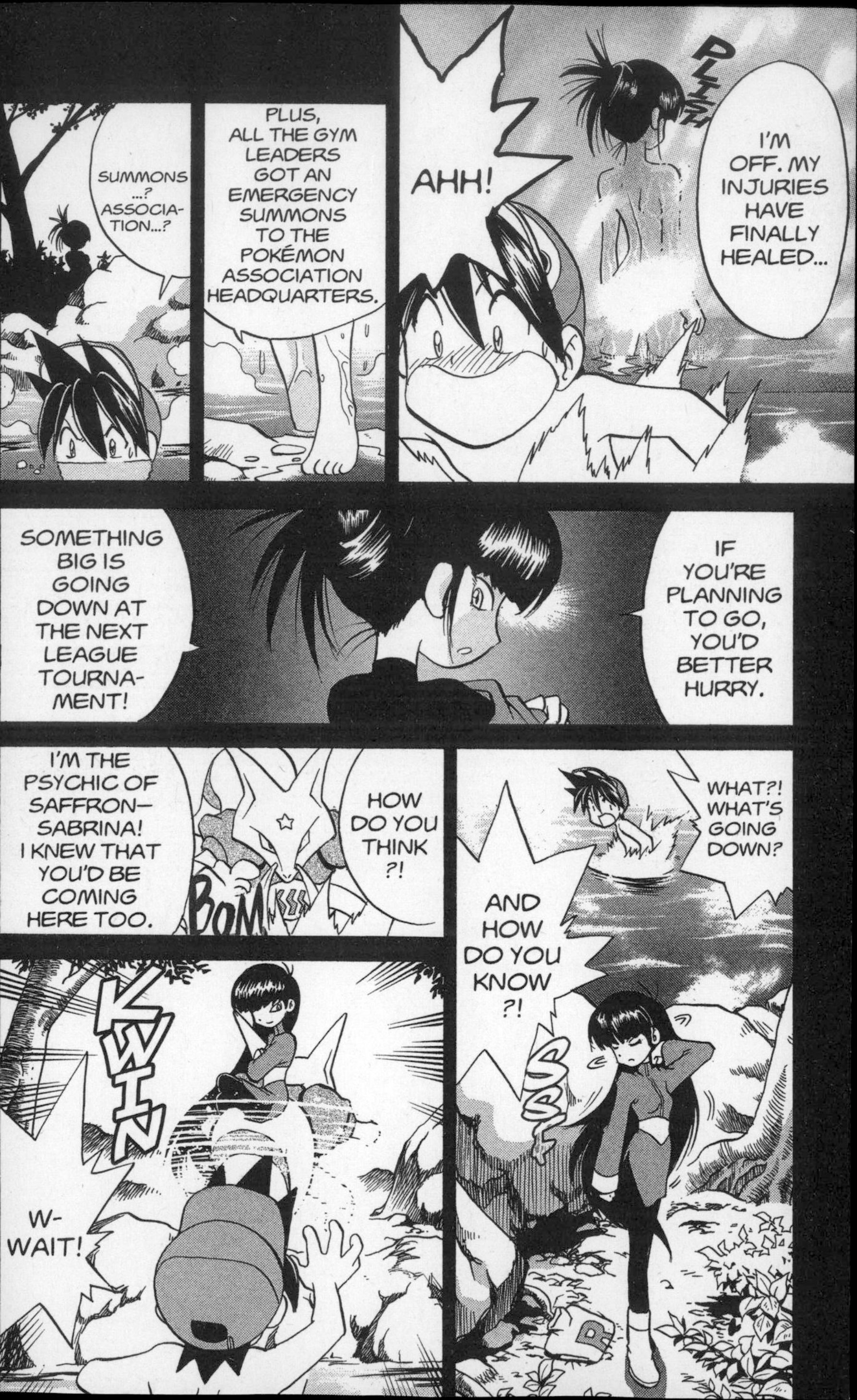
PLISH
I'M OFF. MY INJURIES HAVE FINALLY HEALED...
AHH!
PLUS, ALL THE GYM LEADERS GOT AN EMERGENCY SUMMONS TO THE POKÉMON ASSOCIATION HEADQUARTERS.
SUMMONS ...? ASSOCIA-TION...?
IF YOU'RE PLANNING TO GO, YOU'D BETTER HURRY.
SOMETHING BIG IS GOING DOWN AT THE NEXT LEAGUE TOURNA-MENT!
WHAT?! WHAT'S GOING DOWN?
AND HOW DO YOU KNOW ?!
SS
HOW DO YOU THINK ?!
I'M THE PSYCHIC OF SAFFRON— SABRINA! I KNEW THAT YOU'D BE COMING HERE TOO.
BOM
KWIN
W-WAIT!

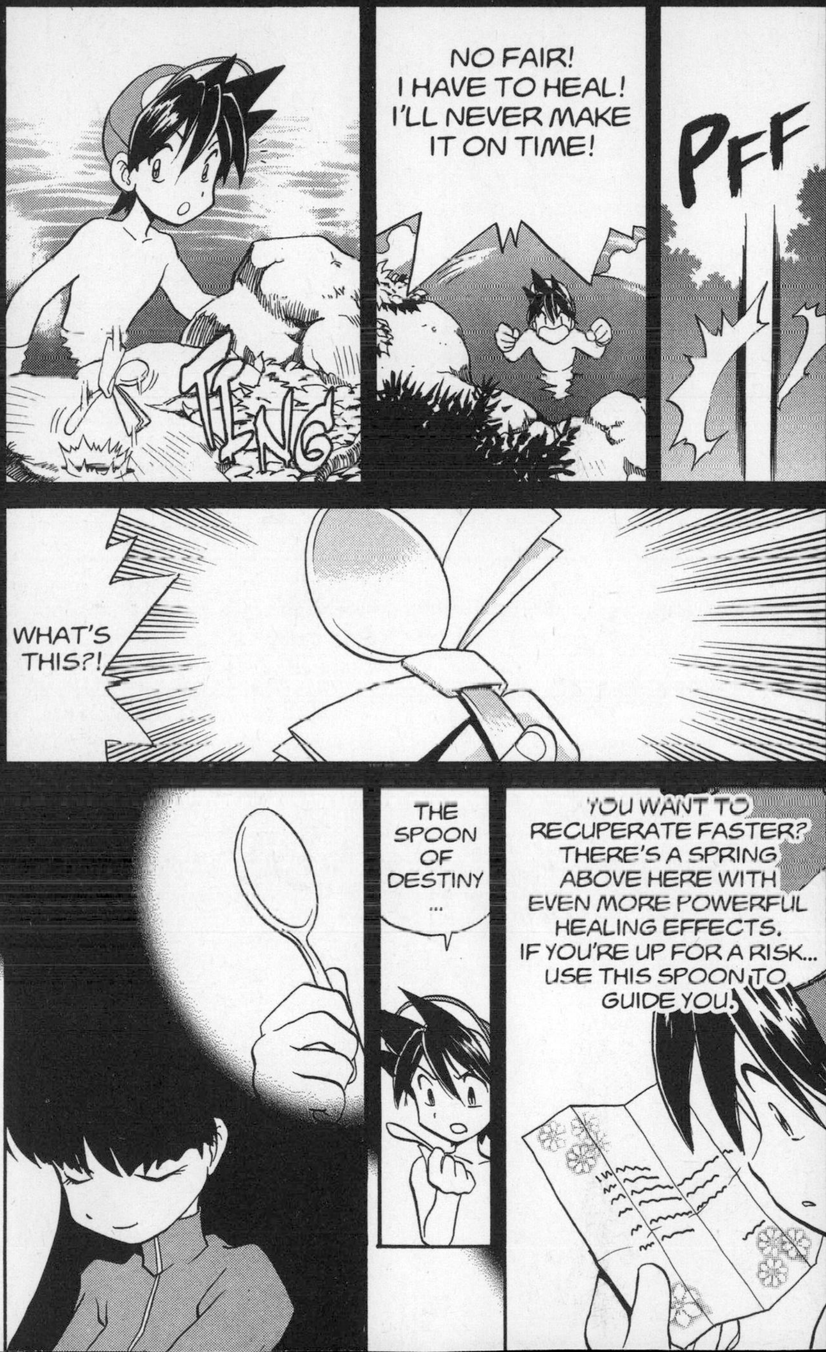
PFF
NO FAIR! I HAVE TO HEAL! I'LL NEVER MAKE IT ON TIME!
TING
WHAT'S THIS?!
YOU WANT TO RECUPERATE FASTER? THERE'S A SPRING ABOVE HERE WITH EVEN MORE POWERFUL HEALING EFFECTS. IF YOU'RE UP FOR A RISK... USE THIS SPOON TO GUIDE YOU.
THE SPOON OF DESTINY ...

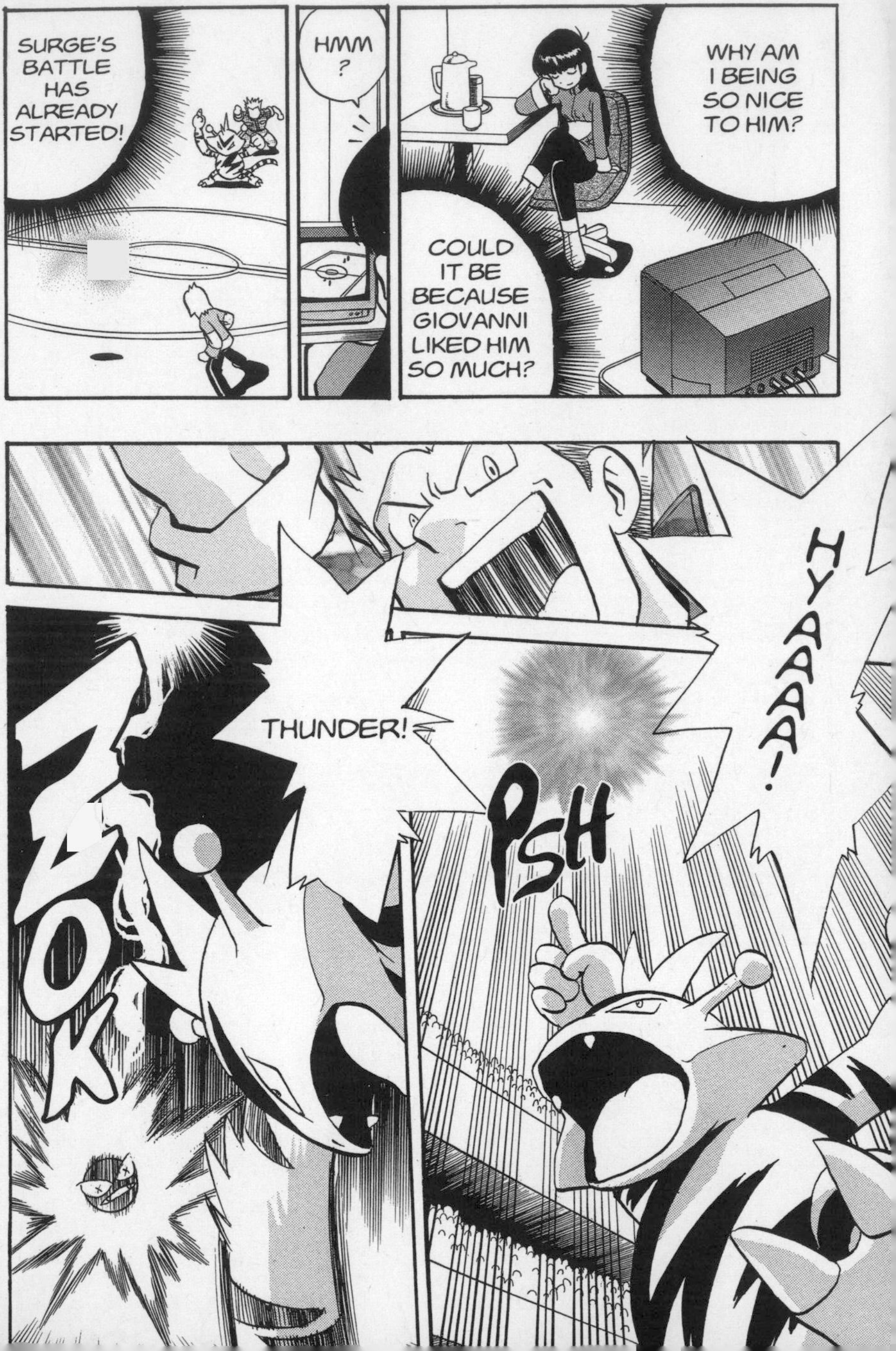
WHY AM I BEING SO NICE TO HIM?
COULD IT BE BECAUSE GIOVANNI LIKED HIM SO MUCH?
HMM ?
SURGE'S BATTLE HAS ALREADY STARTED!
HYAAAA!
THUNDER!
PSH
ZOK

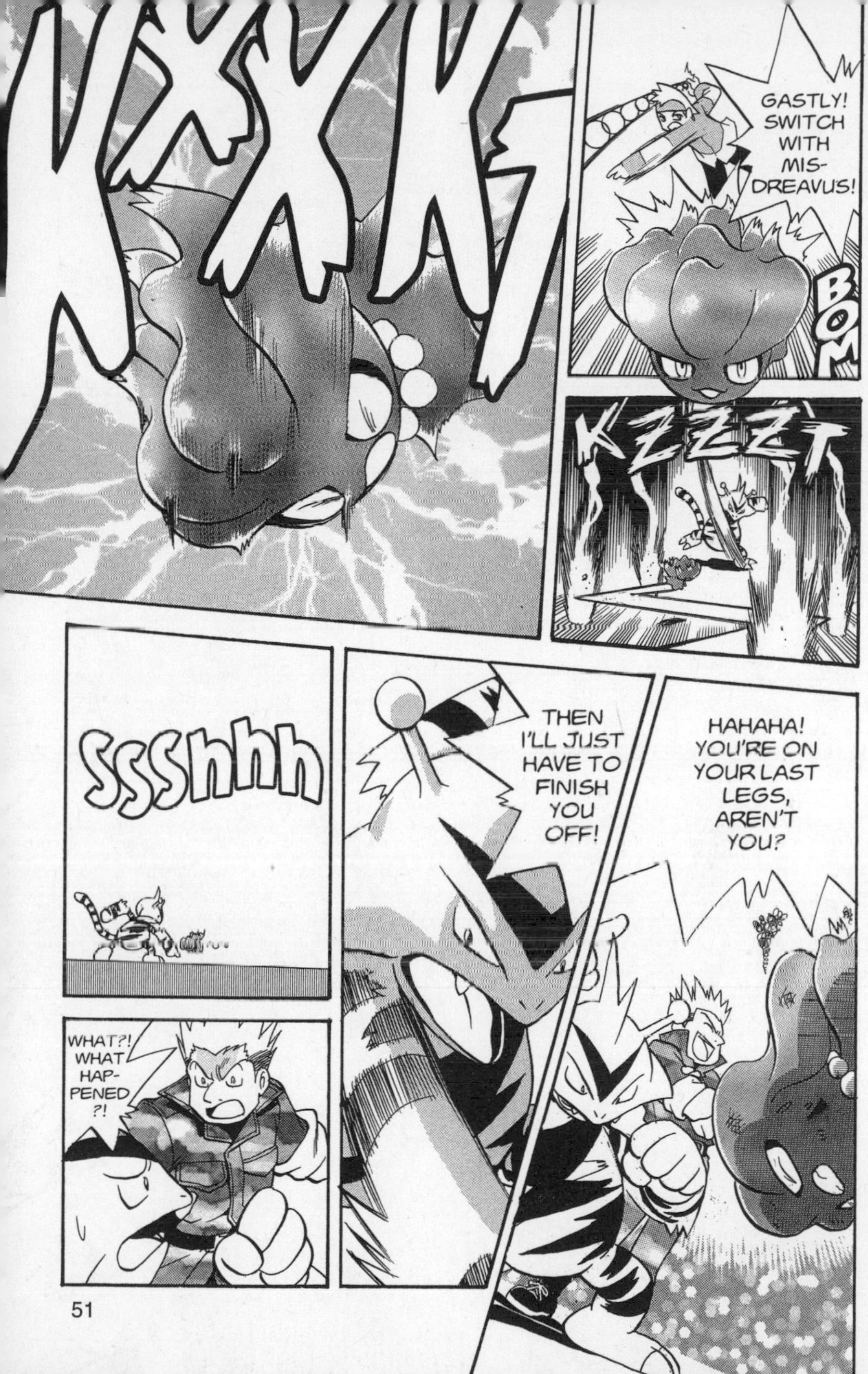
GASTLY! SWITCH WITH MIS-DREAVUS!
BOM
KZZZT
HAHAHA! YOU'RE ON YOUR LAST LEGS, AREN'T YOU?
THEN I'LL JUST HAVE TO FINISH YOU OFF!
SSShhh
WHAT?! WHAT HAP-PENED?!

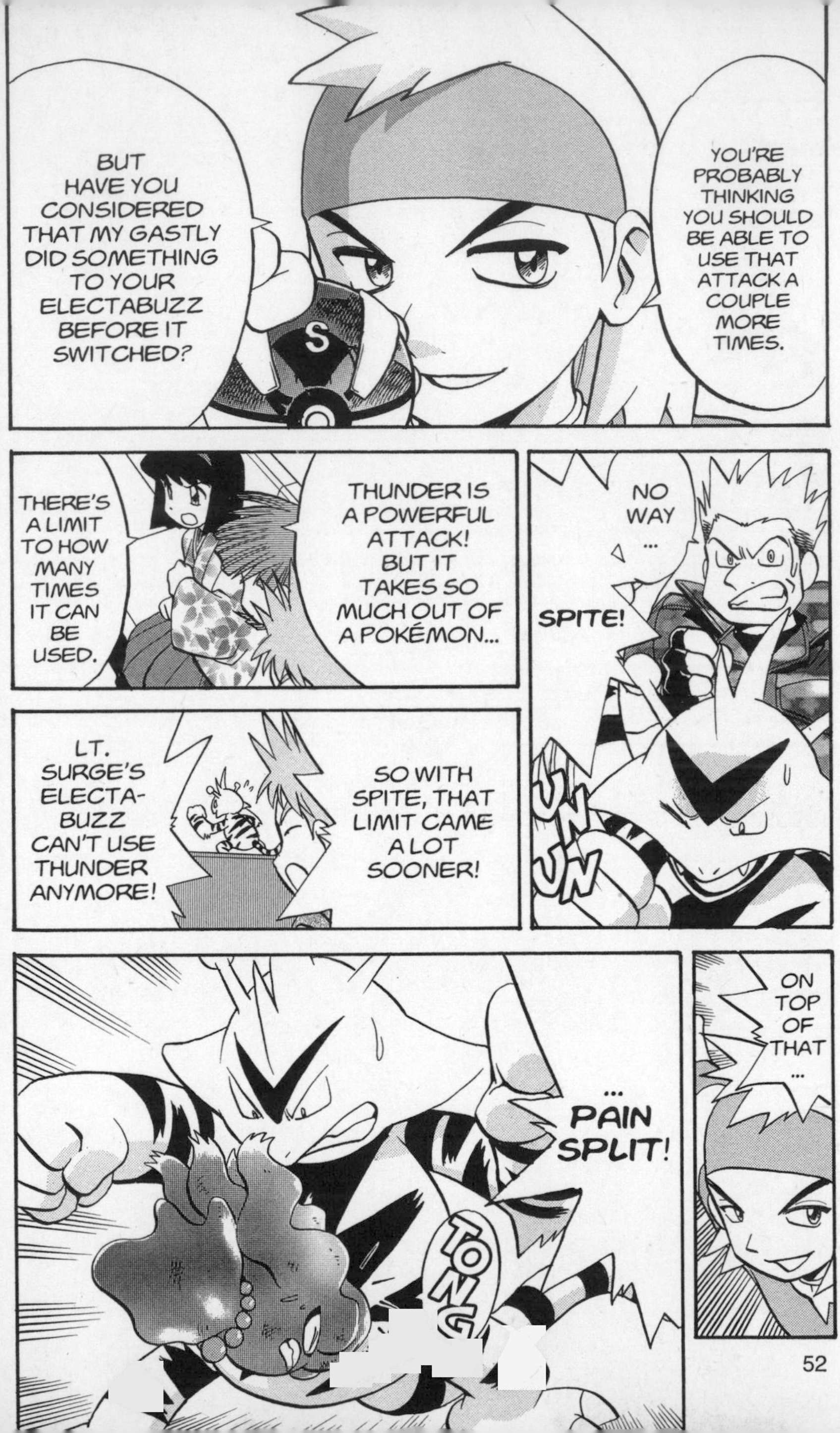
YOU'RE PROBABLY THINKING YOU SHOULD BE ABLE TO USE THAT ATTACK A COUPLE MORE TIMES.
BUT HAVE YOU CONSIDERED THAT MY GASTLY DID SOMETHING TO YOUR ELECTABUZZ BEFORE IT SWITCHED?
NO WAY ...
SPITE!
UN UN UN
THUNDER IS A POWERFUL ATTACK! BUT IT TAKES SO MUCH OUT OF A POKÉMON...
THERE'S A LIMIT TO HOW MANY TIMES IT CAN BE USED.
SO WITH SPITE, THAT LIMIT CAME A LOT SOONER!
LT. SURGE'S ELECTA-BUZZ CAN'T USE THUNDER ANYMORE!
ON TOP OF THAT ...
... PAIN SPLIT!
TONG

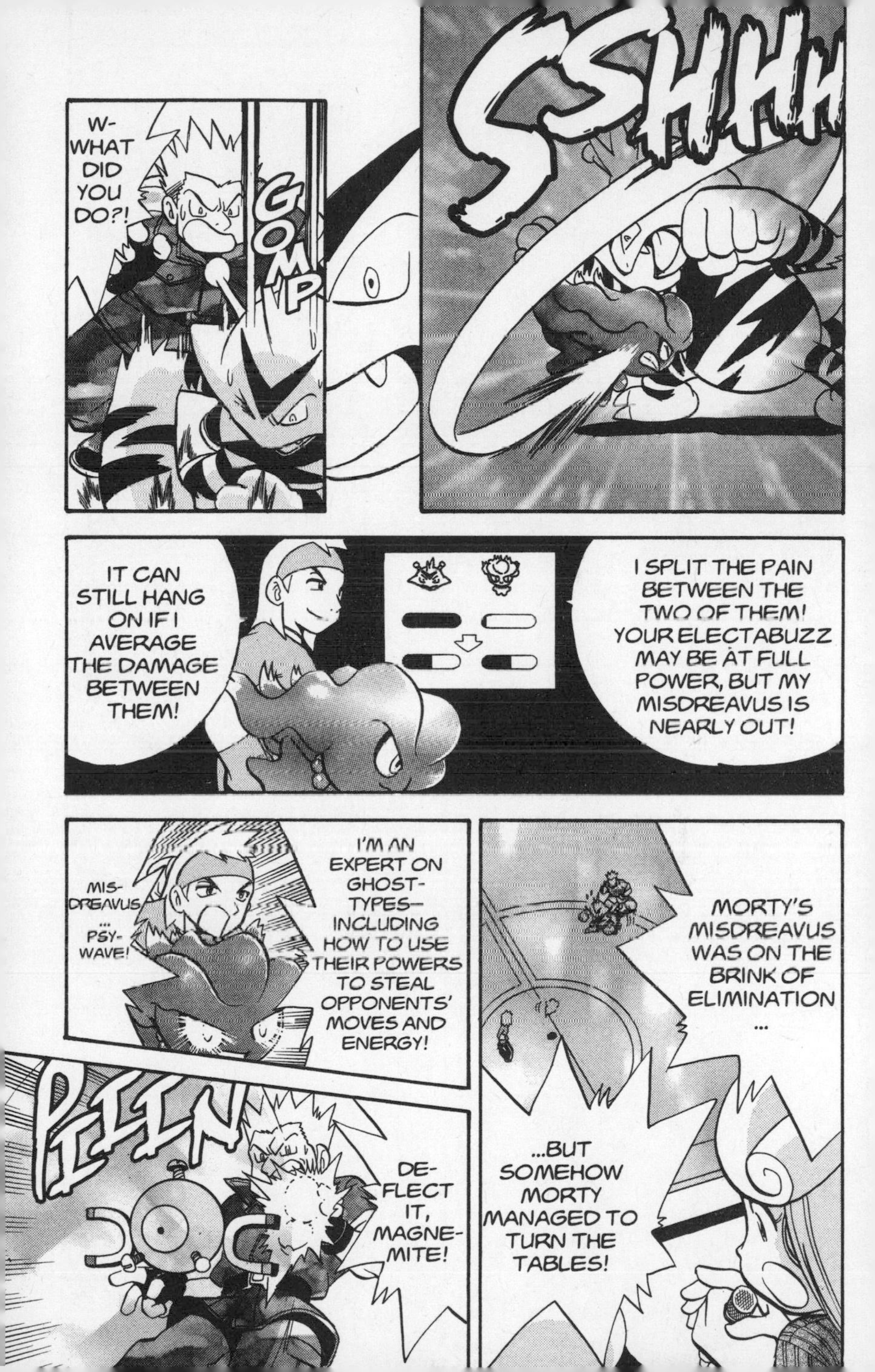
SSHHH
W-WHAT DID YOU DO?!
GOMP
I SPLIT THE PAIN BETWEEN THE TWO OF THEM! YOUR ELECTABUZZ MAY BE AT FULL POWER, BUT MY MISDREAVUS IS NEARLY OUT!
IT CAN STILL HANG ON IF I AVERAGE THE DAMAGE BETWEEN THEM!
MORTY'S MISDREAVUS WAS ON THE BRINK OF ELIMINATION ...
...BUT SOMEHOW MORTY MANAGED TO TURN THE TABLES!
I'M AN EXPERT ON GHOST-TYPES—INCLUDING HOW TO USE THEIR POWERS TO STEAL OPPONENTS' MOVES AND ENERGY!
MISDREAVUS ... PSYWAVE!
PIIIN
DEFLECT IT, MAGNEMITE!

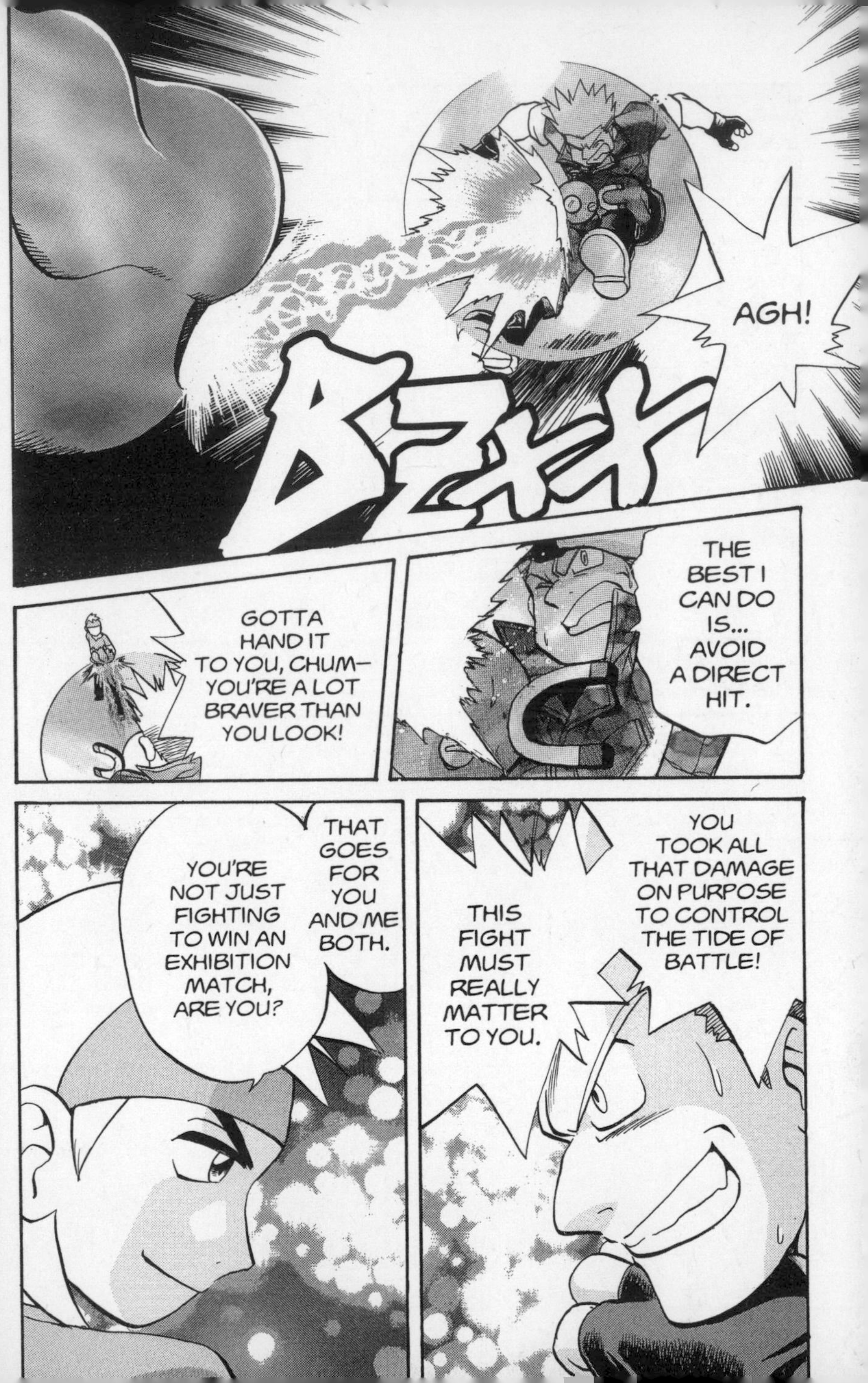
AGH!
THE BEST I CAN DO IS... AVOID A DIRECT HIT.
GOTTA HAND IT TO YOU, CHUM— YOU'RE A LOT BRAVER THAN YOU LOOK!
YOU TOOK ALL THAT DAMAGE ON PURPOSE TO CONTROL THE TIDE OF BATTLE!
THIS FIGHT MUST REALLY MATTER TO YOU.
THAT GOES FOR YOU AND ME BOTH.
YOU'RE NOT JUST FIGHTING TO WIN AN EXHIBITION MATCH, ARE YOU?

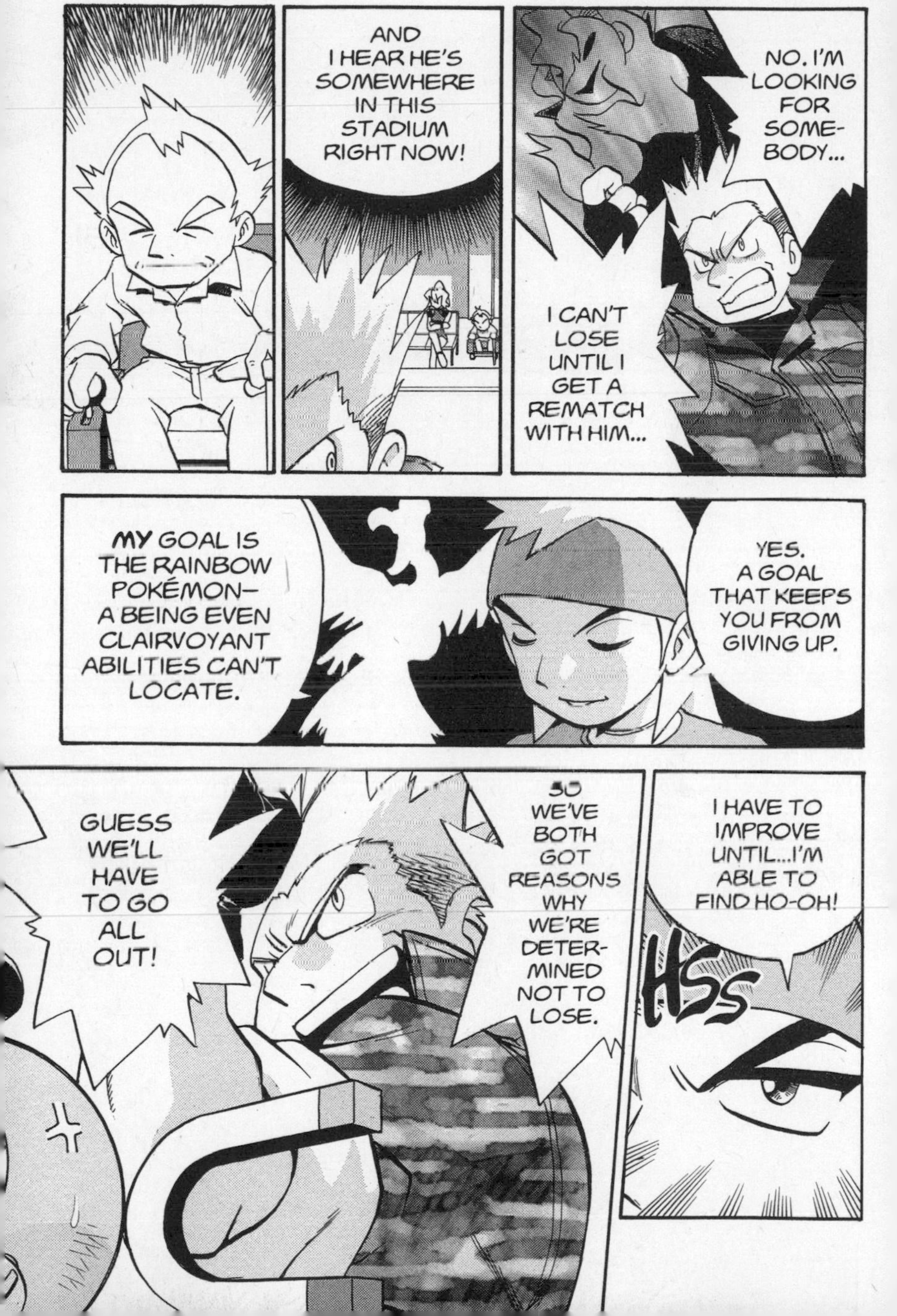
NO. I'M LOOKING FOR SOMEBODY...
I CAN'T LOSE UNTIL I GET A REMATCH WITH HIM...
AND I HEAR HE'S SOMEWHERE IN THIS STADIUM RIGHT NOW!
YES. A GOAL THAT KEEPS YOU FROM GIVING UP.
MY GOAL IS THE RAINBOW POKÉMON—A BEING EVEN CLAIRVOYANT ABILITIES CAN'T LOCATE.
I HAVE TO IMPROVE UNTIL...I'M ABLE TO FIND HO-OH!
HSS
SO WE'VE BOTH GOT REASONS WHY WE'RE DETERMINED NOT TO LOSE.
GUESS WE'LL HAVE TO GO ALL OUT!

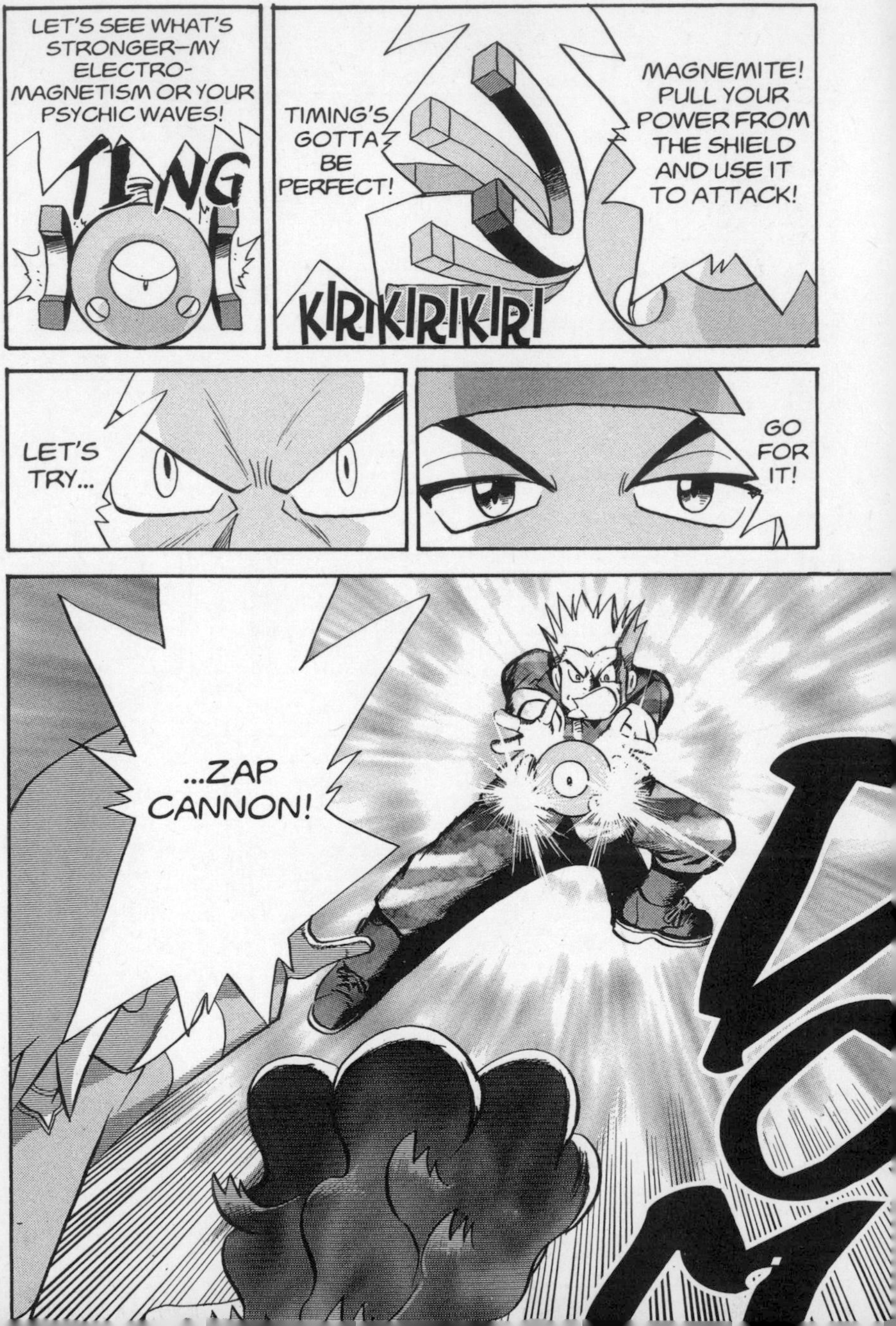
MAGNEMITE! PULL YOUR POWER FROM THE SHIELD AND USE IT TO ATTACK!
TIMING'S GOTTA BE PERFECT!
KIRIKIRIKIRI
LET'S SEE WHAT'S STRONGER—MY ELECTRO-MAGNETISM OR YOUR PSYCHIC WAVES!
TING
GO FOR IT!
LET'S TRY...
...ZAP CANNON!

158 Silly Scyther

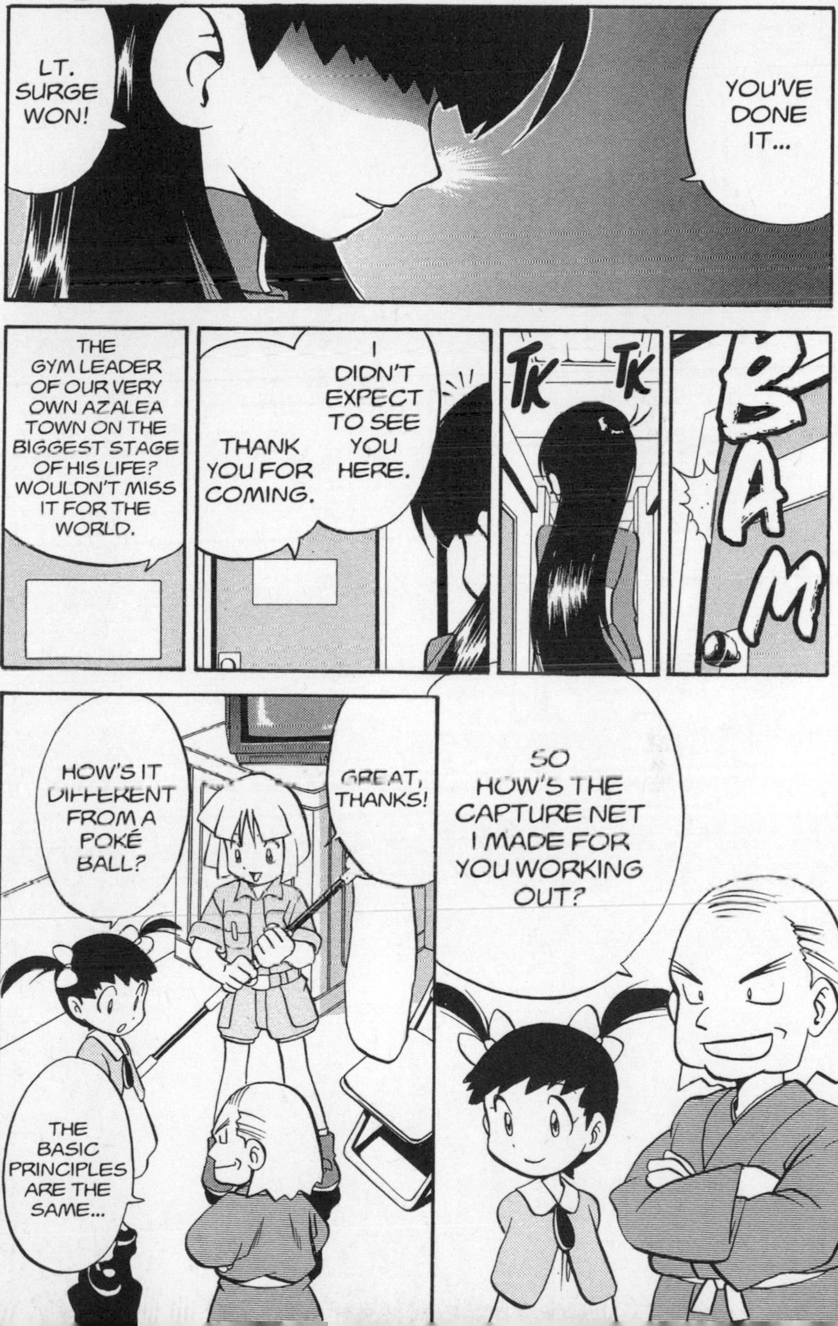
YOU'VE DONE IT...
LT. SURGE WON!
BAM
TK TK
I DIDN'T EXPECT TO SEE YOU HERE.
THANK YOU FOR COMING.
THE GYM LEADER OF OUR VERY OWN AZALEA TOWN ON THE BIGGEST STAGE OF HIS LIFE? WOULDN'T MISS IT FOR THE WORLD.
SO HOW'S THE CAPTURE NET I MADE FOR YOU WORKING OUT?
GREAT, THANKS!
HOW'S IT DIFFERENT FROM A POKÉ BALL?
THE BASIC PRINCIPLES ARE THE SAME...

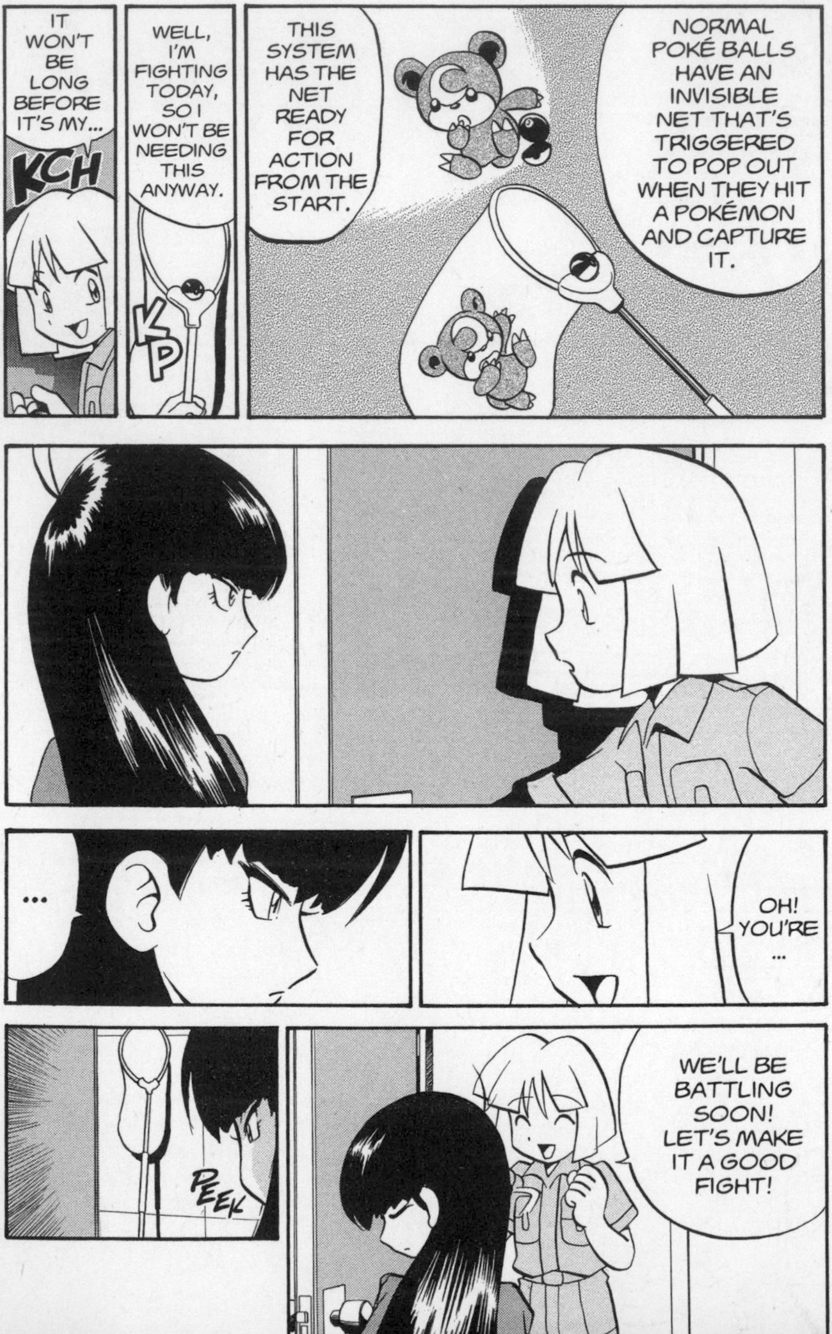
NORMAL POKÉ BALLS HAVE AN INVISIBLE NET THAT'S TRIGGERED TO POP OUT WHEN THEY HIT A POKÉMON AND CAPTURE IT.
THIS SYSTEM HAS THE NET READY FOR ACTION FROM THE START.
WELL, I'M FIGHTING TODAY, SO I WON'T BE NEEDING THIS ANYWAY.
KP
IT WON'T BE LONG BEFORE IT'S MY...
KCH
OH! YOU'RE ...
...
WE'LL BE BATTLING SOON! LET'S MAKE IT A GOOD FIGHT!
PEEK

158 Silly Scyther

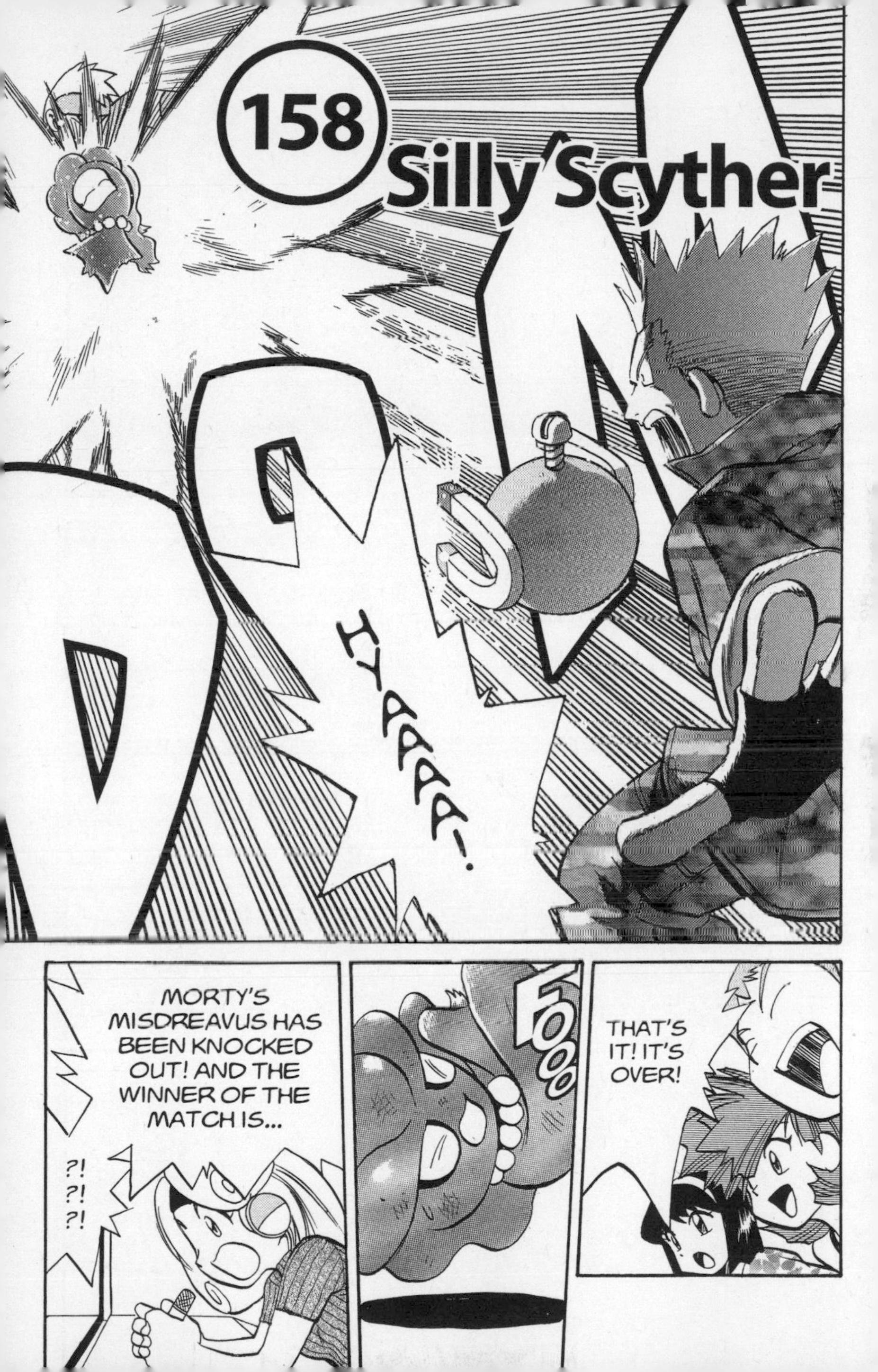
HYAAAA!
THAT'S IT! IT'S OVER!
FOOO
MORTY'S MISDREAVUS HAS BEEN KNOCKED OUT! AND THE WINNER OF THE MATCH IS...
?! ?! ?!

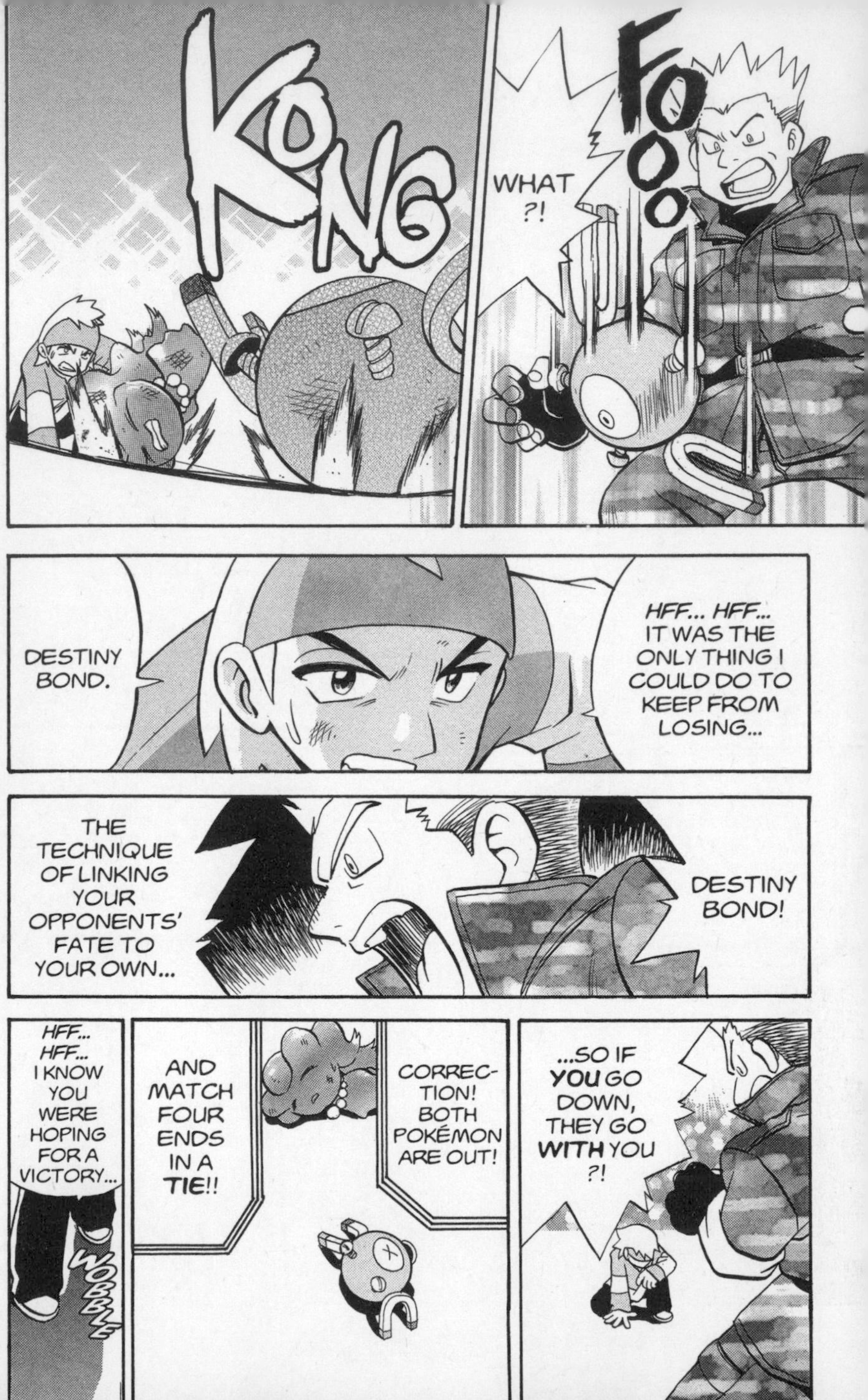
FOOOO
WHAT?!
KONG
HFF... HFF... IT WAS THE ONLY THING I COULD DO TO KEEP FROM LOSING...
DESTINY BOND.
DESTINY BOND!
THE TECHNIQUE OF LINKING YOUR OPPONENTS' FATE TO YOUR OWN...
...SO IF **YOU** GO DOWN, THEY GO **WITH** YOU?!
CORREC-TION! BOTH POKÉMON ARE OUT!
AND MATCH FOUR ENDS IN A **TIE**!!
HFF... HFF... I KNOW YOU WERE HOPING FOR A VICTORY...
WOBBLE

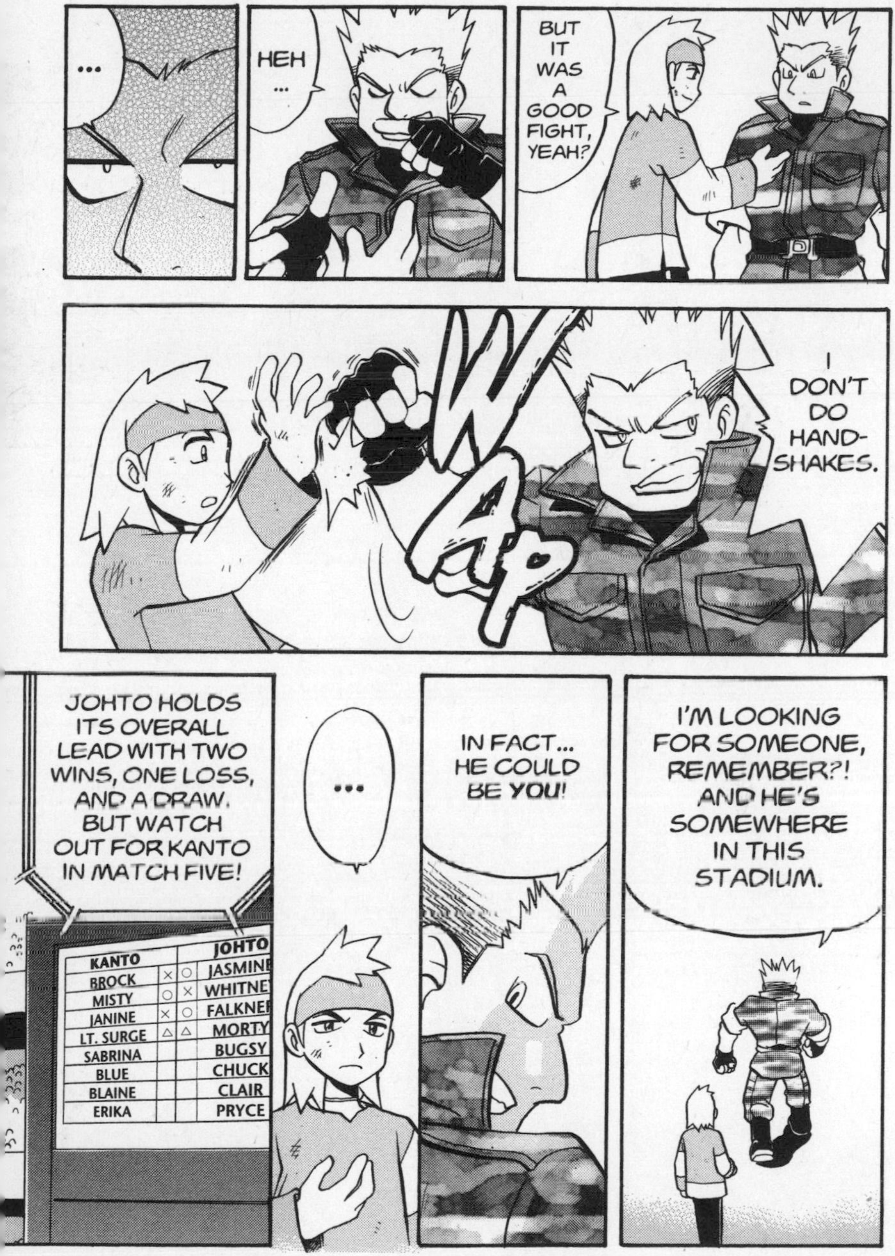
BUT IT WAS A GOOD FIGHT, YEAH?
HEH ...
...
I DON'T DO HAND-SHAKES.
WAP
I'M LOOKING FOR SOMEONE, REMEMBER?! AND HE'S SOMEWHERE IN THIS STADIUM.
IN FACT... HE COULD BE YOU!
...
JOHTO HOLDS ITS OVERALL LEAD WITH TWO WINS, ONE LOSS, AND A DRAW. BUT WATCH OUT FOR KANTO IN MATCH FIVE!
KANTO
JOHTO
BROCK × ○ JASMINE
MISTY ○ × WHITNEY
JANINE × ○ FALKNER
LT. SURGE △ △ MORTY
SABRINA BUGSY
BLUE CHUCK
BLAINE CLAIR
ERIKA PRYCE

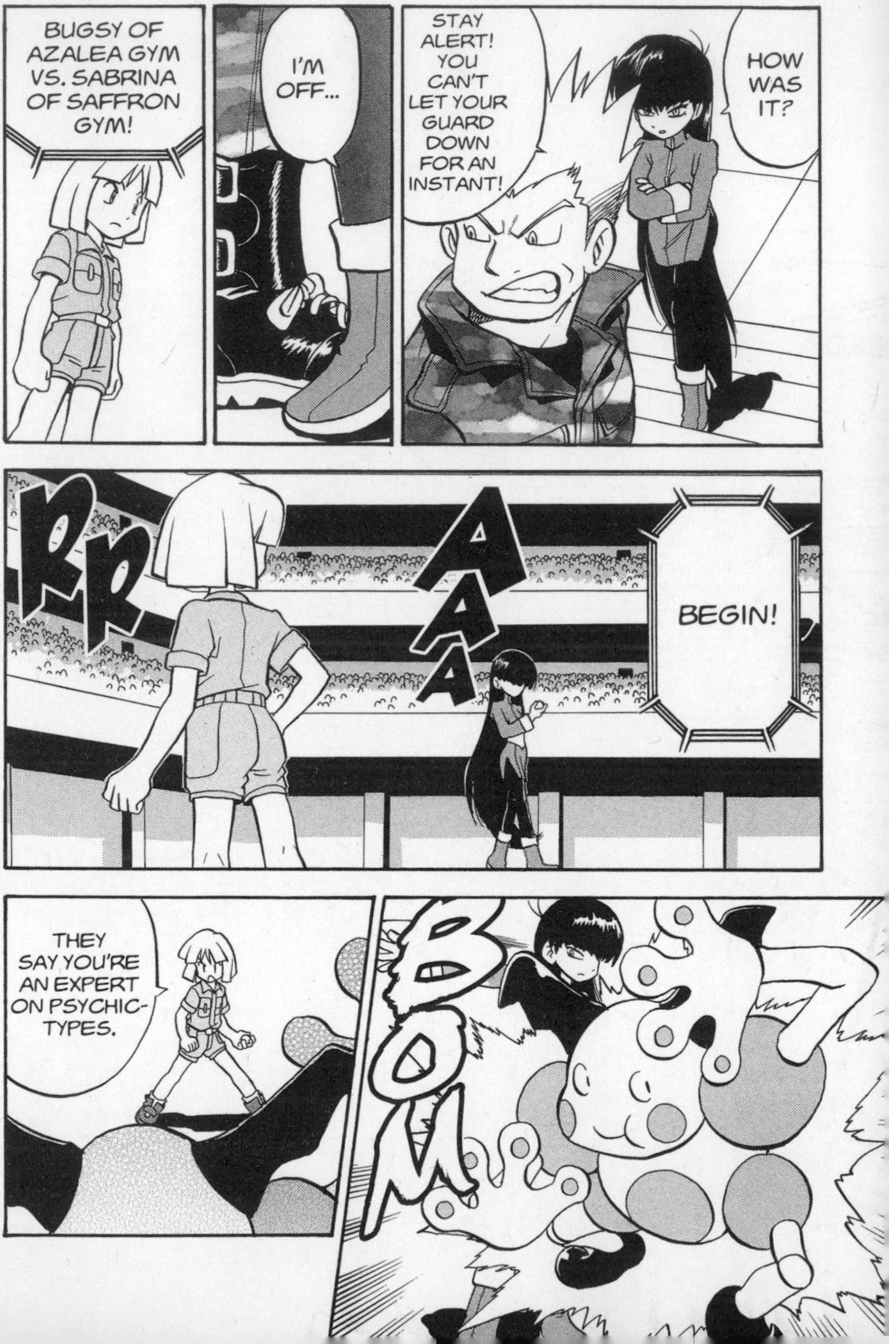
HOW WAS IT?
STAY ALERT! YOU CAN'T LET YOUR GUARD DOWN FOR AN INSTANT!
I'M OFF...
BUGSY OF AZALEA GYM VS. SABRINA OF SAFFRON GYM!
BEGIN!
AAAA
RR
BOM
THEY SAY YOU'RE AN EXPERT ON PSYCHIC-TYPES.

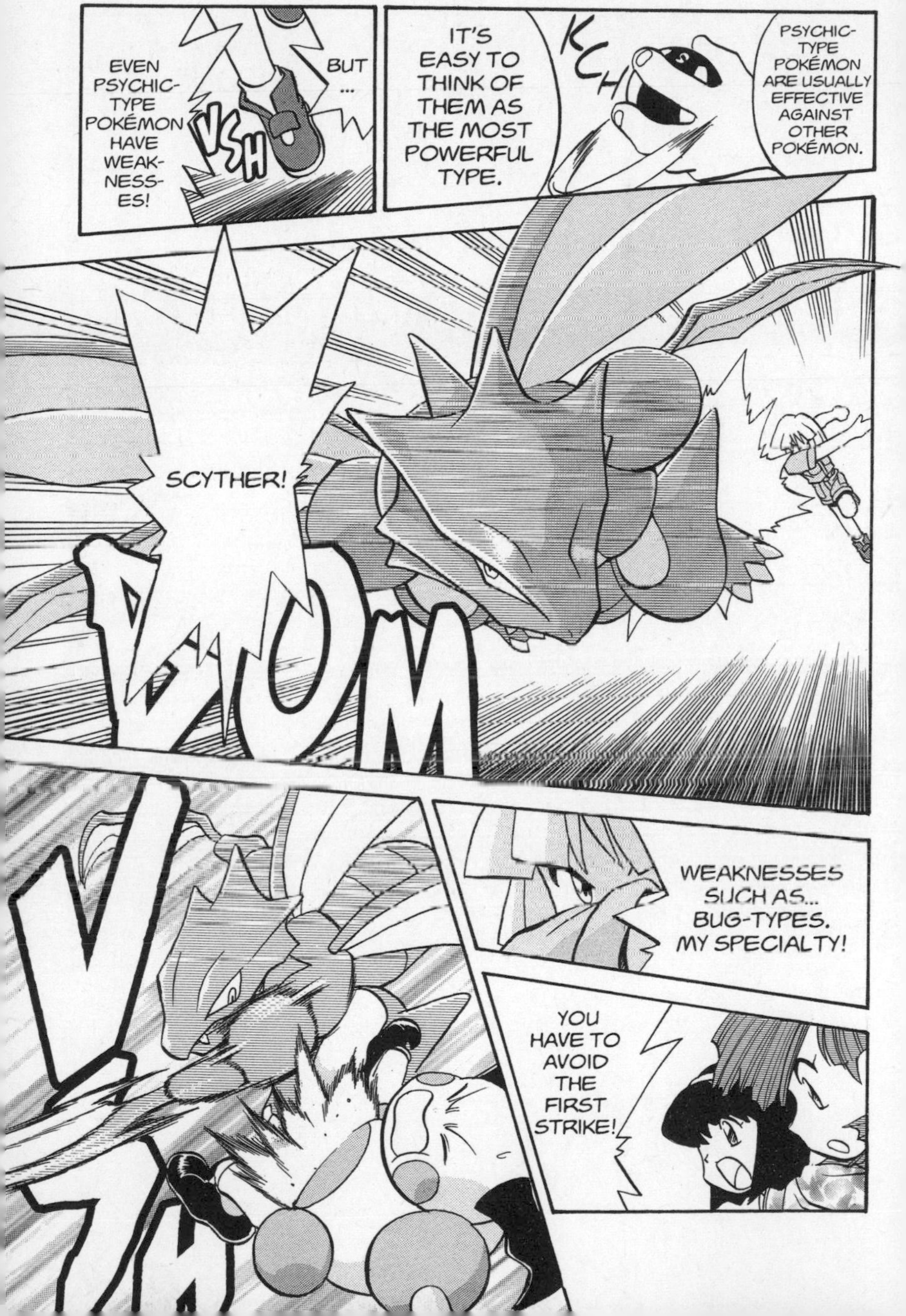
PSYCHIC-TYPE POKÉMON ARE USUALLY EFFECTIVE AGAINST OTHER POKÉMON.
KCH
IT'S EASY TO THINK OF THEM AS THE MOST POWERFUL TYPE.
BUT ...
EVEN PSYCHIC-TYPE POKÉMON HAVE WEAKNESSES!
VSH
SCYTHER!
WEAKNESSES SUCH AS... BUG-TYPES. MY SPECIALTY!
YOU HAVE TO AVOID THE FIRST STRIKE!

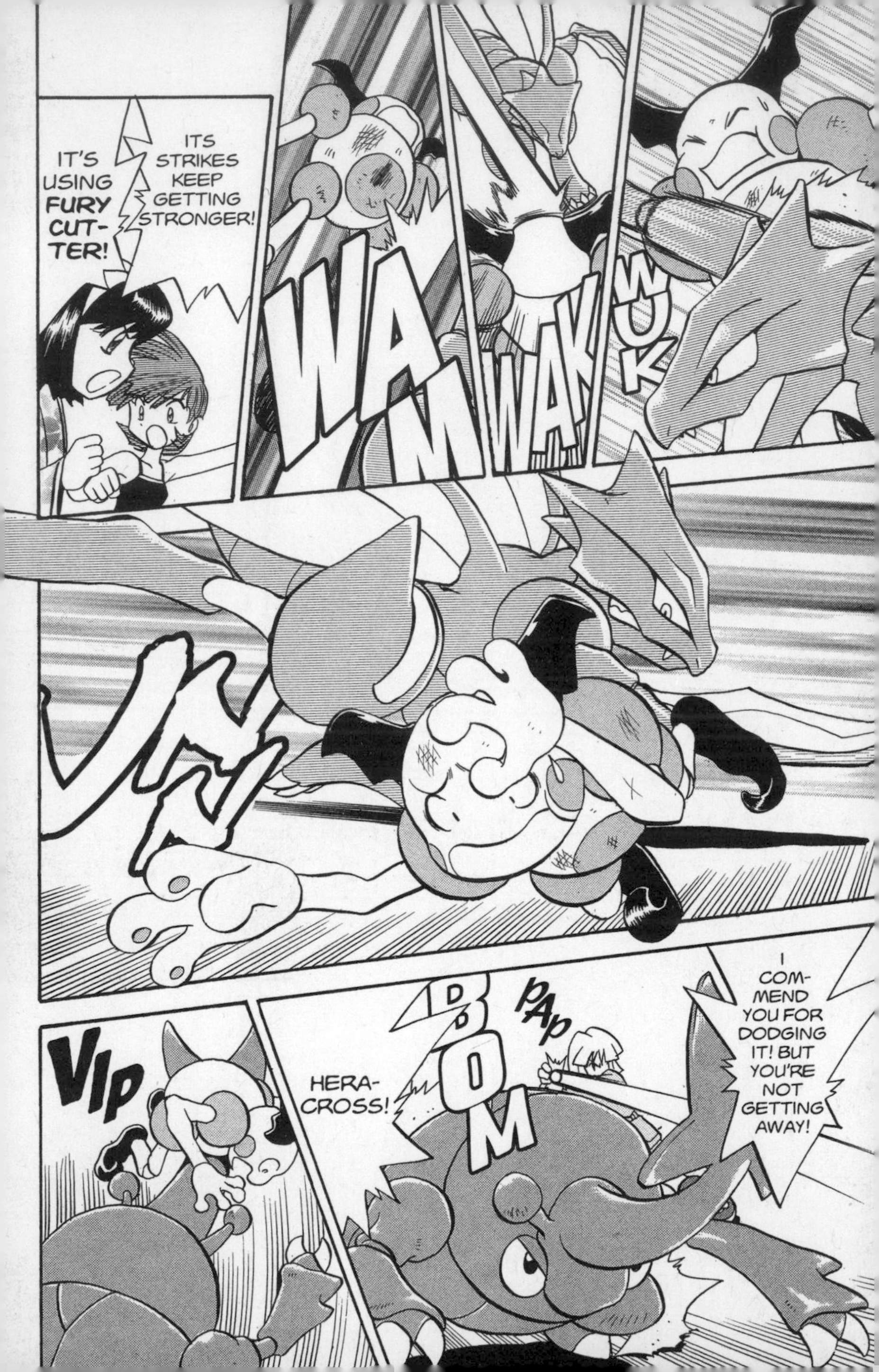
WUK
WAK
WAM
ITS STRIKES KEEP GETTING STRONGER!
IT'S USING FURY CUTTER!
I COM-MEND YOU FOR DODGING IT! BUT YOU'RE NOT GETTING AWAY!
PAP
DOOM
HERA-CROSS!
VIP

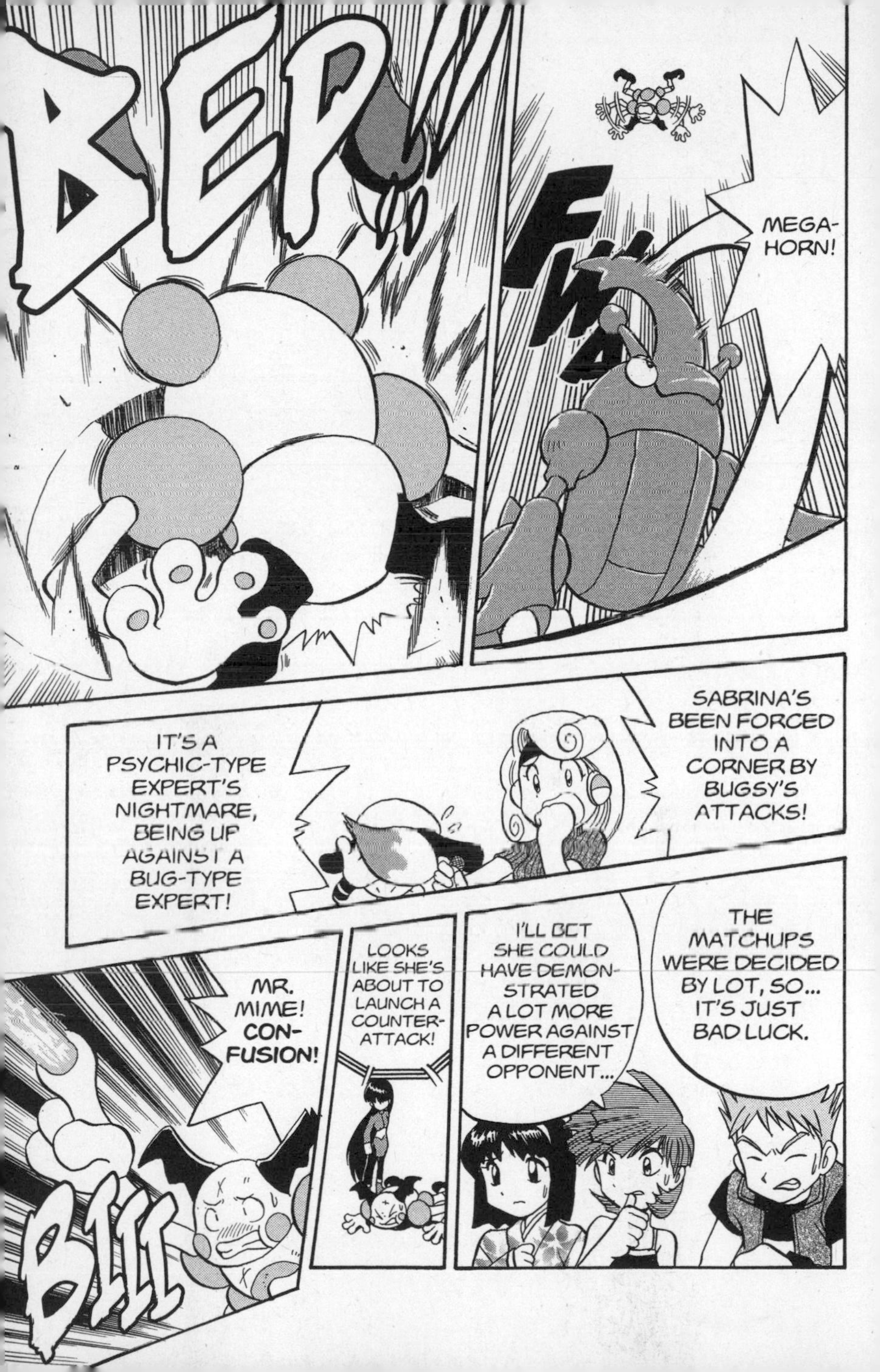
MEGA-HORN!
BEP!!
SABRINA'S BEEN FORCED INTO A CORNER BY BUGSY'S ATTACKS!
IT'S A PSYCHIC-TYPE EXPERT'S NIGHTMARE, BEING UP AGAINST A BUG-TYPE EXPERT!
THE MATCHUPS WERE DECIDED BY LOT, SO... IT'S JUST BAD LUCK.
I'LL BET SHE COULD HAVE DEMON-STRATED A LOT MORE POWER AGAINST A DIFFERENT OPPONENT...
LOOKS LIKE SHE'S ABOUT TO LAUNCH A COUNTER-ATTACK!
MR. MIME! CON-FUSION!
BIII

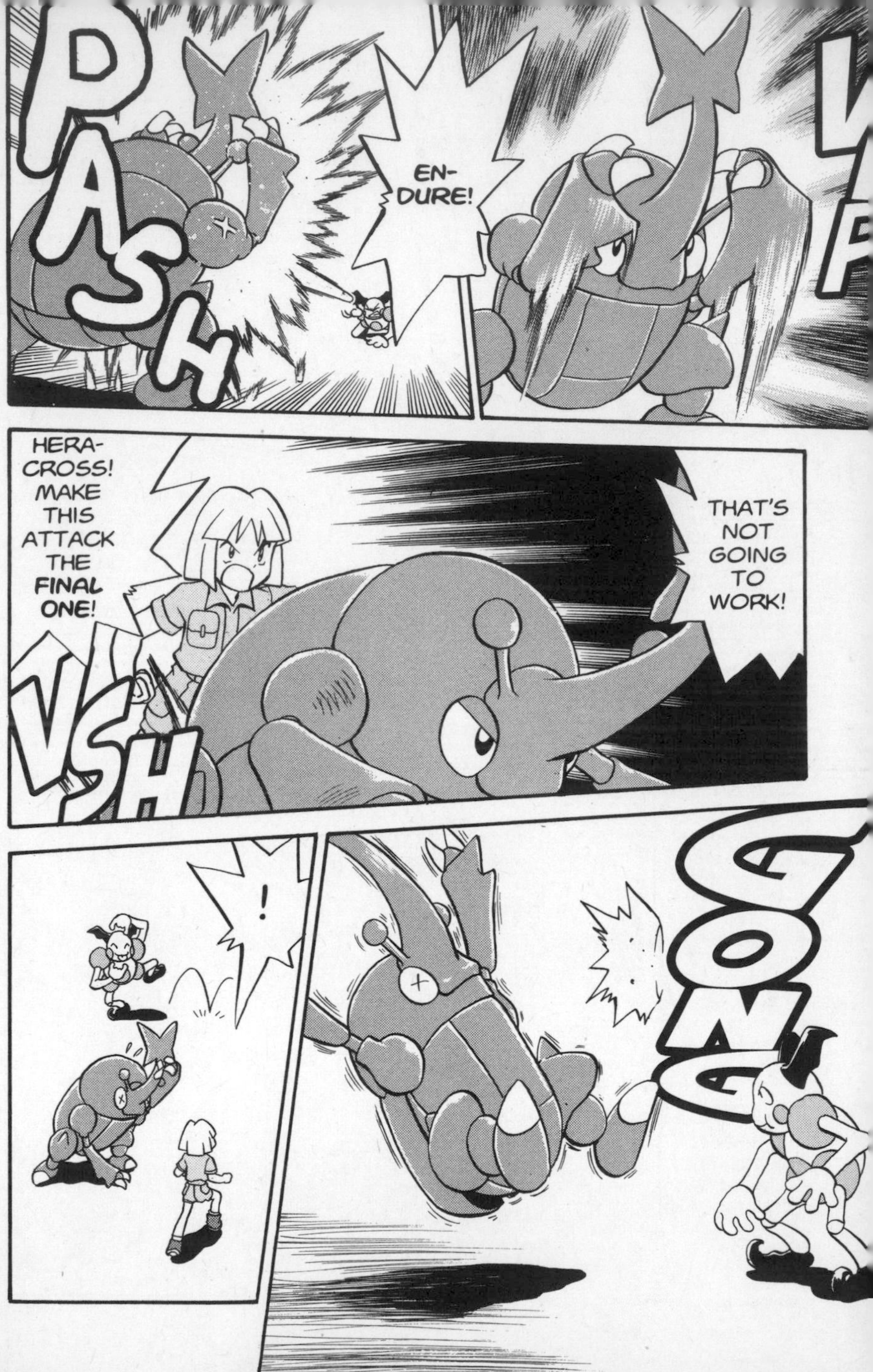
EN-DURE!
PASH
THAT'S NOT GOING TO WORK!
HERA-CROSS! MAKE THIS ATTACK THE FINAL ONE!
VSH
GONG
!

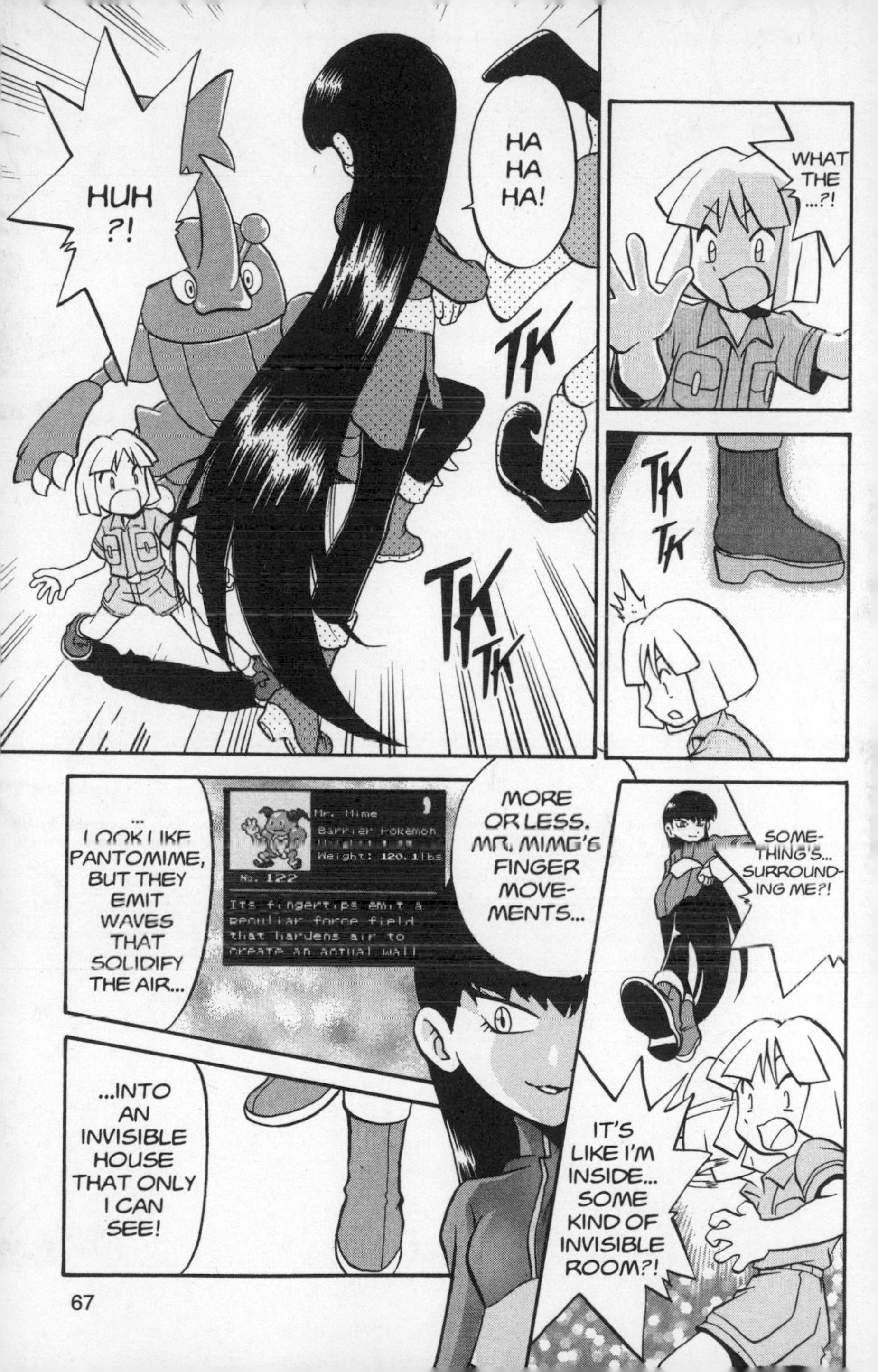
WHAT THE ...?!
TK TK
HA HA HA!
TK
TK TK
HUH ?!
SOME-THING'S... SURROUND-ING ME?!
IT'S LIKE I'M INSIDE... SOME KIND OF INVISIBLE ROOM?!
MORE OR LESS. MR. MIME'S FINGER MOVEMENTS...
...LOOK LIKE PANTOMIME, BUT THEY EMIT WAVES THAT SOLIDIFY THE AIR...
Mr. Mime
Barrier Pokemon
Weight: 120.1lbs
No. 122
Its fingertips emit a peculiar force field that hardens air to create an actual wall
...INTO AN INVISIBLE HOUSE THAT ONLY I CAN SEE!

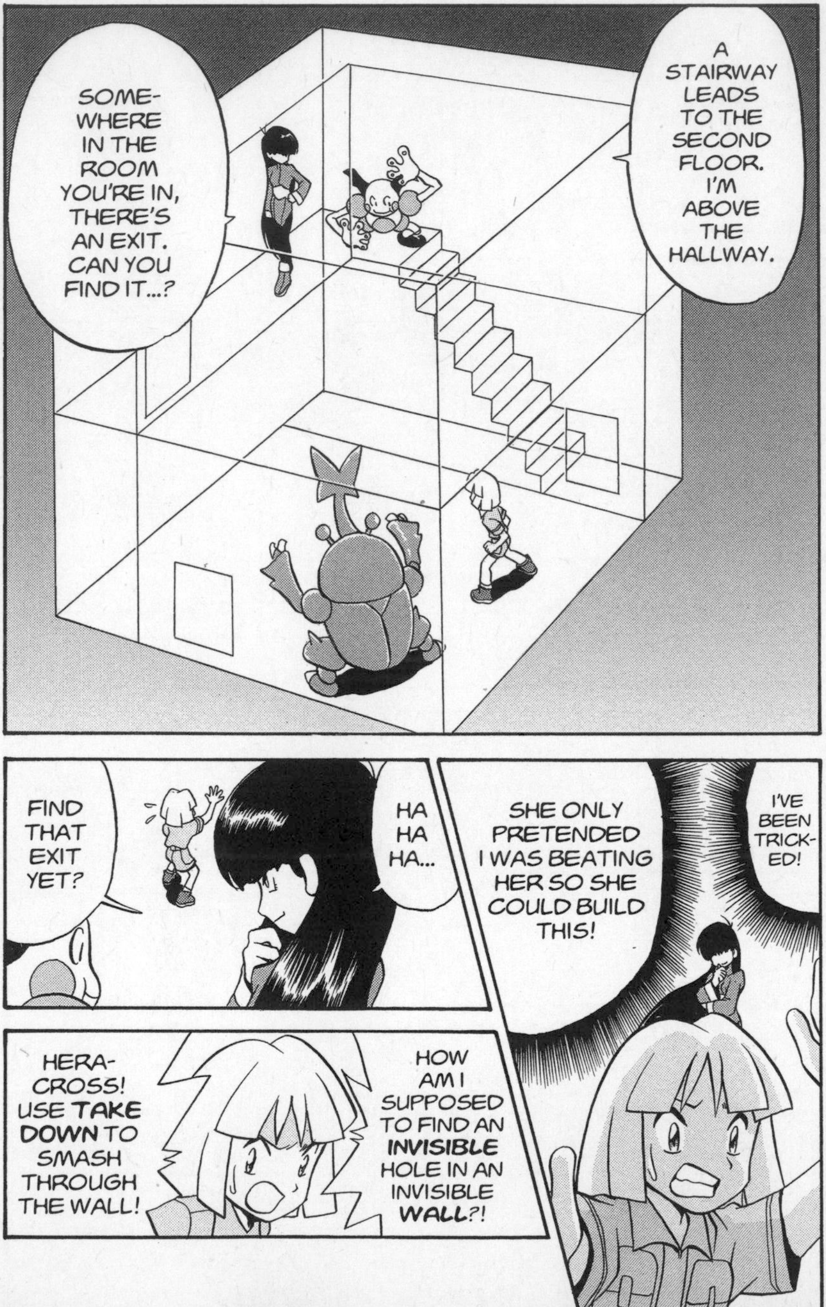
A STAIRWAY LEADS TO THE SECOND FLOOR. I'M ABOVE THE HALLWAY.
SOME-WHERE IN THE ROOM YOU'RE IN, THERE'S AN EXIT. CAN YOU FIND IT...?
I'VE BEEN TRICK-ED!
SHE ONLY PRETENDED I WAS BEATING HER SO SHE COULD BUILD THIS!
HA HA HA...
FIND THAT EXIT YET?
HOW AM I SUPPOSED TO FIND AN **INVISIBLE** HOLE IN AN INVISIBLE **WALL**?!
HERA-CROSS! USE **TAKE DOWN** TO SMASH THROUGH THE WALL!

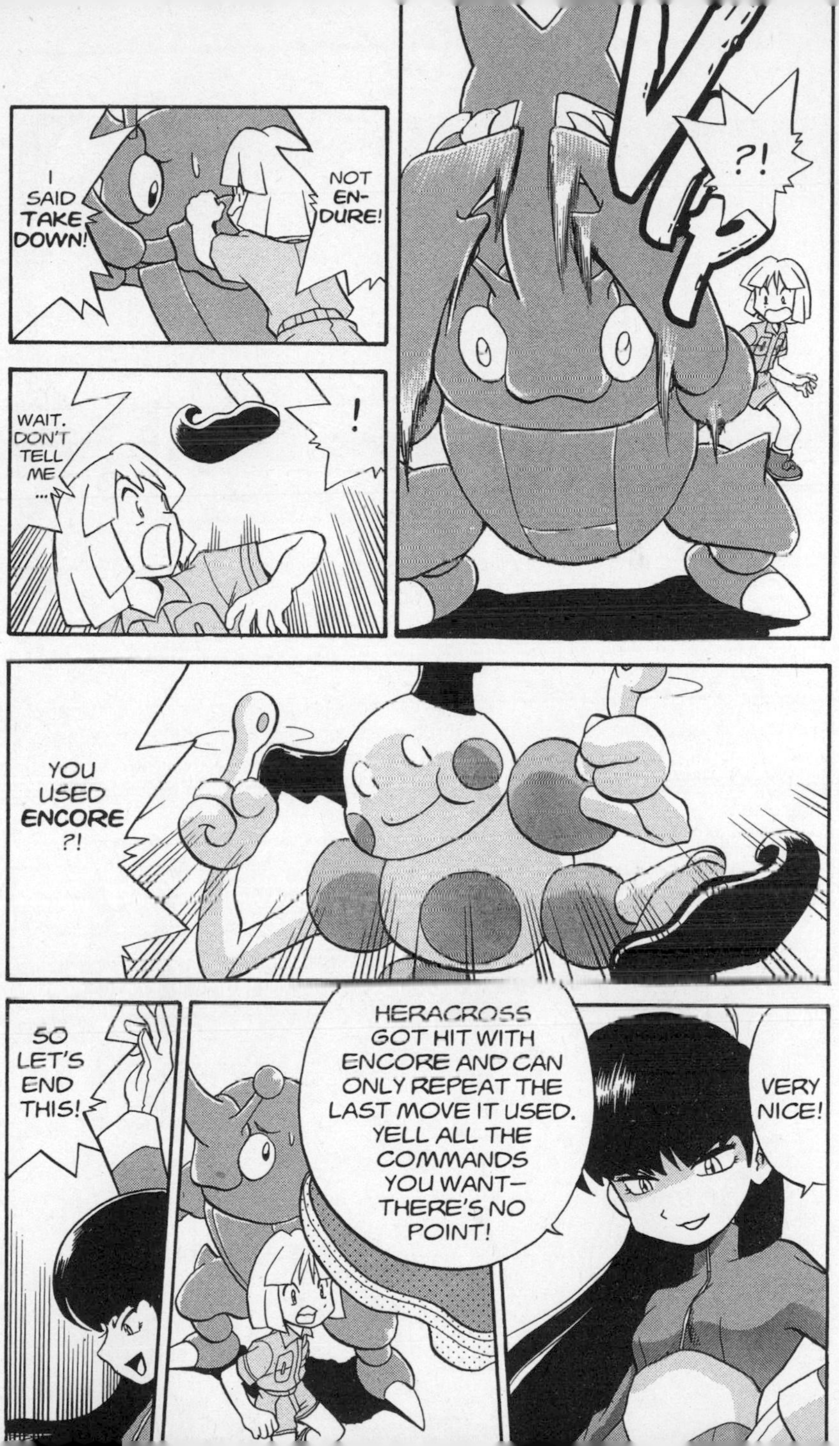

?!
I SAID TAKE DOWN!
NOT ENDURE!
!
WAIT. DON'T TELL ME ...
YOU USED ENCORE ?!
VERY NICE!
HERACROSS GOT HIT WITH ENCORE AND CAN ONLY REPEAT THE LAST MOVE IT USED. YELL ALL THE COMMANDS YOU WANT—THERE'S NO POINT!
SO LET'S END THIS!

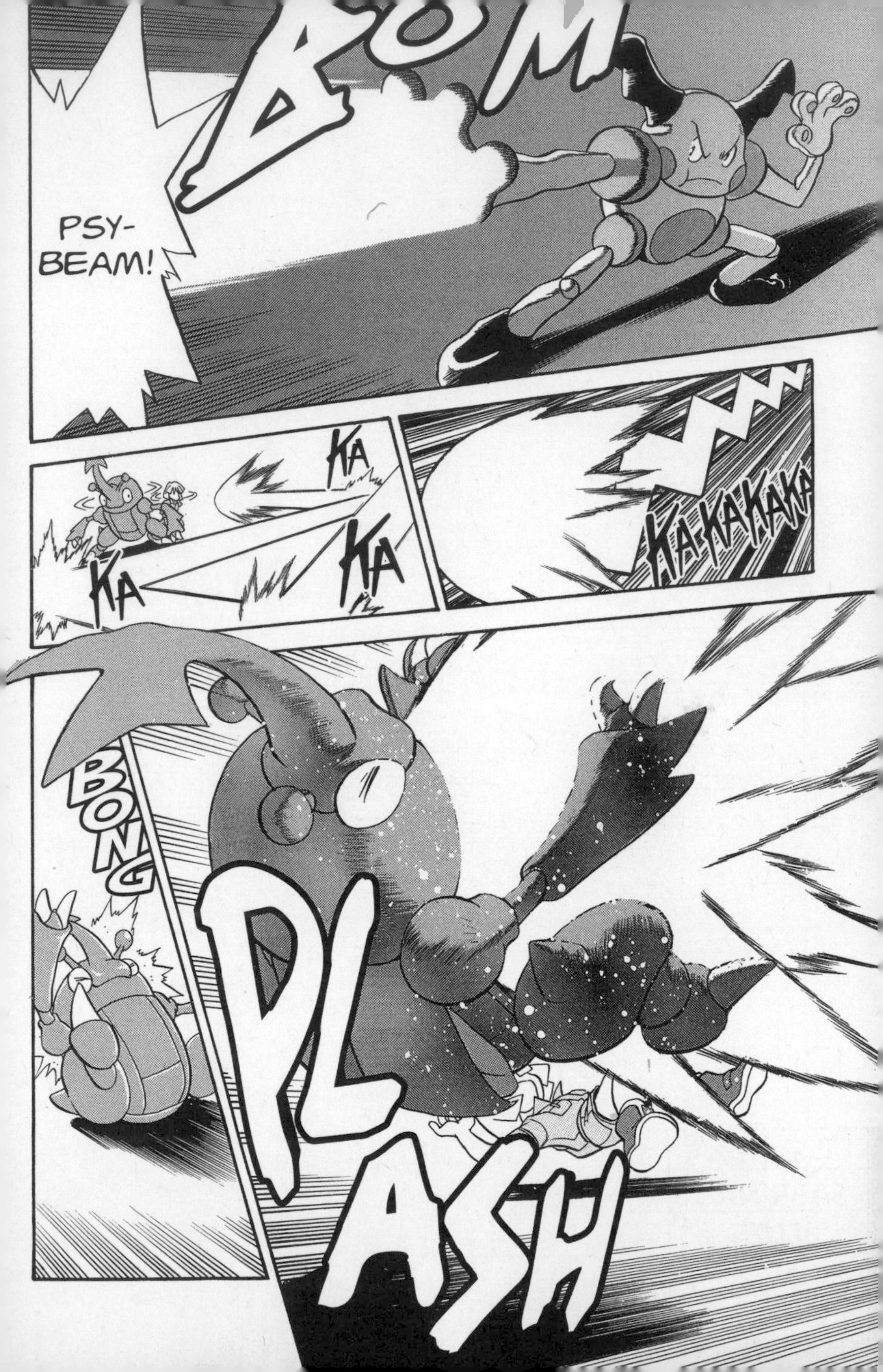
BOOM
PSY-BEAM!
KA-KAKAKA
KA
KA
KA
BONG
PLASH

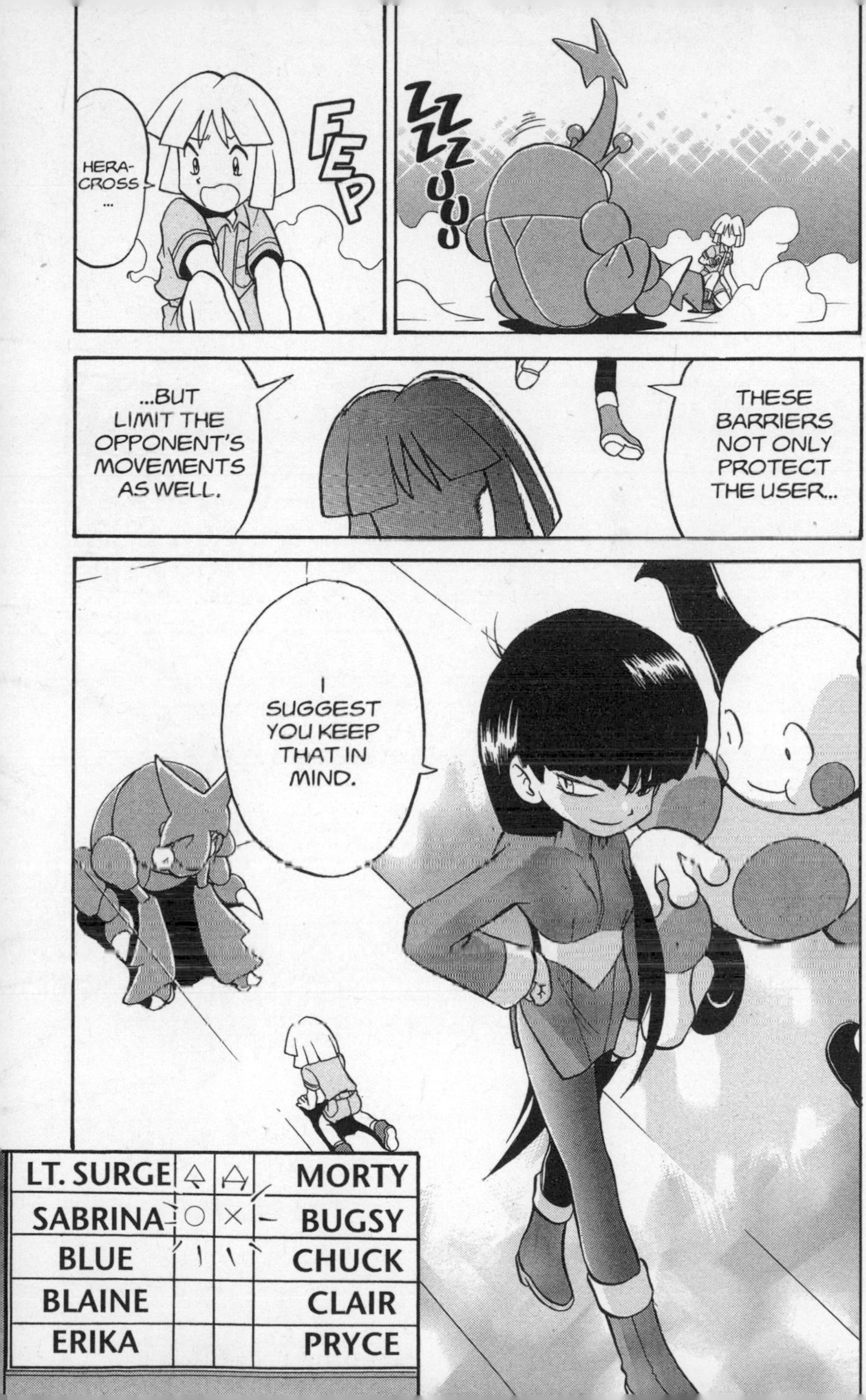
ZZZZUUU
FEP
HERA-CROSS ...
THESE BARRIERS NOT ONLY PROTECT THE USER...
...BUT LIMIT THE OPPONENT'S MOVEMENTS AS WELL.
I SUGGEST YOU KEEP THAT IN MIND.
LT. SURGE
SABRINA
BLUE
BLAINE
ERIKA
MORTY
BUGSY
CHUCK
CLAIR
PRYCE

159 Popular Pupitar

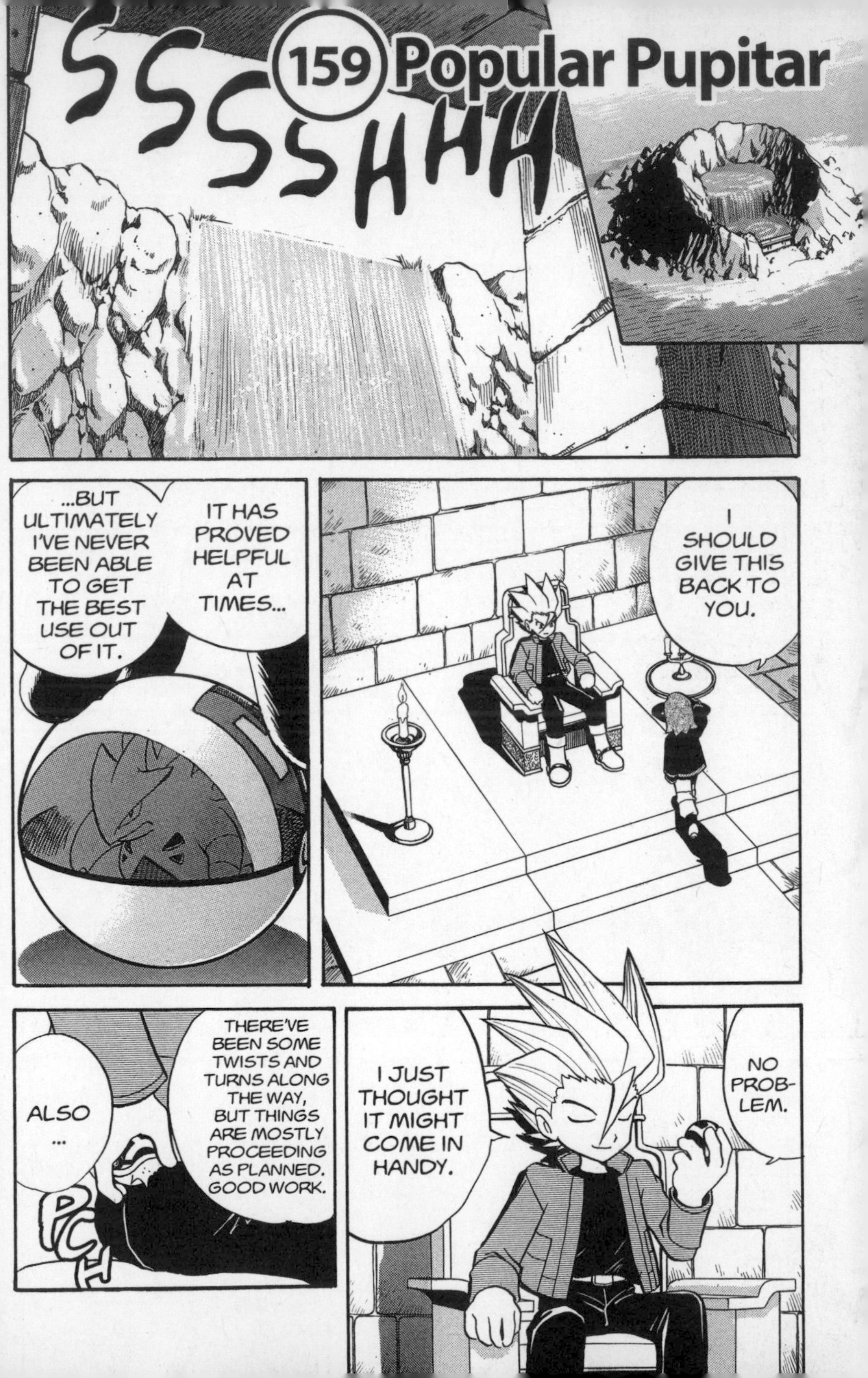
SSSSHHH
I SHOULD GIVE THIS BACK TO YOU.
IT HAS PROVED HELPFUL AT TIMES...
...BUT ULTIMATELY I'VE NEVER BEEN ABLE TO GET THE BEST USE OUT OF IT.
NO PROB-LEM.
I JUST THOUGHT IT MIGHT COME IN HANDY.
THERE'VE BEEN SOME TWISTS AND TURNS ALONG THE WAY, BUT THINGS ARE MOSTLY PROCEEDING AS PLANNED. GOOD WORK.
ALSO ...
PCH

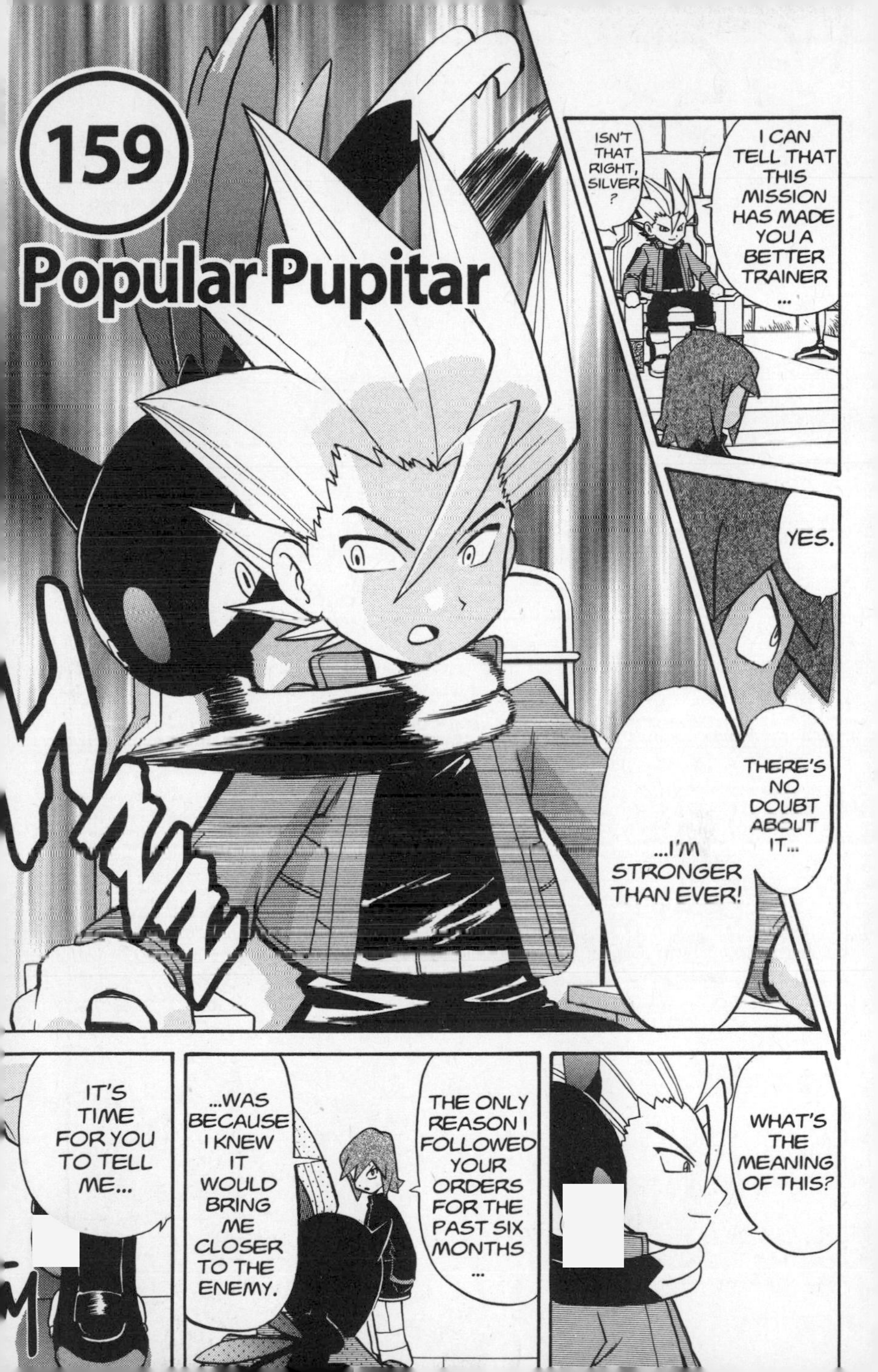
I CAN TELL THAT THIS MISSION HAS MADE YOU A BETTER TRAINER ...
ISN'T THAT RIGHT, SILVER?
YES.
159
Popular Pupitar
THERE'S NO DOUBT ABOUT IT...
...I'M STRONGER THAN EVER!
WHAT'S THE MEANING OF THIS?
THE ONLY REASON I FOLLOWED YOUR ORDERS FOR THE PAST SIX MONTHS ...
...WAS BECAUSE I KNEW IT WOULD BRING ME CLOSER TO THE ENEMY.
IT'S TIME FOR YOU TO TELL ME...

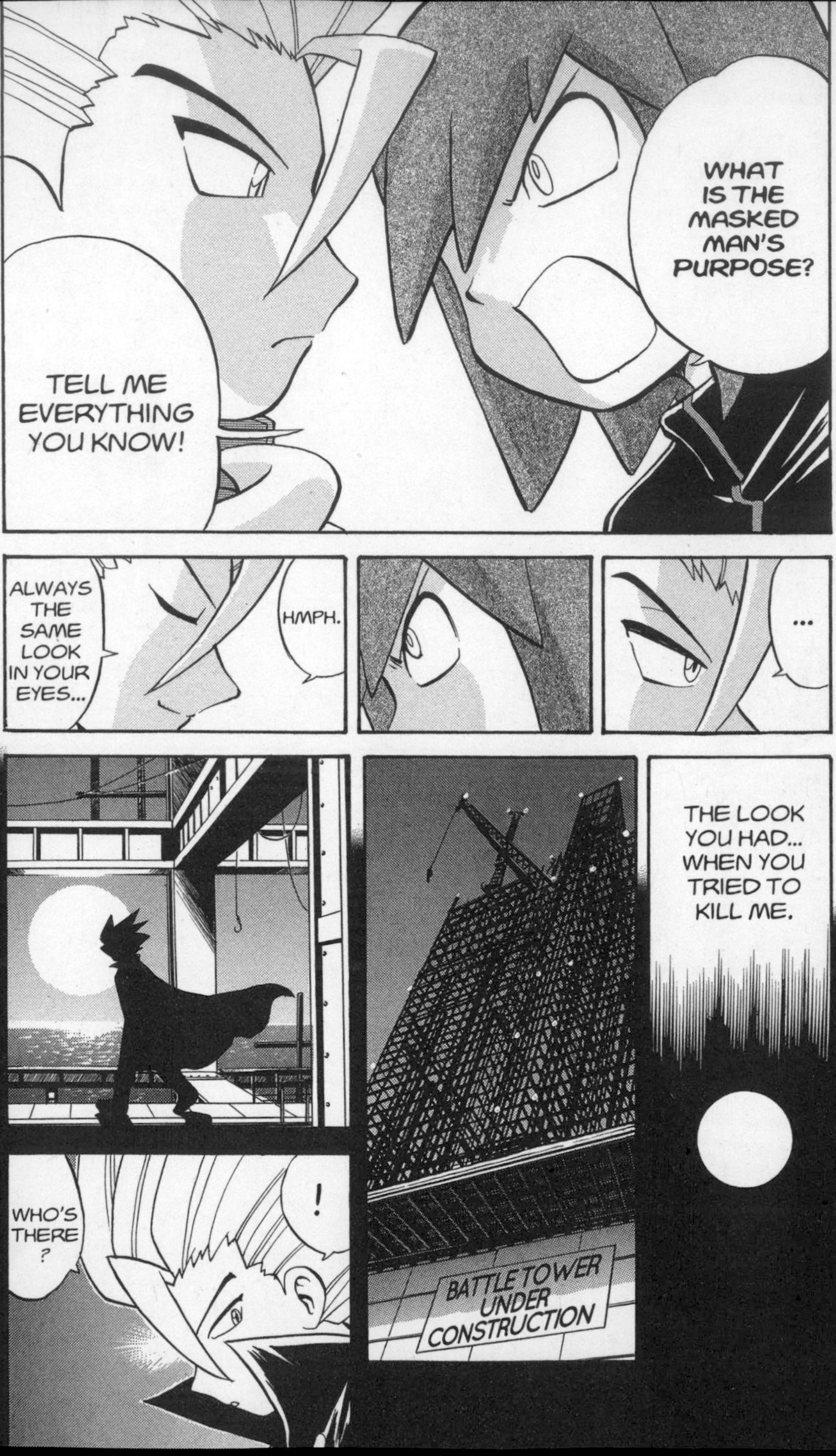
WHAT IS THE MASKED MAN'S PURPOSE?
TELL ME EVERYTHING YOU KNOW!
...
HMPH.
ALWAYS THE SAME LOOK IN YOUR EYES...
THE LOOK YOU HAD... WHEN YOU TRIED TO KILL ME.
BATTLE TOWER UNDER CONSTRUCTION
!
WHO'S THERE?

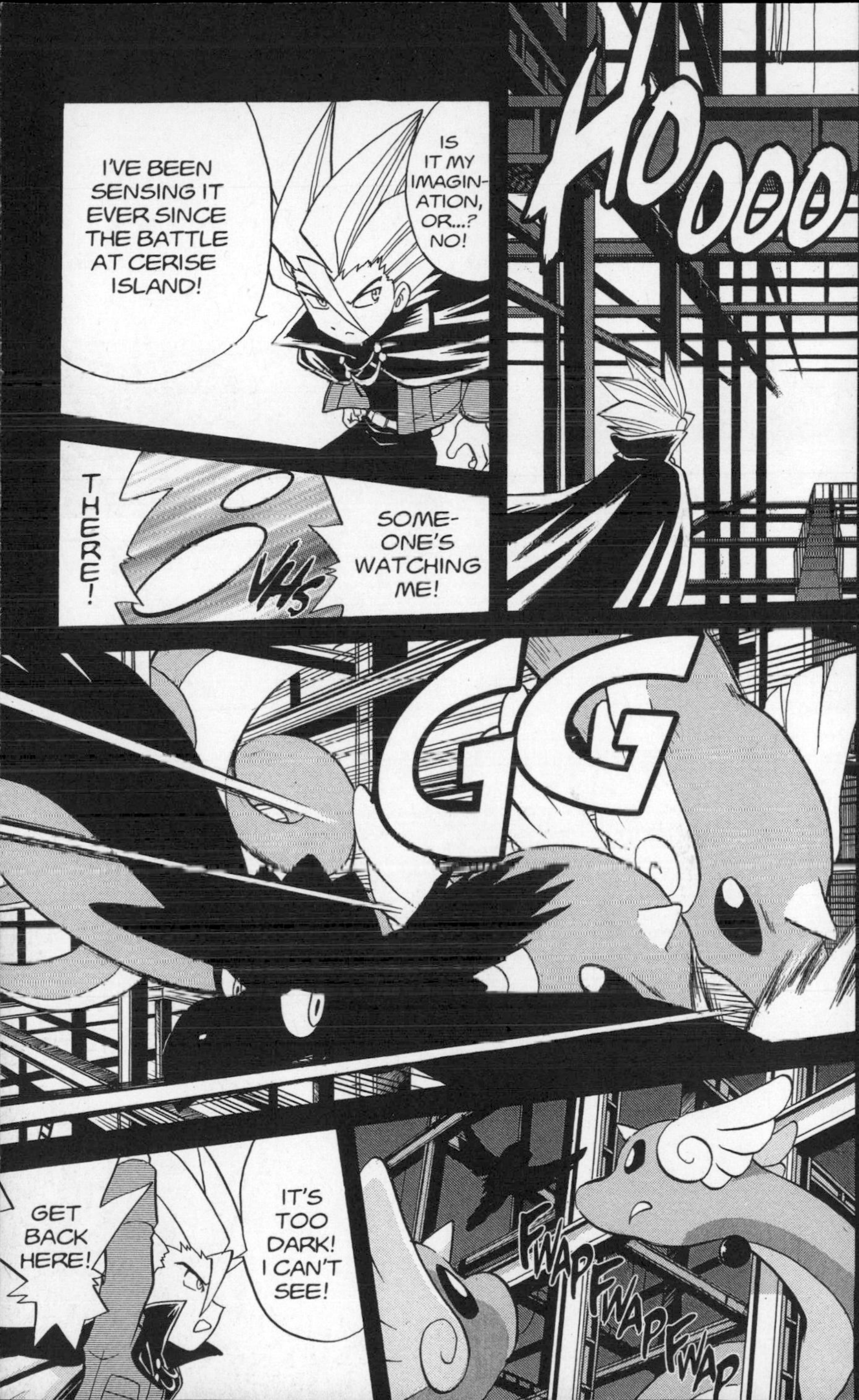
HOOOO
IS IT MY IMAGINATION, OR...? NO!
I'VE BEEN SENSING IT EVER SINCE THE BATTLE AT CERISE ISLAND!
SOME-ONE'S WATCHING ME!
VHS
THERE!
GG
FWAP FWAP FWAP
IT'S TOO DARK! I CAN'T SEE!
GET BACK HERE!

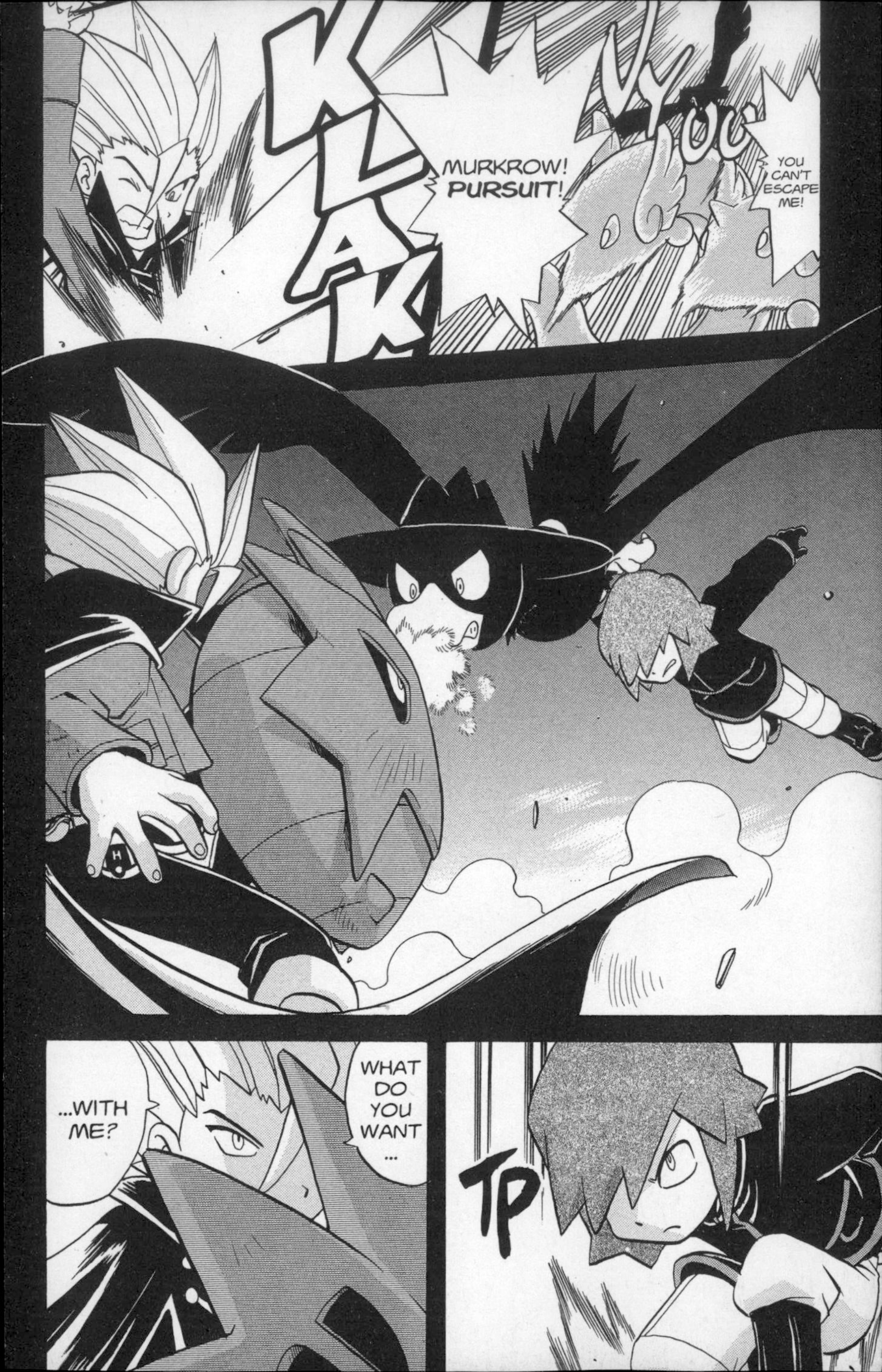
YOU CAN'T ESCAPE ME!
MURKROW! PURSUIT!
KLAK
TP
WHAT DO YOU WANT ...
...WITH ME?

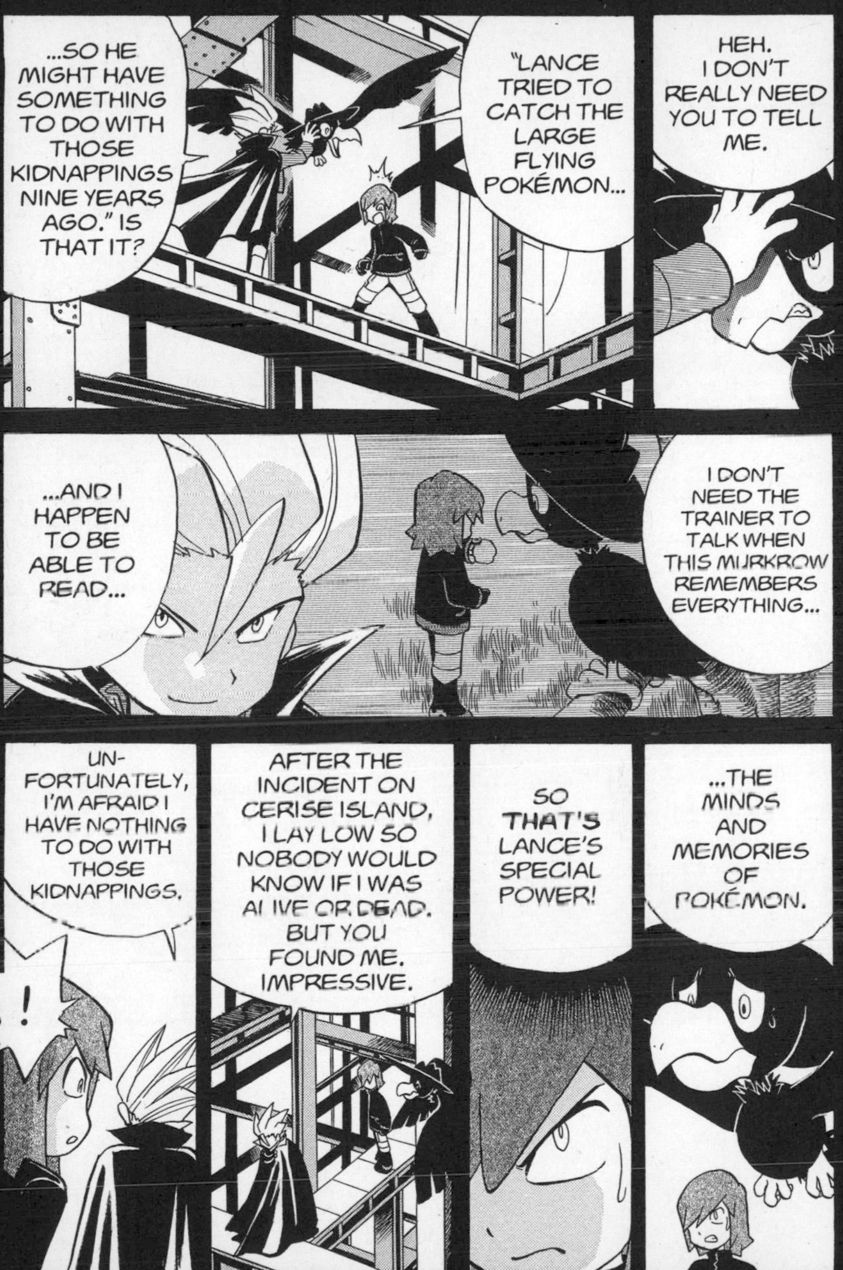
HEH. I DON'T REALLY NEED YOU TO TELL ME.
"LANCE TRIED TO CATCH THE LARGE FLYING POKÉMON...
...SO HE MIGHT HAVE SOMETHING TO DO WITH THOSE KIDNAPPINGS NINE YEARS AGO." IS THAT IT?
I DON'T NEED THE TRAINER TO TALK WHEN THIS MURKROW REMEMBERS EVERYTHING...
...AND I HAPPEN TO BE ABLE TO READ...
...THE MINDS AND MEMORIES OF POKÉMON.
SO THAT'S LANCE'S SPECIAL POWER!
AFTER THE INCIDENT ON CERISE ISLAND, I LAY LOW SO NOBODY WOULD KNOW IF I WAS ALIVE OR DEAD. BUT YOU FOUND ME. IMPRESSIVE.
UN-FORTUNATELY, I'M AFRAID I HAVE NOTHING TO DO WITH THOSE KIDNAPPINGS.
!

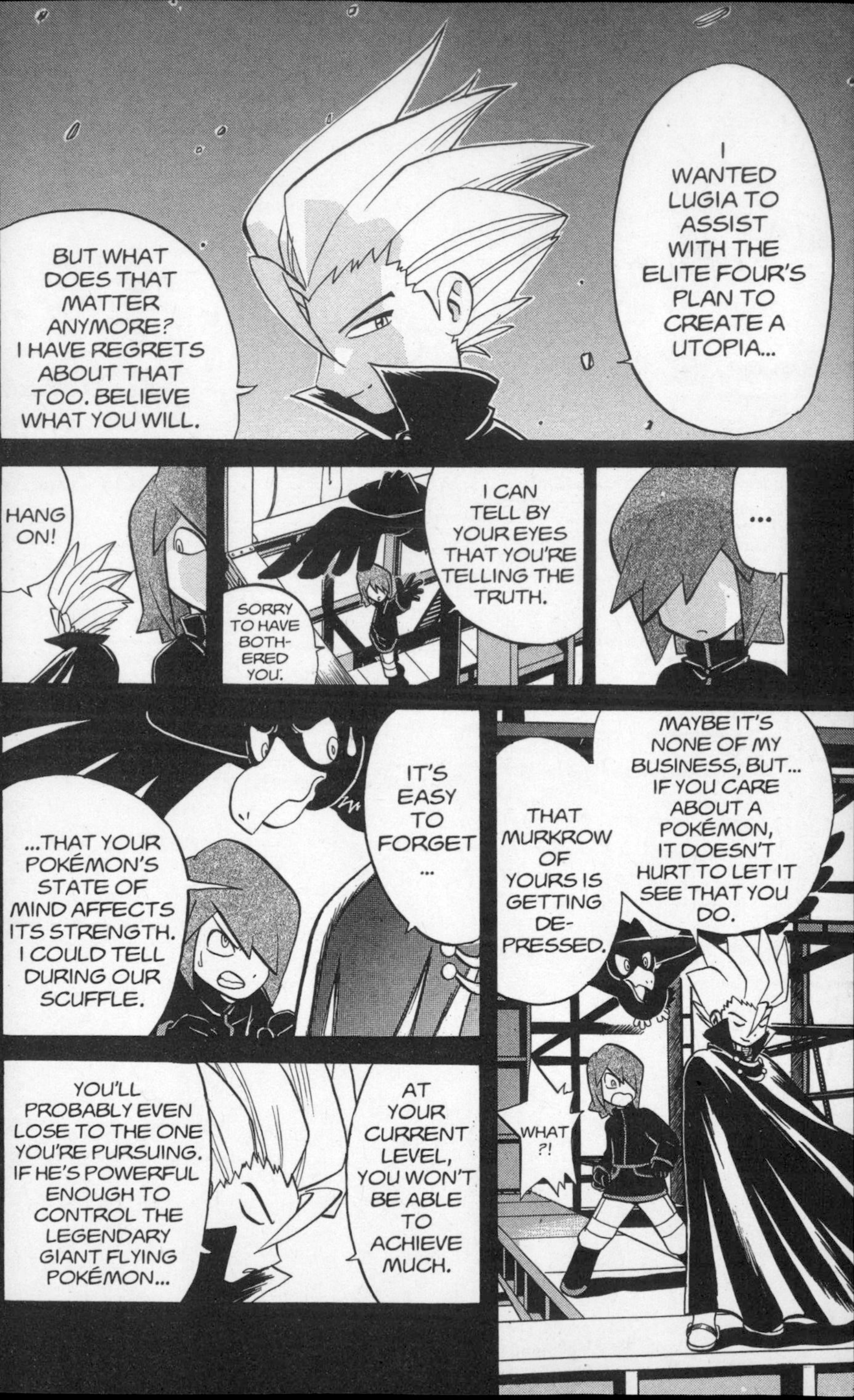

I WANTED LUGIA TO ASSIST WITH THE ELITE FOUR'S PLAN TO CREATE A UTOPIA...
BUT WHAT DOES THAT MATTER ANYMORE? I HAVE REGRETS ABOUT THAT TOO. BELIEVE WHAT YOU WILL.
...
I CAN TELL BY YOUR EYES THAT YOU'RE TELLING THE TRUTH.
SORRY TO HAVE BOTHERED YOU.
HANG ON!
MAYBE IT'S NONE OF MY BUSINESS, BUT... IF YOU CARE ABOUT A POKÉMON, IT DOESN'T HURT TO LET IT SEE THAT YOU DO.
THAT MURKROW OF YOURS IS GETTING DE-PRESSED.
WHAT?!
IT'S EASY TO FORGET...
...THAT YOUR POKÉMON'S STATE OF MIND AFFECTS ITS STRENGTH. I COULD TELL DURING OUR SCUFFLE.
AT YOUR CURRENT LEVEL, YOU WON'T BE ABLE TO ACHIEVE MUCH.
YOU'LL PROBABLY EVEN LOSE TO THE ONE YOU'RE PURSUING. IF HE'S POWERFUL ENOUGH TO CONTROL THE LEGENDARY GIANT FLYING POKÉMON...

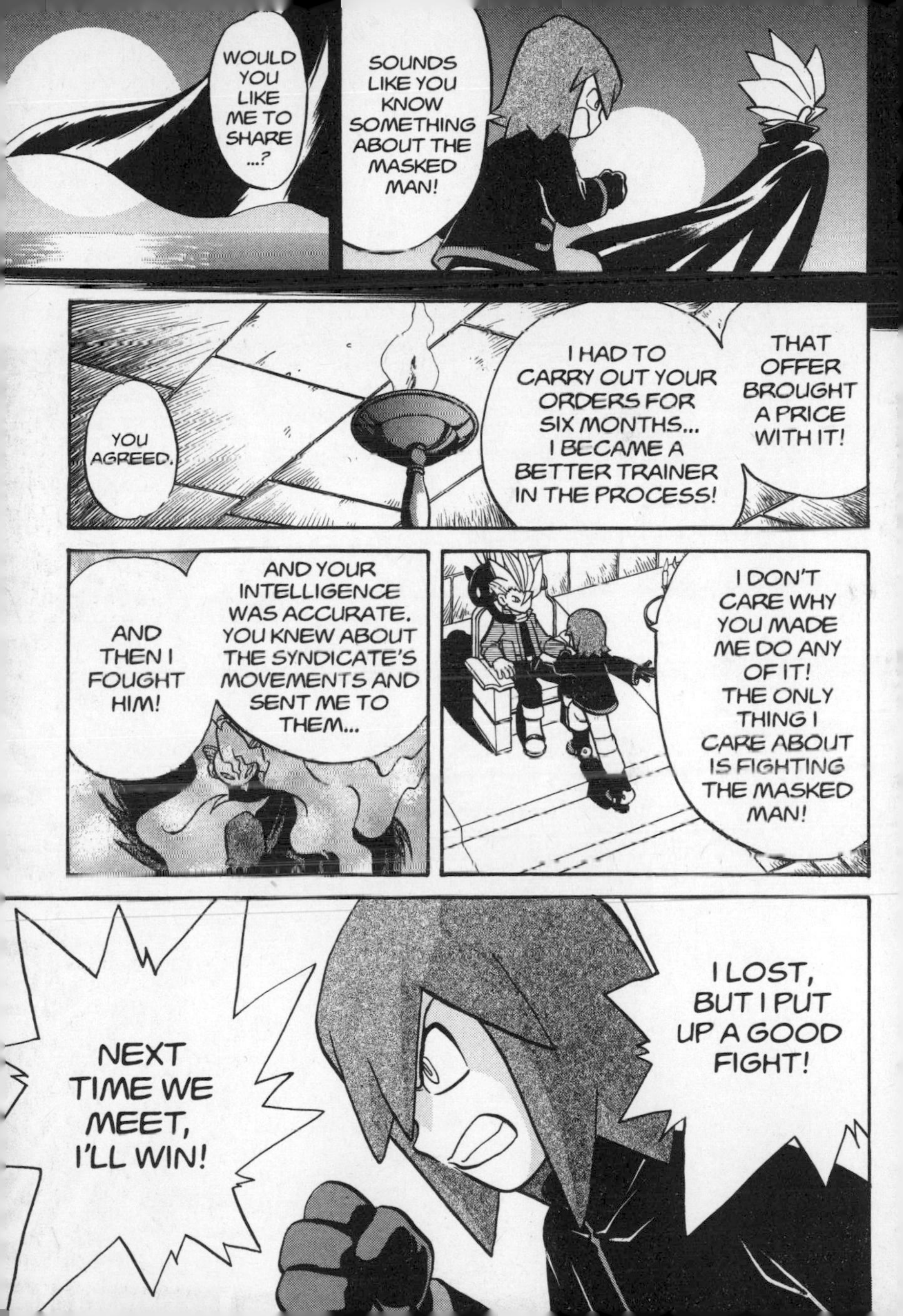
SOUNDS LIKE YOU KNOW SOMETHING ABOUT THE MASKED MAN!
WOULD YOU LIKE ME TO SHARE ...?
THAT OFFER BROUGHT A PRICE WITH IT!
I HAD TO CARRY OUT YOUR ORDERS FOR SIX MONTHS... I BECAME A BETTER TRAINER IN THE PROCESS!
YOU AGREED.
I DON'T CARE WHY YOU MADE ME DO ANY OF IT! THE ONLY THING I CARE ABOUT IS FIGHTING THE MASKED MAN!
AND YOUR INTELLIGENCE WAS ACCURATE. YOU KNEW ABOUT THE SYNDICATE'S MOVEMENTS AND SENT ME TO THEM...
AND THEN I FOUGHT HIM!
I LOST, BUT I PUT UP A GOOD FIGHT!
NEXT TIME WE MEET, I'LL WIN!

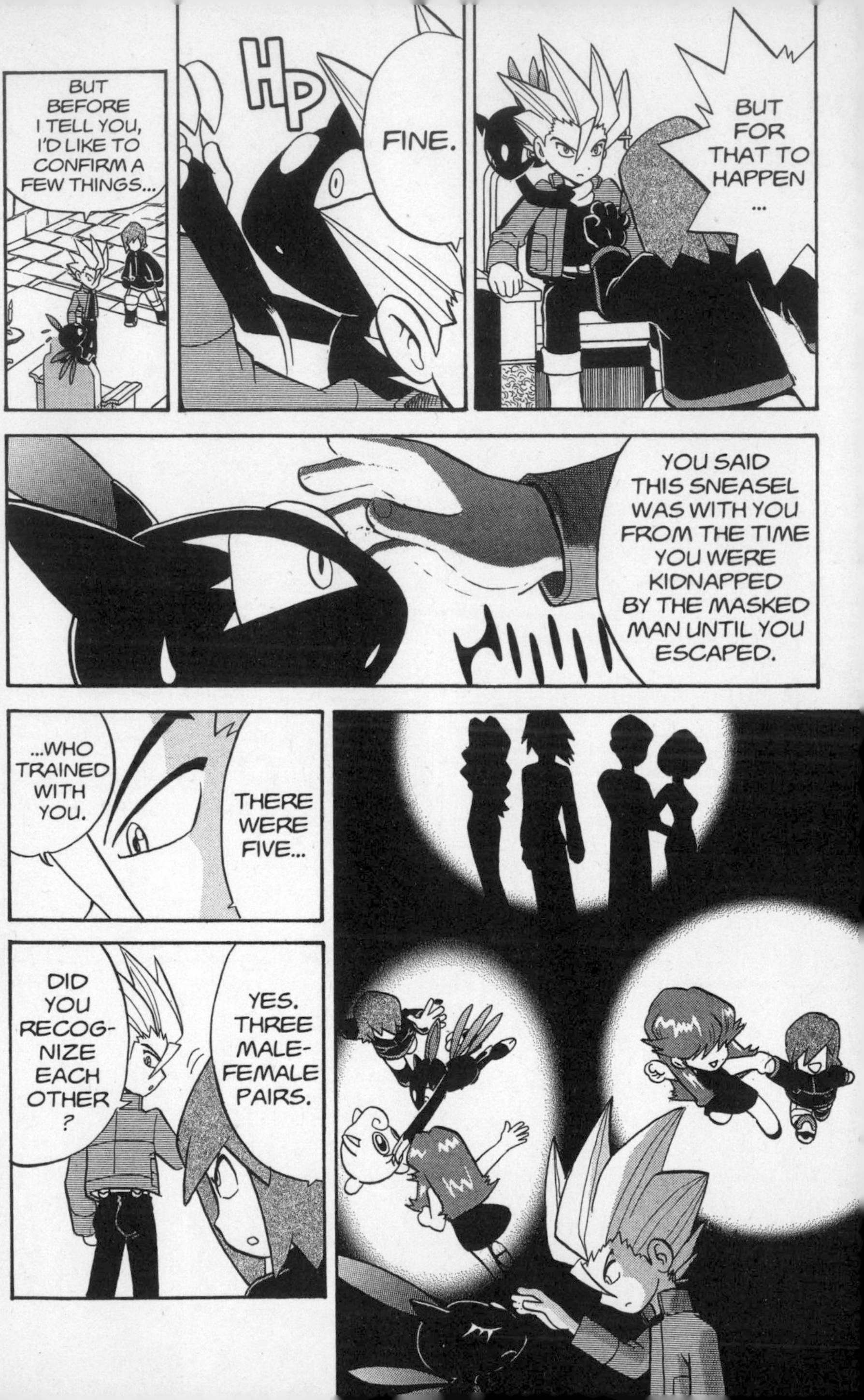

BUT FOR THAT TO HAPPEN ...
HP
FINE.
BUT BEFORE I TELL YOU, I'D LIKE TO CONFIRM A FEW THINGS...
YOU SAID THIS SNEASEL WAS WITH YOU FROM THE TIME YOU WERE KIDNAPPED BY THE MASKED MAN UNTIL YOU ESCAPED.
THERE WERE FIVE...
...WHO TRAINED WITH YOU.
YES. THREE MALE-FEMALE PAIRS.
DID YOU RECOGNIZE EACH OTHER?

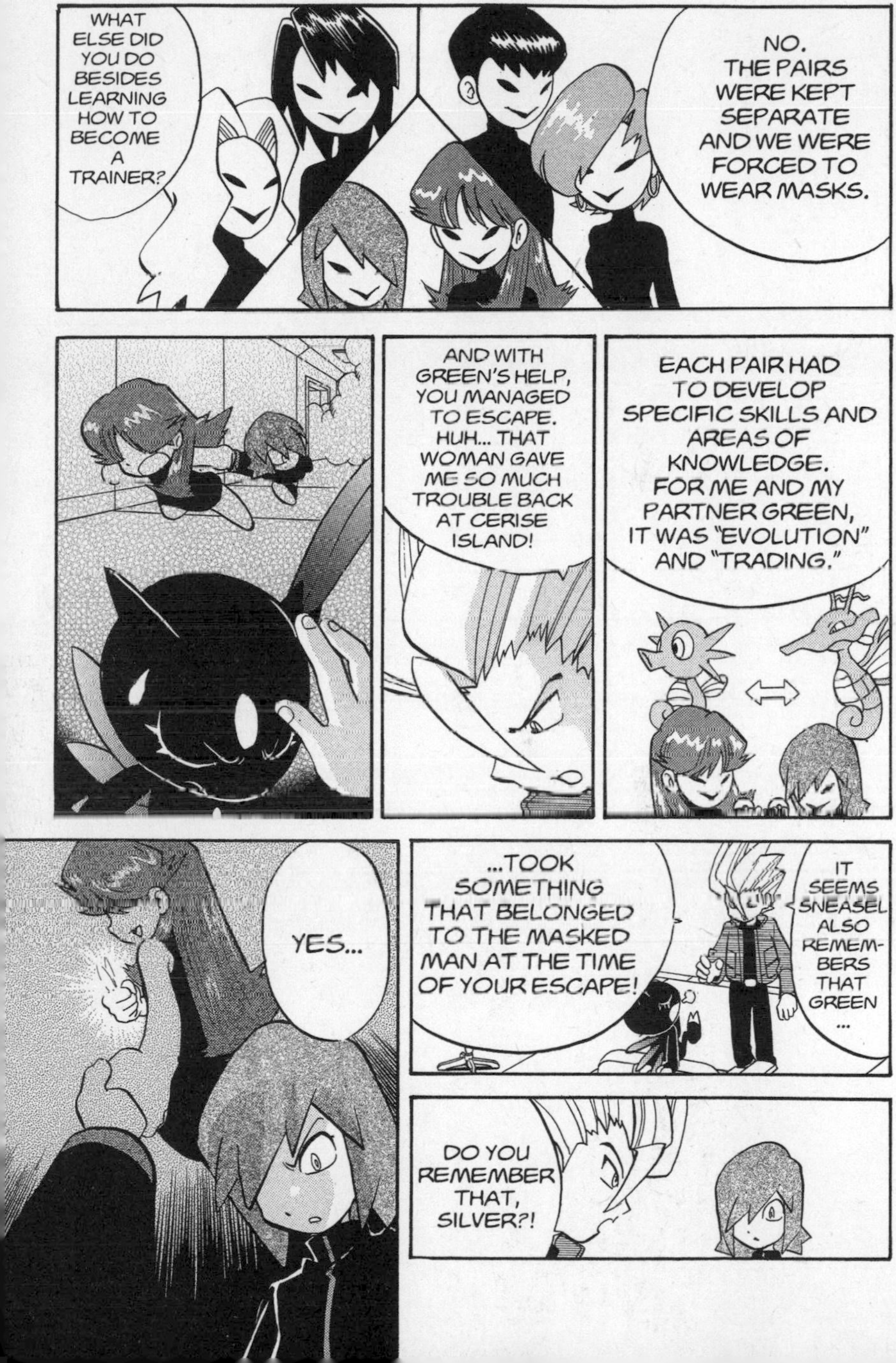
NO. THE PAIRS WERE KEPT SEPARATE AND WE WERE FORCED TO WEAR MASKS.
WHAT ELSE DID YOU DO BESIDES LEARNING HOW TO BECOME A TRAINER?
EACH PAIR HAD TO DEVELOP SPECIFIC SKILLS AND AREAS OF KNOWLEDGE. FOR ME AND MY PARTNER GREEN, IT WAS "EVOLUTION" AND "TRADING."
AND WITH GREEN'S HELP, YOU MANAGED TO ESCAPE. HUH... THAT WOMAN GAVE ME SO MUCH TROUBLE BACK AT CERISE ISLAND!
IT SEEMS SNEASEL ALSO REMEMBERS THAT GREEN...
...TOOK SOMETHING THAT BELONGED TO THE MASKED MAN AT THE TIME OF YOUR ESCAPE!
DO YOU REMEMBER THAT, SILVER?!
YES...

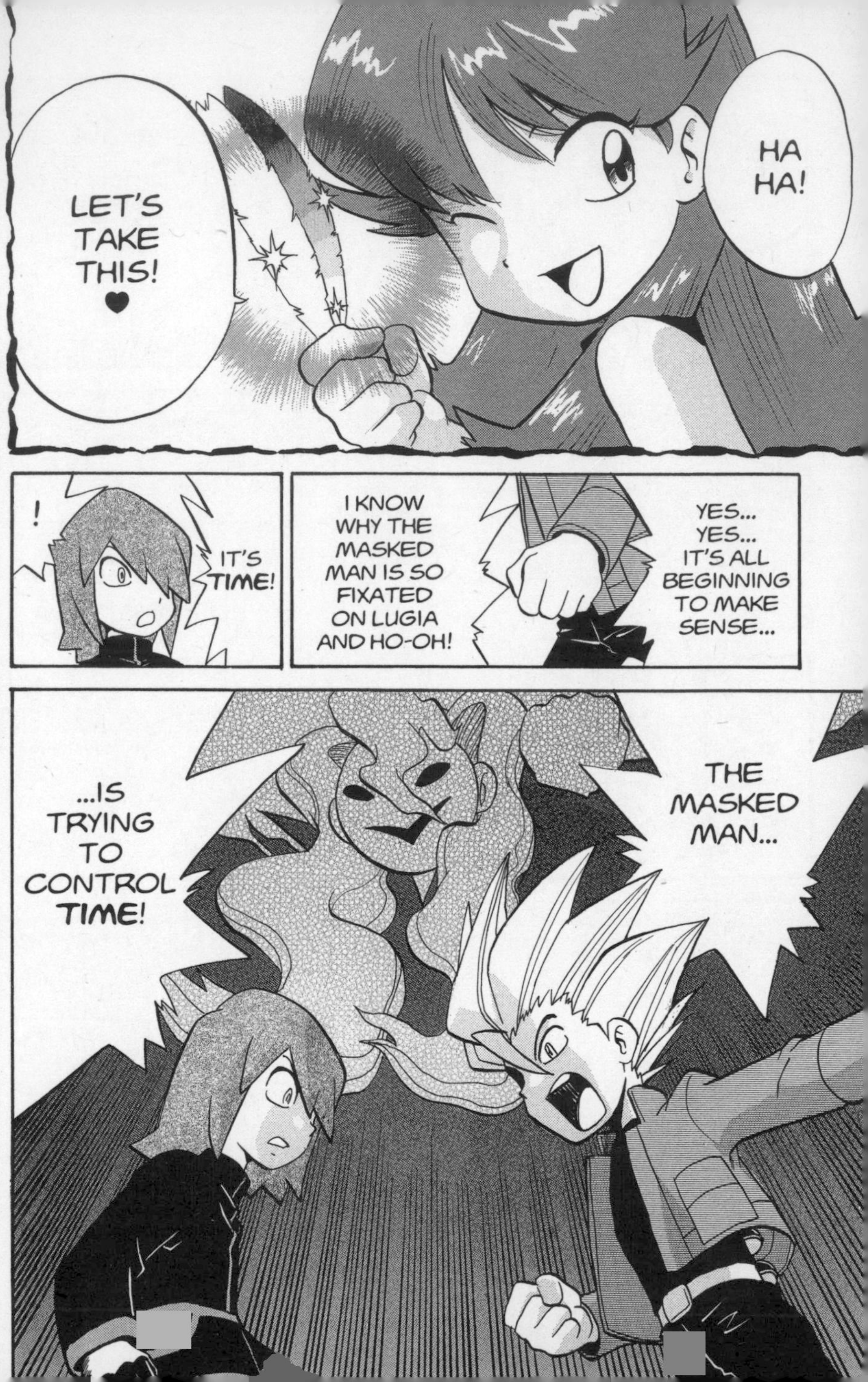
HA HA!
LET'S TAKE THIS! ♥
YES... YES... IT'S ALL BEGINNING TO MAKE SENSE...
I KNOW WHY THE MASKED MAN IS SO FIXATED ON LUGIA AND HO-OH!
!
IT'S TIME!
THE MASKED MAN...
...IS TRYING TO CONTROL TIME!

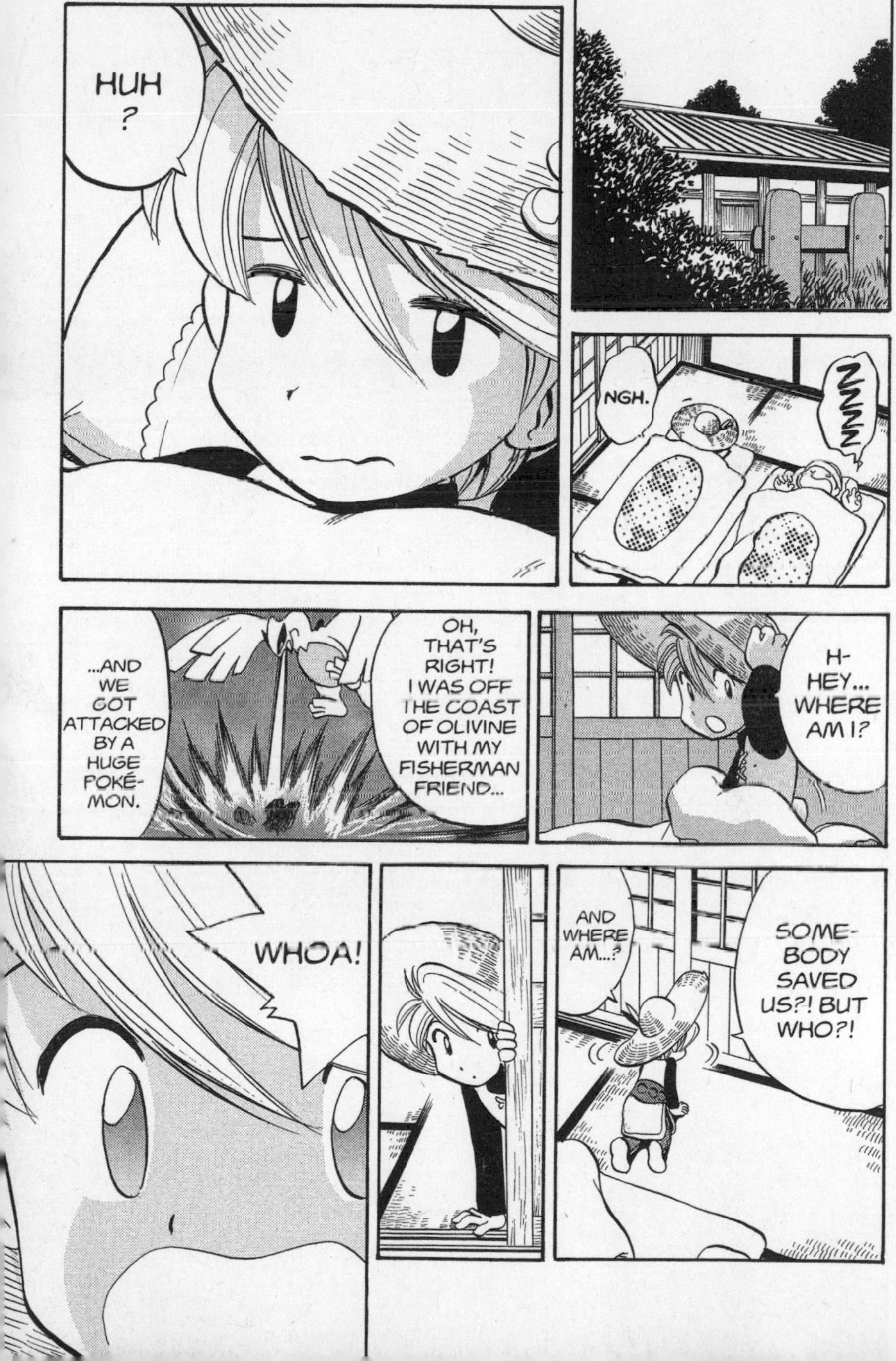
ZZZZ
NGH.
HUH?
H-HEY... WHERE AM I?
OH, THAT'S RIGHT! I WAS OFF THE COAST OF OLIVINE WITH MY FISHERMAN FRIEND...
...AND WE GOT ATTACKED BY A HUGE POKÉMON.
SOMEBODY SAVED US?! BUT WHO?!
AND WHERE AM...?
WHOA!

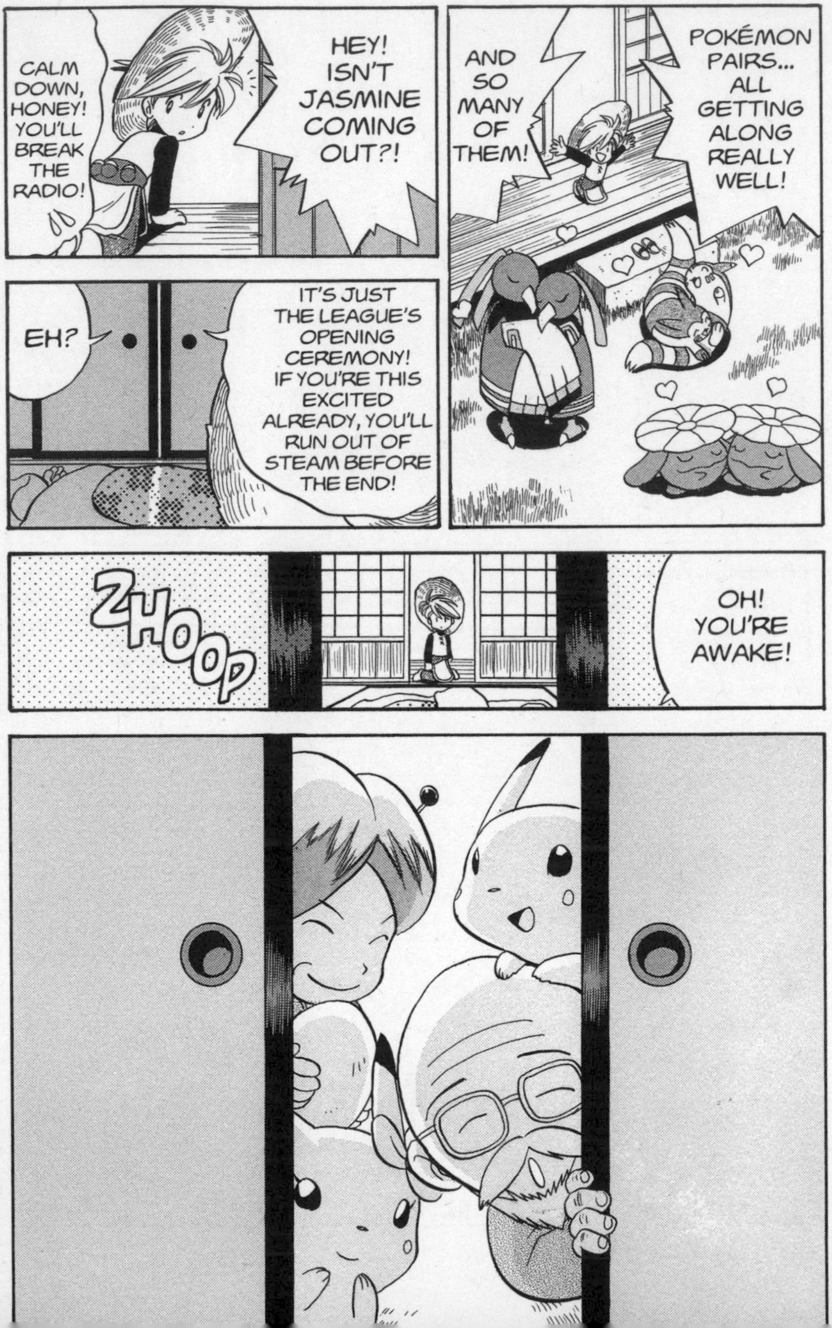
POKÉMON PAIRS... ALL GETTING ALONG REALLY WELL!
AND SO MANY OF THEM!
HEY! ISN'T JASMINE COMING OUT?!
CALM DOWN, HONEY! YOU'LL BREAK THE RADIO!
IT'S JUST THE LEAGUE'S OPENING CEREMONY! IF YOU'RE THIS EXCITED ALREADY, YOU'LL RUN OUT OF STEAM BEFORE THE END!
EH?
OH! YOU'RE AWAKE!
ZHOOP

160 Playful Porygon2

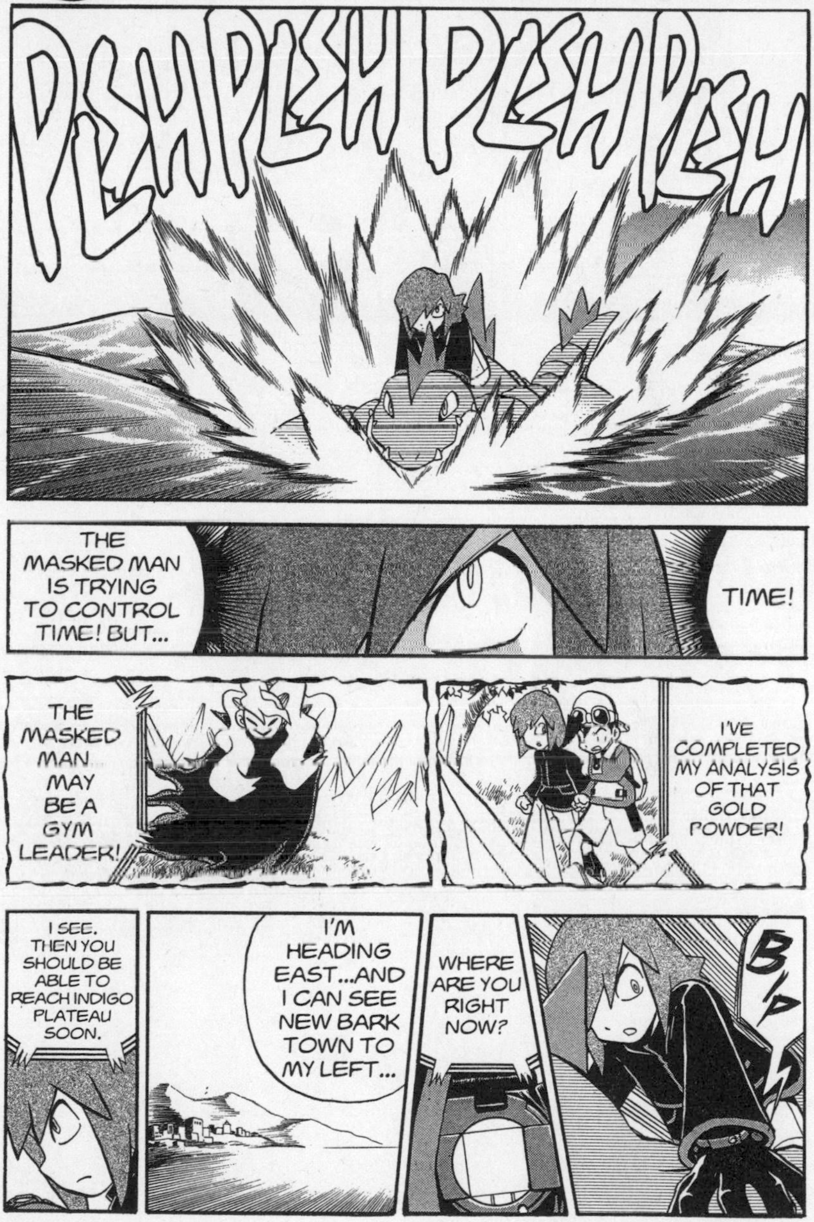
PLSH PLSH PLSH PLSH
TIME!
THE MASKED MAN IS TRYING TO CONTROL TIME! BUT...
I'VE COMPLETED MY ANALYSIS OF THAT GOLD POWDER!
THE MASKED MAN MAY BE A GYM LEADER!
BIP
WHERE ARE YOU RIGHT NOW?
I'M HEADING EAST...AND I CAN SEE NEW BARK TOWN TO MY LEFT...
I SEE. THEN YOU SHOULD BE ABLE TO REACH INDIGO PLATEAU SOON.

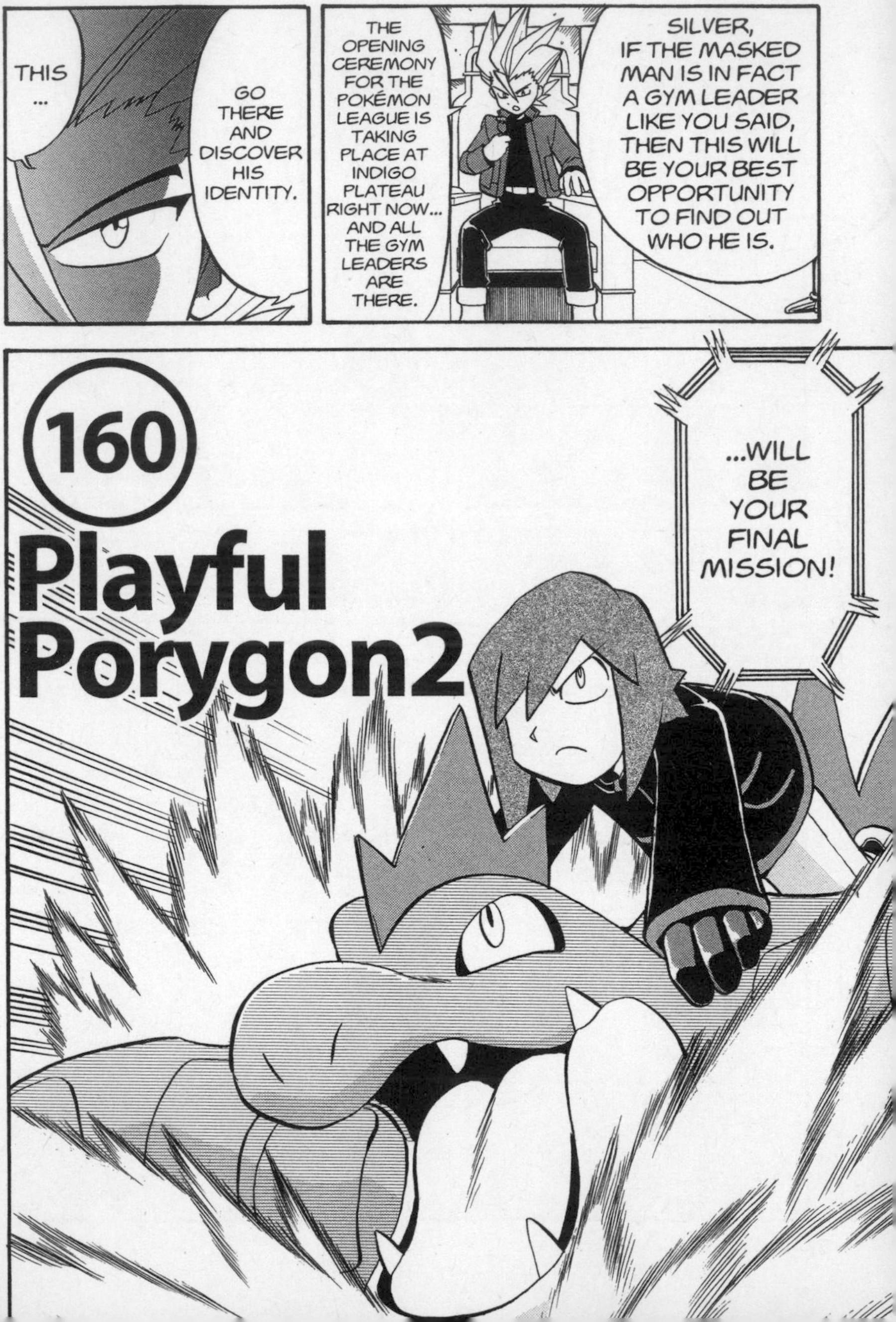

SILVER, IF THE MASKED MAN IS IN FACT A GYM LEADER LIKE YOU SAID, THEN THIS WILL BE YOUR BEST OPPORTUNITY TO FIND OUT WHO HE IS.
THE OPENING CEREMONY FOR THE POKÉMON LEAGUE IS TAKING PLACE AT INDIGO PLATEAU RIGHT NOW... AND ALL THE GYM LEADERS ARE THERE.
GO THERE AND DISCOVER HIS IDENTITY.
THIS ...
160
Playful Porygon2
...WILL BE YOUR FINAL MISSION!

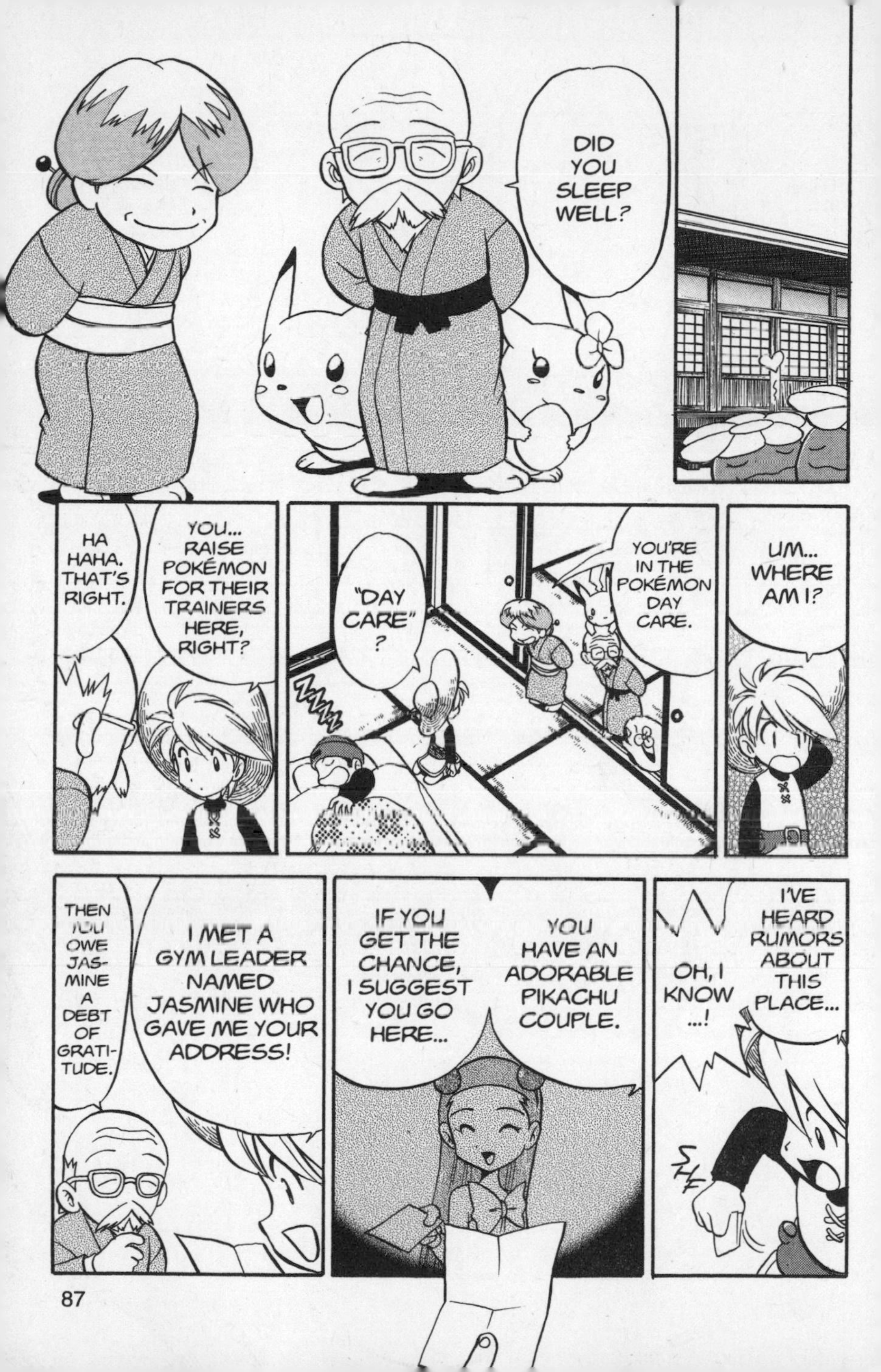
DID YOU SLEEP WELL?
UM... WHERE AM I?
YOU'RE IN THE POKÉMON DAY CARE.
"DAY CARE" ?
YOU... RAISE POKÉMON FOR THEIR TRAINERS HERE, RIGHT?
HA HAHA. THAT'S RIGHT.
I'VE HEARD RUMORS ABOUT THIS PLACE...
OH, I KNOW ...!
YOU HAVE AN ADORABLE PIKACHU COUPLE.
IF YOU GET THE CHANCE, I SUGGEST YOU GO HERE...
I MET A GYM LEADER NAMED JASMINE WHO GAVE ME YOUR ADDRESS!
THEN YOU OWE JASMINE A DEBT OF GRATITUDE.

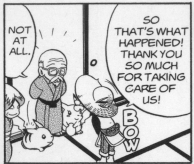

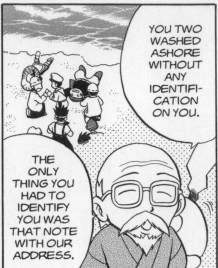

YOU TWO WASHED ASHORE WITHOUT ANY IDENTIFI-CATION ON YOU.
THE ONLY THING YOU HAD TO IDENTIFY YOU WAS THAT NOTE WITH OUR ADDRESS.
SO THAT'S WHAT HAPPENED! THANK YOU SO MUCH FOR TAKING CARE OF US!
BOW
NOT AT ALL.
HUH? PIKA AND CHUCHU... WHAT'S THAT?
AN... AN EGG ?!
YES INDEEDY. I LEFT THESE TWO PIKACHU TOGETHER ...
AND THE NEXT THING I KNEW— THERE WAS THIS EGG!
WHAT ?!
GONG
COME ALONG NOW. YOU CAN CONTINUE YOUR SMALL TALK LATER!

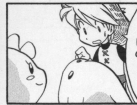

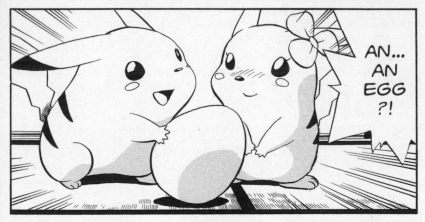

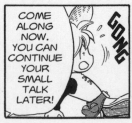

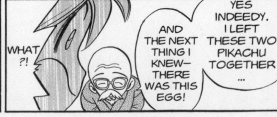

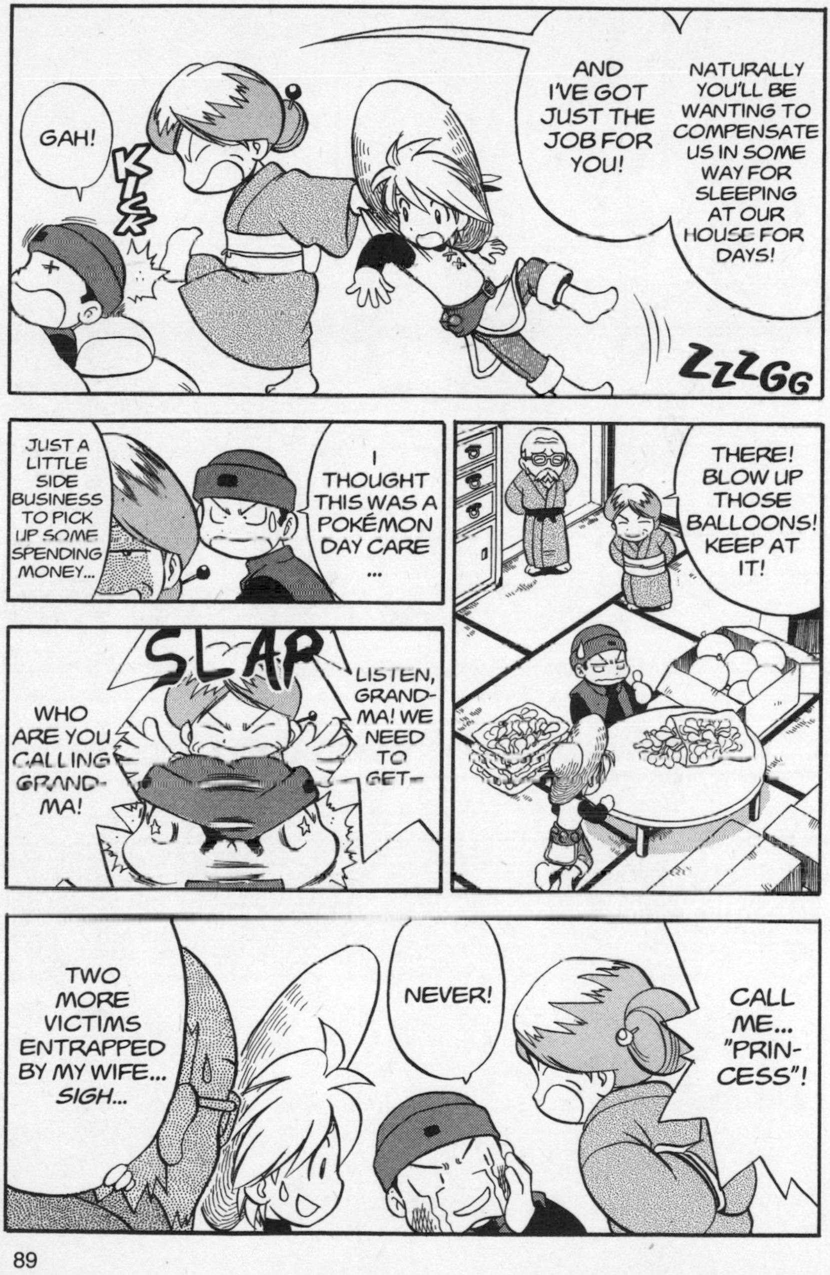
NATURALLY YOU'LL BE WANTING TO COMPENSATE US IN SOME WAY FOR SLEEPING AT OUR HOUSE FOR DAYS!
AND I'VE GOT JUST THE JOB FOR YOU!
KICK
GAH!
ZZZGG
THERE! BLOW UP THOSE BALLOONS! KEEP AT IT!
I THOUGHT THIS WAS A POKÉMON DAY CARE...
JUST A LITTLE SIDE BUSINESS TO PICK UP SOME SPENDING MONEY...
SLAP
LISTEN, GRANDMA! WE NEED TO GET—
WHO ARE YOU CALLING GRANDMA!
CALL ME... "PRINCESS"!
NEVER!
TWO MORE VICTIMS ENTRAPPED BY MY WIFE... SIGH...

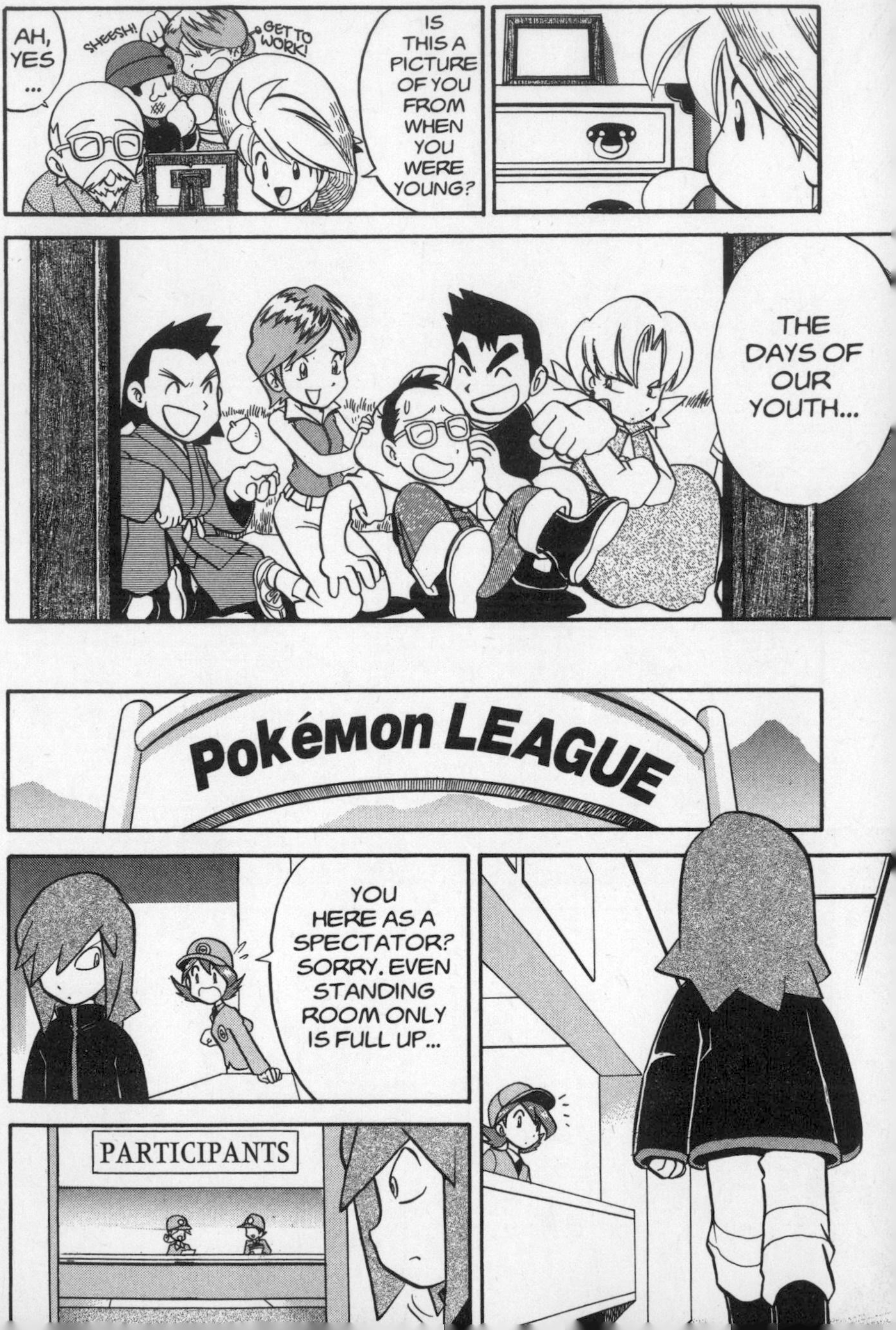
IS THIS A PICTURE OF YOU FROM WHEN YOU WERE YOUNG?
GET TO WORK!
SHEESH!
AH, YES ...
THE DAYS OF OUR YOUTH...
Pokémon LEAGUE
YOU HERE AS A SPECTATOR? SORRY. EVEN STANDING ROOM ONLY IS FULL UP...
PARTICIPANTS

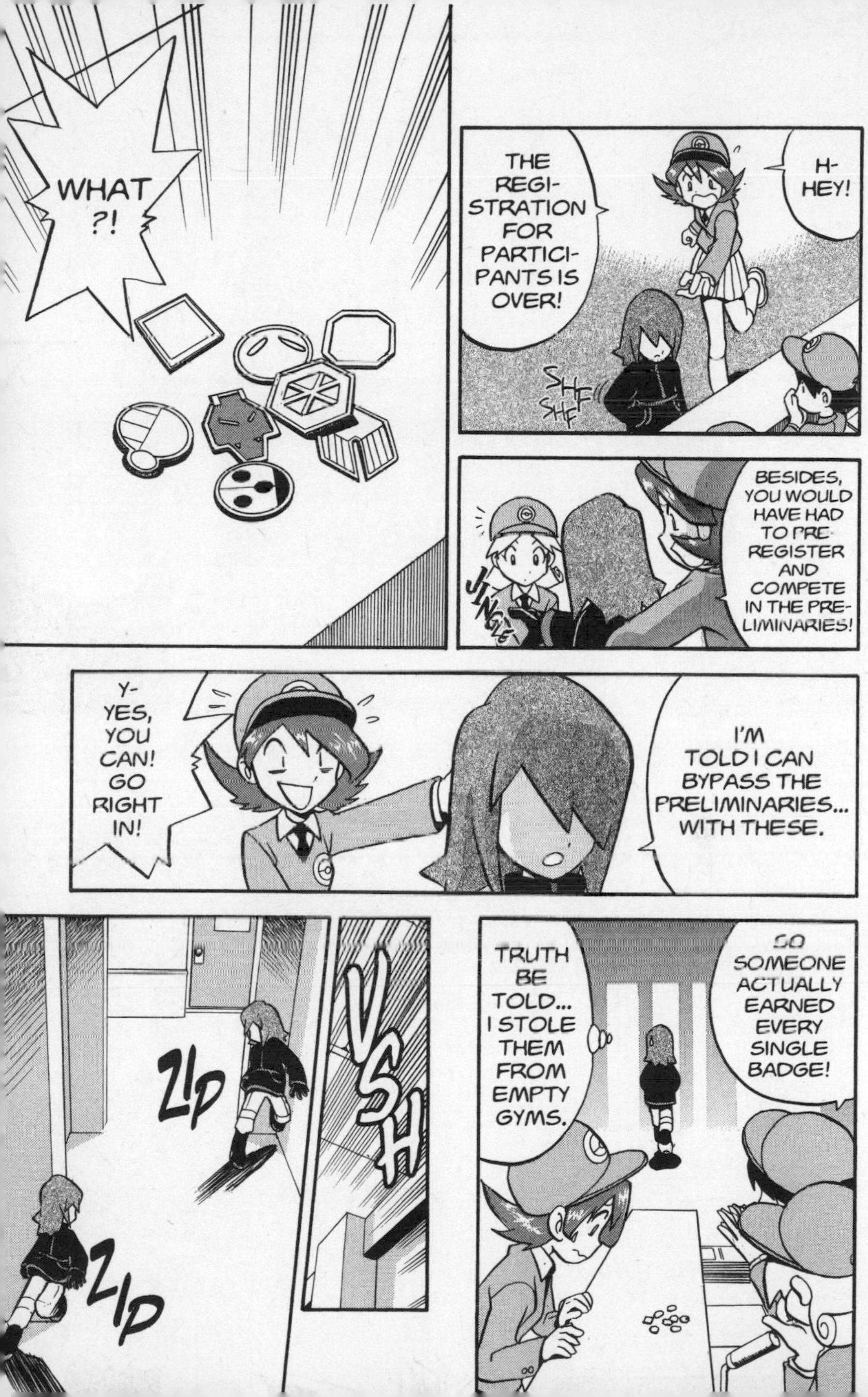
H- HEY!
THE REGISTRATION FOR PARTICIPANTS IS OVER!
SHF SHF
BESIDES, YOU WOULD HAVE HAD TO PRE-REGISTER AND COMPETE IN THE PRELIMINARIES!
JINGLE
WHAT ?!
I'M TOLD I CAN BYPASS THE PRELIMINARIES... WITH THESE.
Y- YES, YOU CAN! GO RIGHT IN!
SO SOMEONE ACTUALLY EARNED EVERY SINGLE BADGE!
TRUTH BE TOLD... I STOLE THEM FROM EMPTY GYMS.
VSH
ZIP
ZIP

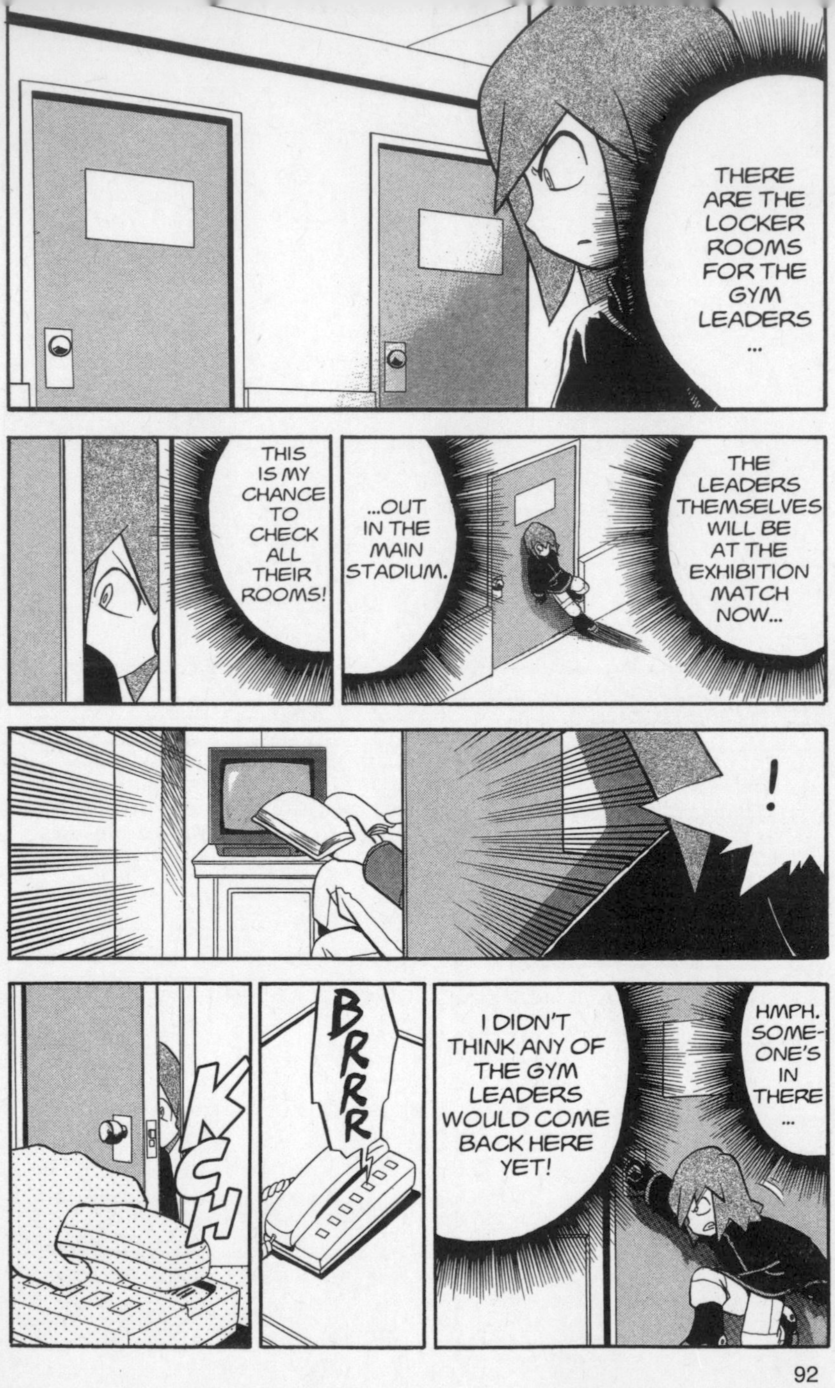
THERE ARE THE LOCKER ROOMS FOR THE GYM LEADERS ...
THE LEADERS THEMSELVES WILL BE AT THE EXHIBITION MATCH NOW...
...OUT IN THE MAIN STADIUM.
THIS IS MY CHANCE TO CHECK ALL THEIR ROOMS!
!
HMPH. SOME-ONE'S IN THERE ...
I DIDN'T THINK ANY OF THE GYM LEADERS WOULD COME BACK HERE YET!
BRRR
KCH

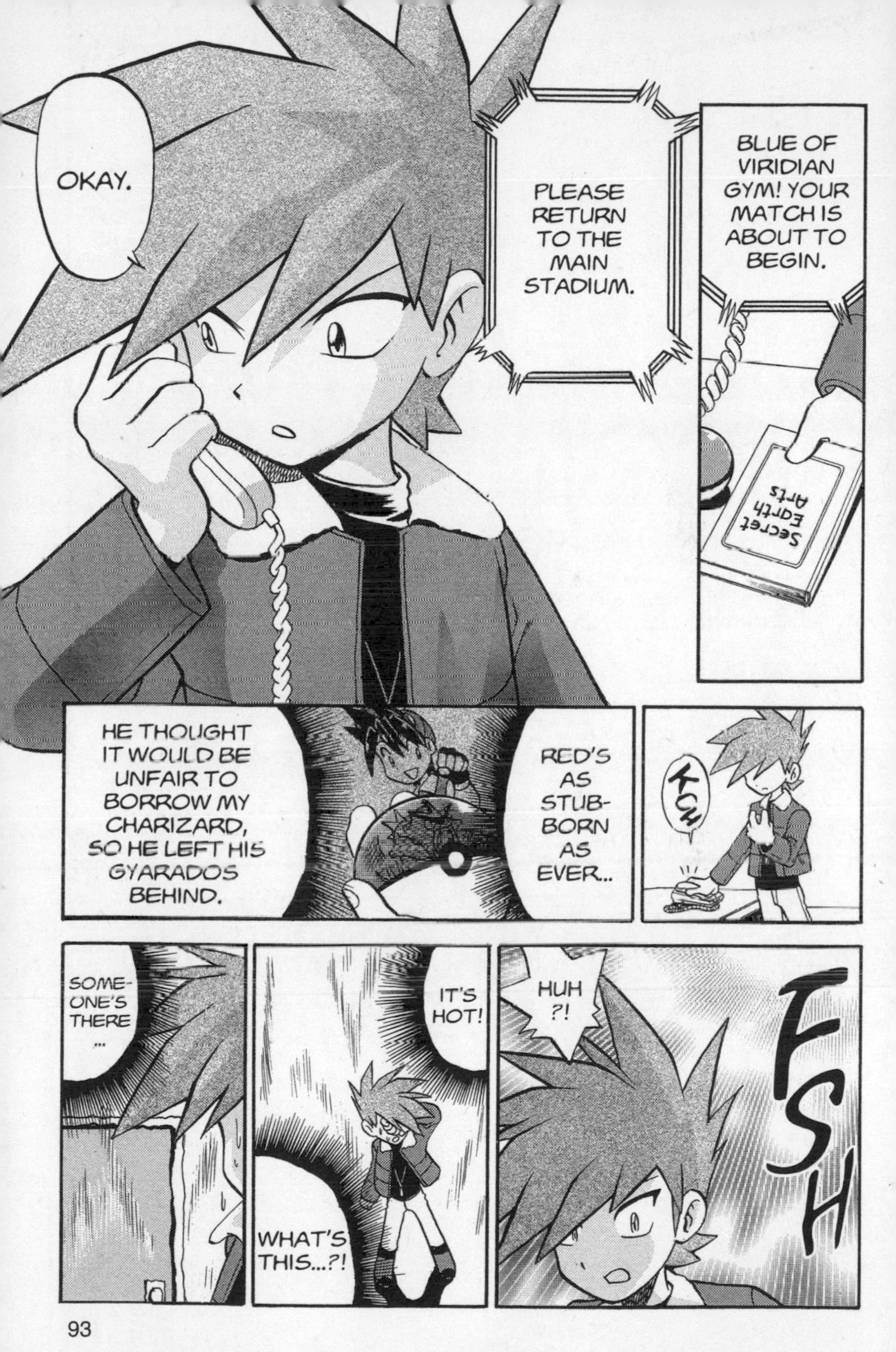
BLUE OF VIRIDIAN GYM! YOUR MATCH IS ABOUT TO BEGIN.
Secret Earth Arts
PLEASE RETURN TO THE MAIN STADIUM.
OKAY.
KCH
RED'S AS STUB-BORN AS EVER...
HE THOUGHT IT WOULD BE UNFAIR TO BORROW MY CHARIZARD, SO HE LEFT HIS GYARADOS BEHIND.
FSH
HUH ?!
IT'S HOT!
WHAT'S THIS...?!
SOME-ONE'S THERE ...

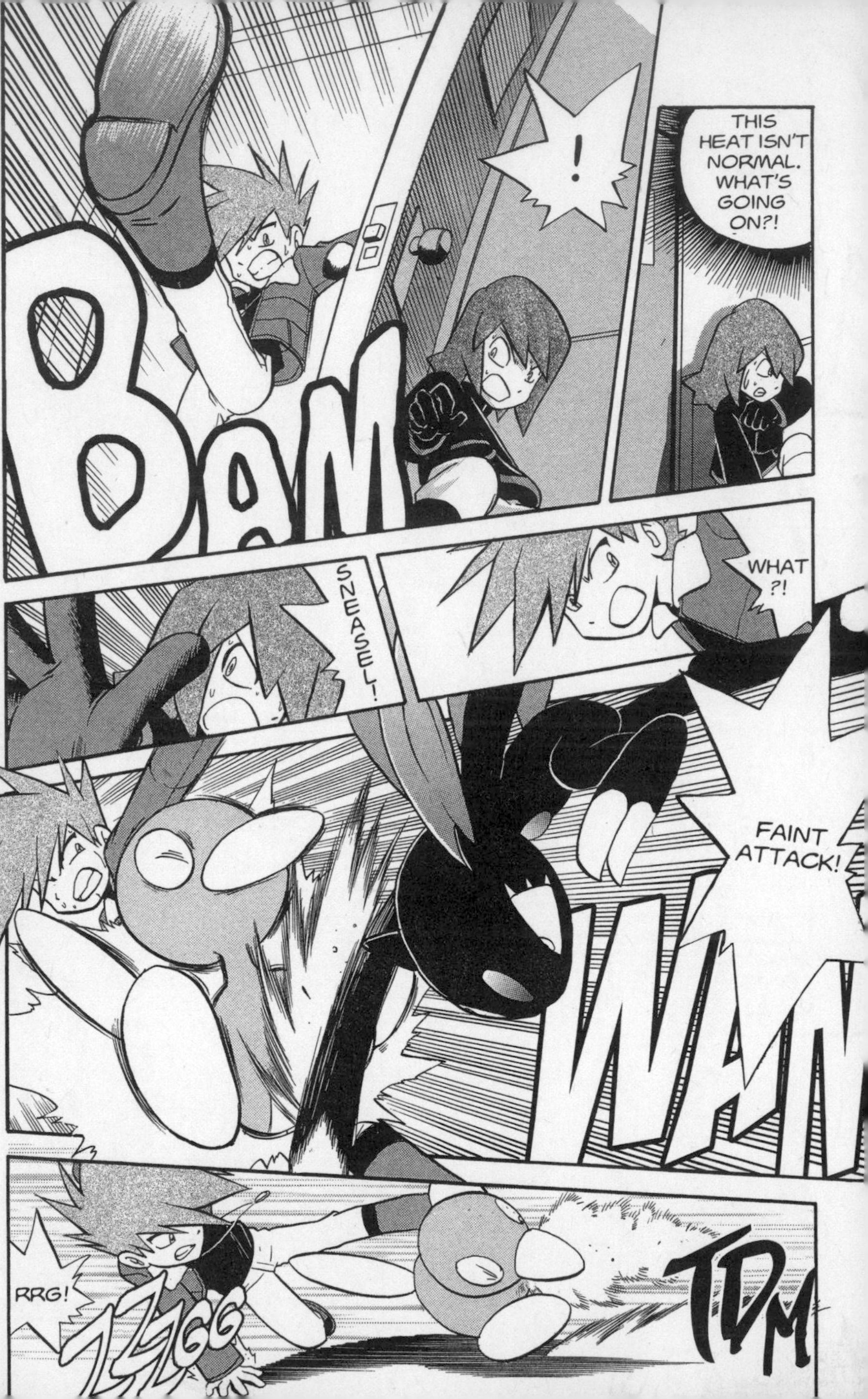
THIS HEAT ISN'T NORMAL. WHAT'S GOING ON?!
!
BAM
WHAT?!
SNEASEL!
FAINT ATTACK!
WAM
TDM
RRG!

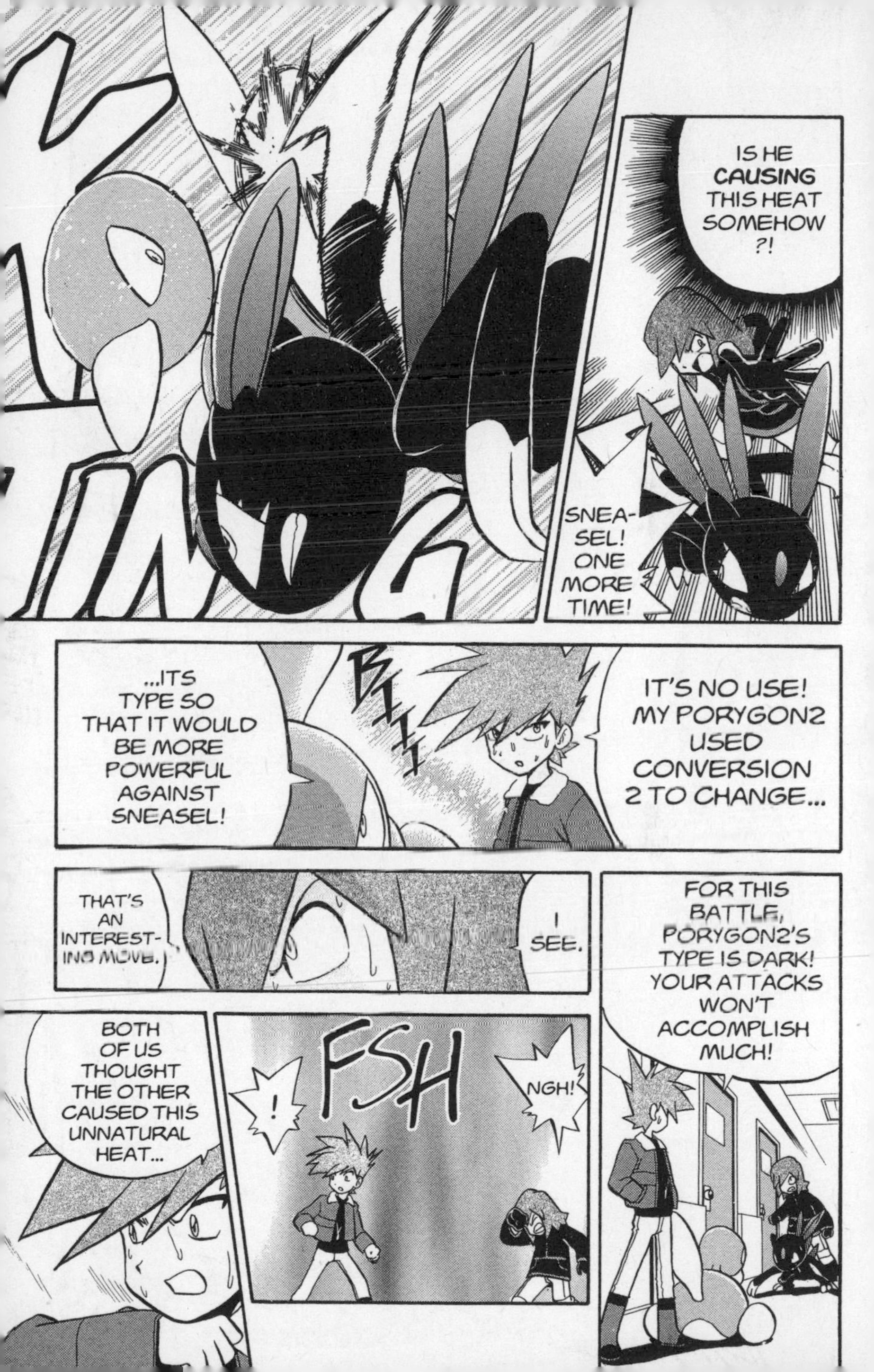
IS HE CAUSING THIS HEAT SOMEHOW?!
SNEASEL! ONE MORE TIME!
IT'S NO USE! MY PORYGON2 USED CONVERSION 2 TO CHANGE...
...ITS TYPE SO THAT IT WOULD BE MORE POWERFUL AGAINST SNEASEL!
FOR THIS BATTLE, PORYGON2'S TYPE IS DARK! YOUR ATTACKS WON'T ACCOMPLISH MUCH!
I SEE.
THAT'S AN INTERESTING MOVE.
NGH!
FSH
!
BOTH OF US THOUGHT THE OTHER CAUSED THIS UNNATURAL HEAT...

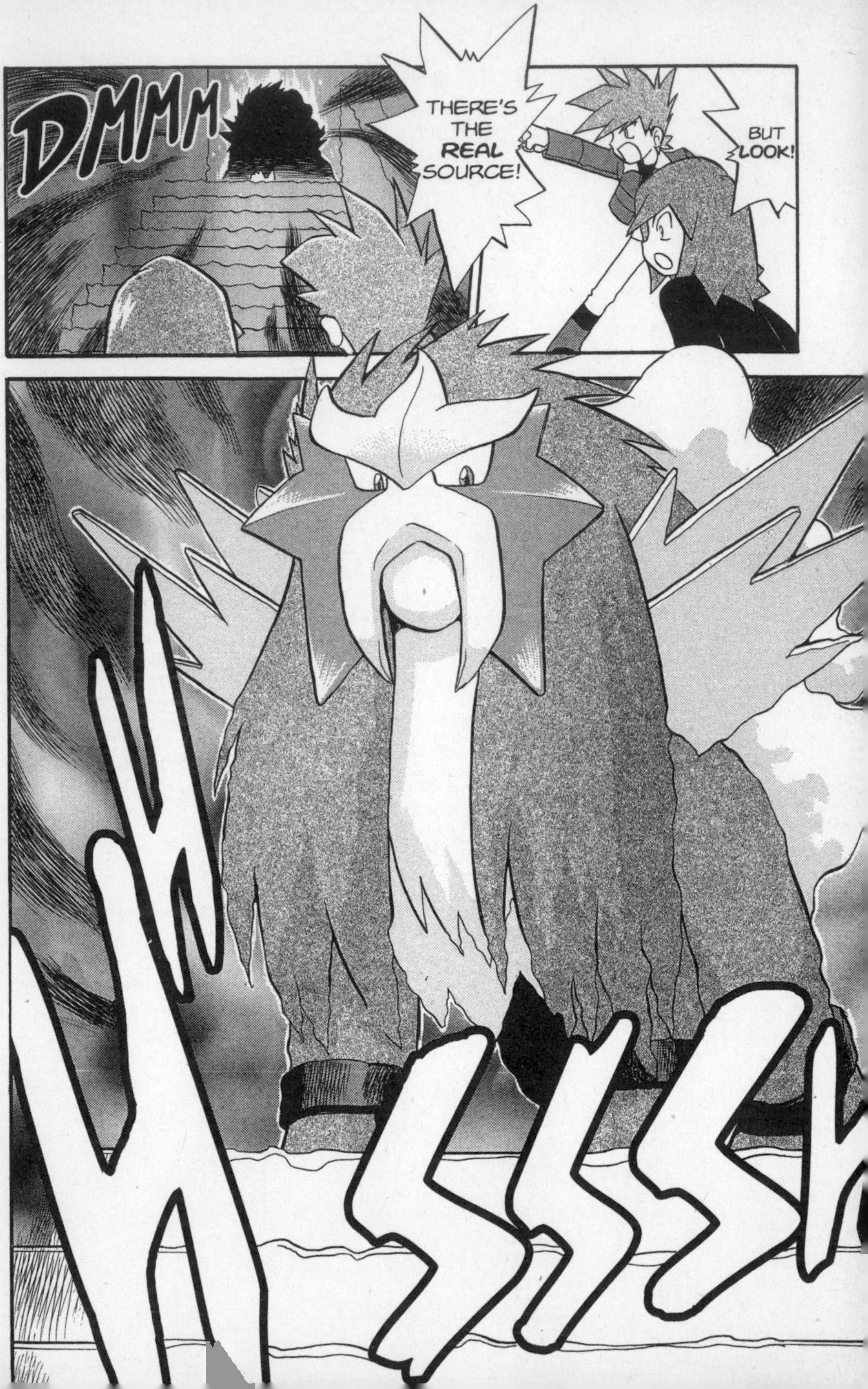
BUT LOOK!
THERE'S THE **REAL** SOURCE!
DMMM
WHSSS

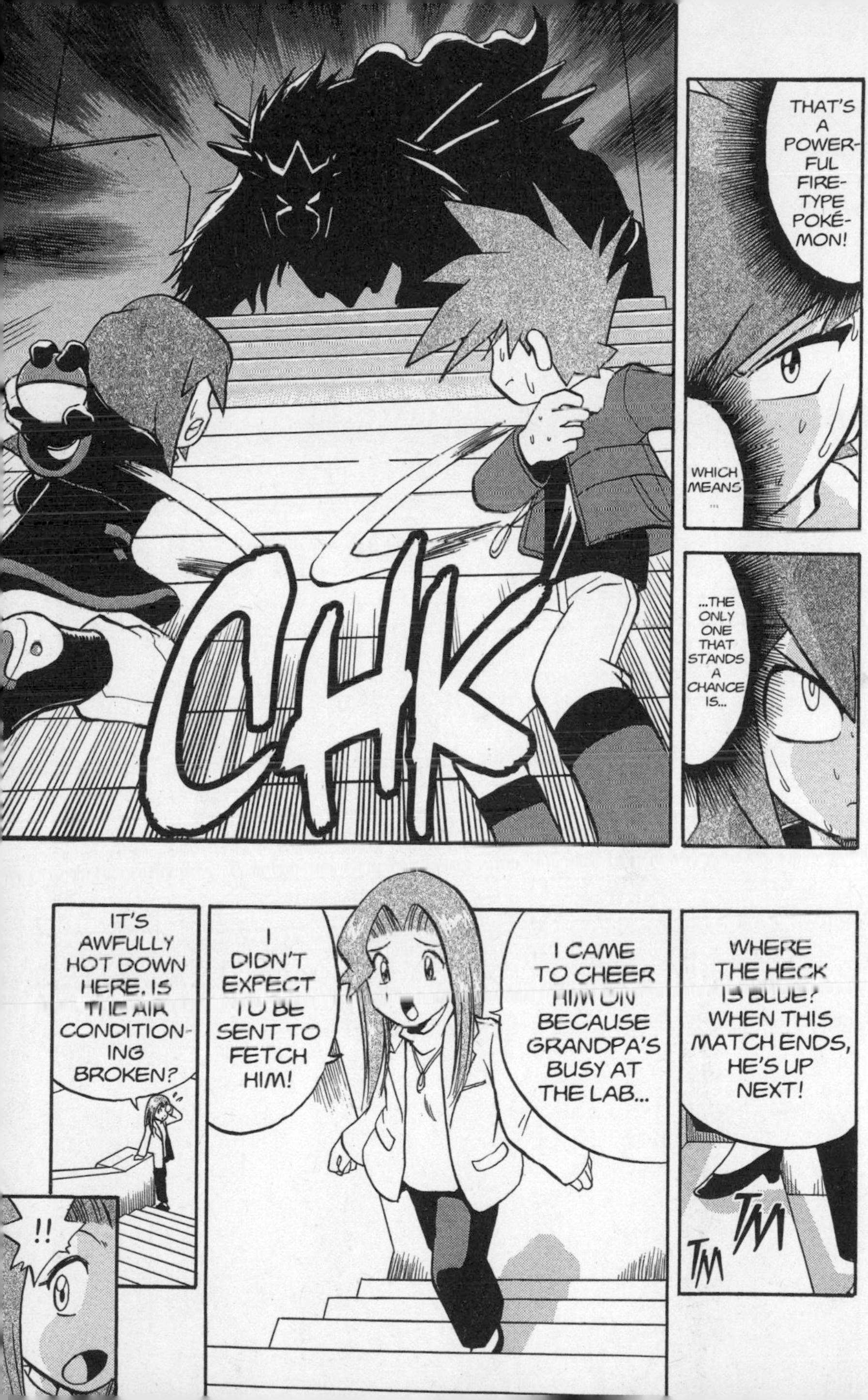
THAT'S A POWERFUL FIRE-TYPE POKÉMON!
WHICH MEANS...
...THE ONLY ONE THAT STANDS A CHANCE IS...
CHK
WHERE THE HECK IS BLUE? WHEN THIS MATCH ENDS, HE'S UP NEXT!
TM TM
I CAME TO CHEER HIM ON BECAUSE GRANDPA'S BUSY AT THE LAB...
I DIDN'T EXPECT TO BE SENT TO FETCH HIM!
IT'S AWFULLY HOT DOWN HERE. IS THE AIR CONDITIONING BROKEN?
!!

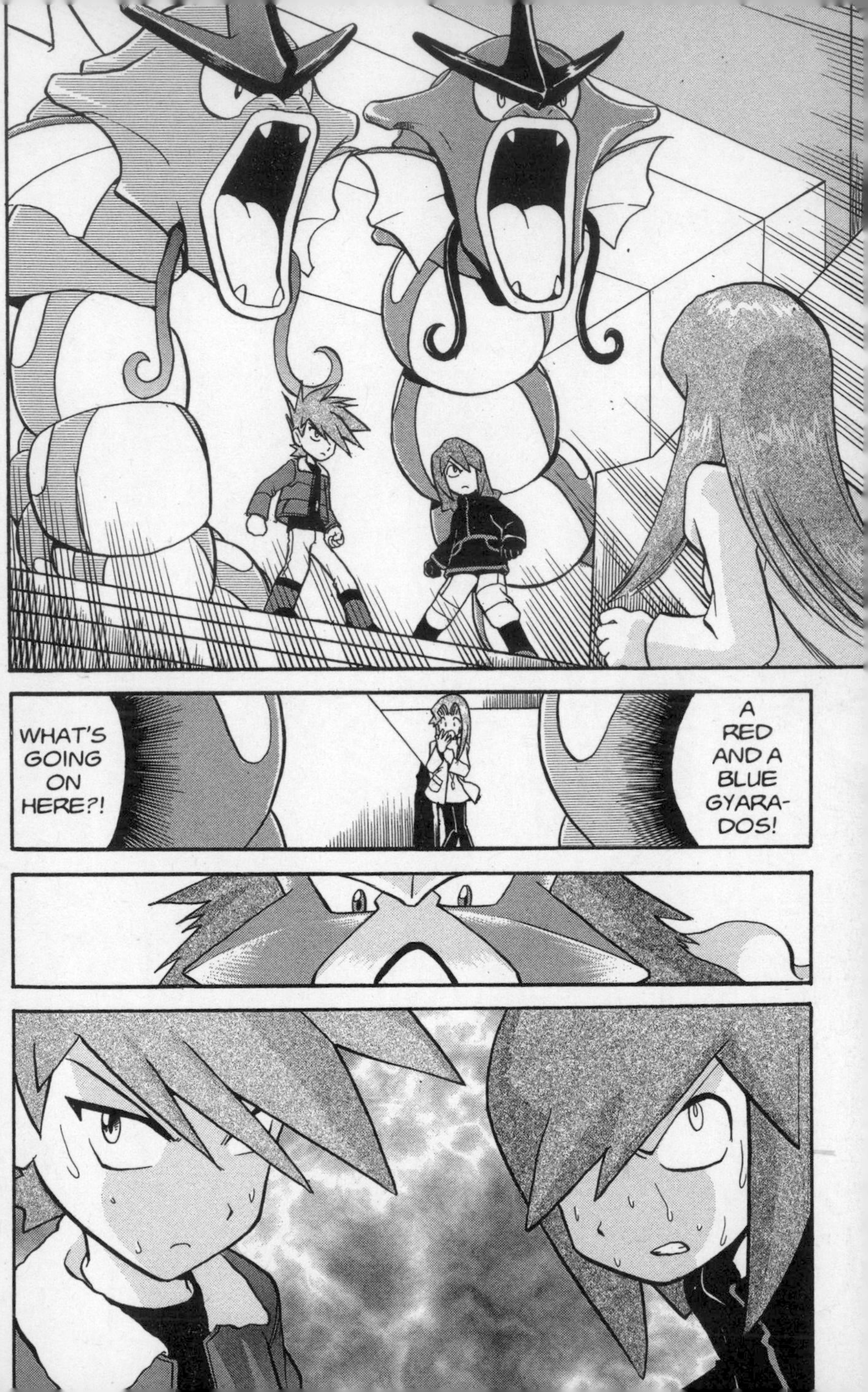
A RED AND A BLUE GYARADOS!
WHAT'S GOING ON HERE?!

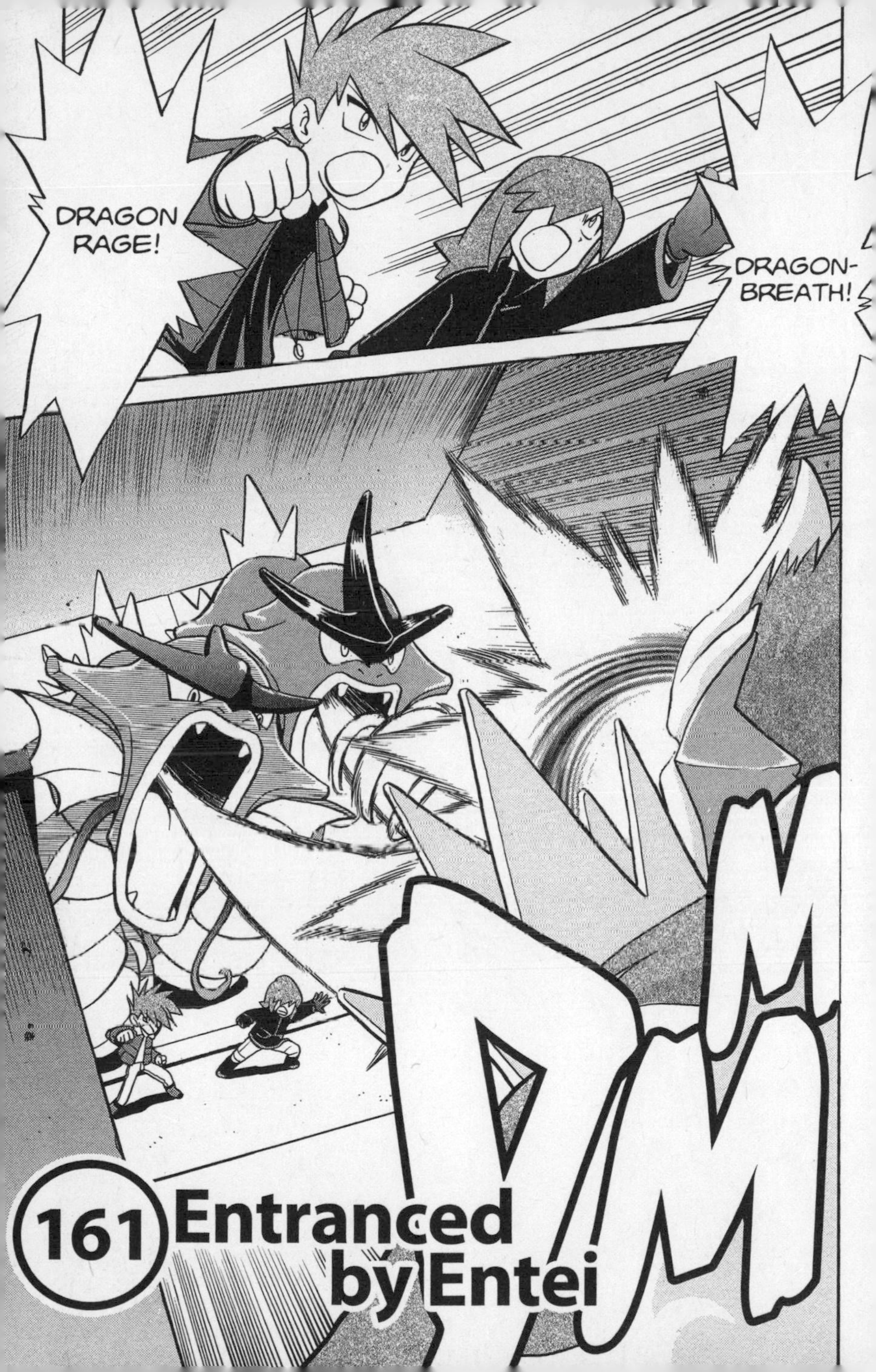
DRAGON-BREATH!
DRAGON RAGE!

161 Entranced by Entei

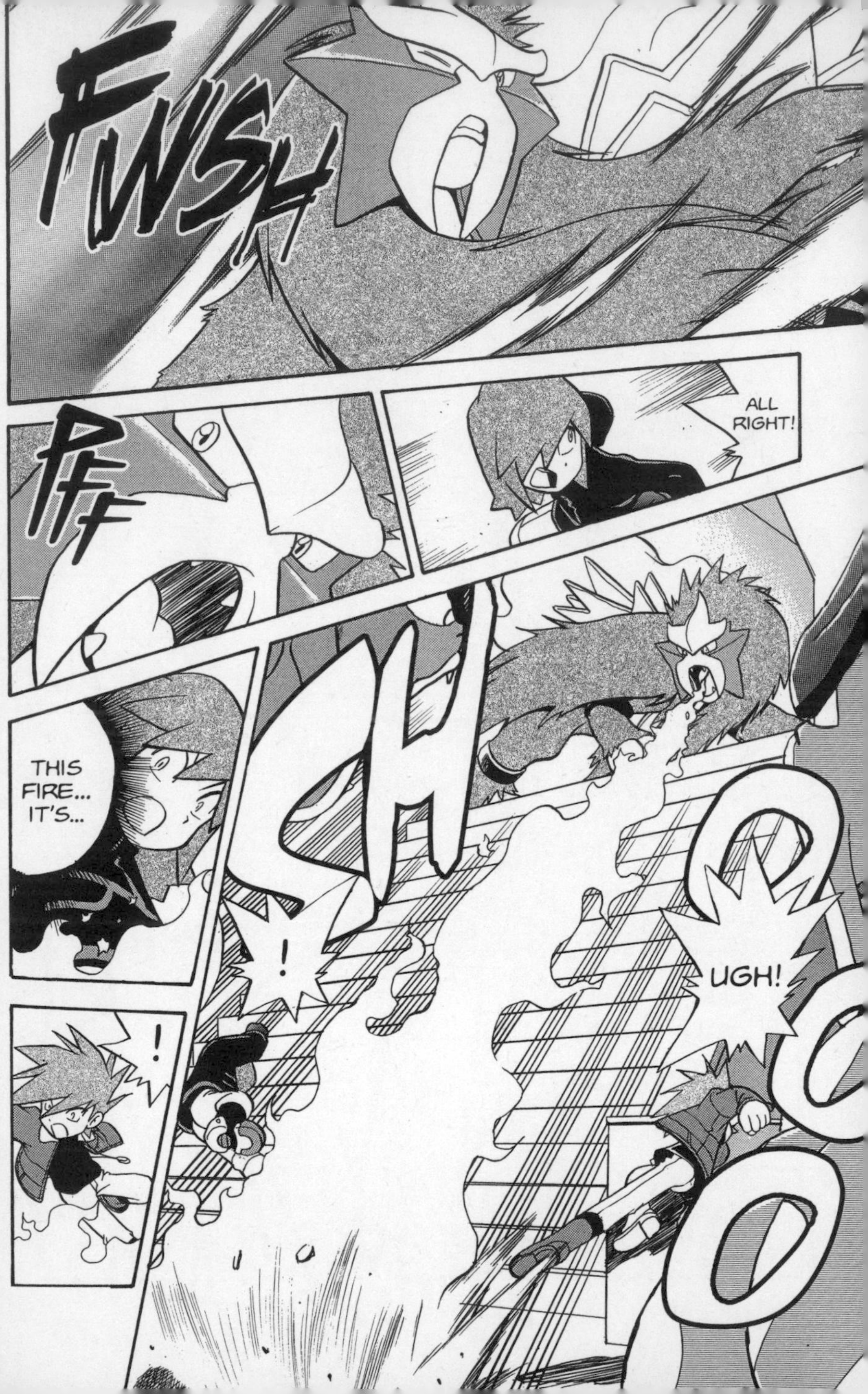
FWSH
ALL RIGHT!
PFF
SH
!
UGH!
THIS FIRE... IT'S...
!

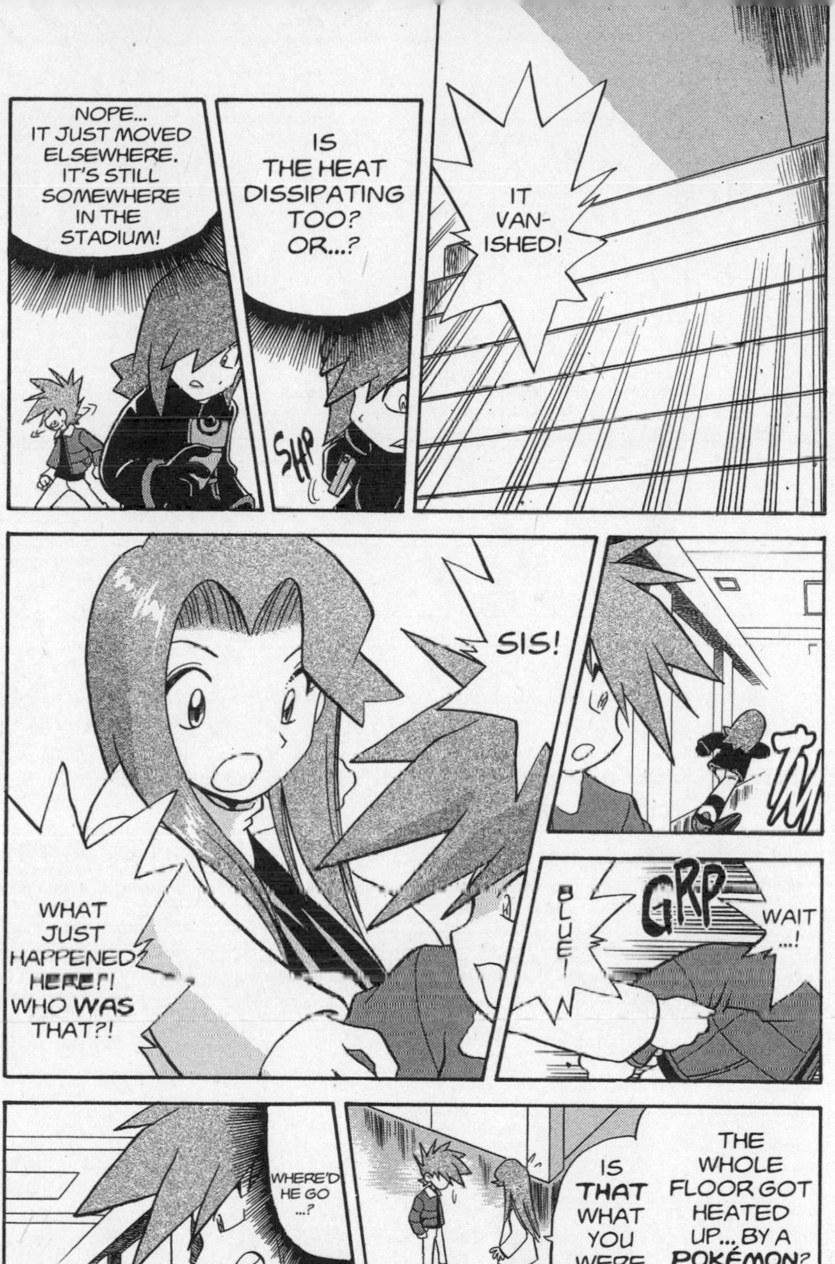
IT VAN-ISHED!
IS THE HEAT DISSIPATING TOO? OR...?
SHP
NOPE... IT JUST MOVED ELSEWHERE. IT'S STILL SOMEWHERE IN THE STADIUM!
WAIT ...!
GRP
BLUE!
SIS!
WHAT JUST HAPPENED HERE?! WHO WAS THAT?!
THE WHOLE FLOOR GOT HEATED UP... BY A POKÉMON?
IS THAT WHAT YOU WERE FIGHT-ING?
WHERE'D HE GO ...?

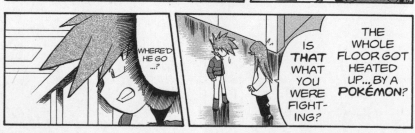

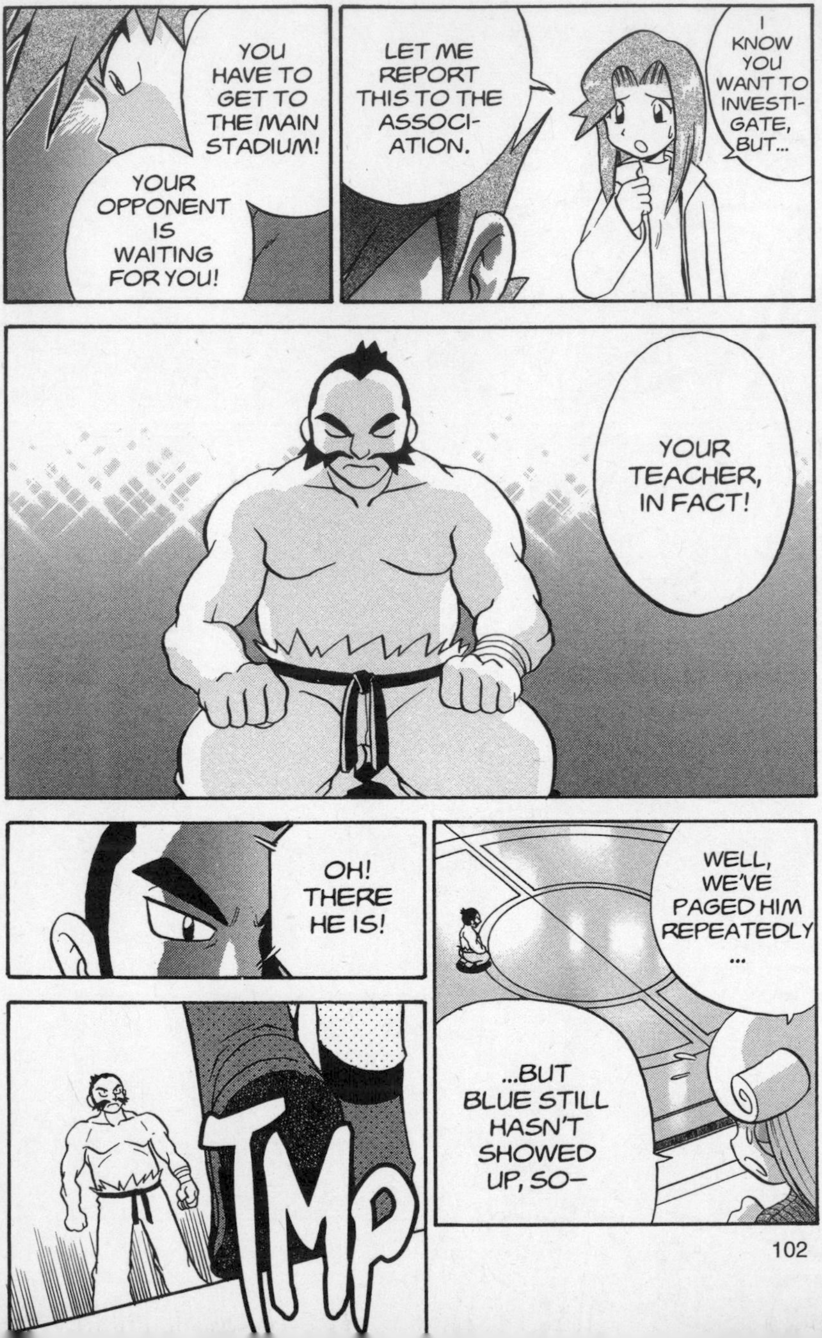
I KNOW YOU WANT TO INVESTIGATE, BUT...
LET ME REPORT THIS TO THE ASSOCIATION.
YOU HAVE TO GET TO THE MAIN STADIUM!
YOUR OPPONENT IS WAITING FOR YOU!
YOUR TEACHER, IN FACT!
WELL, WE'VE PAGED HIM REPEATEDLY...
...BUT BLUE STILL HASN'T SHOWED UP, SO—
OH! THERE HE IS!
TMP

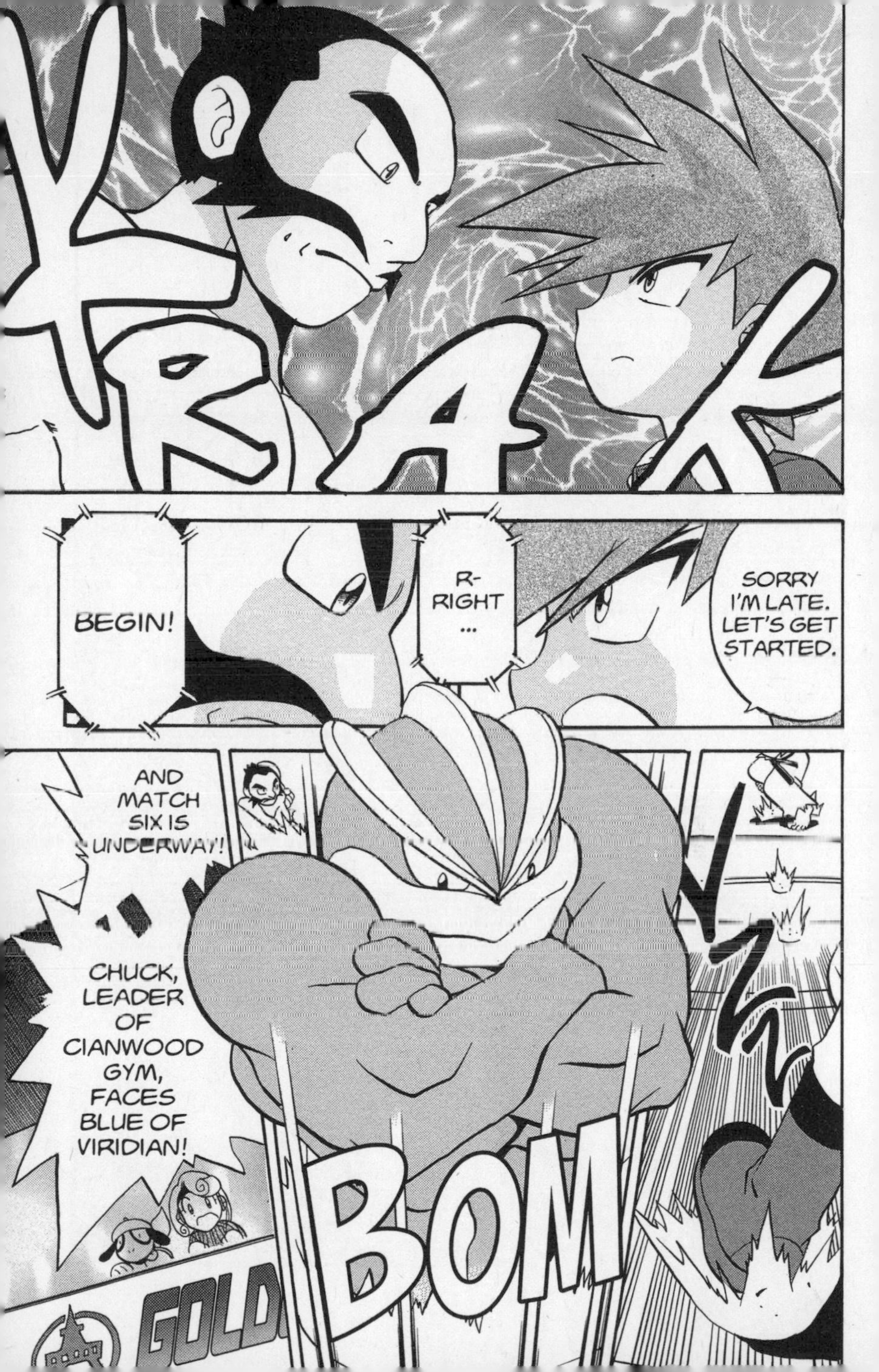
KRAK
SORRY I'M LATE. LET'S GET STARTED.
R-RIGHT ...
BEGIN!
AND MATCH SIX IS UNDERWAY!
CHUCK, LEADER OF CIANWOOD GYM, FACES BLUE OF VIRIDIAN!
BOM
GOLD

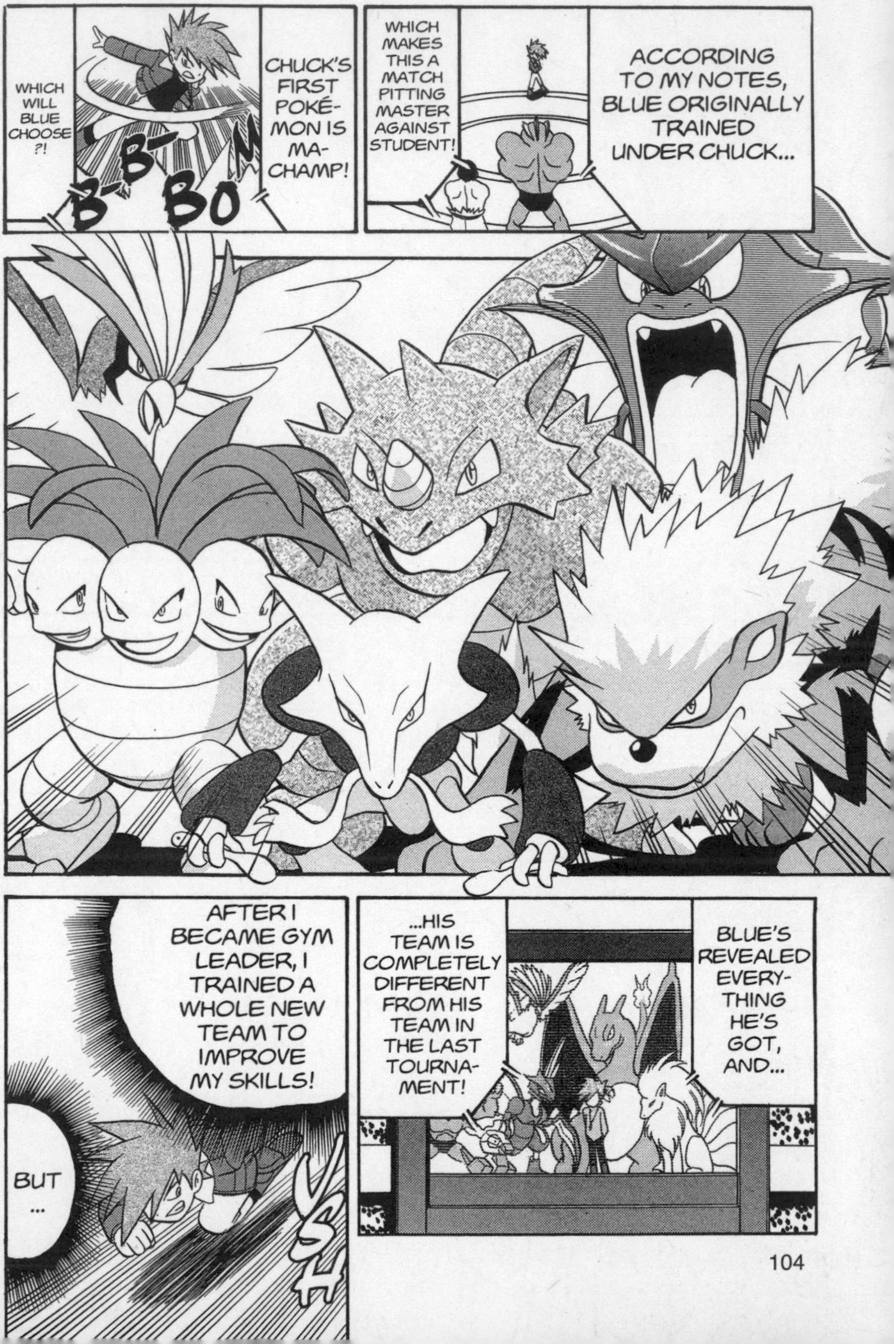
ACCORDING TO MY NOTES, BLUE ORIGINALLY TRAINED UNDER CHUCK...
WHICH MAKES THIS A MATCH PITTING MASTER AGAINST STUDENT!
CHUCK'S FIRST POKÉMON IS MACHAMP!
B-B-B-BOOM
WHICH WILL BLUE CHOOSE?!
BLUE'S REVEALED EVERYTHING HE'S GOT, AND...
...HIS TEAM IS COMPLETELY DIFFERENT FROM HIS TEAM IN THE LAST TOURNAMENT!
AFTER I BECAME GYM LEADER, I TRAINED A WHOLE NEW TEAM TO IMPROVE MY SKILLS!
BUT...

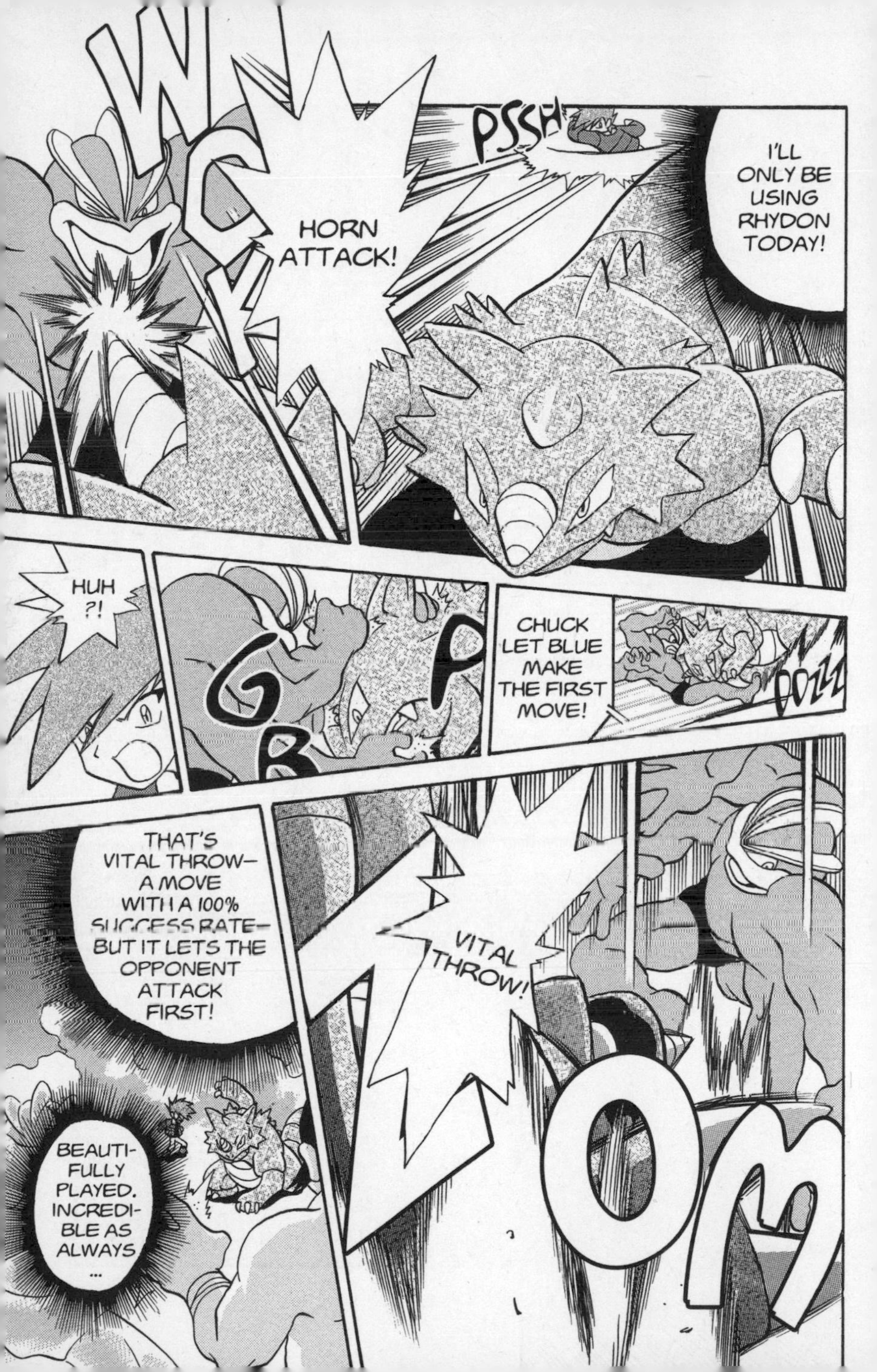
I'LL ONLY BE USING RHYDON TODAY!
PSSH
HORN ATTACK!
CHUCK LET BLUE MAKE THE FIRST MOVE!
HUH ?!
VITAL THROW!
THAT'S VITAL THROW— A MOVE WITH A 100% SUCCESS RATE— BUT IT LETS THE OPPONENT ATTACK FIRST!
BEAUTI-FULLY PLAYED. INCREDI-BLE AS ALWAYS ...

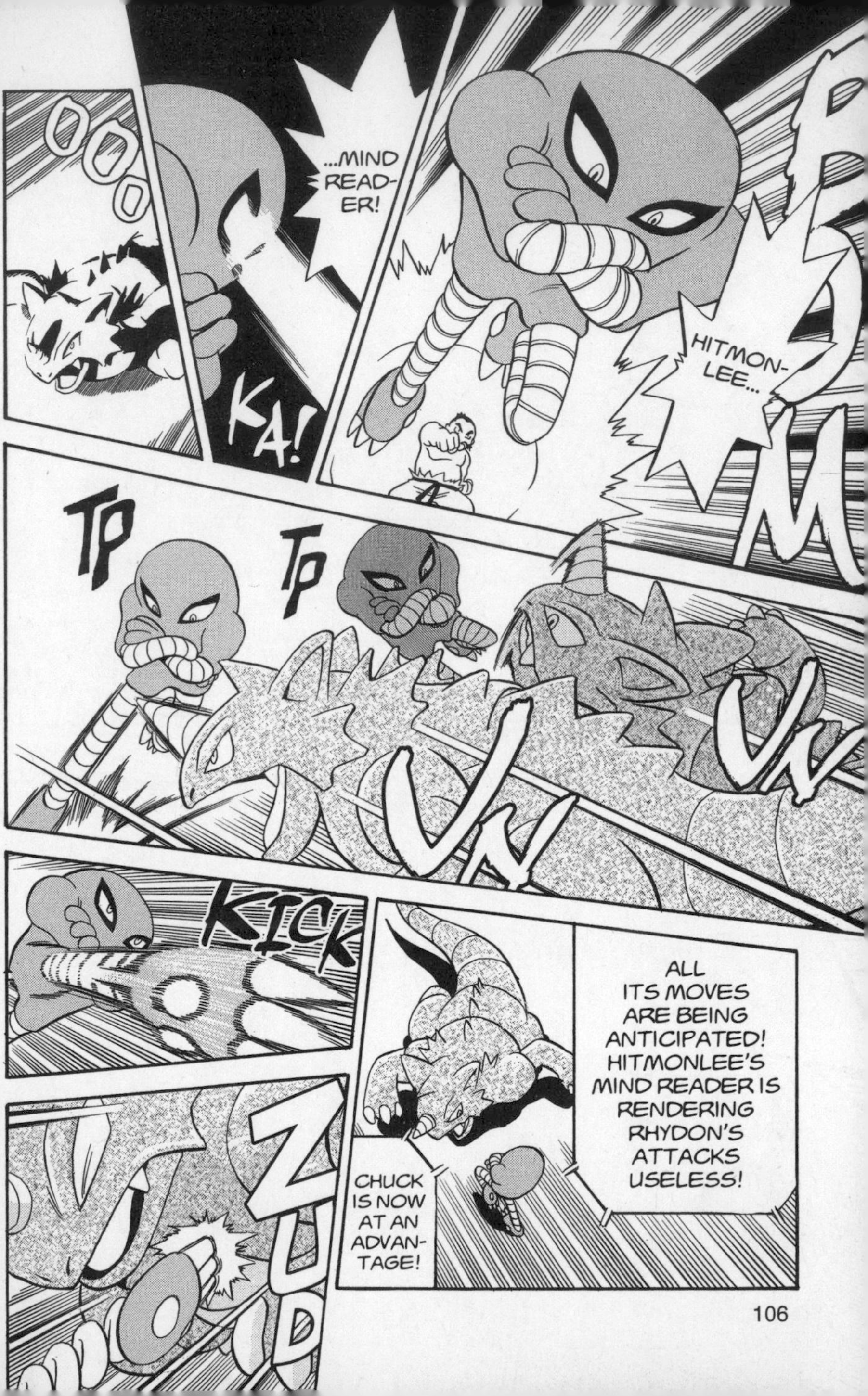
HITMON-
LEE...
...MIND
READ-
ER!
KA!
TP
TP
ALL
ITS MOVES
ARE BEING
ANTICIPATED!
HITMONLEE'S
MIND READER IS
RENDERING
RHYDON'S
ATTACKS
USELESS!
CHUCK
IS NOW
AT AN
ADVAN-
TAGE!
KICK
ZUD

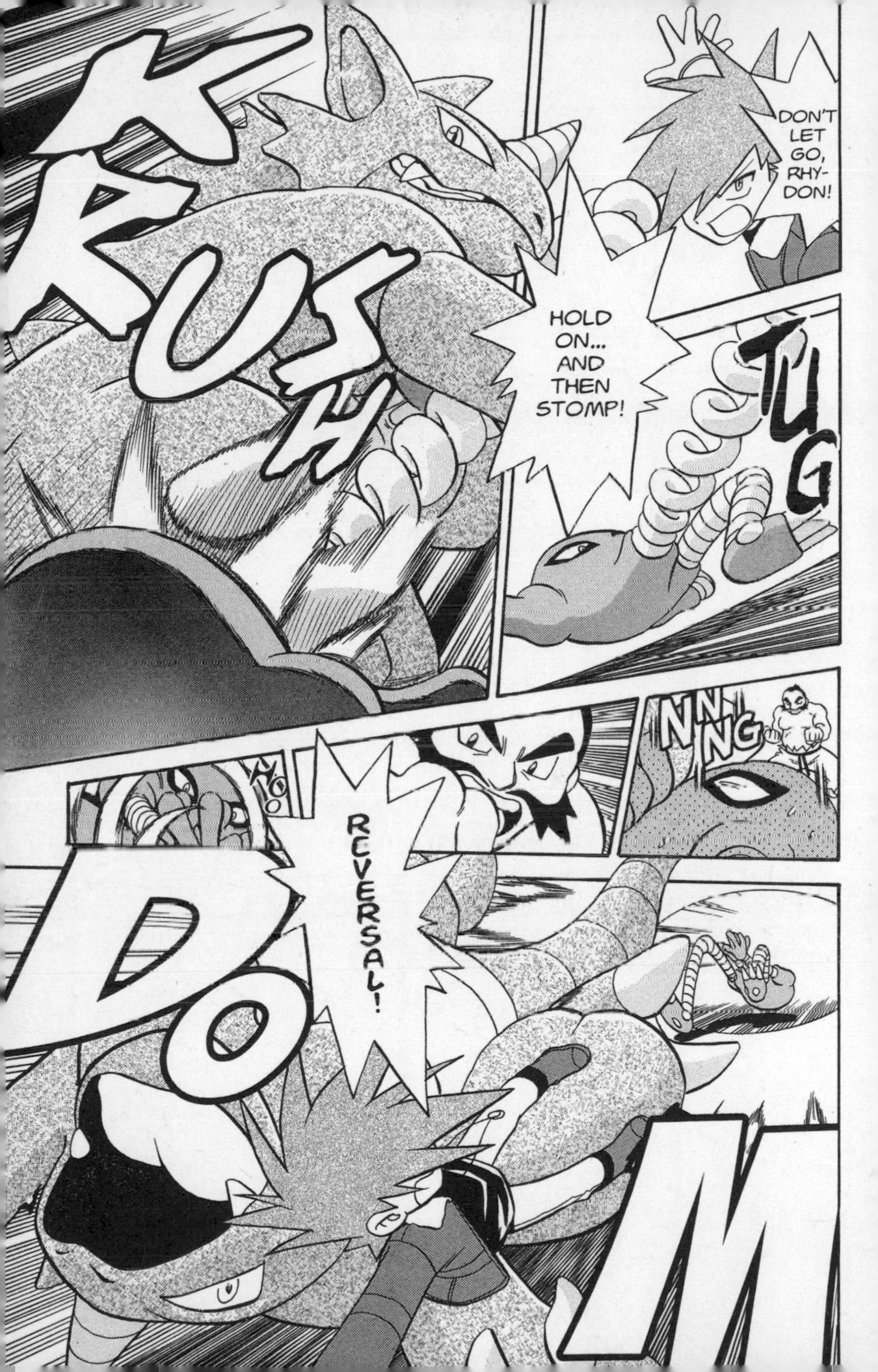
DON'T LET GO, RHY-DON!
KRUSH
HOLD ON... AND THEN STOMP!
TUG
NNNG
REVERSAL!
DOM

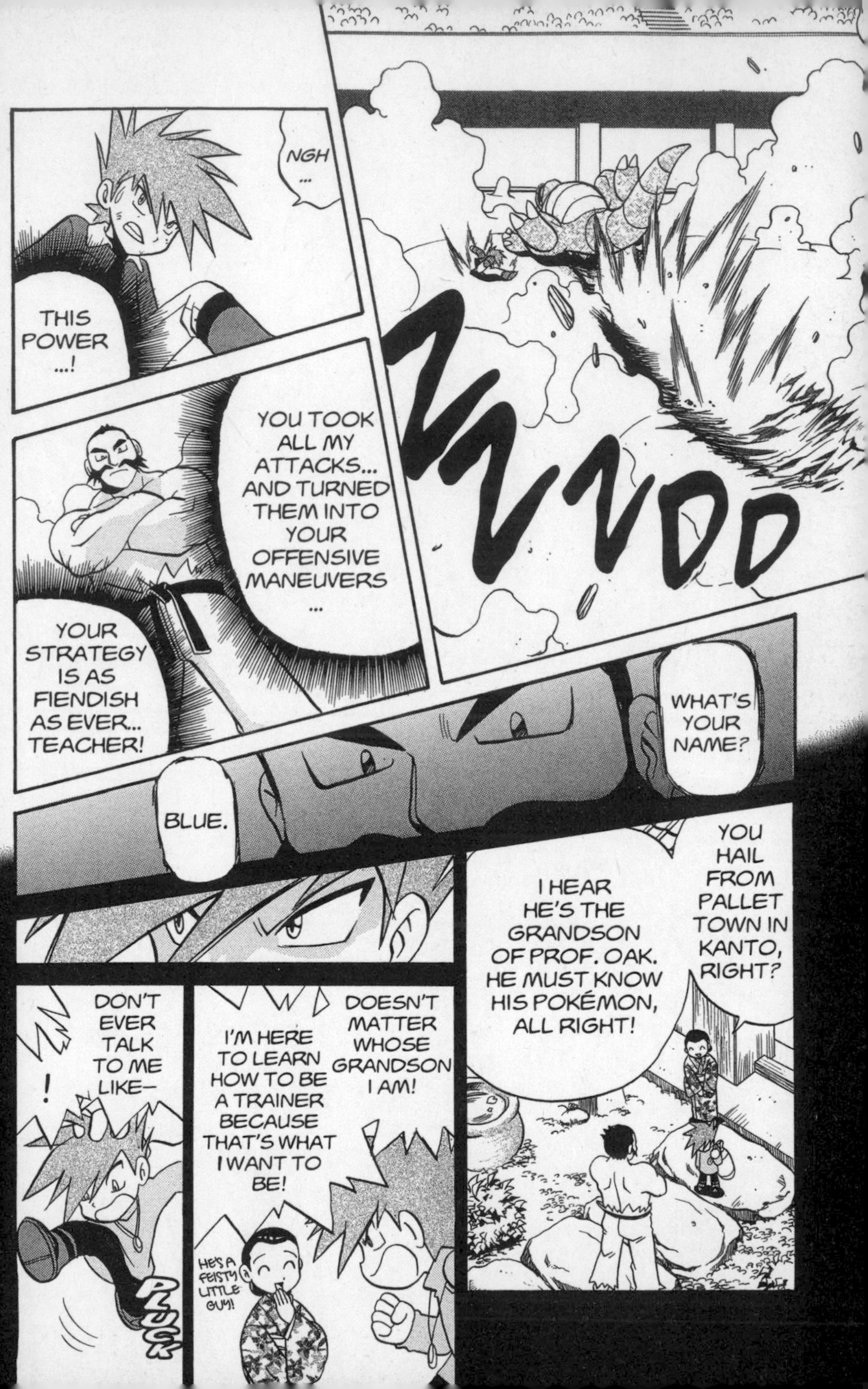
NGH...
THIS POWER...!
YOU TOOK ALL MY ATTACKS... AND TURNED THEM INTO YOUR OFFENSIVE MANEUVERS...
YOUR STRATEGY IS AS FIENDISH AS EVER... TEACHER!
WHAT'S YOUR NAME?
BLUE.
YOU HAIL FROM PALLET TOWN IN KANTO, RIGHT?
I HEAR HE'S THE GRANDSON OF PROF. OAK. HE MUST KNOW HIS POKÉMON, ALL RIGHT!
DOESN'T MATTER WHOSE GRANDSON I AM!
I'M HERE TO LEARN HOW TO BE A TRAINER BECAUSE THAT'S WHAT I WANT TO BE!
HE'S A FEISTY LITTLE GUY!
!
DON'T EVER TALK TO ME LIKE—
PLUCK

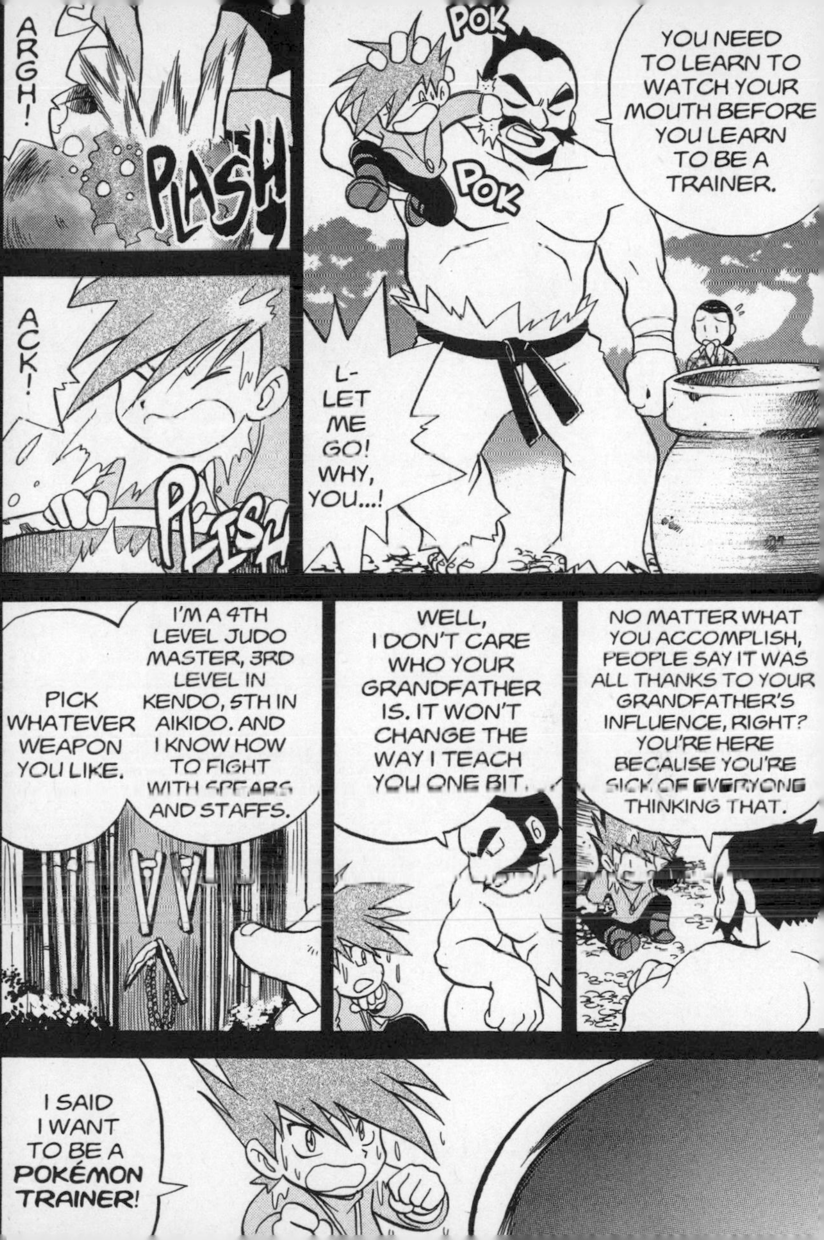
POK
YOU NEED TO LEARN TO WATCH YOUR MOUTH BEFORE YOU LEARN TO BE A TRAINER.
POK
L- LET ME GO! WHY, YOU...!
ARGH!
PLASH
ACK!
PLISH
NO MATTER WHAT YOU ACCOMPLISH, PEOPLE SAY IT WAS ALL THANKS TO YOUR GRANDFATHER'S INFLUENCE, RIGHT? YOU'RE HERE BECAUSE YOU'RE SICK OF EVERYONE THINKING THAT.
WELL, I DON'T CARE WHO YOUR GRANDFATHER IS. IT WON'T CHANGE THE WAY I TEACH YOU ONE BIT.
I'M A 4TH LEVEL JUDO MASTER, 3RD LEVEL IN KENDO, 5TH IN AIKIDO. AND I KNOW HOW TO FIGHT WITH SPEARS AND STAFFS.
PICK WHATEVER WEAPON YOU LIKE.
I SAID I WANT TO BE A POKÉMON TRAINER!

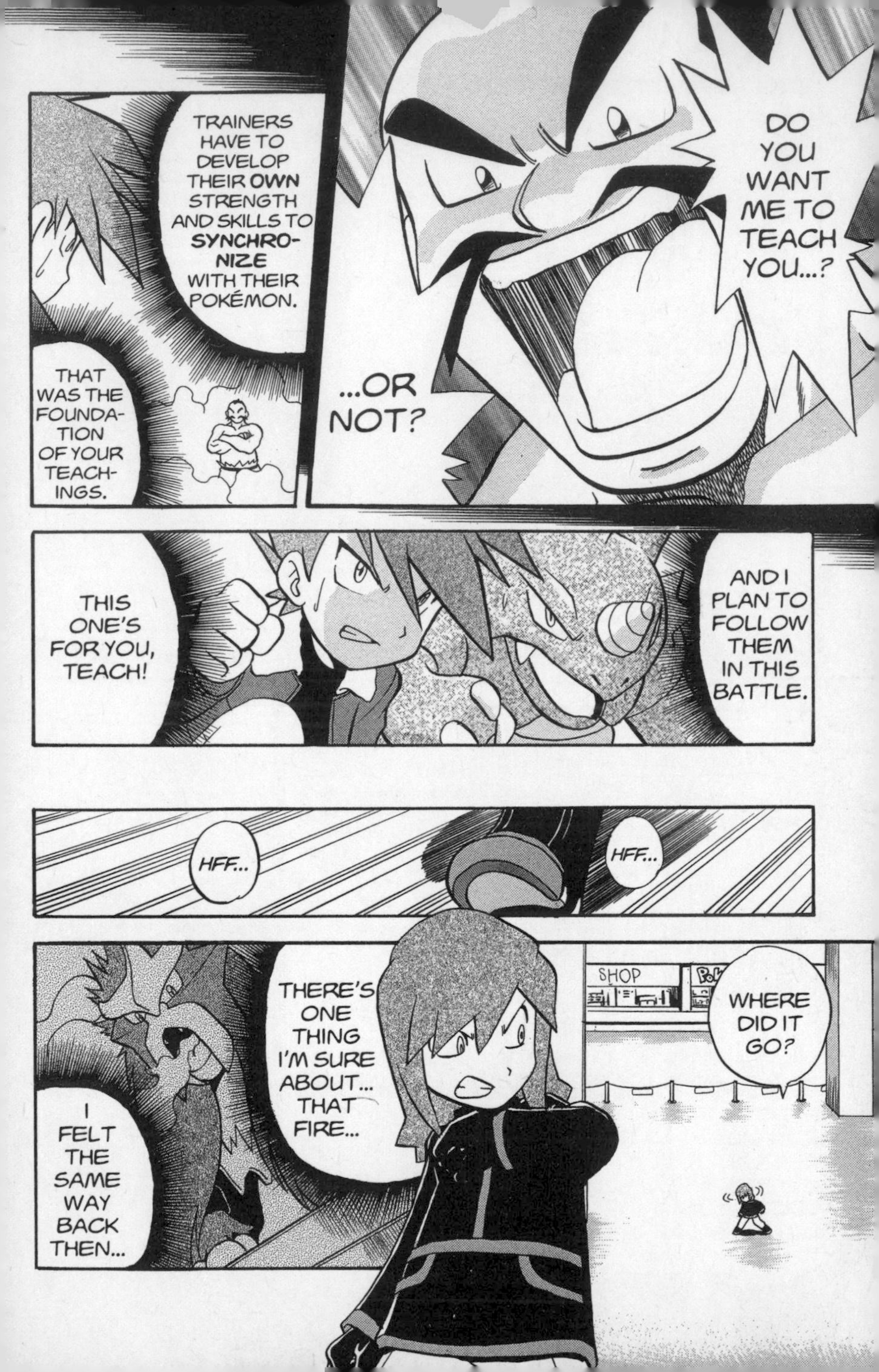
DO YOU WANT ME TO TEACH YOU...?
...OR NOT?
TRAINERS HAVE TO DEVELOP THEIR **OWN** STRENGTH AND SKILLS TO **SYNCHRO-NIZE** WITH THEIR POKÉMON.
THAT WAS THE FOUNDA-TION OF YOUR TEACH-INGS.
AND I PLAN TO FOLLOW THEM IN THIS BATTLE.
THIS ONE'S FOR YOU, TEACH!
HFF...
HFF...
SHOP
WHERE DID IT GO?
THERE'S ONE THING I'M SURE ABOUT... THAT FIRE...
I FELT THE SAME WAY BACK THEN...

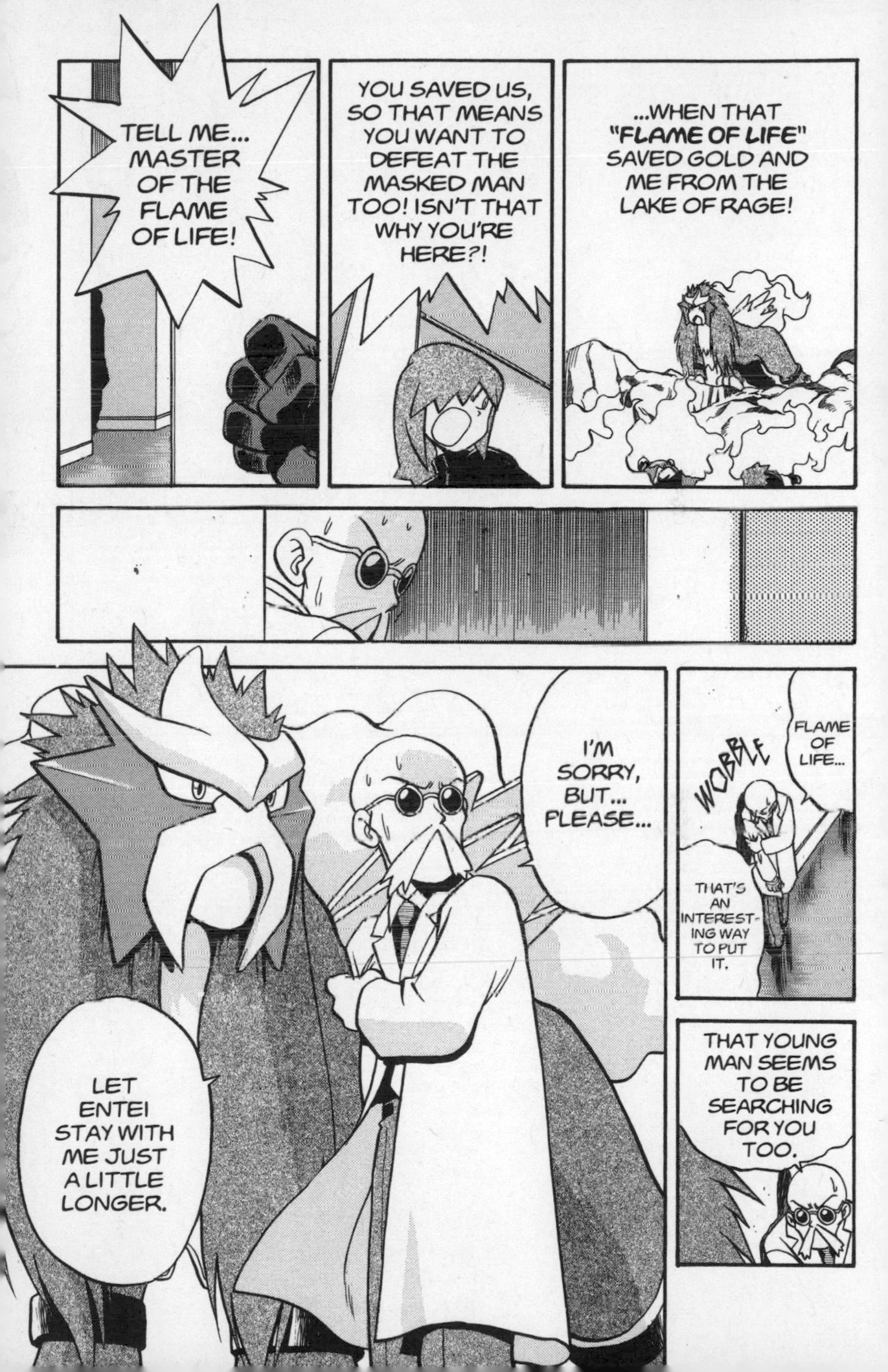
...WHEN THAT "**FLAME OF LIFE**" SAVED GOLD AND ME FROM THE LAKE OF RAGE!
YOU SAVED US, SO THAT MEANS YOU WANT TO DEFEAT THE MASKED MAN TOO! ISN'T THAT WHY YOU'RE HERE?!
TELL ME... MASTER OF THE FLAME OF LIFE!
FLAME OF LIFE...
WOBBLE
THAT'S AN INTEREST-ING WAY TO PUT IT.
THAT YOUNG MAN SEEMS TO BE SEARCHING FOR YOU TOO.
I'M SORRY, BUT... PLEASE...
LET ENTEI STAY WITH ME JUST A LITTLE LONGER.

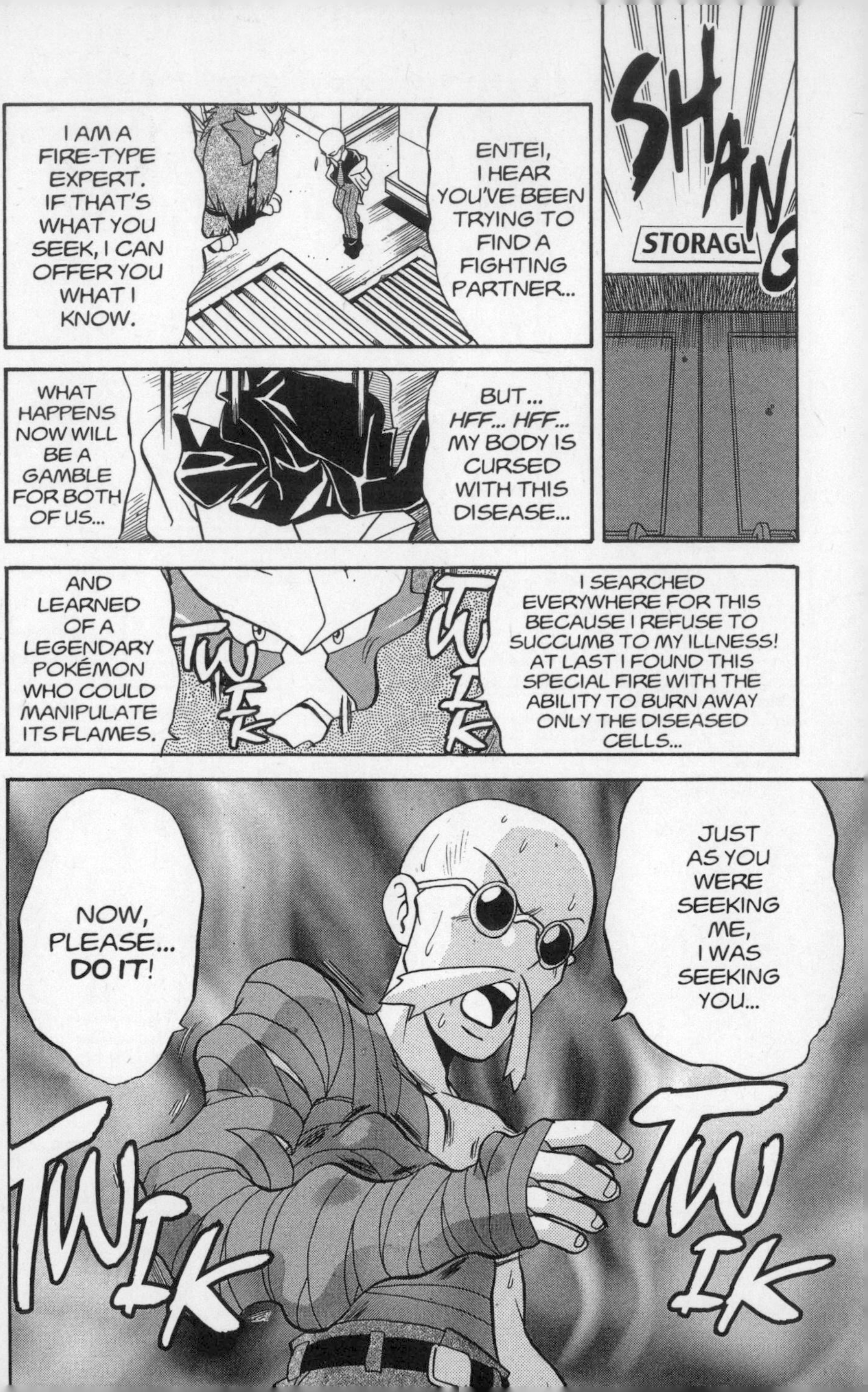
SHANG
STORAGE
ENTEI, I HEAR YOU'VE BEEN TRYING TO FIND A FIGHTING PARTNER...
I AM A FIRE-TYPE EXPERT. IF THAT'S WHAT YOU SEEK, I CAN OFFER YOU WHAT I KNOW.
BUT... *HFF... HFF...* MY BODY IS CURSED WITH THIS DISEASE...
WHAT HAPPENS NOW WILL BE A GAMBLE FOR BOTH OF US...
I SEARCHED EVERYWHERE FOR THIS BECAUSE I REFUSE TO SUCCUMB TO MY ILLNESS! AT LAST I FOUND THIS SPECIAL FIRE WITH THE ABILITY TO BURN AWAY ONLY THE DISEASED CELLS...
TWIK
TWIK
AND LEARNED OF A LEGENDARY POKÉMON WHO COULD MANIPULATE ITS FLAMES.
JUST AS YOU WERE SEEKING ME, I WAS SEEKING YOU...
NOW, PLEASE... **DO IT**!
TWIK
TWIK

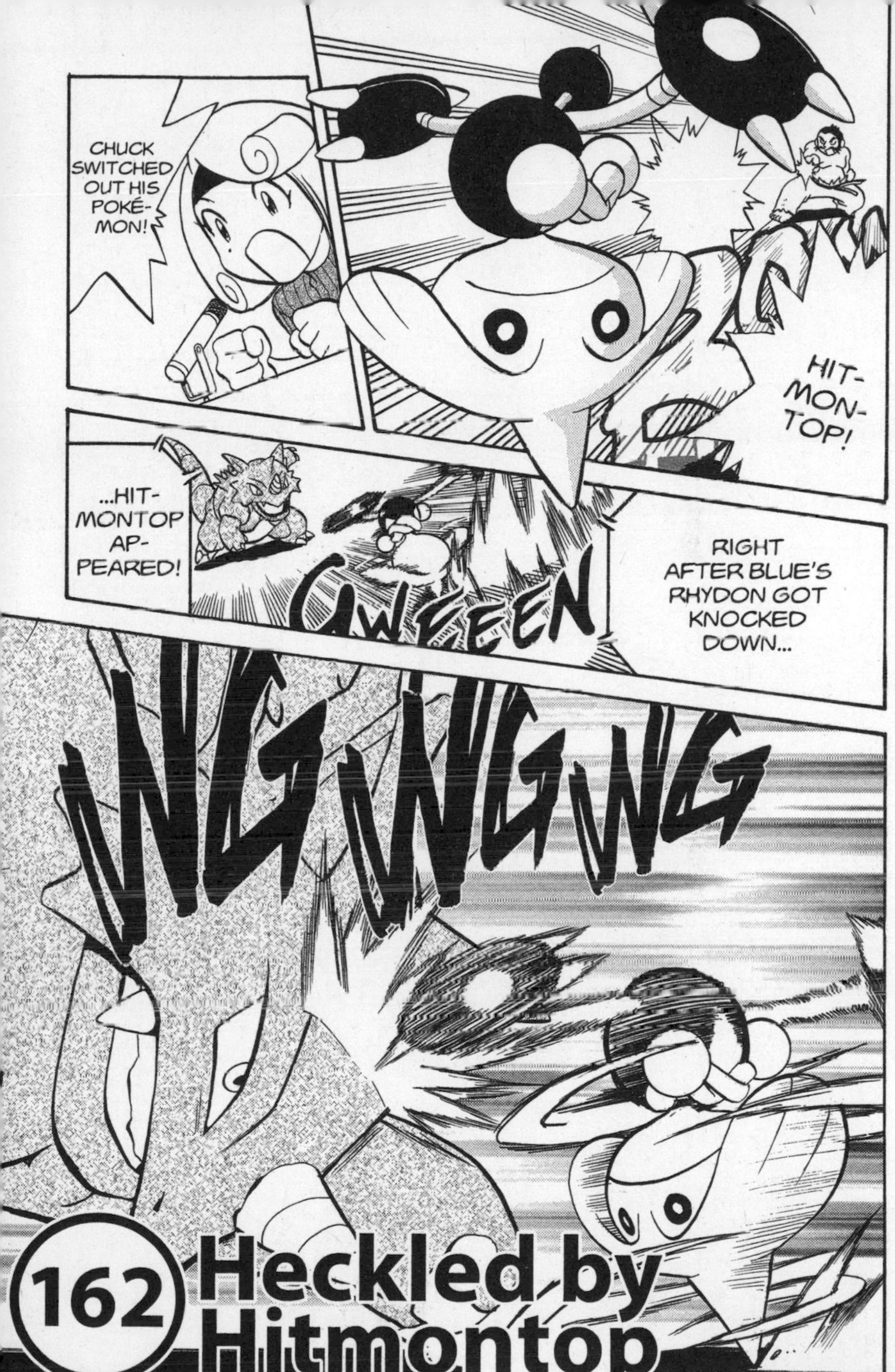
HIT-MONTOP!
CHUCK SWITCHED OUT HIS POKÉMON!
RIGHT AFTER BLUE'S RHYDON GOT KNOCKED DOWN...
...HIT-MONTOP AP-PEARED!
GWEEEN
WNG WNG WNG
162 Heckled by Hitmontop

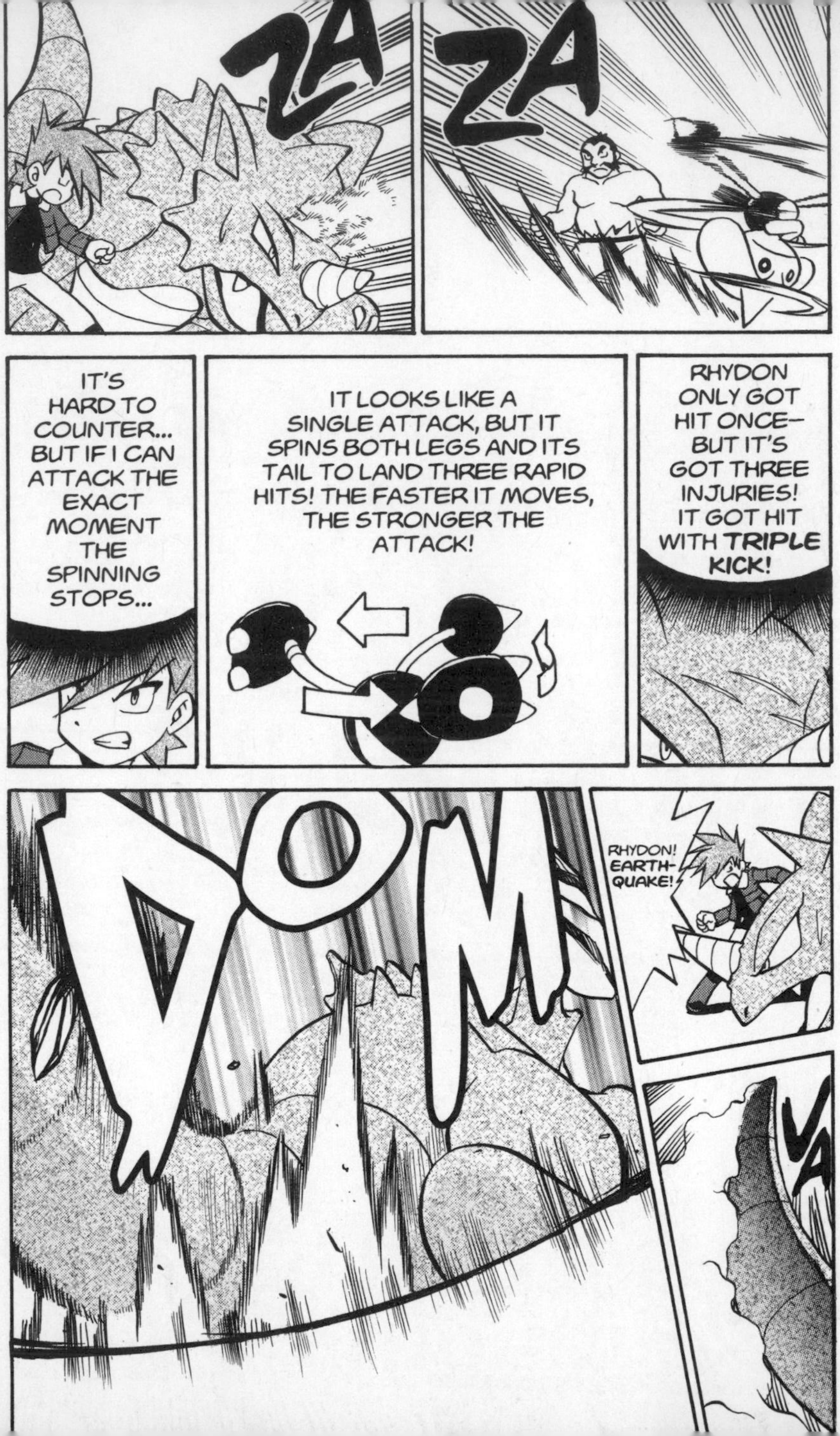
ZA ZA
RHYDON ONLY GOT HIT ONCE—BUT IT'S GOT THREE INJURIES! IT GOT HIT WITH **TRIPLE KICK!**
IT LOOKS LIKE A SINGLE ATTACK, BUT IT SPINS BOTH LEGS AND ITS TAIL TO LAND THREE RAPID HITS! THE FASTER IT MOVES, THE STRONGER THE ATTACK!
IT'S HARD TO COUNTER... BUT IF I CAN ATTACK THE EXACT MOMENT THE SPINNING STOPS...
RHYDON! EARTH-QUAKE!
DOM

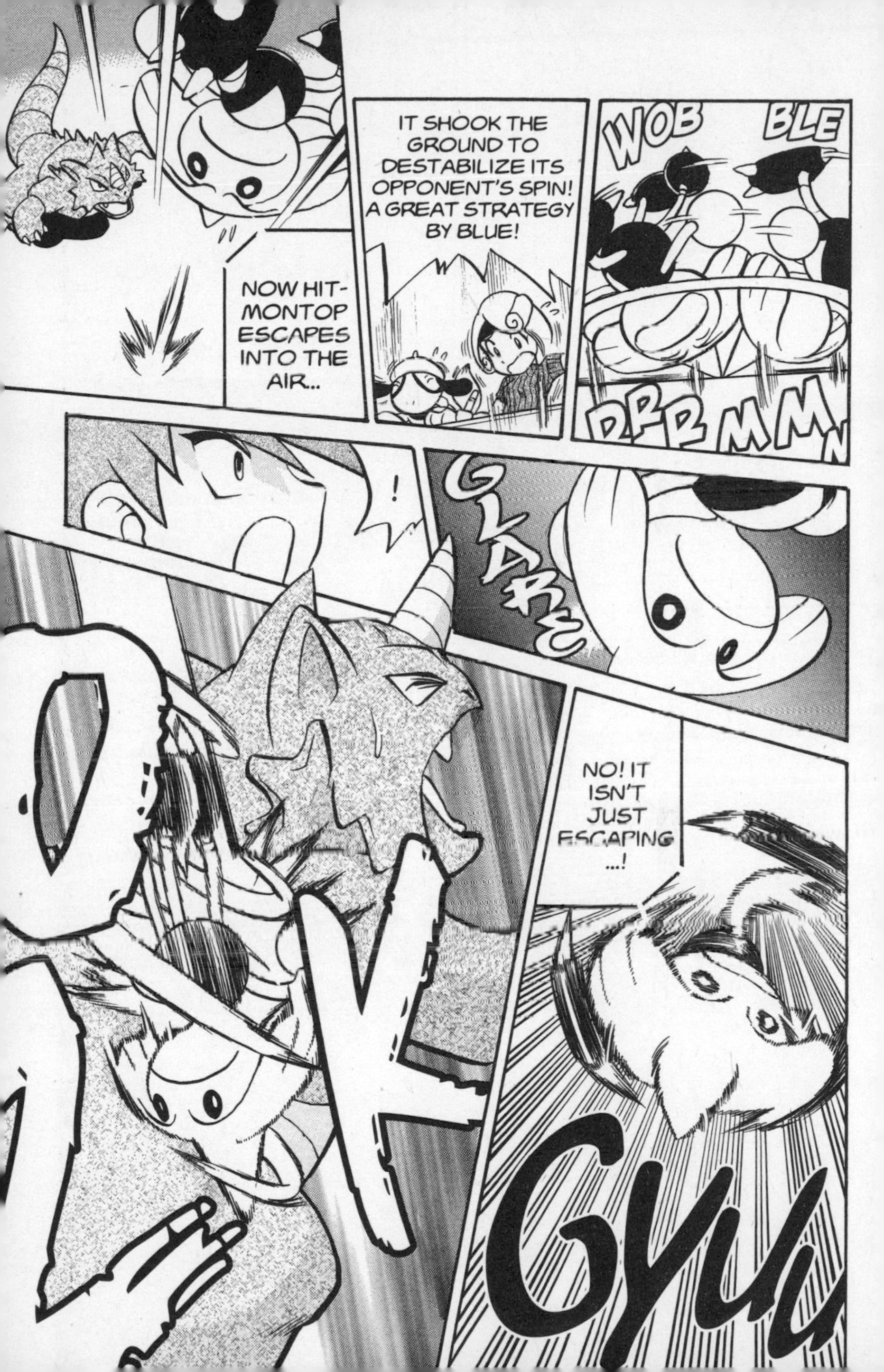
WOB BLE
DRRMMMN
IT SHOOK THE GROUND TO DESTABILIZE ITS OPPONENT'S SPIN! A GREAT STRATEGY BY BLUE!
NOW HIT-MONTOP ESCAPES INTO THE AIR...
!
NO! IT ISN'T JUST ESCAPING ...!

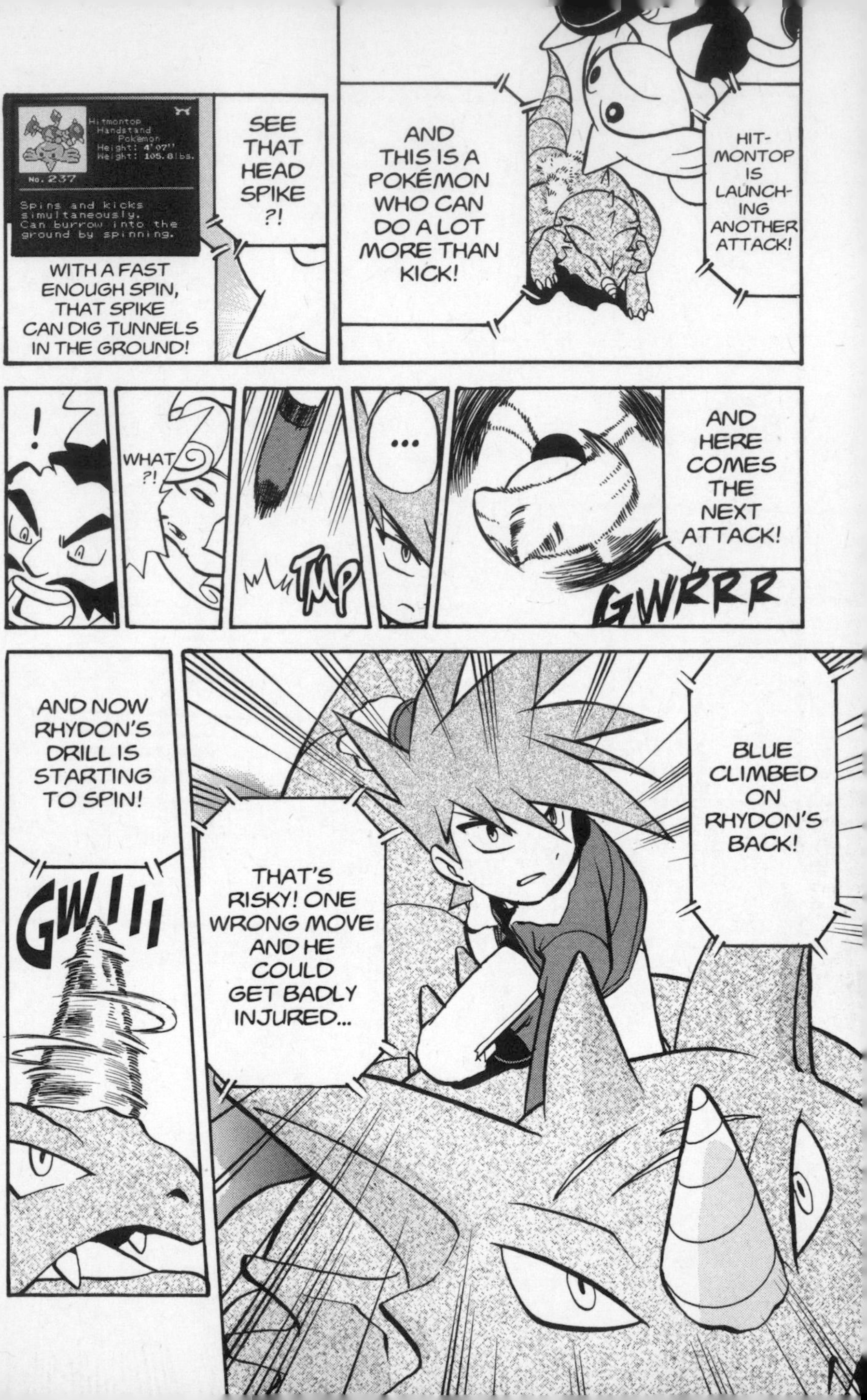
HIT-MONTOP IS LAUNCHING ANOTHER ATTACK!
AND THIS IS A POKÉMON WHO CAN DO A LOT MORE THAN KICK!
SEE THAT HEAD SPIKE ?!
Hitmontop Handstand Pokémon Height: 4'07'' Weight: 105.8lbs.
No. 237
Spins and kicks simultaneously. Can burrow into the ground by spinning.
WITH A FAST ENOUGH SPIN, THAT SPIKE CAN DIG TUNNELS IN THE GROUND!
AND HERE COMES THE NEXT ATTACK!
GWRRR
...
TMP
WHAT ?!
!
BLUE CLIMBED ON RHYDON'S BACK!
THAT'S RISKY! ONE WRONG MOVE AND HE COULD GET BADLY INJURED...
AND NOW RHYDON'S DRILL IS STARTING TO SPIN!
GWIIII

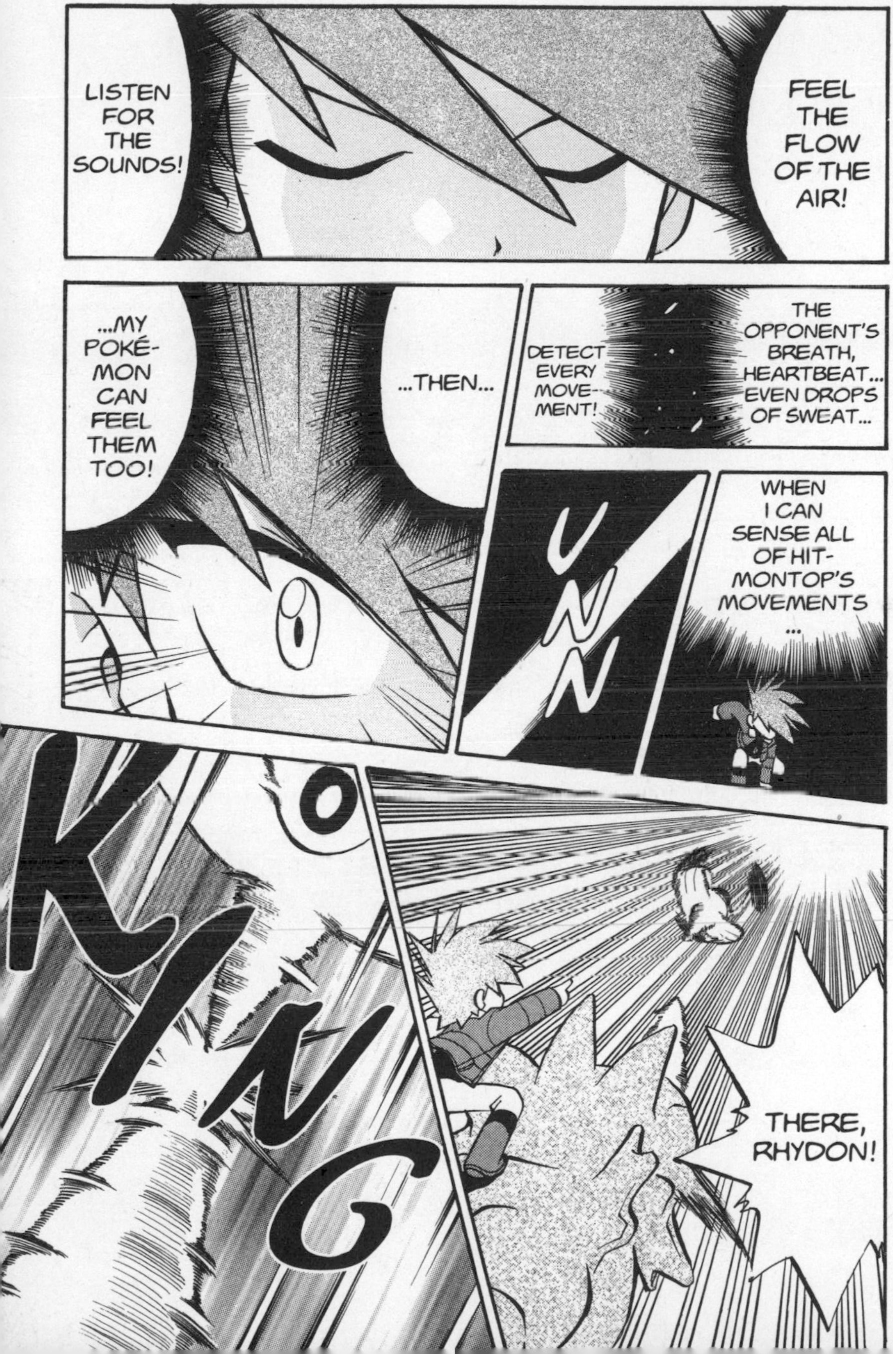
FEEL THE FLOW OF THE AIR!
LISTEN FOR THE SOUNDS!
THE OPPONENT'S BREATH, HEARTBEAT... EVEN DROPS OF SWEAT...
DETECT EVERY MOVE-MENT!
WHEN I CAN SENSE ALL OF HIT-MONTOP'S MOVEMENTS...
UNNN
...THEN...
...MY POKÉ-MON CAN FEEL THEM TOO!
THERE, RHYDON!
KWING

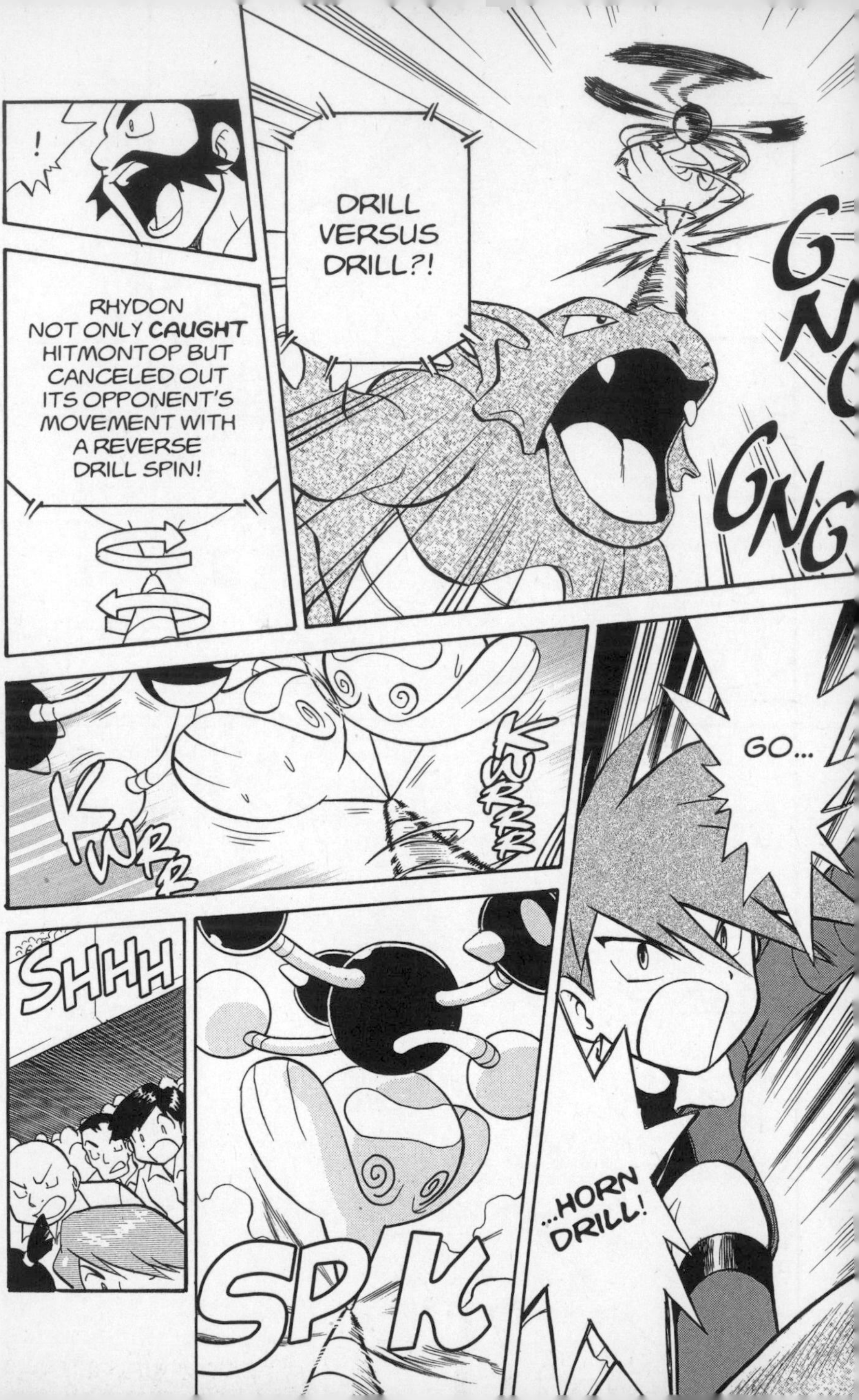
GNG
GNG
DRILL VERSUS DRILL?!
!
RHYDON NOT ONLY **CAUGHT** HITMONTOP BUT CANCELED OUT ITS OPPONENT'S MOVEMENT WITH A REVERSE DRILL SPIN!
GO...
...HORN DRILL!
KURRRR
KURR
SPK
SHHH

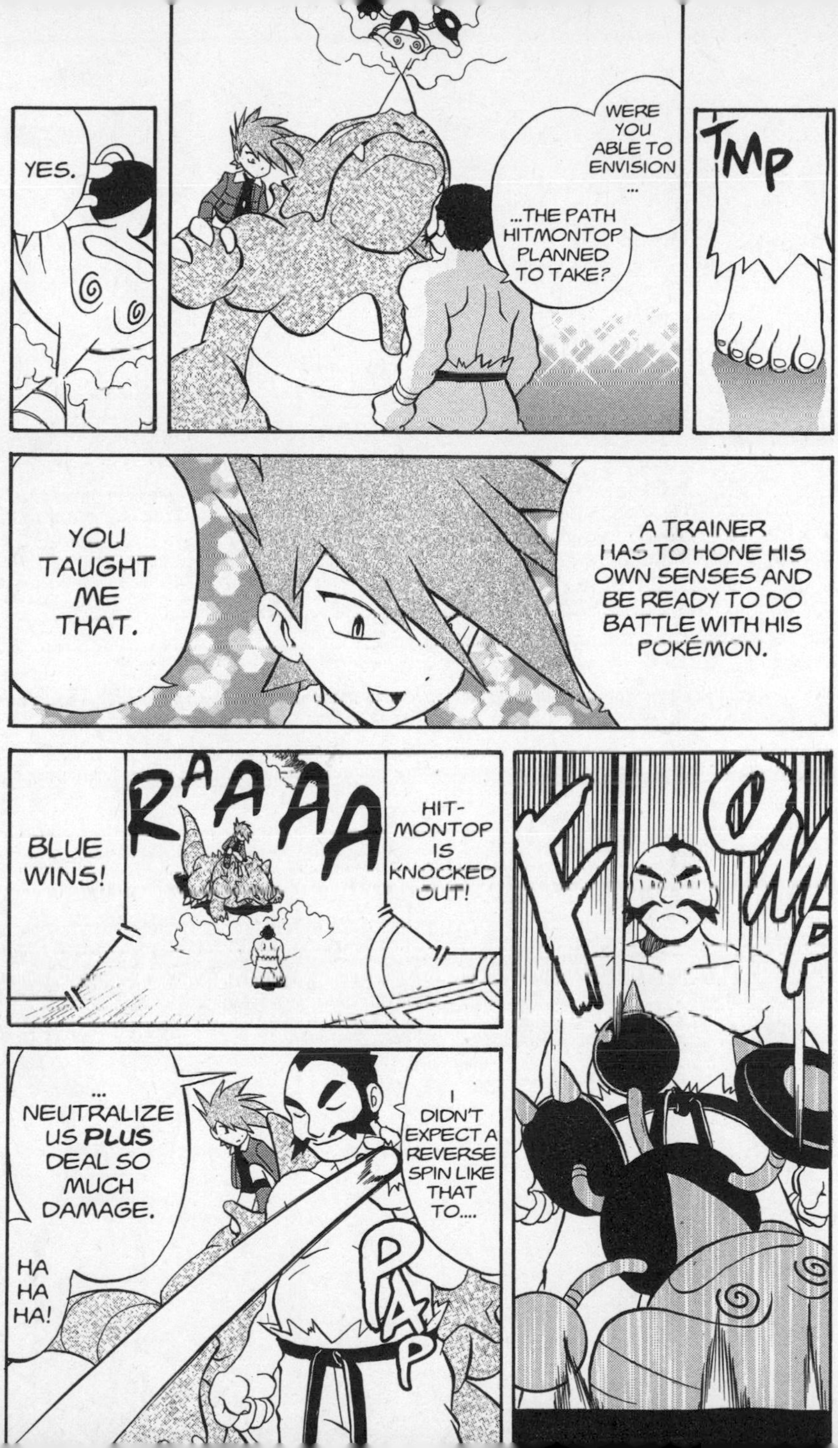
TMP
WERE YOU ABLE TO ENVISION ...
...THE PATH HITMONTOP PLANNED TO TAKE?
YES.
A TRAINER HAS TO HONE HIS OWN SENSES AND BE READY TO DO BATTLE WITH HIS POKÉMON.
YOU TAUGHT ME THAT.
RAAAA
HIT-MONTOP IS KNOCKED OUT!
BLUE WINS!
I DIDN'T EXPECT A REVERSE SPIN LIKE THAT TO....
... NEUTRALIZE US **PLUS** DEAL SO MUCH DAMAGE.
HA HA HA!
PAP

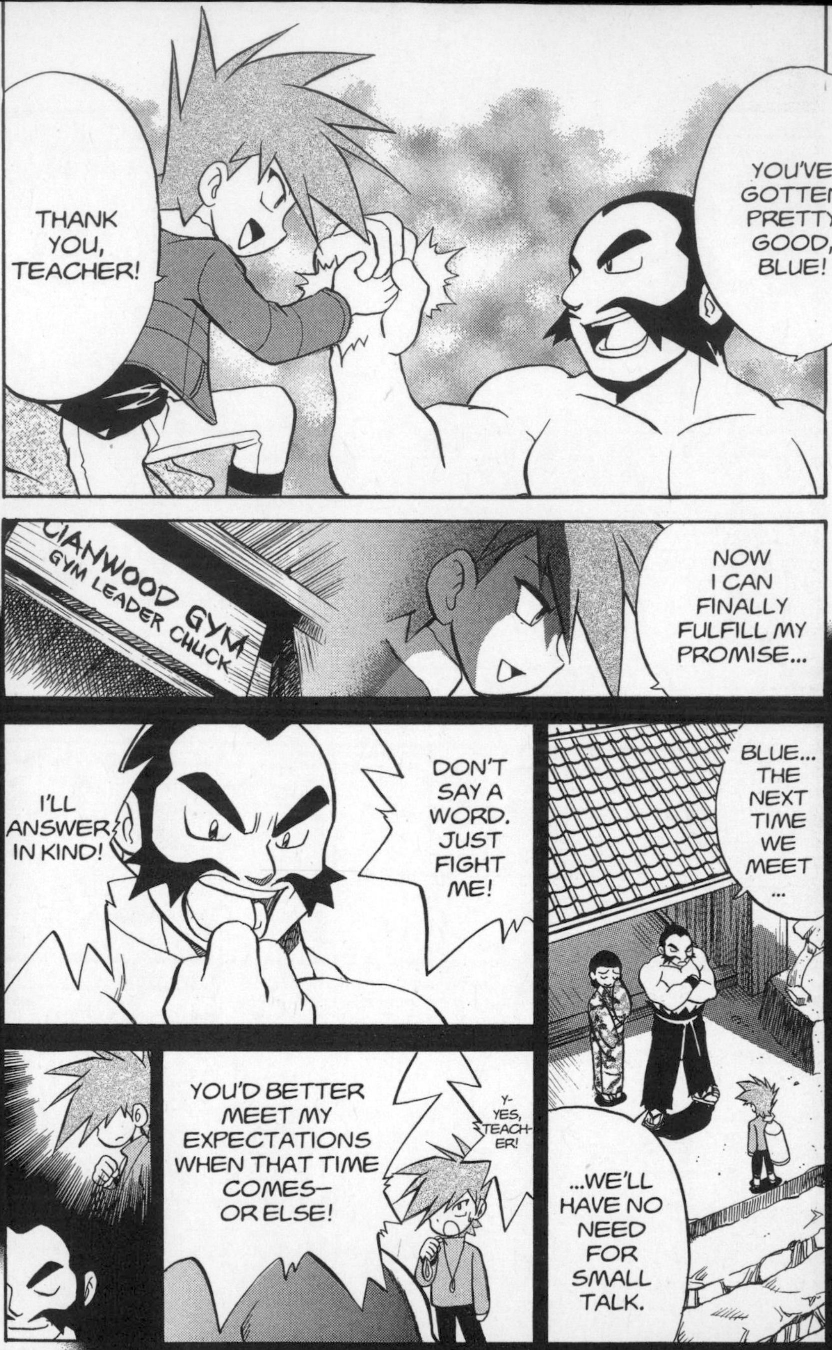
YOU'VE GOTTEN PRETTY GOOD, BLUE!
THANK YOU, TEACHER!
NOW I CAN FINALLY FULFILL MY PROMISE...
CIANWOOD GYM
GYM LEADER CHUCK
BLUE... THE NEXT TIME WE MEET ...
...WE'LL HAVE NO NEED FOR SMALL TALK.
DON'T SAY A WORD. JUST FIGHT ME!
I'LL ANSWER IN KIND!
YOU'D BETTER MEET MY EXPECTATIONS WHEN THAT TIME COMES— OR ELSE!
Y-YES, TEACHER!

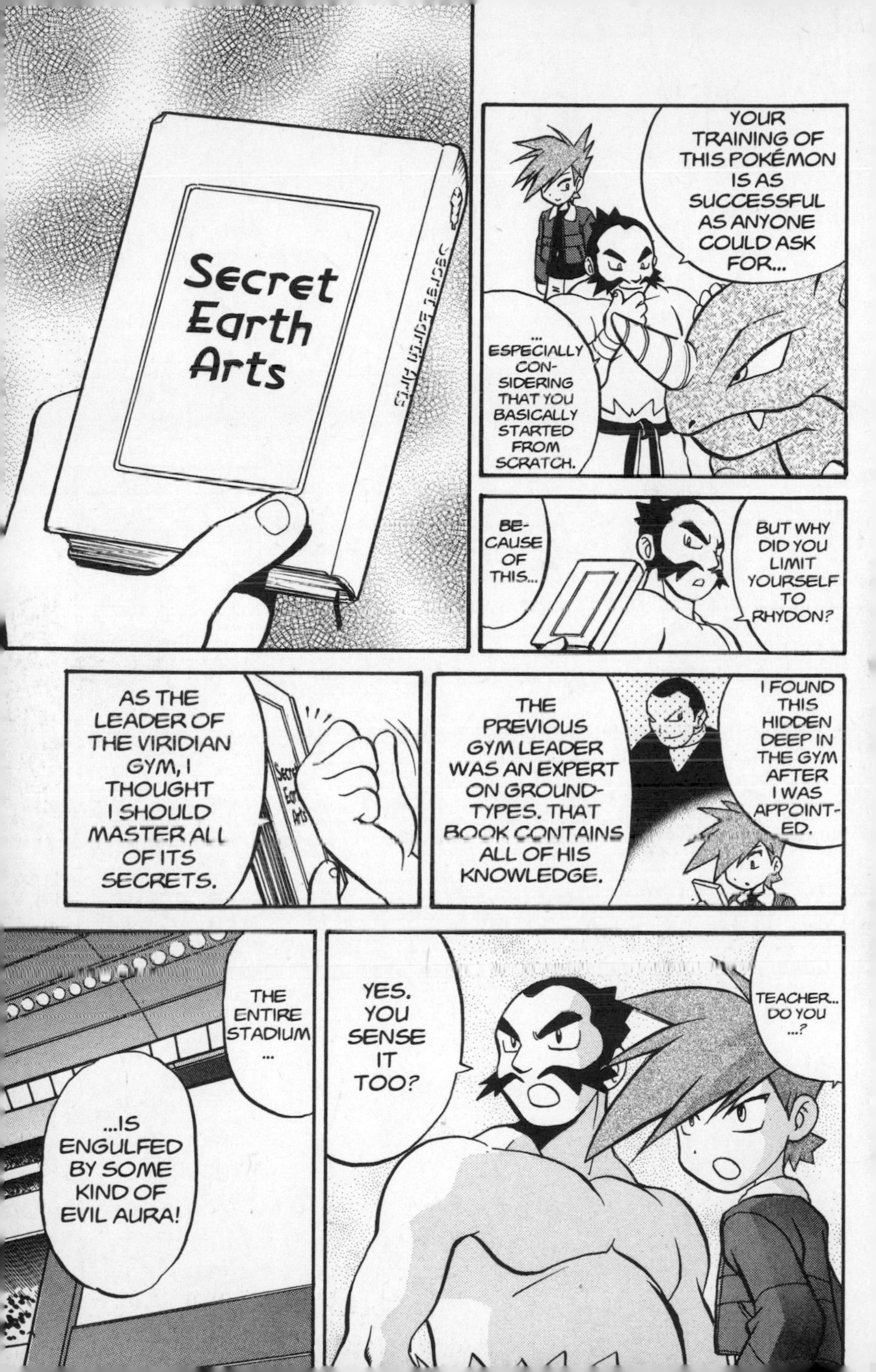
YOUR TRAINING OF THIS POKÉMON IS AS SUCCESSFUL AS ANYONE COULD ASK FOR...
...ESPECIALLY CON-SIDERING THAT YOU BASICALLY STARTED FROM SCRATCH.
BUT WHY DID YOU LIMIT YOURSELF TO RHYDON?
BE-CAUSE OF THIS...
Secret Earth Arts
Secret Earth Arts
I FOUND THIS HIDDEN DEEP IN THE GYM AFTER I WAS APPOINT-ED.
THE PREVIOUS GYM LEADER WAS AN EXPERT ON GROUND-TYPES. THAT BOOK CONTAINS ALL OF HIS KNOWLEDGE.
AS THE LEADER OF THE VIRIDIAN GYM, I THOUGHT I SHOULD MASTER ALL OF ITS SECRETS.
Secret Earth Arts
TEACHER... DO YOU ...?
YES. YOU SENSE IT TOO?
THE ENTIRE STADIUM ...
...IS ENGULFED BY SOME KIND OF EVIL AURA!

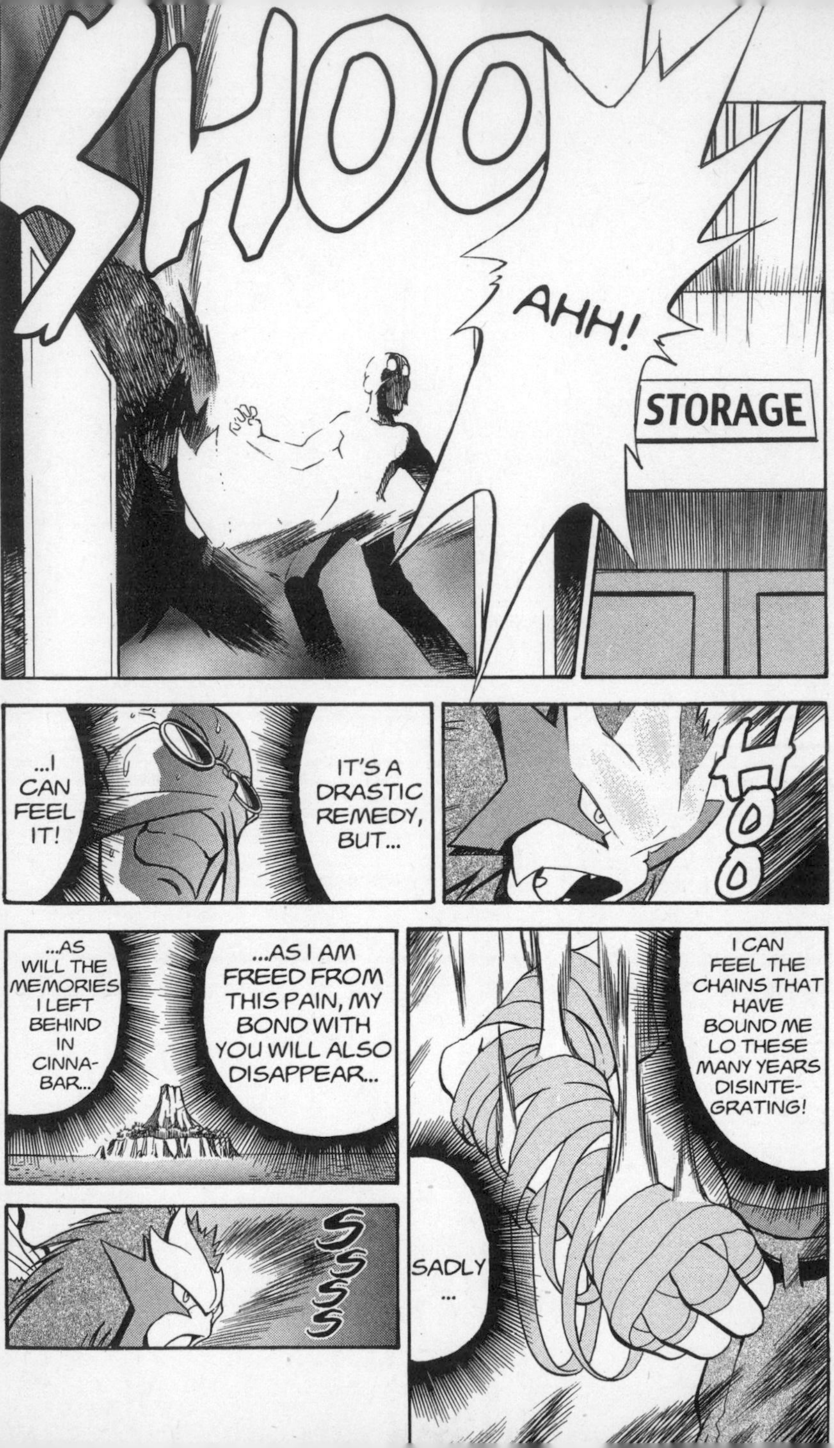
SHOO
AHH!
STORAGE
HOOO
IT'S A DRASTIC REMEDY, BUT...
...I CAN FEEL IT!
I CAN FEEL THE CHAINS THAT HAVE BOUND ME LO THESE MANY YEARS DISINTE-GRATING!
SADLY ...
...AS I AM FREED FROM THIS PAIN, MY BOND WITH YOU WILL ALSO DISAPPEAR...
...AS WILL THE MEMORIES I LEFT BEHIND IN CINNA-BAR...
SSSS

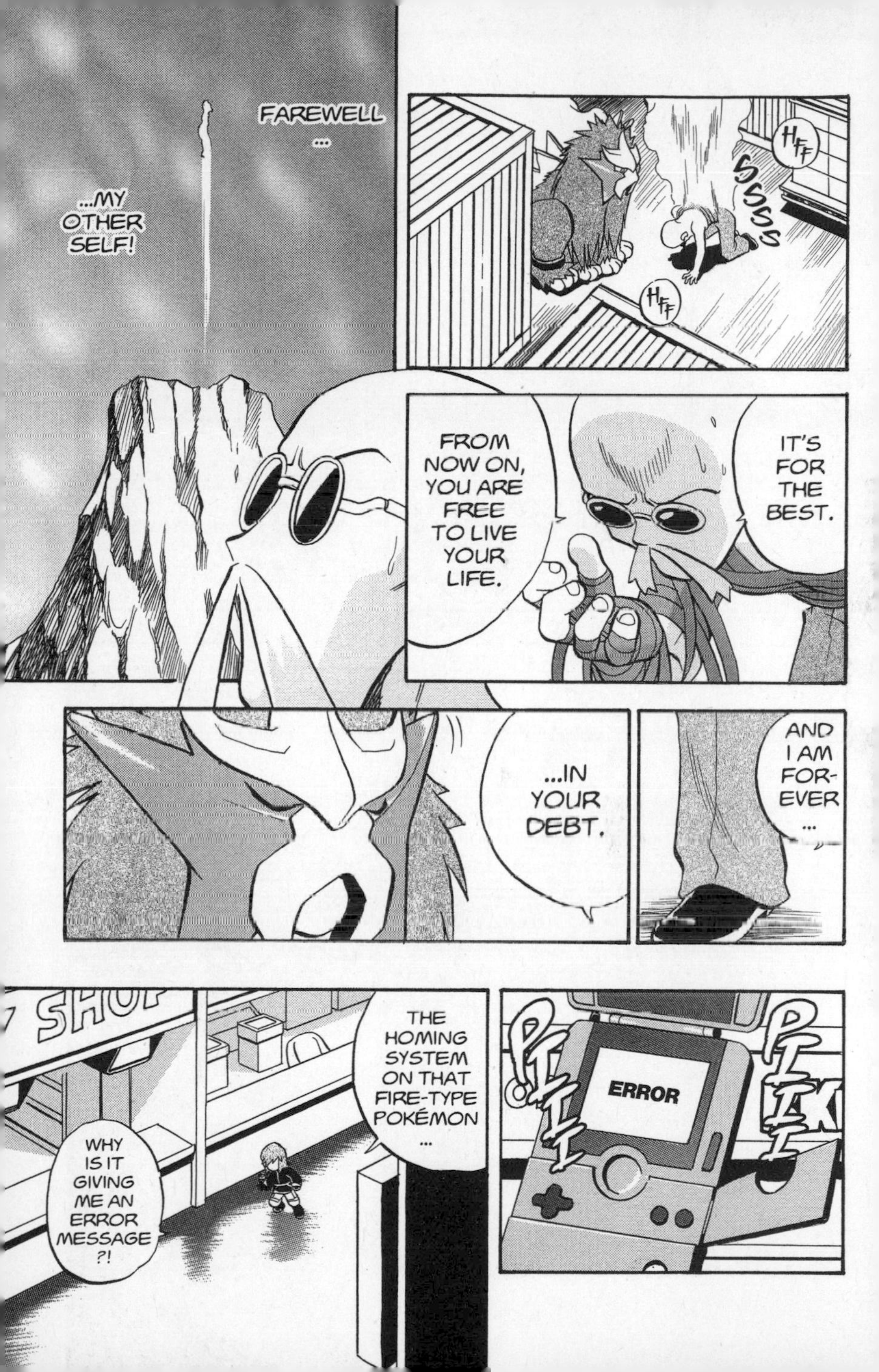
HFF
SSSS
HFF
IT'S FOR THE BEST.
FROM NOW ON, YOU ARE FREE TO LIVE YOUR LIFE.
FAREWELL ...
...MY OTHER SELF!
AND I AM FOR-EVER ...
...IN YOUR DEBT.
ERROR
THE HOMING SYSTEM ON THAT FIRE-TYPE POKÉMON ...
WHY IS IT GIVING ME AN ERROR MESSAGE ?!
SHOP

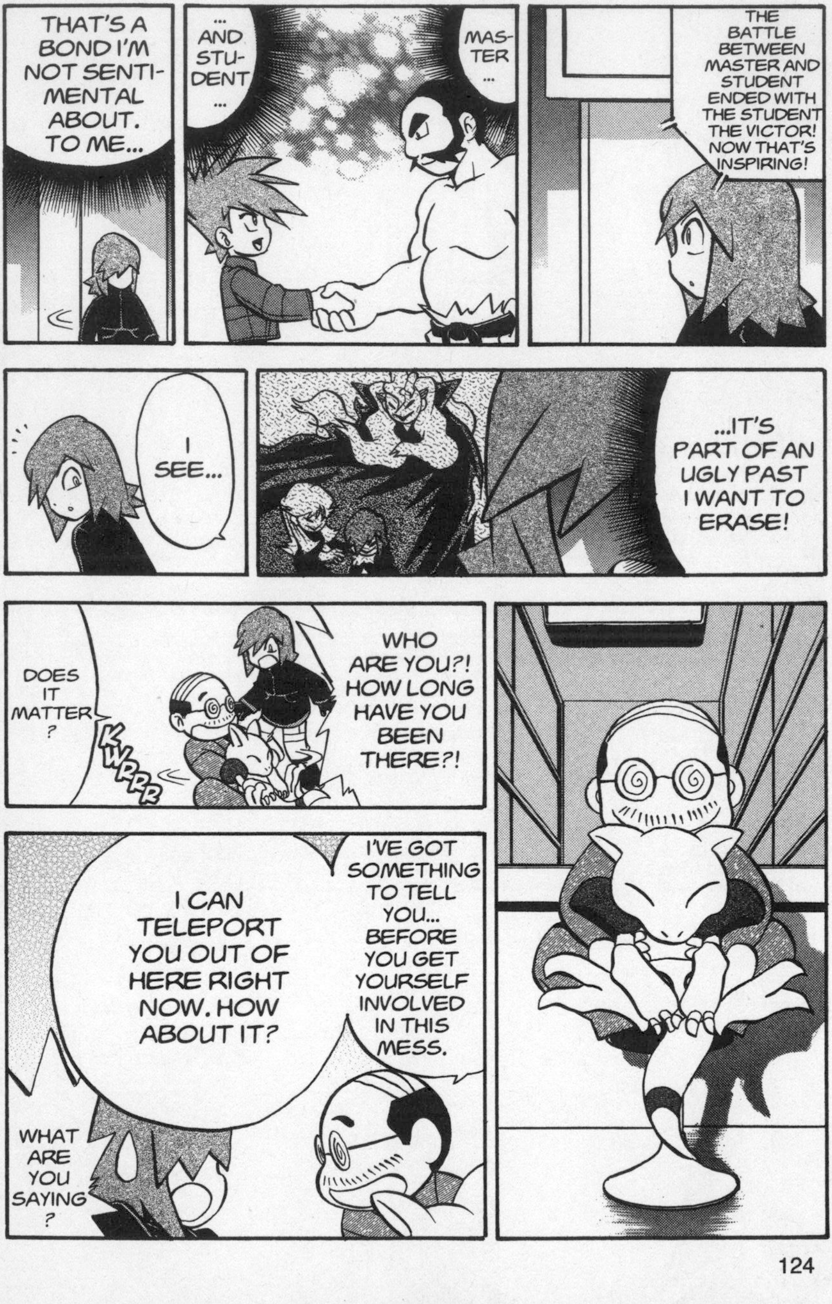
THE BATTLE BETWEEN MASTER AND STUDENT ENDED WITH THE STUDENT THE VICTOR! NOW THAT'S INSPIRING!
MAS-TER ...
... AND STU-DENT ...
THAT'S A BOND I'M NOT SENTI-MENTAL ABOUT. TO ME...
...IT'S PART OF AN UGLY PAST I WANT TO ERASE!
I SEE...
WHO ARE YOU?! HOW LONG HAVE YOU BEEN THERE?!
KWRRR
DOES IT MATTER?
I'VE GOT SOMETHING TO TELL YOU... BEFORE YOU GET YOURSELF INVOLVED IN THIS MESS.
I CAN TELEPORT YOU OUT OF HERE RIGHT NOW. HOW ABOUT IT?
WHAT ARE YOU SAYING?

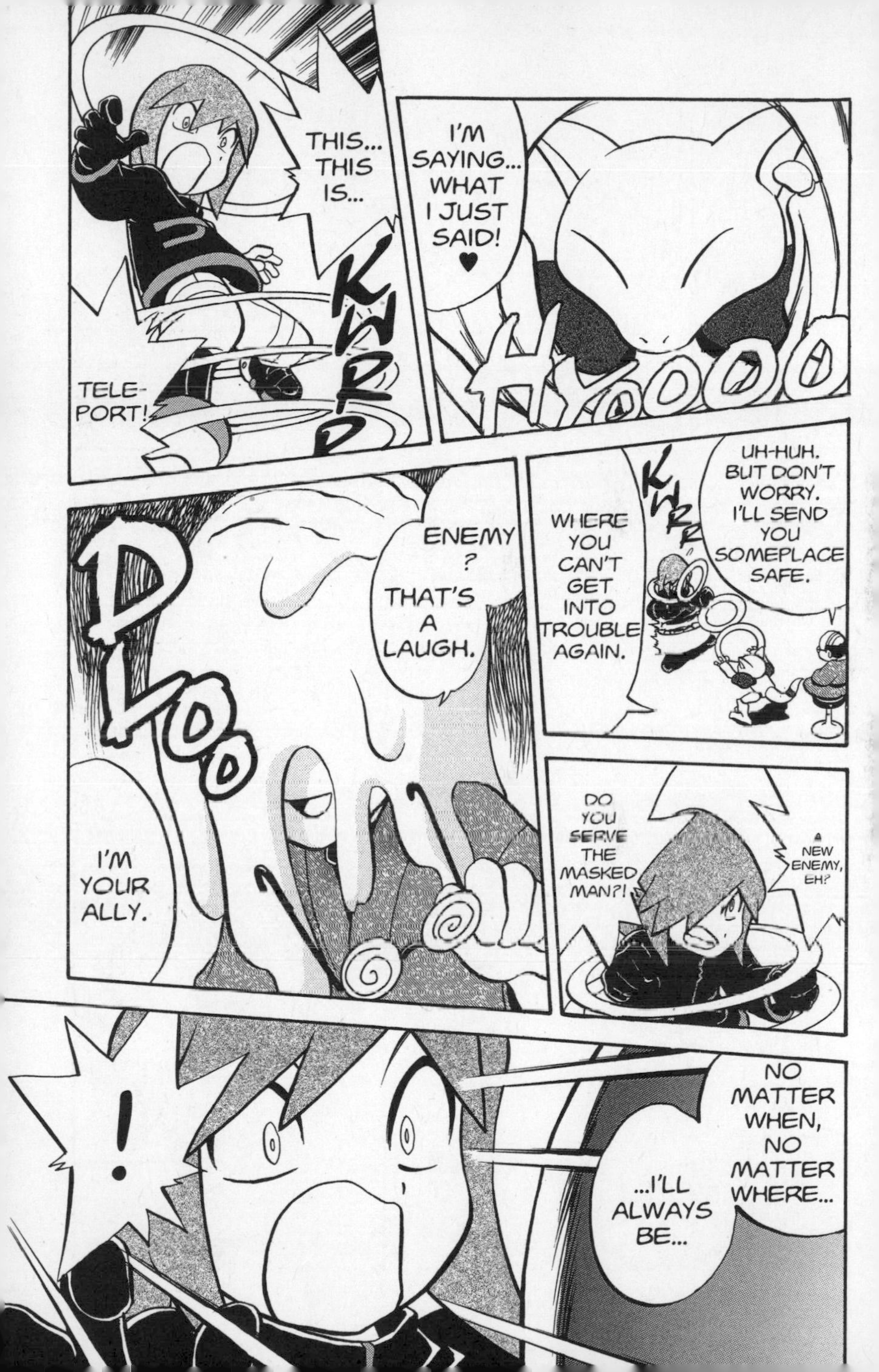
I'M SAYING... WHAT I JUST SAID! ♥
HYOOOO
THIS... THIS IS...
KWRRR
TELE-PORT!
UH-HUH. BUT DON'T WORRY. I'LL SEND YOU SOMEPLACE SAFE.
KWRR
WHERE YOU CAN'T GET INTO TROUBLE AGAIN.
A NEW ENEMY, EH?
DO YOU SERVE THE MASKED MAN?!
ENEMY? THAT'S A LAUGH.
DOOO
I'M YOUR ALLY.
NO MATTER WHEN, NO MATTER WHERE...
...I'LL ALWAYS BE...
!

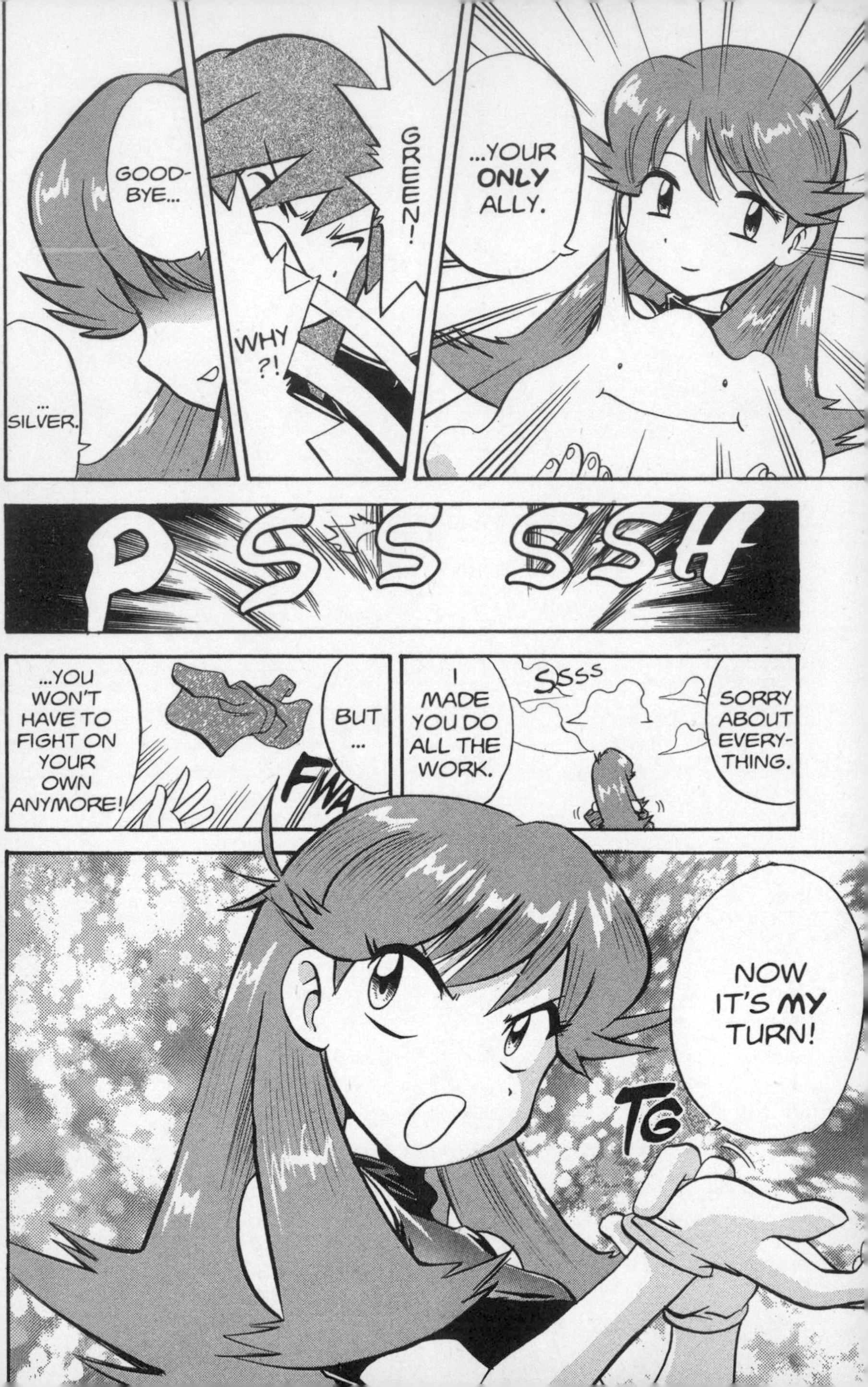
...YOUR ONLY ALLY.
GREEN!
WHY?!
GOOD-BYE...
... SILVER.
PSSSSH
SORRY ABOUT EVERYTHING.
SSSS
I MADE YOU DO ALL THE WORK.
BUT ...
...YOU WON'T HAVE TO FIGHT ON YOUR OWN ANYMORE!
FWA
NOW IT'S MY TURN!
TG

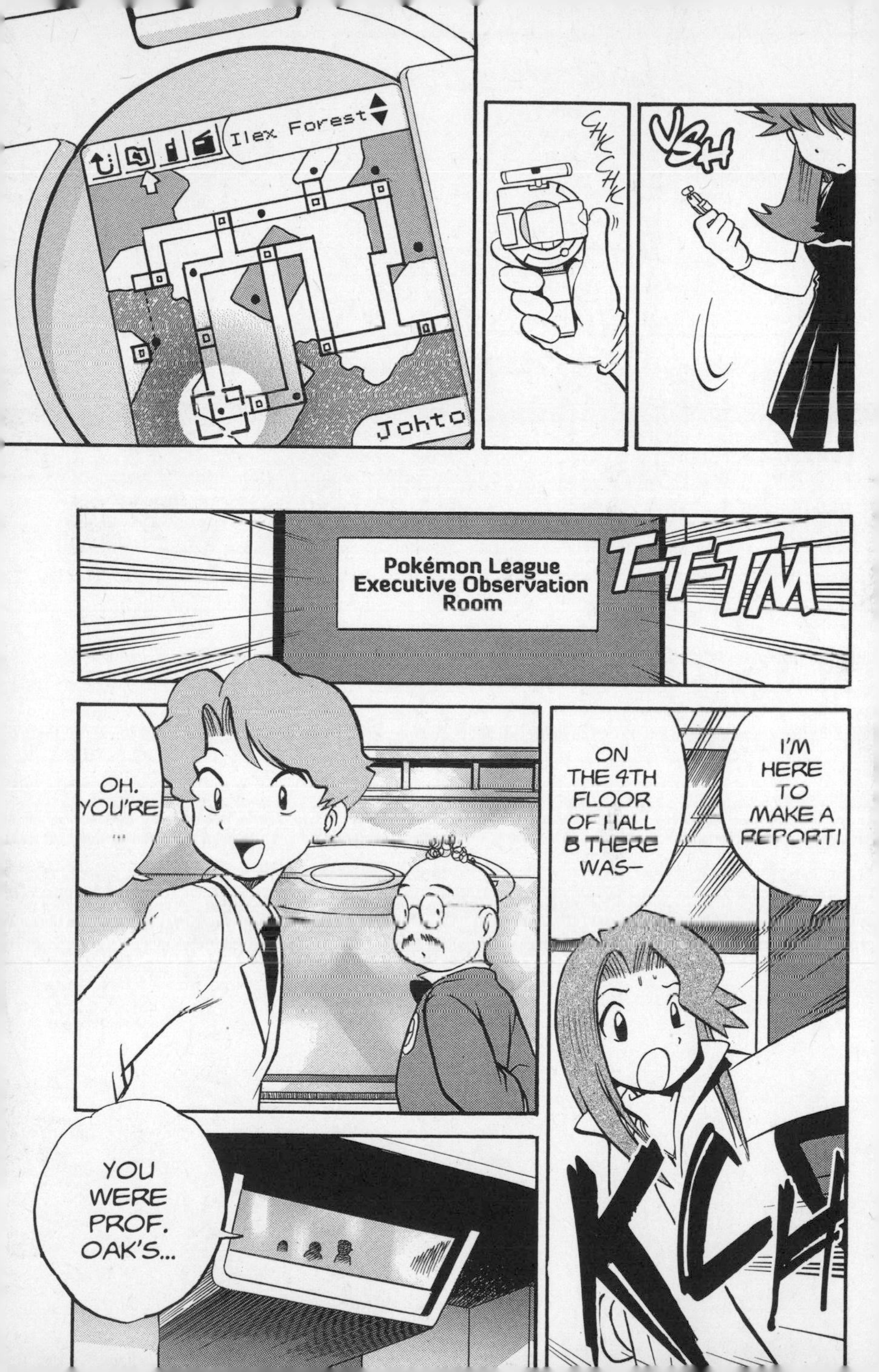
VSH
CHK CHK CHK
Ilex Forest
Johto
Pokémon League Executive Observation Room
T-T-TM
I'M HERE TO MAKE A REPORT!
ON THE 4TH FLOOR OF HALL B THERE WAS—
KCHY
OH. YOU'RE ...
YOU WERE PROF. OAK'S...

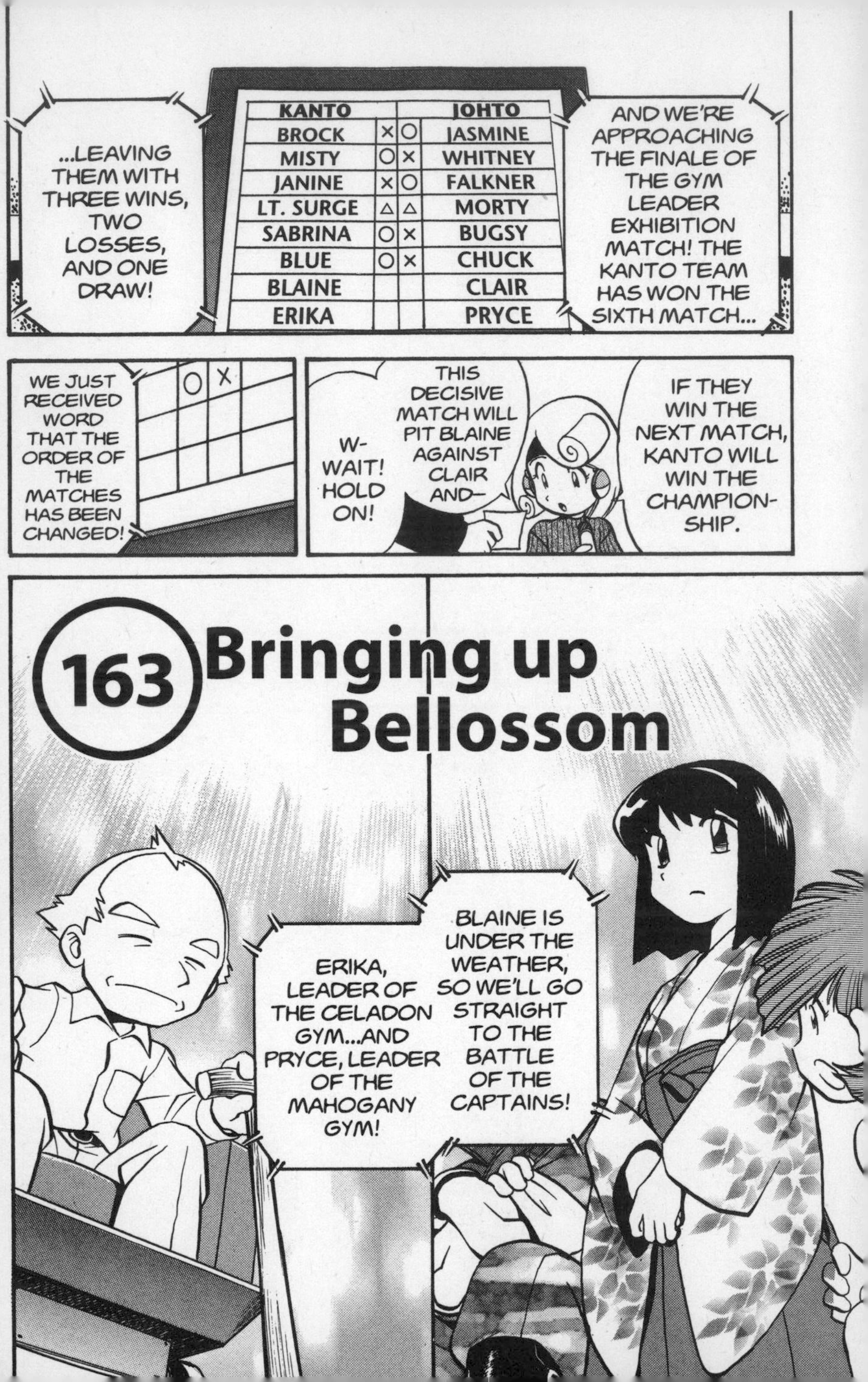
AND WE'RE APPROACHING THE FINALE OF THE GYM LEADER EXHIBITION MATCH! THE KANTO TEAM HAS WON THE SIXTH MATCH...
KANTO JOHTO
BROCK × ○ JASMINE
MISTY ○ × WHITNEY
JANINE × ○ FALKNER
LT. SURGE △ △ MORTY
SABRINA ○ × BUGSY
BLUE ○ × CHUCK
BLAINE CLAIR
ERIKA PRYCE
...LEAVING THEM WITH THREE WINS, TWO LOSSES, AND ONE DRAW!
IF THEY WIN THE NEXT MATCH, KANTO WILL WIN THE CHAMPIONSHIP.
THIS DECISIVE MATCH WILL PIT BLAINE AGAINST CLAIR AND—
W-WAIT! HOLD ON!
WE JUST RECEIVED WORD THAT THE ORDER OF THE MATCHES HAS BEEN CHANGED!
163 Bringing up Bellossom
BLAINE IS UNDER THE WEATHER, SO WE'LL GO STRAIGHT TO THE BATTLE OF THE CAPTAINS!
ERIKA, LEADER OF THE CELADON GYM...AND PRYCE, LEADER OF THE MAHOGANY GYM!

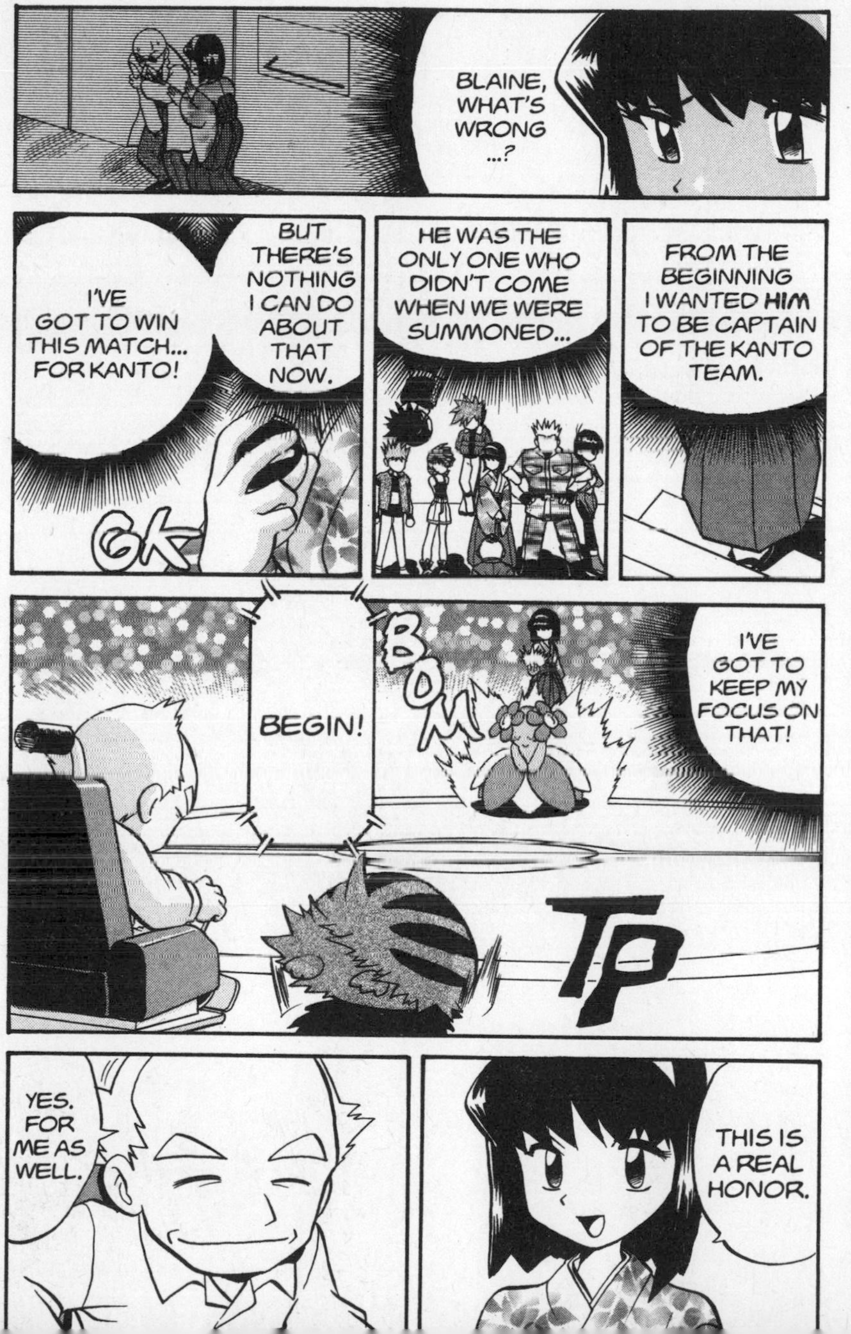
BLAINE, WHAT'S WRONG ...?
FROM THE BEGINNING I WANTED **HIM** TO BE CAPTAIN OF THE KANTO TEAM.
HE WAS THE ONLY ONE WHO DIDN'T COME WHEN WE WERE SUMMONED...
BUT THERE'S NOTHING I CAN DO ABOUT THAT NOW.
I'VE GOT TO WIN THIS MATCH... FOR KANTO!
GK
I'VE GOT TO KEEP MY FOCUS ON THAT!
BOM
BEGIN!
TP
THIS IS A REAL HONOR.
YES. FOR ME AS WELL.

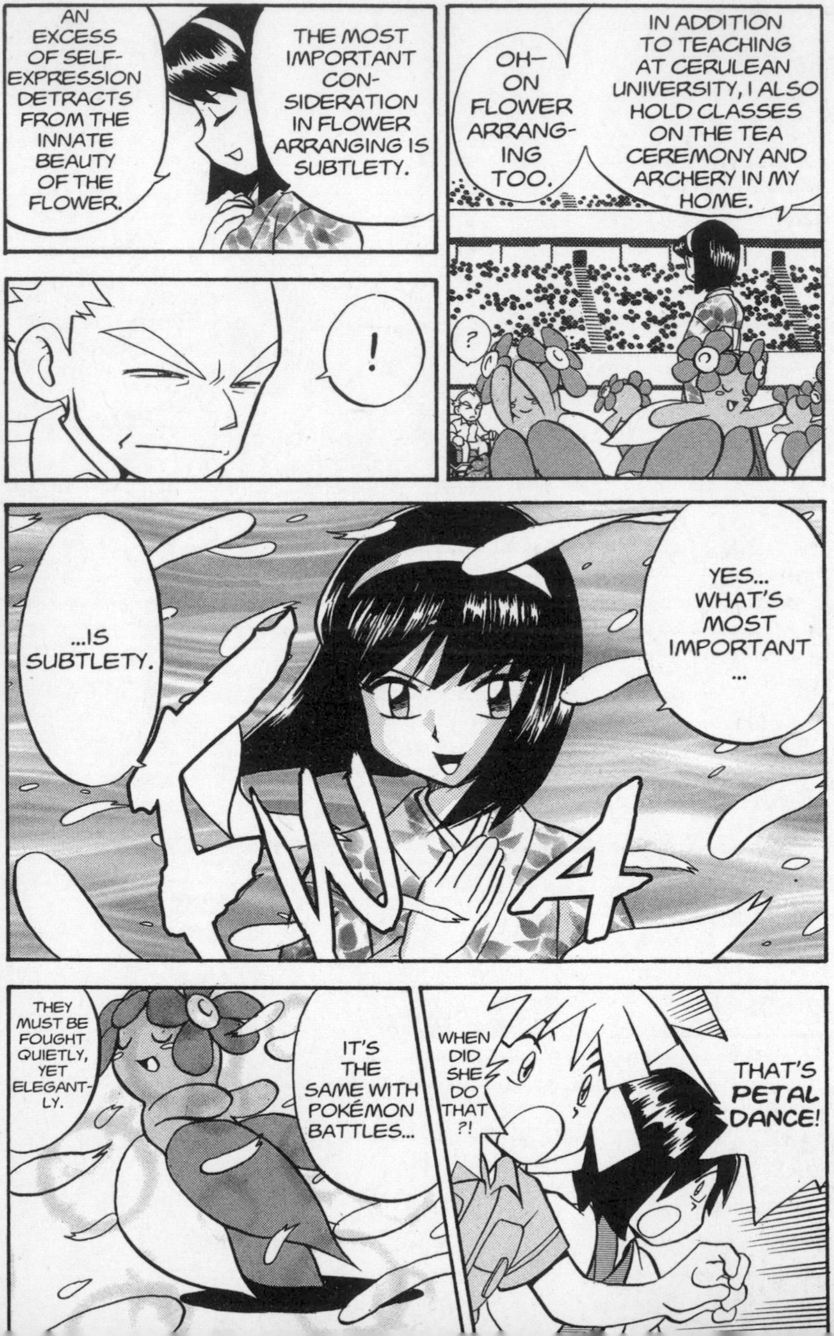
IN ADDITION TO TEACHING AT CERULEAN UNIVERSITY, I ALSO HOLD CLASSES ON THE TEA CEREMONY AND ARCHERY IN MY HOME.
OH— ON FLOWER ARRANG-ING TOO.
THE MOST IMPORTANT CON-SIDERATION IN FLOWER ARRANGING IS SUBTLETY.
AN EXCESS OF SELF-EXPRESSION DETRACTS FROM THE INNATE BEAUTY OF THE FLOWER.
?
!
YES... WHAT'S MOST IMPORTANT ...
...IS SUBTLETY.
THAT'S **PETAL DANCE**!
WHEN DID SHE DO THAT?!
IT'S THE SAME WITH POKÉMON BATTLES...
THEY MUST BE FOUGHT QUIETLY, YET ELEGANT-LY.

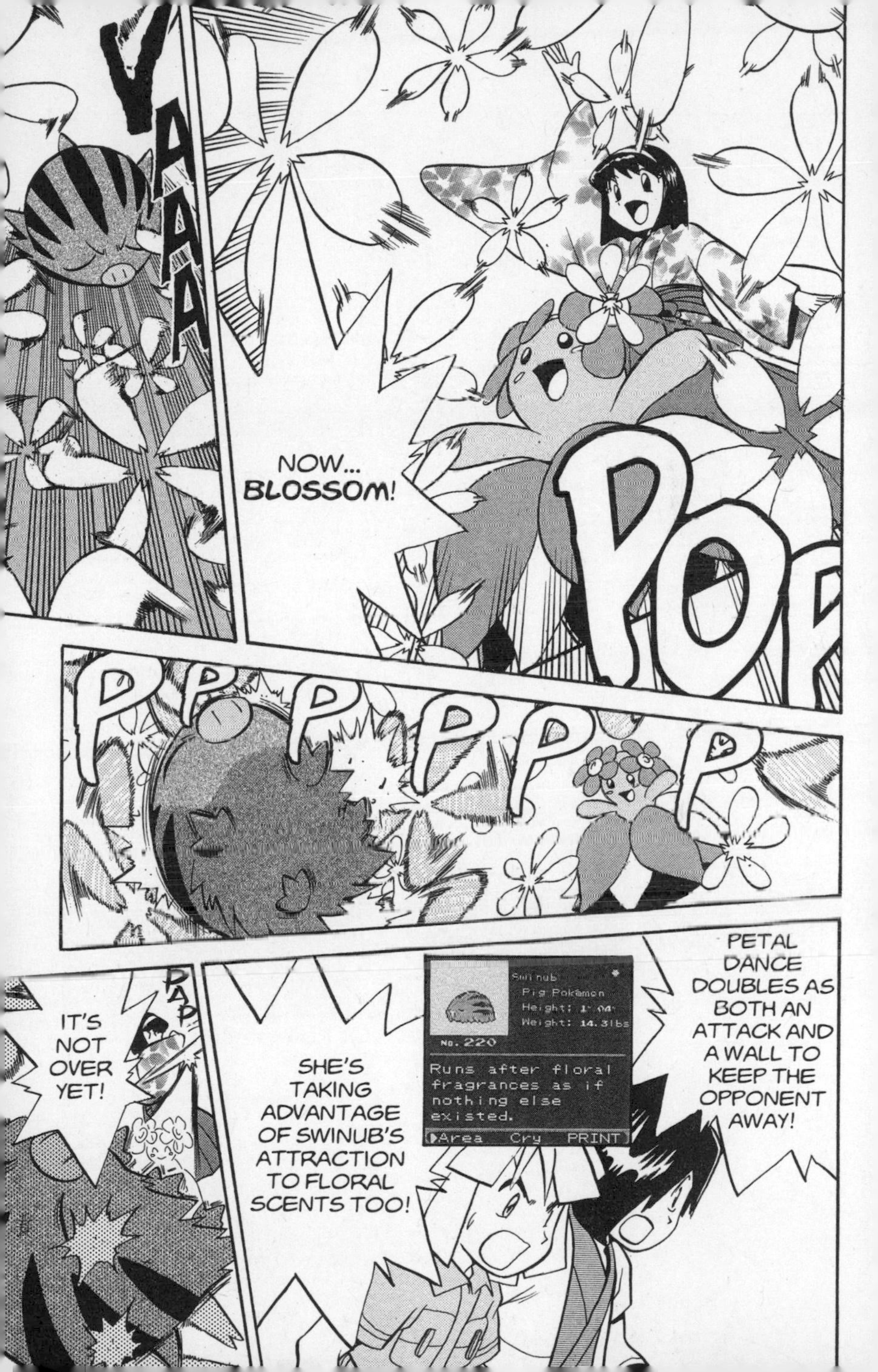
NOW... BLOSSOM!
POP
YAAAA
P P P P P P
PETAL DANCE DOUBLES AS BOTH AN ATTACK AND A WALL TO KEEP THE OPPONENT AWAY!
Swinub
Pig Pokémon
Height: 1'04"
Weight: 14.3lbs
No. 220
Runs after floral fragrances as if nothing else existed.
Area Cry PRINT
SHE'S TAKING ADVANTAGE OF SWINUB'S ATTRACTION TO FLORAL SCENTS TOO!
PAP
IT'S NOT OVER YET!

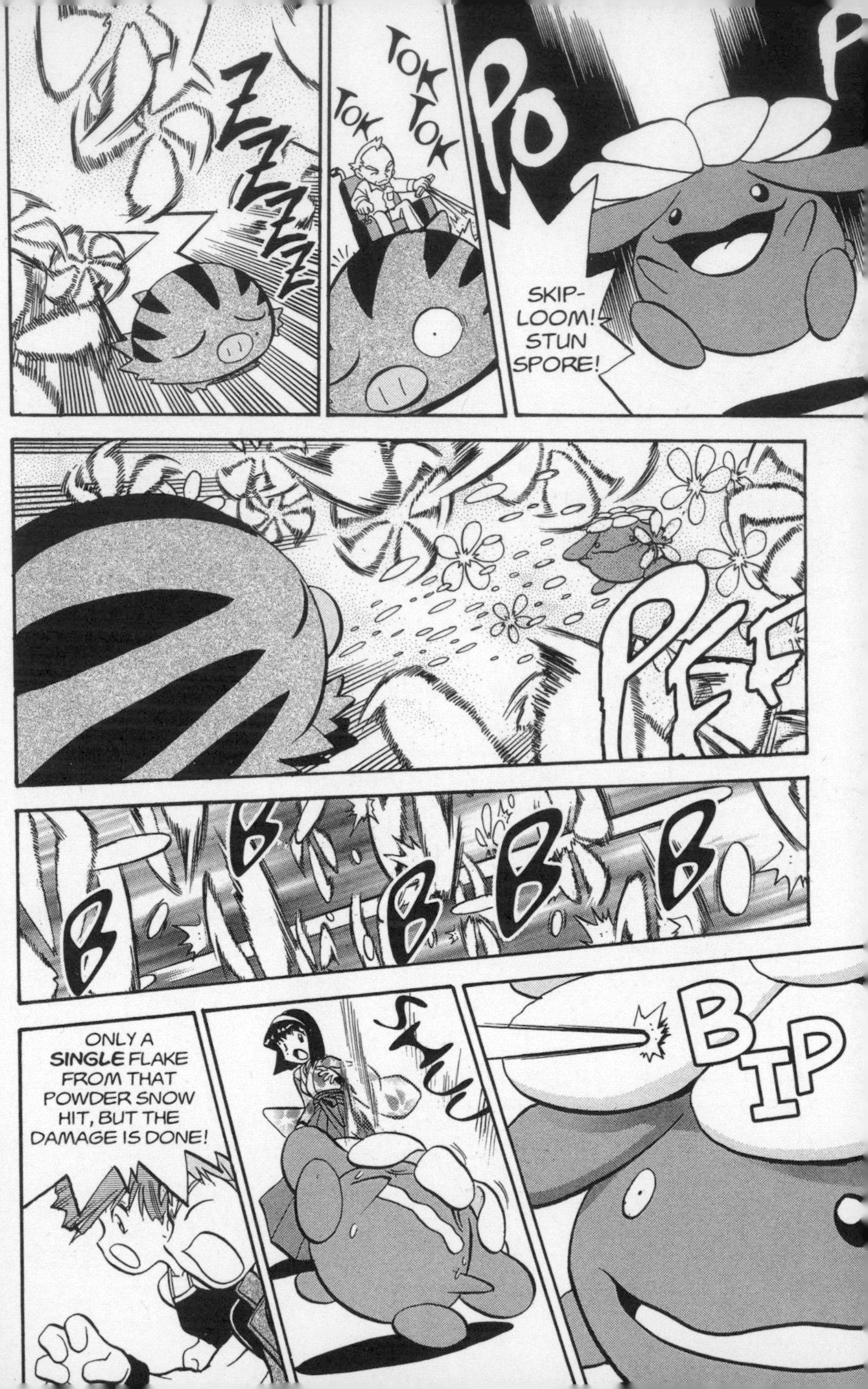
PO
SKIP-LOOM! STUN SPORE!
TOK TOK TOK
BIP
ONLY A **SINGLE** FLAKE FROM THAT POWDER SNOW HIT, BUT THE DAMAGE IS DONE!

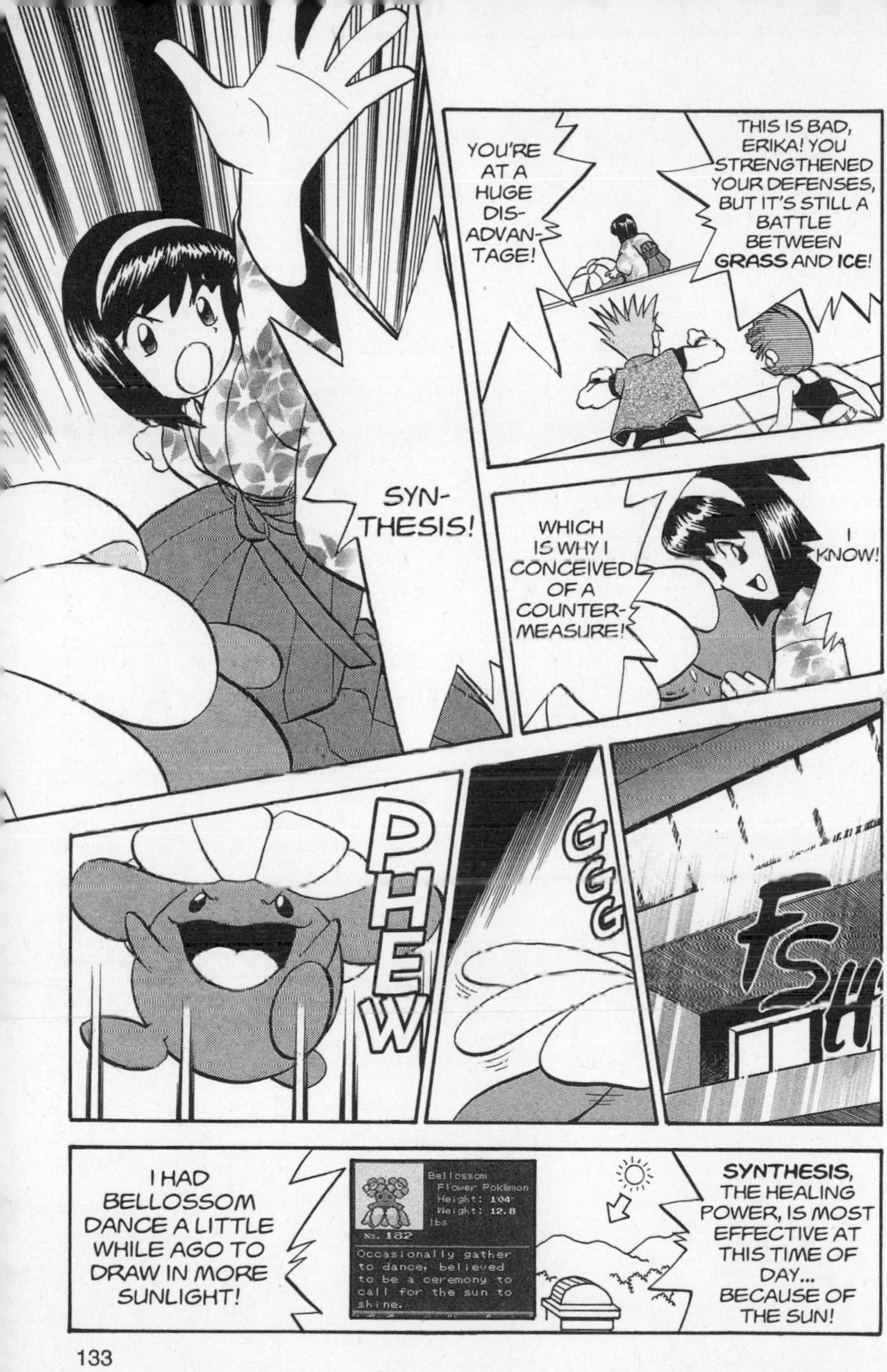
THIS IS BAD, ERIKA! YOU STRENGTHENED YOUR DEFENSES, BUT IT'S STILL A BATTLE BETWEEN **GRASS** AND **ICE**!
YOU'RE AT A HUGE DIS-ADVAN-TAGE!
I KNOW!
WHICH IS WHY I CONCEIVED OF A COUNTER-MEASURE!
SYN-THESIS!
GGG
PHEW
SYNTHESIS, THE HEALING POWER, IS MOST EFFECTIVE AT THIS TIME OF DAY... BECAUSE OF THE SUN!
Bellossom
Flower Pokémon
Height: 1'04"
Weight: 12.8 lbs
No. 182
Occasionally gather to dance, believed to be a ceremony to call for the sun to shine.
I HAD BELLOSSOM DANCE A LITTLE WHILE AGO TO DRAW IN MORE SUNLIGHT!

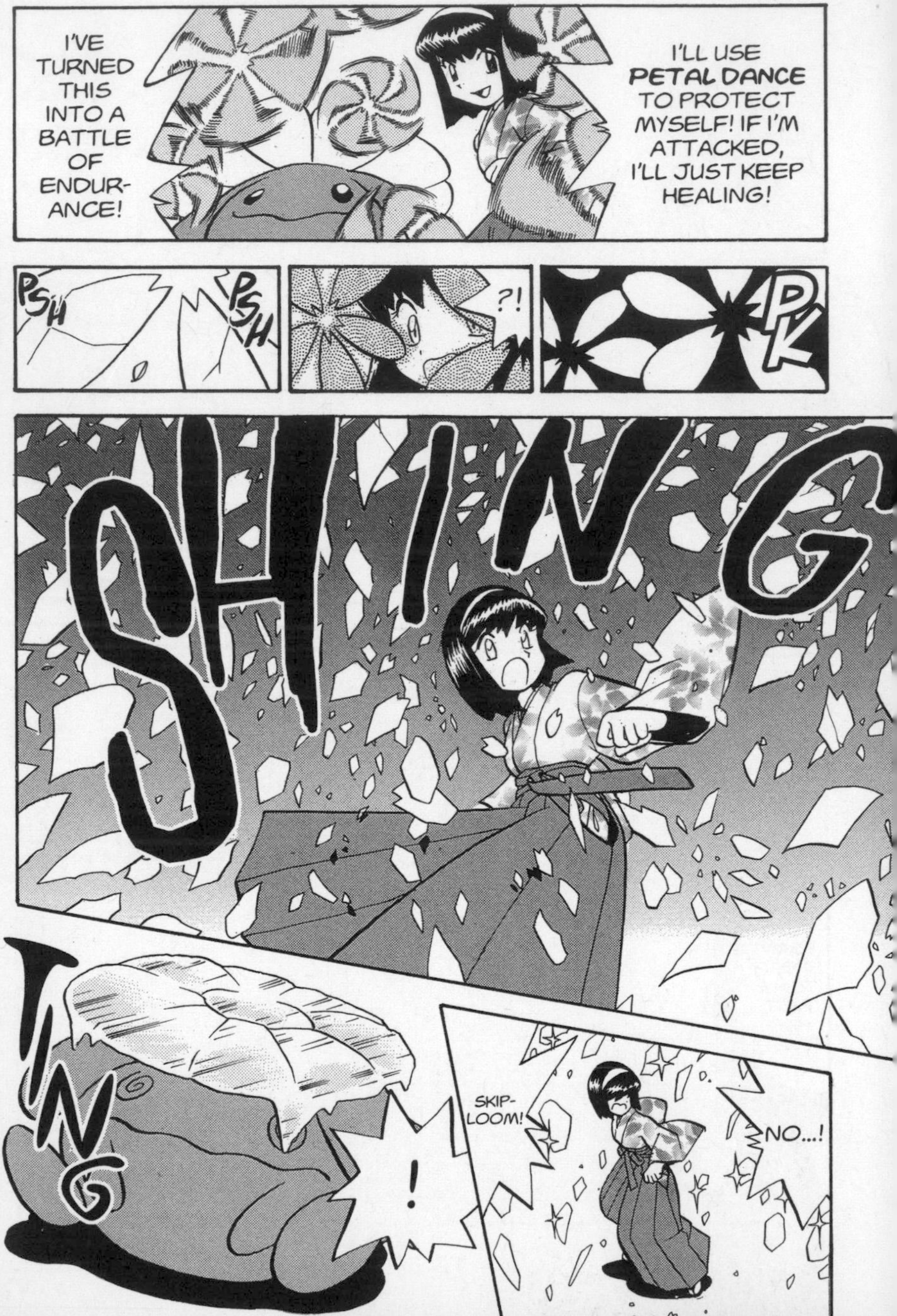
I'LL USE PETAL DANCE TO PROTECT MYSELF! IF I'M ATTACKED, I'LL JUST KEEP HEALING!
I'VE TURNED THIS INTO A BATTLE OF ENDUR-ANCE!
PK
?!
PSH
PSH
SHING
NO...!
SKIP-LOOM!
!
TING

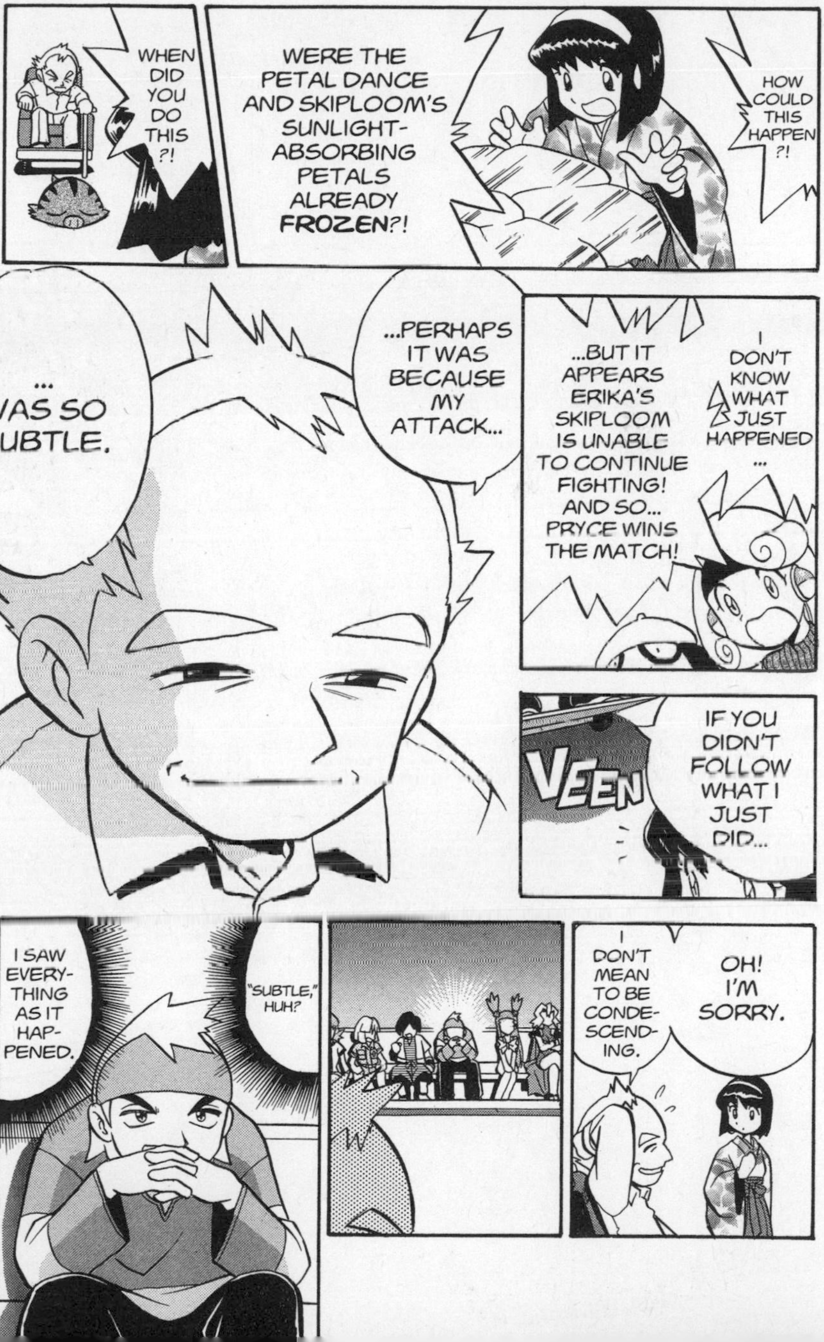
HOW COULD THIS HAPPEN?!
WERE THE PETAL DANCE AND SKIPLOOM'S SUNLIGHT-ABSORBING PETALS ALREADY FROZEN?!
WHEN DID YOU DO THIS?!
I DON'T KNOW WHAT JUST HAPPENED...
...BUT IT APPEARS ERIKA'S SKIPLOOM IS UNABLE TO CONTINUE FIGHTING! AND SO... PRYCE WINS THE MATCH!
VEEN
IF YOU DIDN'T FOLLOW WHAT I JUST DID...
...PERHAPS IT WAS BECAUSE MY ATTACK...
...WAS SO SUBTLE.
OH! I'M SORRY.
I DON'T MEAN TO BE CONDESCENDING.
"SUBTLE," HUH?
I SAW EVERYTHING AS IT HAPPENED.

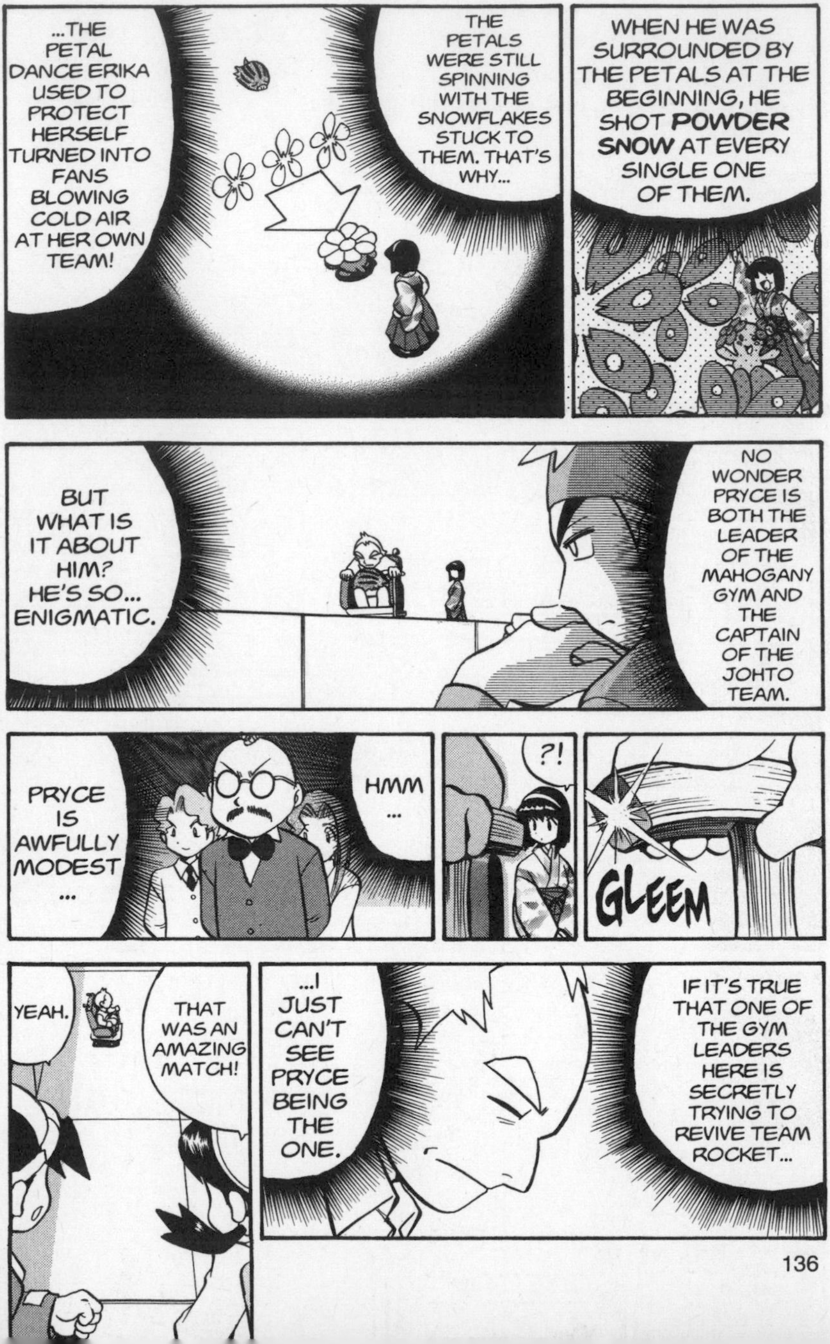
WHEN HE WAS SURROUNDED BY THE PETALS AT THE BEGINNING, HE SHOT **POWDER SNOW** AT EVERY SINGLE ONE OF THEM.
THE PETALS WERE STILL SPINNING WITH THE SNOWFLAKES STUCK TO THEM. THAT'S WHY...
...THE PETAL DANCE ERIKA USED TO PROTECT HERSELF TURNED INTO FANS BLOWING COLD AIR AT HER OWN TEAM!
NO WONDER PRYCE IS BOTH THE LEADER OF THE MAHOGANY GYM AND THE CAPTAIN OF THE JOHTO TEAM.
BUT WHAT IS IT ABOUT HIM? HE'S SO... ENIGMATIC.
GLEEM
?!
HMM ...
PRYCE IS AWFULLY MODEST ...
IF IT'S TRUE THAT ONE OF THE GYM LEADERS HERE IS SECRETLY TRYING TO REVIVE TEAM ROCKET...
...I JUST CAN'T SEE PRYCE BEING THE ONE.
THAT WAS AN AMAZING MATCH!
YEAH.

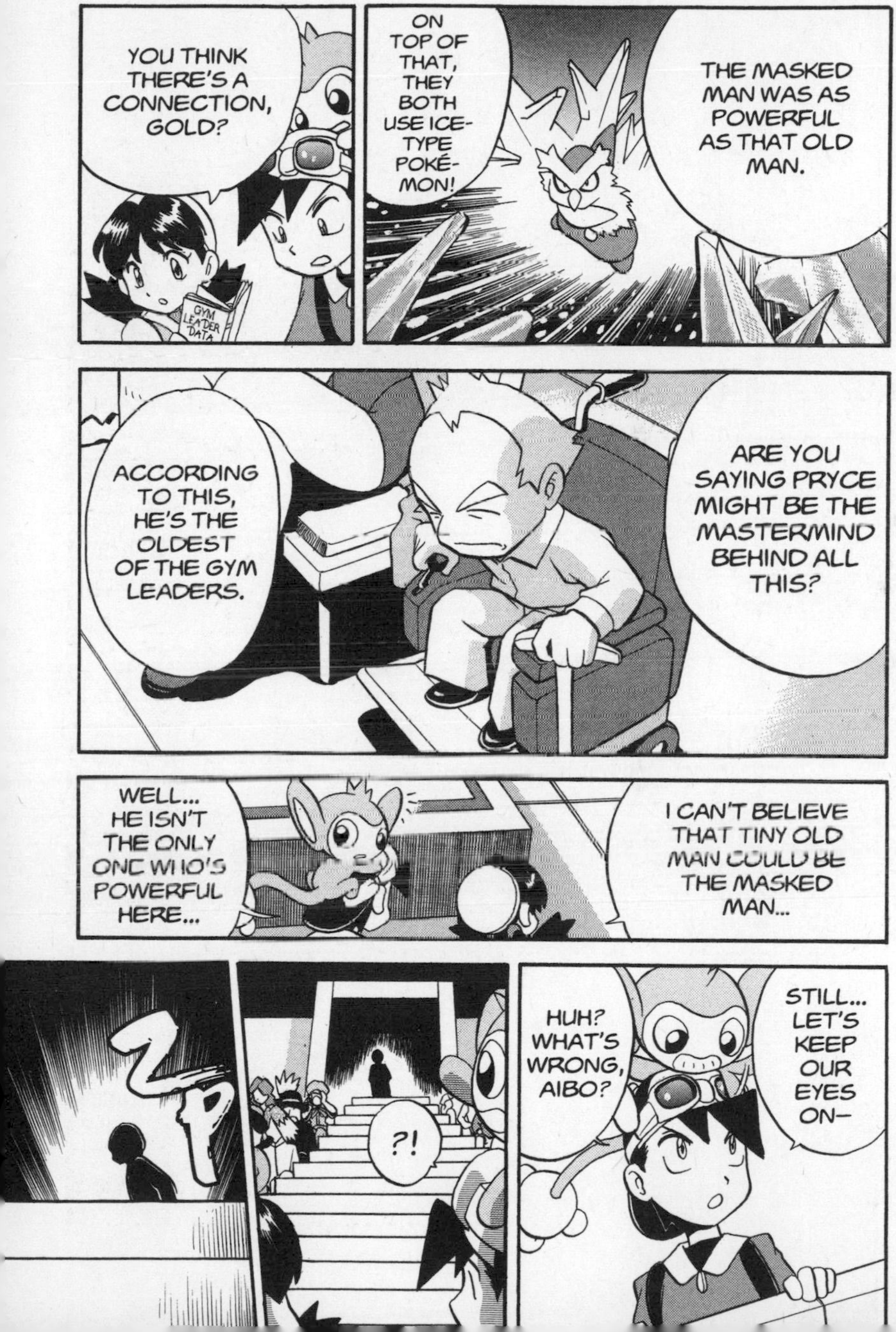
THE MASKED MAN WAS AS POWERFUL AS THAT OLD MAN.
ON TOP OF THAT, THEY BOTH USE ICE-TYPE POKÉMON!
YOU THINK THERE'S A CONNECTION, GOLD?
GYM LEADER DATA
ARE YOU SAYING PRYCE MIGHT BE THE MASTERMIND BEHIND ALL THIS?
ACCORDING TO THIS, HE'S THE OLDEST OF THE GYM LEADERS.
I CAN'T BELIEVE THAT TINY OLD MAN COULD BE THE MASKED MAN...
WELL... HE ISN'T THE ONLY ONE WHO'S POWERFUL HERE...
STILL... LET'S KEEP OUR EYES ON—
HUH? WHAT'S WRONG, AIBO?
?!
ZIP

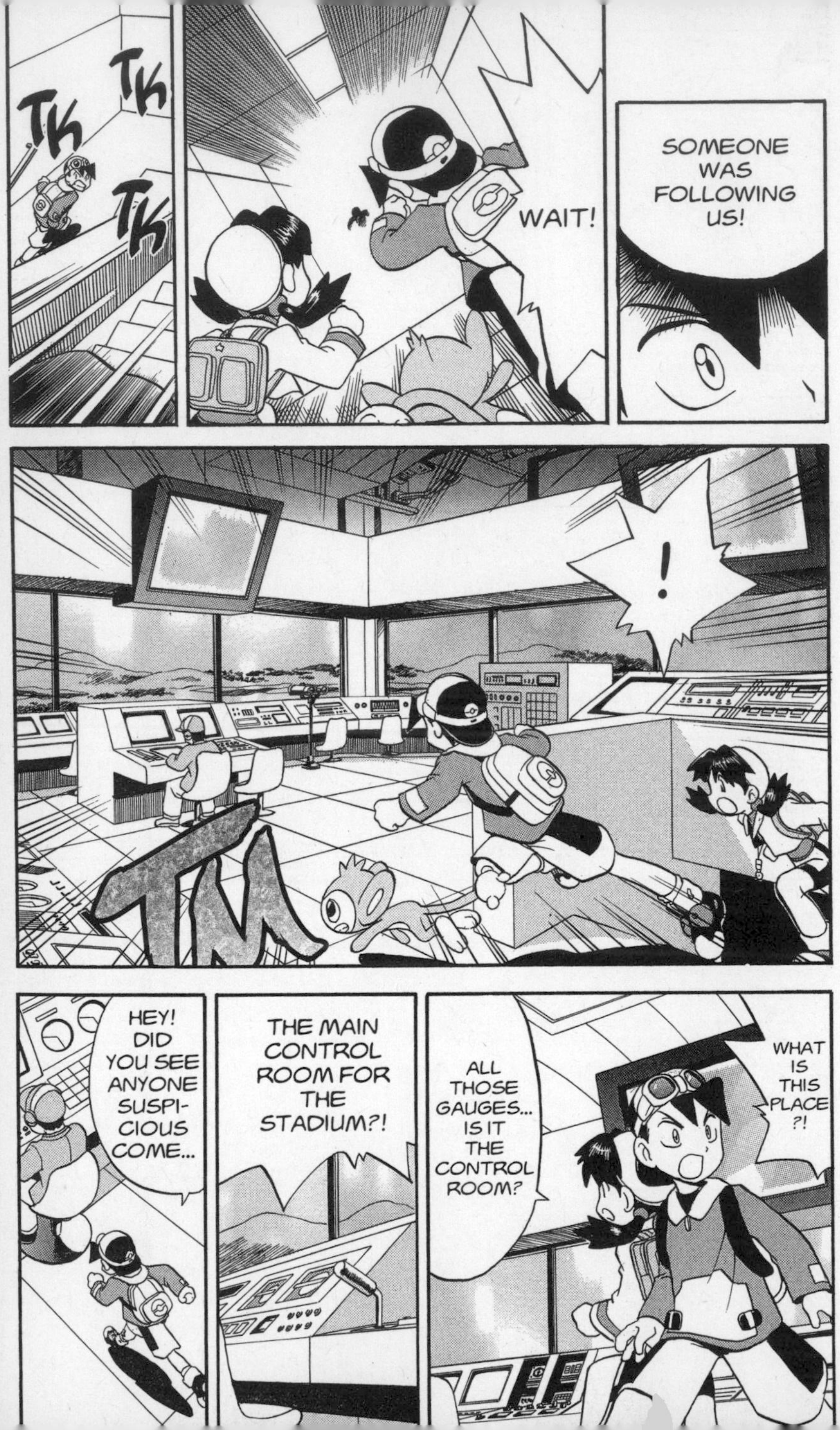
SOMEONE WAS FOLLOWING US!
WAIT!
TK
TK
TK
!
TM
WHAT IS THIS PLACE?!
ALL THOSE GAUGES... IS IT THE CONTROL ROOM?
THE MAIN CONTROL ROOM FOR THE STADIUM?!
HEY! DID YOU SEE ANYONE SUSPICIOUS COME...

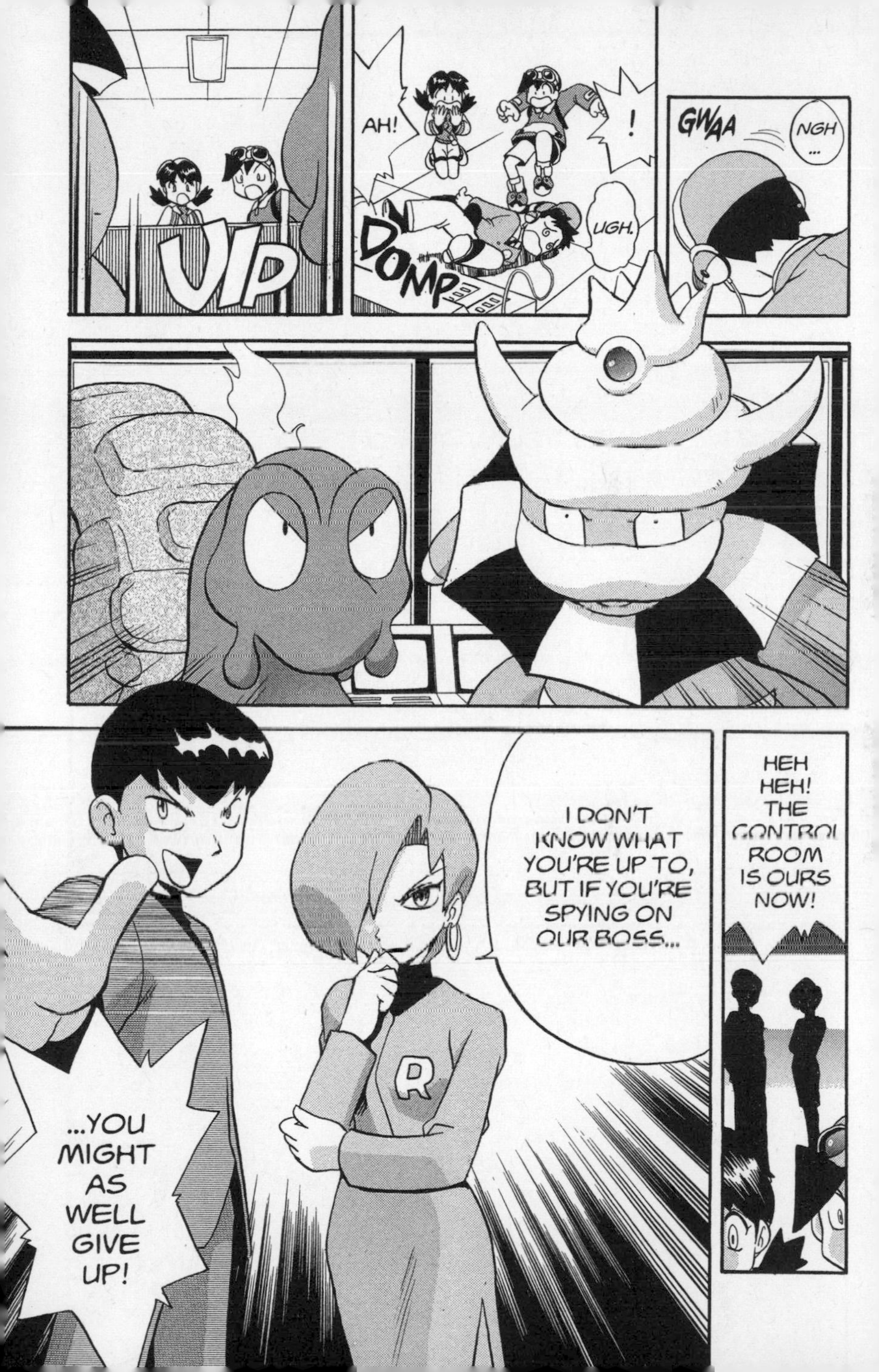
GWAA
NGH ...
!
AH!
UGH.
DOMP
VIP
HEH HEH! THE CONTROL ROOM IS OURS NOW!
I DON'T KNOW WHAT YOU'RE UP TO, BUT IF YOU'RE SPYING ON OUR BOSS...
...YOU MIGHT AS WELL GIVE UP!

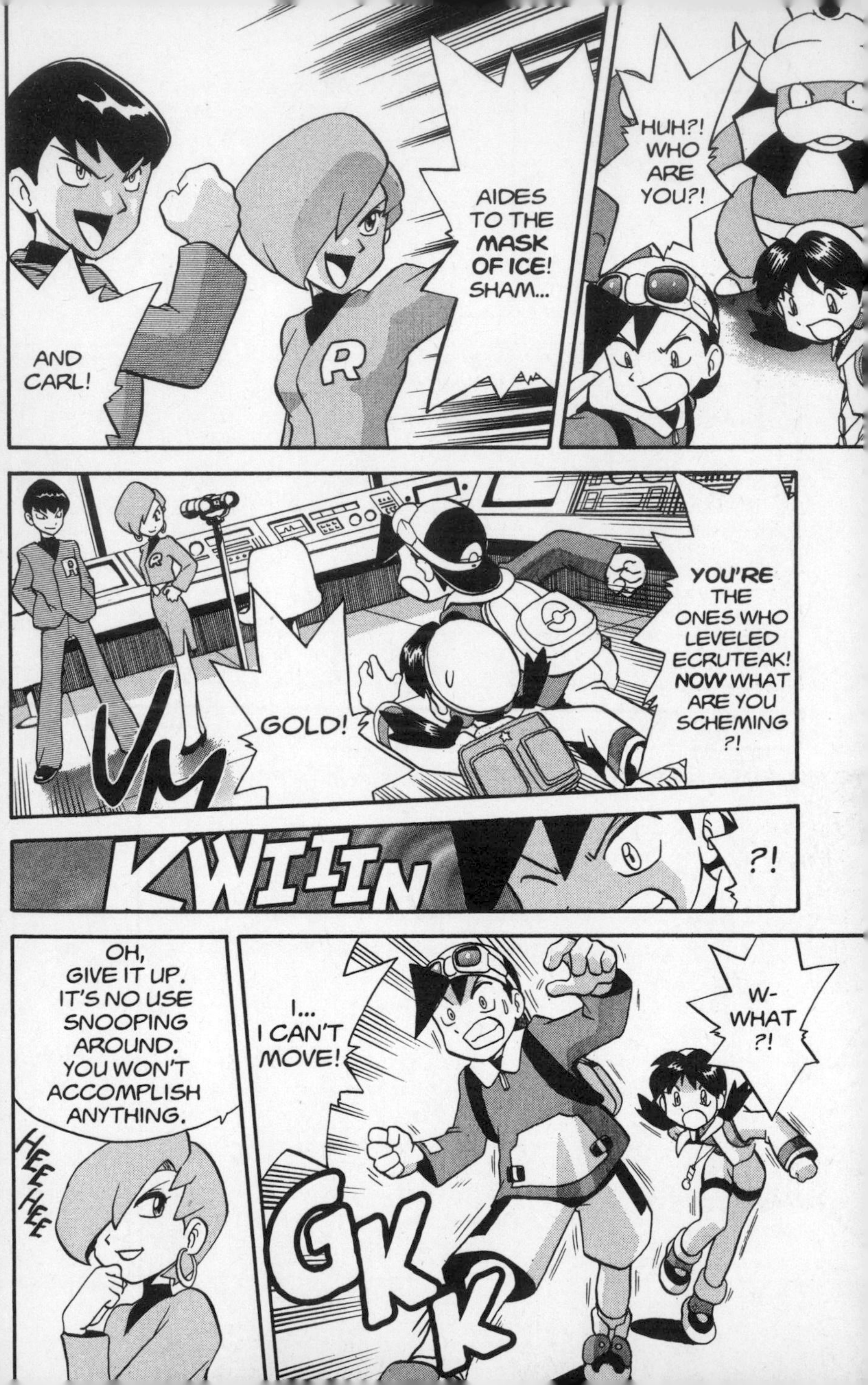
HUH?! WHO ARE YOU?!
AIDES TO THE MASK OF ICE! SHAM...
AND CARL!
YOU'RE THE ONES WHO LEVELED ECRUTEAK! NOW WHAT ARE YOU SCHEMING ?!
GOLD!
?!
KWIIIN
W-WHAT ?!
I... I CAN'T MOVE!
GKK
OH, GIVE IT UP. IT'S NO USE SNOOPING AROUND. YOU WON'T ACCOMPLISH ANYTHING.
HEE HEE

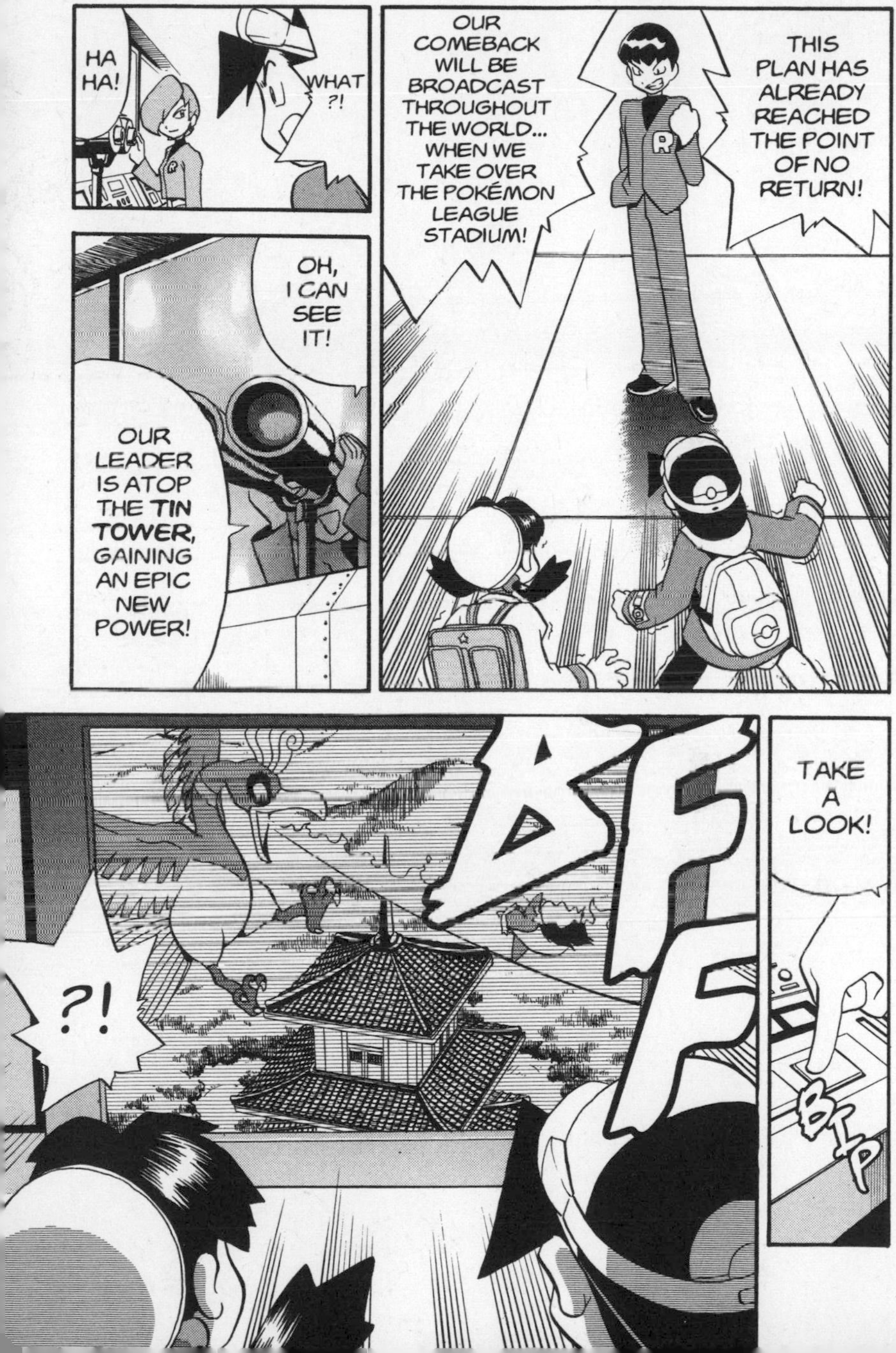
THIS PLAN HAS ALREADY REACHED THE POINT OF NO RETURN!
OUR COMEBACK WILL BE BROADCAST THROUGHOUT THE WORLD... WHEN WE TAKE OVER THE POKÉMON LEAGUE STADIUM!
WHAT ?!
HA HA!
OH, I CAN SEE IT!
OUR LEADER IS ATOP THE TIN TOWER, GAINING AN EPIC NEW POWER!
TAKE A LOOK!
BIP
BFF
?!

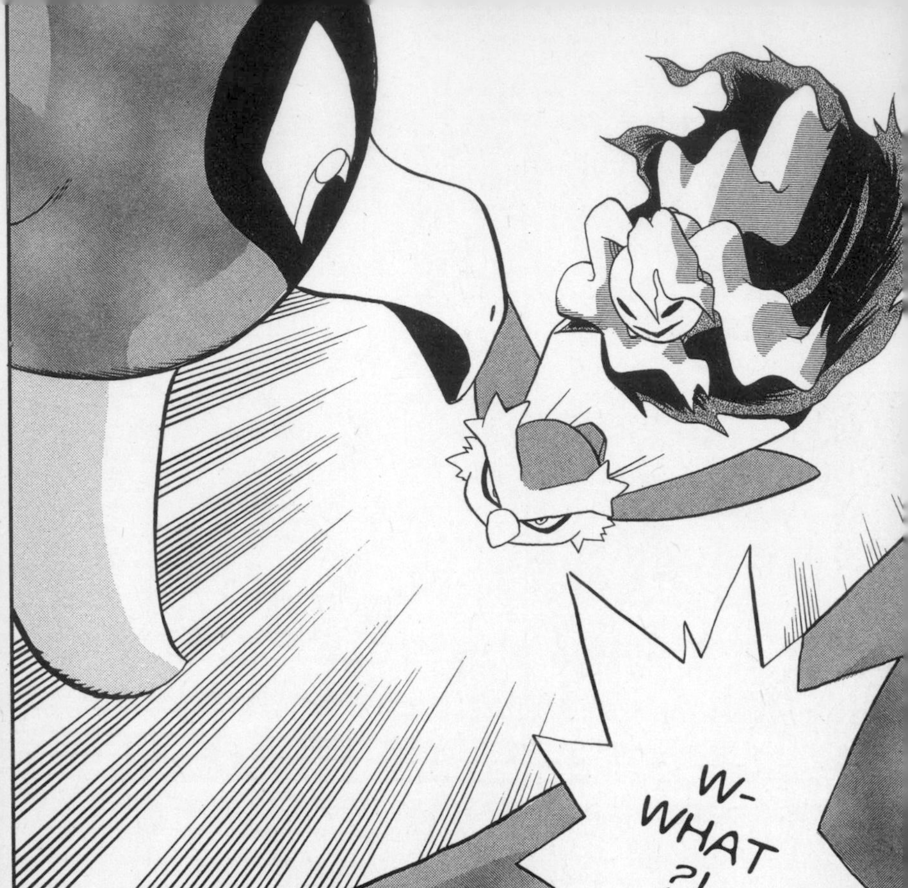
W-WHAT?!

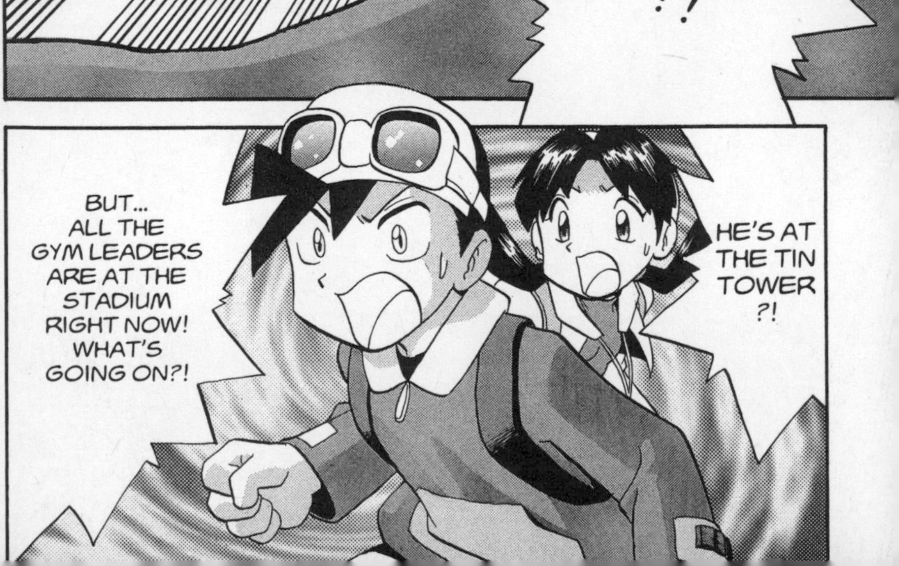
HE'S AT THE TIN TOWER?!
BUT... ALL THE GYM LEADERS ARE AT THE STADIUM RIGHT NOW! WHAT'S GOING ON?!

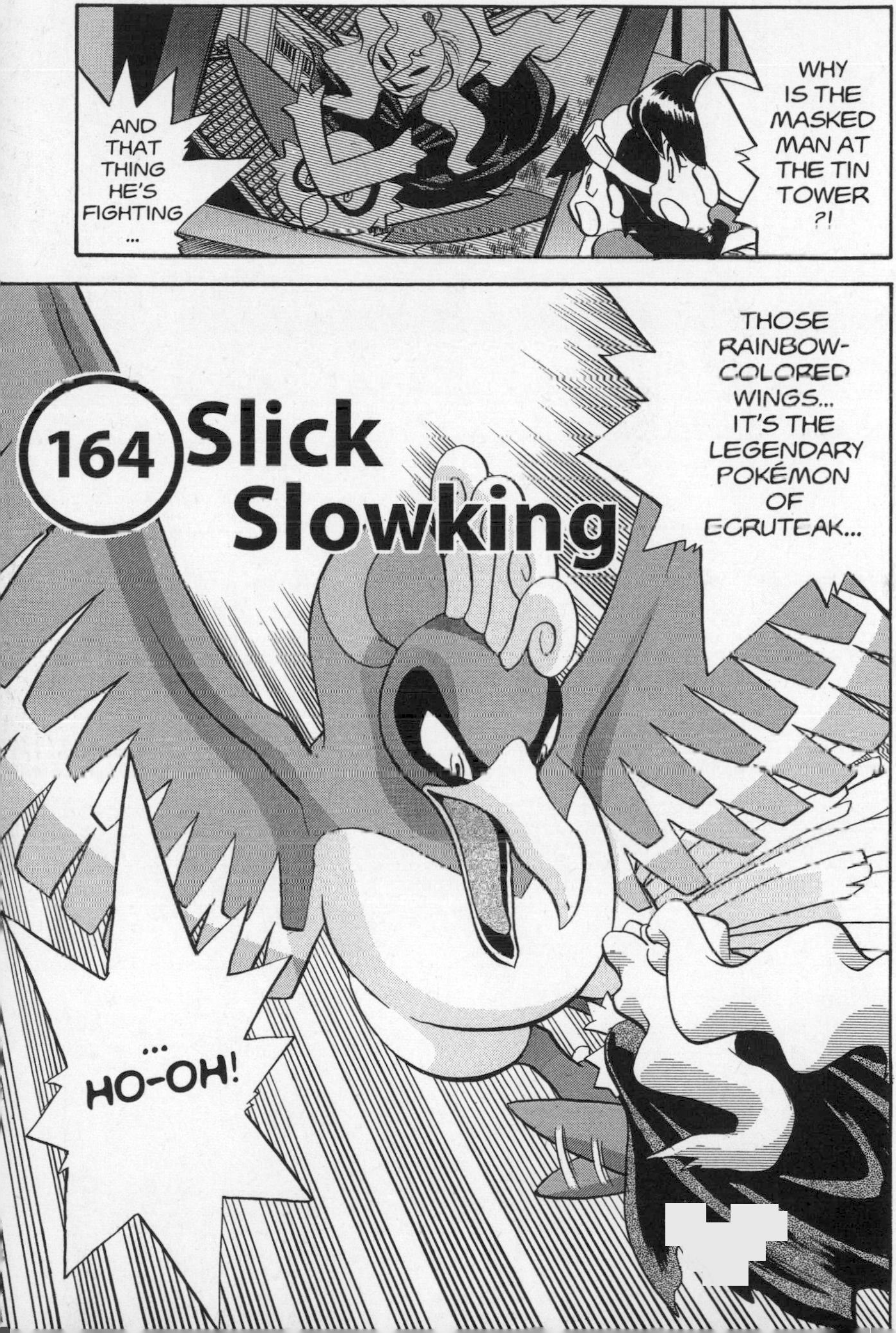
WHY IS THE MASKED MAN AT THE TIN TOWER ?!
AND THAT THING HE'S FIGHTING ...
164 Slick Slowking
THOSE RAINBOW-COLORED WINGS... IT'S THE LEGENDARY POKÉMON OF ECRUTEAK...
... HO-OH!

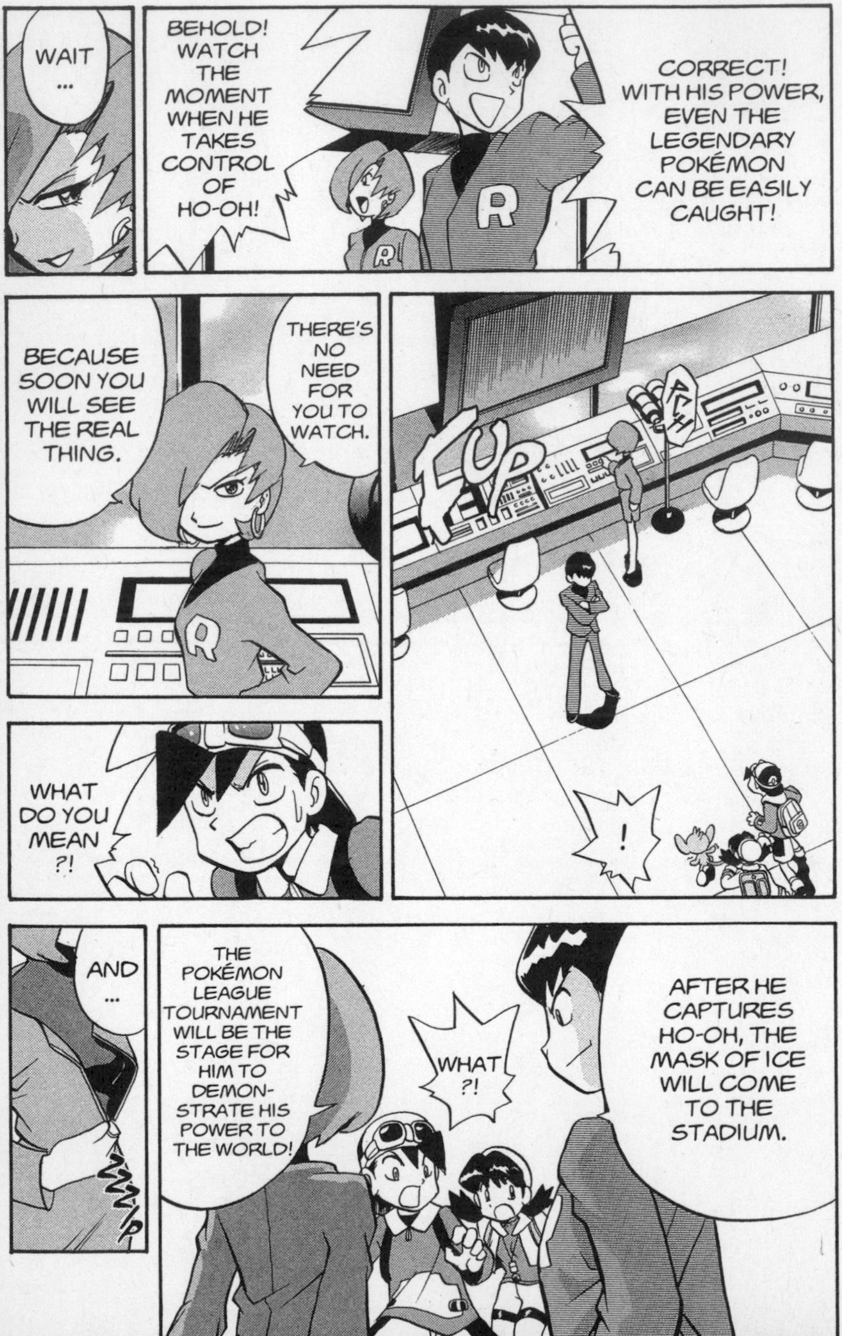
CORRECT! WITH HIS POWER, EVEN THE LEGENDARY POKÉMON CAN BE EASILY CAUGHT!
BEHOLD! WATCH THE MOMENT WHEN HE TAKES CONTROL OF HO-OH!
WAIT ...
!
FUP
THERE'S NO NEED FOR YOU TO WATCH.
BECAUSE SOON YOU WILL SEE THE REAL THING.
WHAT DO YOU MEAN ?!
AFTER HE CAPTURES HO-OH, THE MASK OF ICE WILL COME TO THE STADIUM.
WHAT ?!
THE POKÉMON LEAGUE TOURNAMENT WILL BE THE STAGE FOR HIM TO DEMON-STRATE HIS POWER TO THE WORLD!
AND ...
ZZZIP

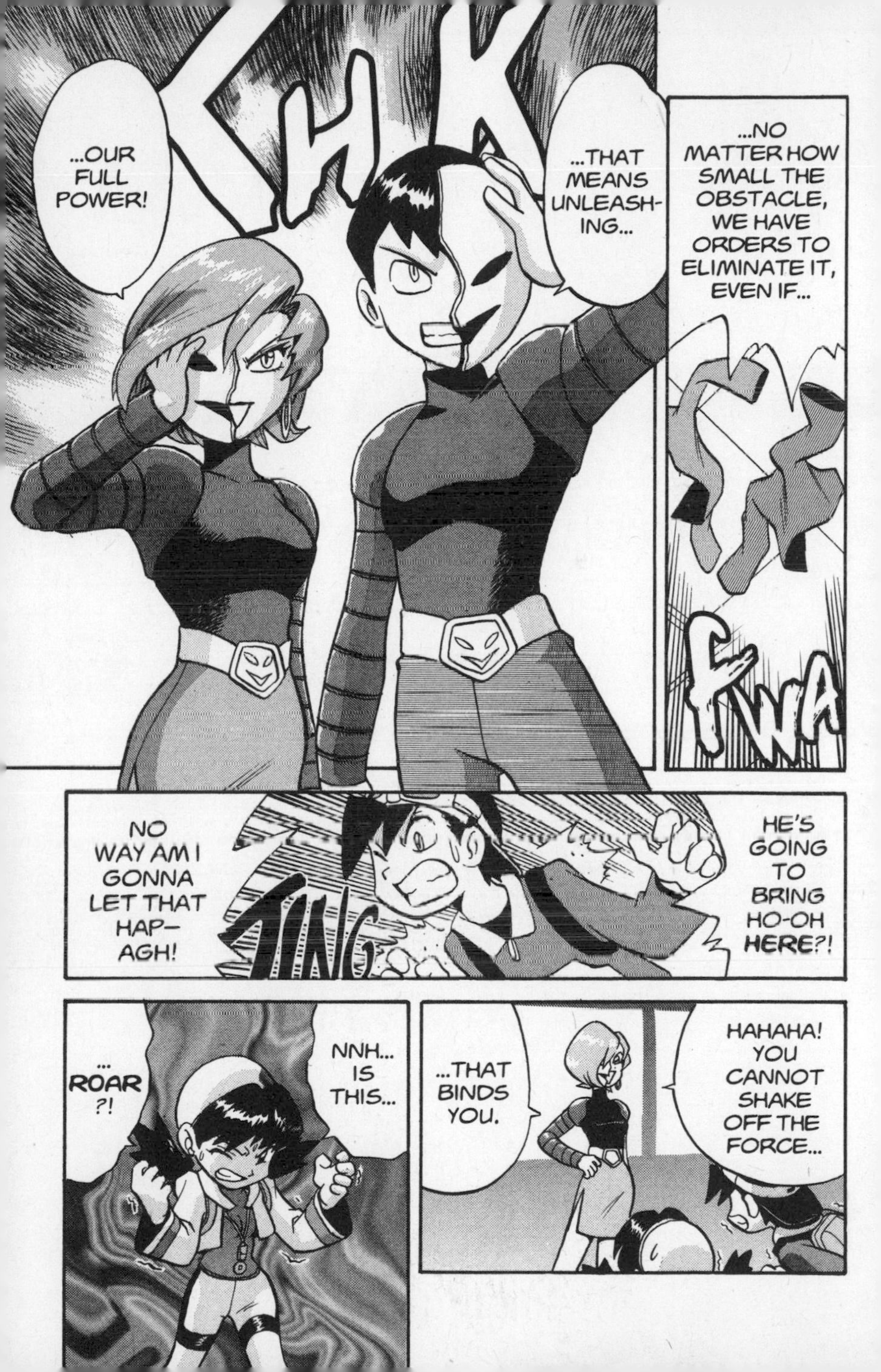
...NO MATTER HOW SMALL THE OBSTACLE, WE HAVE ORDERS TO ELIMINATE IT, EVEN IF...
FWA
...THAT MEANS UNLEASHING...
...OUR FULL POWER!
HE'S GOING TO BRING HO-OH HERE?!
NO WAY AM I GONNA LET THAT HAP—AGH!
TING
HAHAHA! YOU CANNOT SHAKE OFF THE FORCE...
...THAT BINDS YOU.
NNH... IS THIS...
...ROAR?!

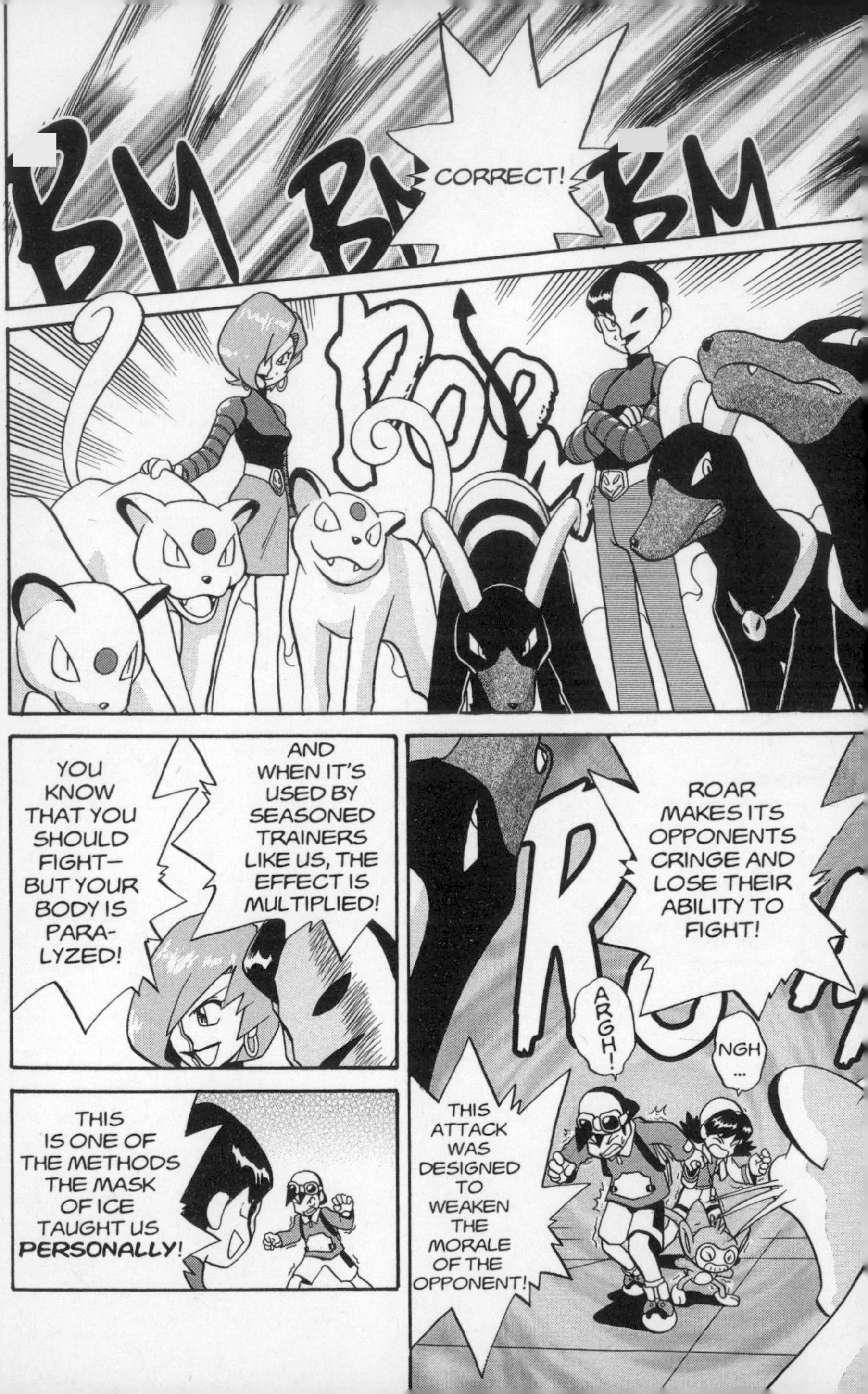

BM
CORRECT!
BM
BM
ROAR MAKES ITS OPPONENTS CRINGE AND LOSE THEIR ABILITY TO FIGHT!
ARGH!
NGH...
THIS ATTACK WAS DESIGNED TO WEAKEN THE MORALE OF THE OPPONENT!
AND WHEN IT'S USED BY SEASONED TRAINERS LIKE US, THE EFFECT IS MULTIPLIED!
YOU KNOW THAT YOU SHOULD FIGHT— BUT YOUR BODY IS PARA-LYZED!
THIS IS ONE OF THE METHODS THE MASK OF ICE TAUGHT US **PERSONALLY**!

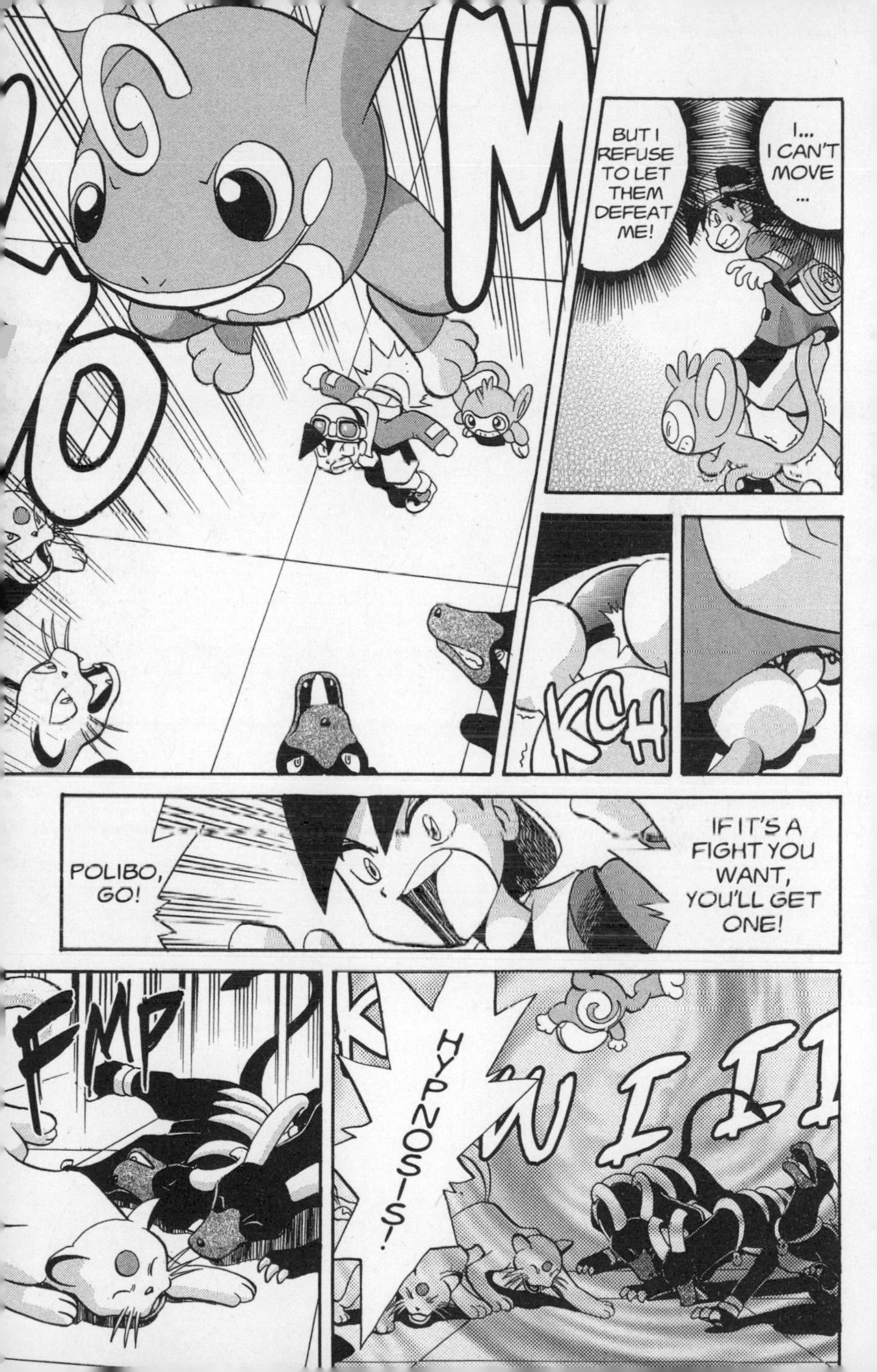
I... I CAN'T MOVE ...
BUT I REFUSE TO LET THEM DEFEAT ME!
KCH
IF IT'S A FIGHT YOU WANT, YOU'LL GET ONE!
POLIBO, GO!
HYPNOSIS!
FMP

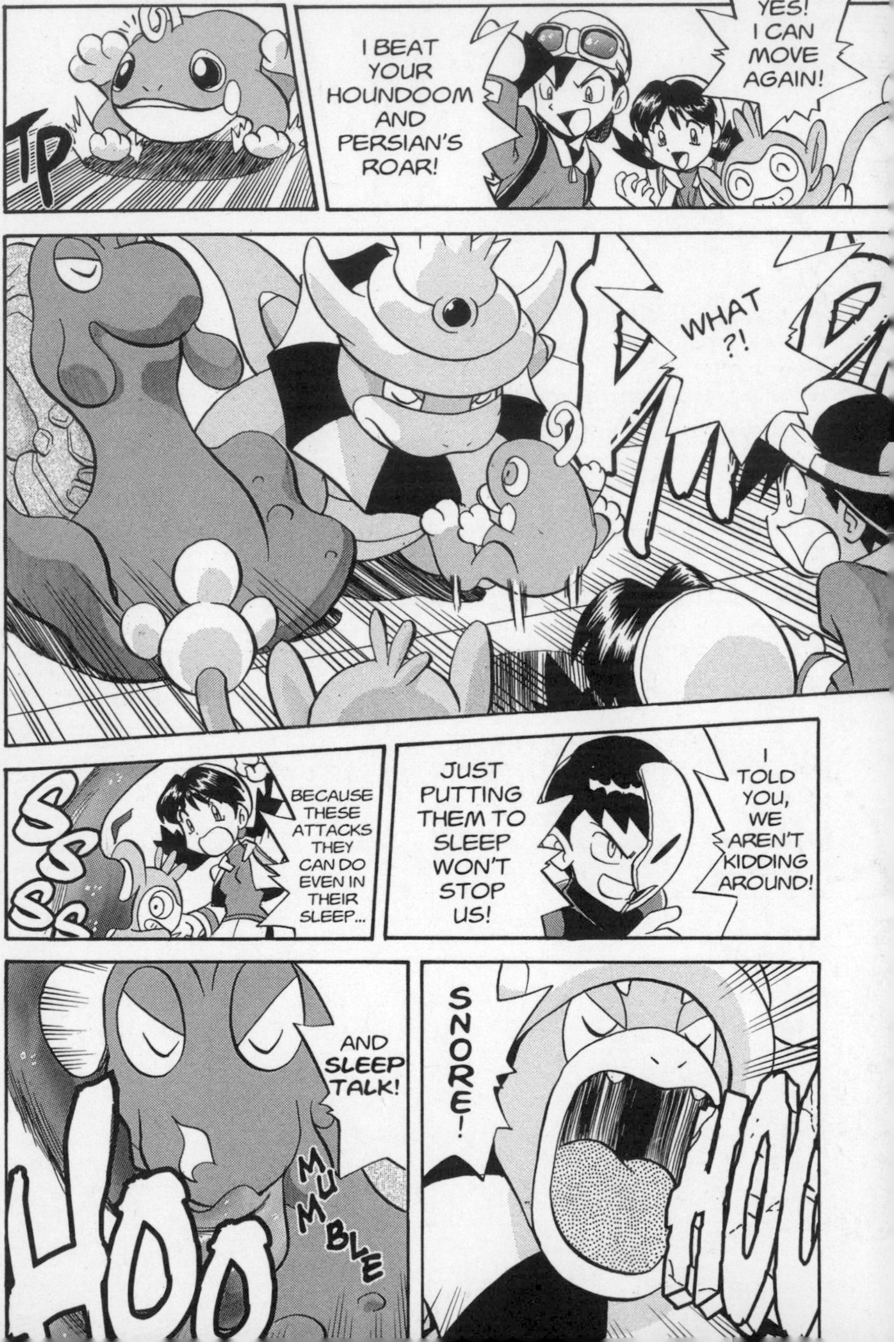
YES! I CAN MOVE AGAIN!
I BEAT YOUR HOUNDOOM AND PERSIAN'S ROAR!
TP
WHAT ?!
I TOLD YOU, WE AREN'T KIDDING AROUND!
JUST PUTTING THEM TO SLEEP WON'T STOP US!
BECAUSE THESE ATTACKS THEY CAN DO EVEN IN THEIR SLEEP...
SSSS
SNORE!
HOO
AND SLEEP TALK!
MUMBLE
HOO

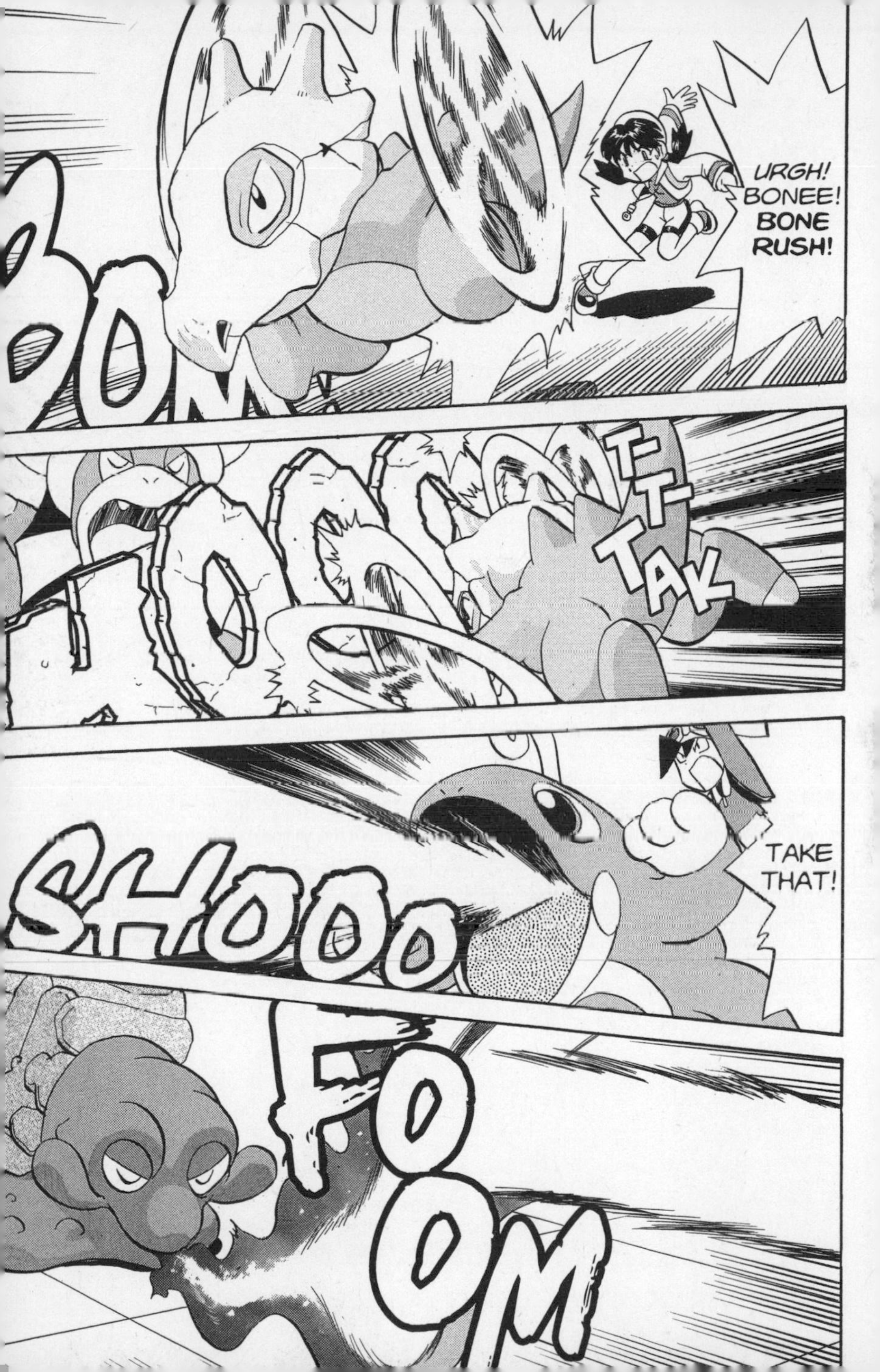
URGH! BONEE! BONE RUSH!
BOOM!
T-T-TAK
TAKE THAT!
SHOOO
FOOOM

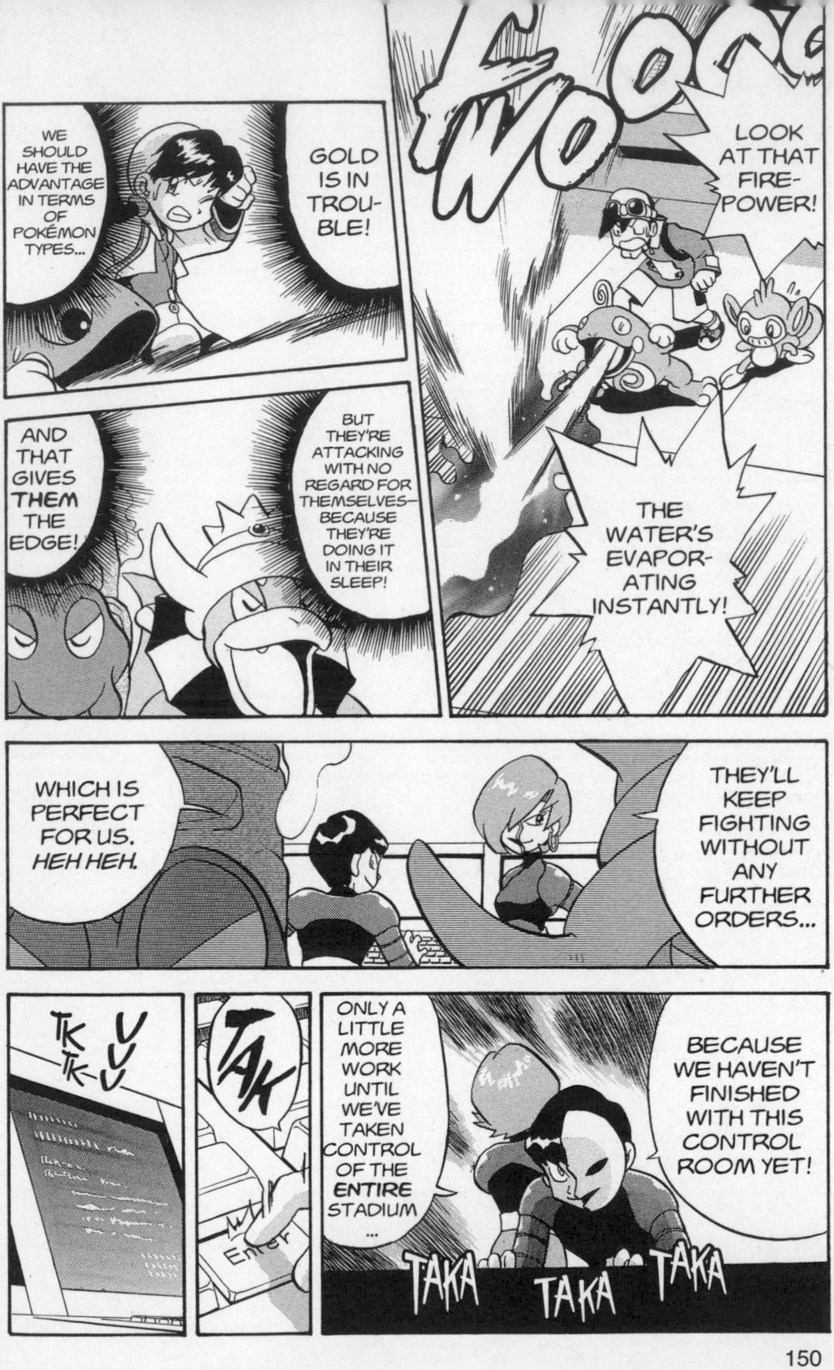
WOOO
LOOK AT THAT FIRE-POWER!
THE WATER'S EVAPORATING INSTANTLY!
GOLD IS IN TROUBLE!
WE SHOULD HAVE THE ADVANTAGE IN TERMS OF POKÉMON TYPES...
BUT THEY'RE ATTACKING WITH NO REGARD FOR THEMSELVES—BECAUSE THEY'RE DOING IT IN THEIR SLEEP!
AND THAT GIVES **THEM** THE EDGE!
THEY'LL KEEP FIGHTING WITHOUT ANY FURTHER ORDERS...
WHICH IS PERFECT FOR US. *HEH HEH.*
BECAUSE WE HAVEN'T FINISHED WITH THIS CONTROL ROOM YET!
ONLY A LITTLE MORE WORK UNTIL WE'VE TAKEN CONTROL OF THE **ENTIRE** STADIUM...
TAKA TAKA TAKA
TAK
Enter
TK TK
VVVV

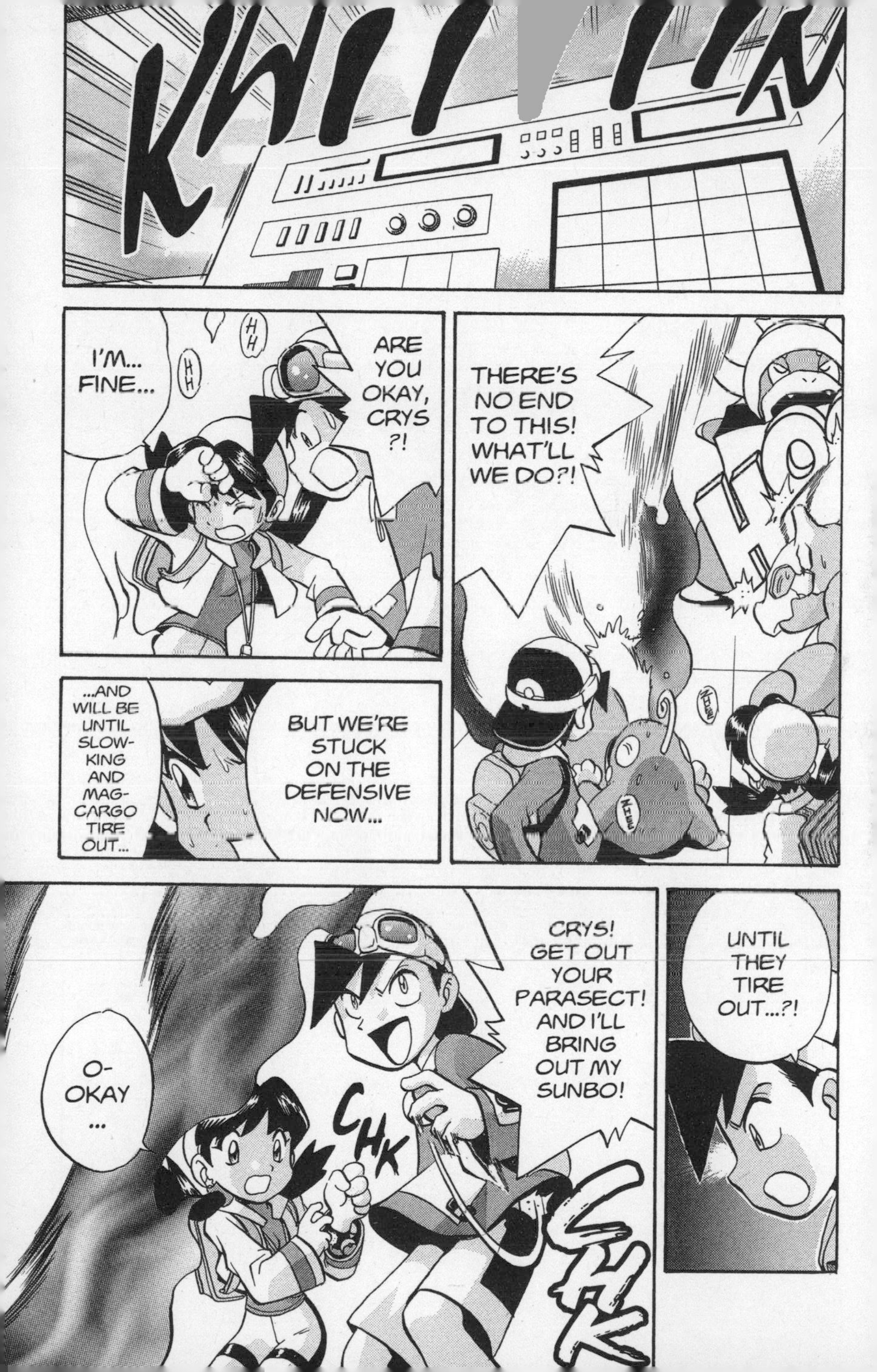
KWIIIIN
THERE'S NO END TO THIS! WHAT'LL WE DO?!
ARE YOU OKAY, CRYS?!
HH
I'M... FINE...
BUT WE'RE STUCK ON THE DEFENSIVE NOW...
...AND WILL BE UNTIL SLOW-KING AND MAG-CARGO TIRE OUT...
UNTIL THEY TIRE OUT...?!
CRYS! GET OUT YOUR PARASECT! AND I'LL BRING OUT MY SUNBO!
CHK
CHK
O-OKAY...

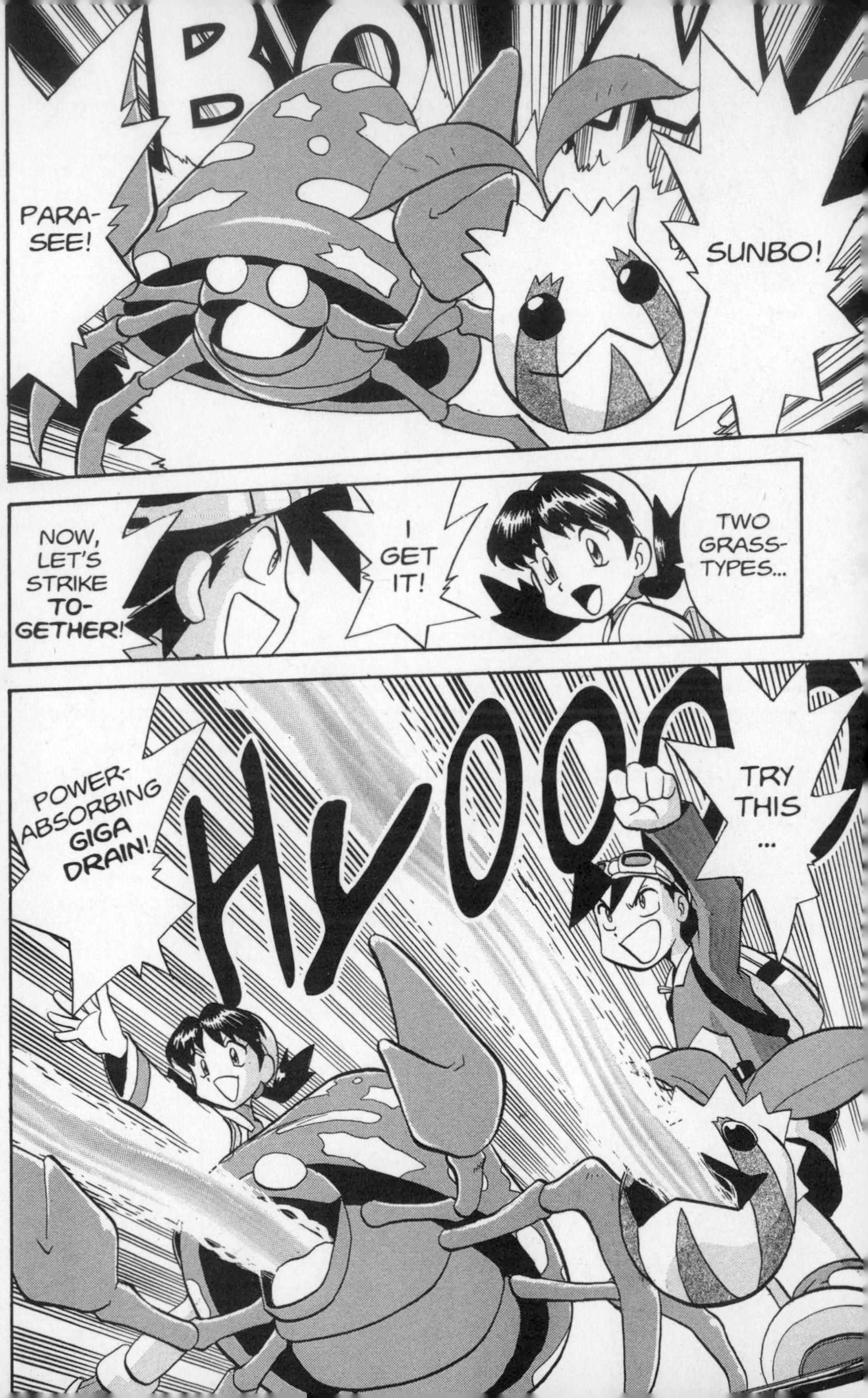
SUNBO!
PARA-SEE!
TWO GRASS-TYPES...
I GET IT!
NOW, LET'S STRIKE TO-GETHER!
TRY THIS ...
POWER-ABSORBING GIGA DRAIN!

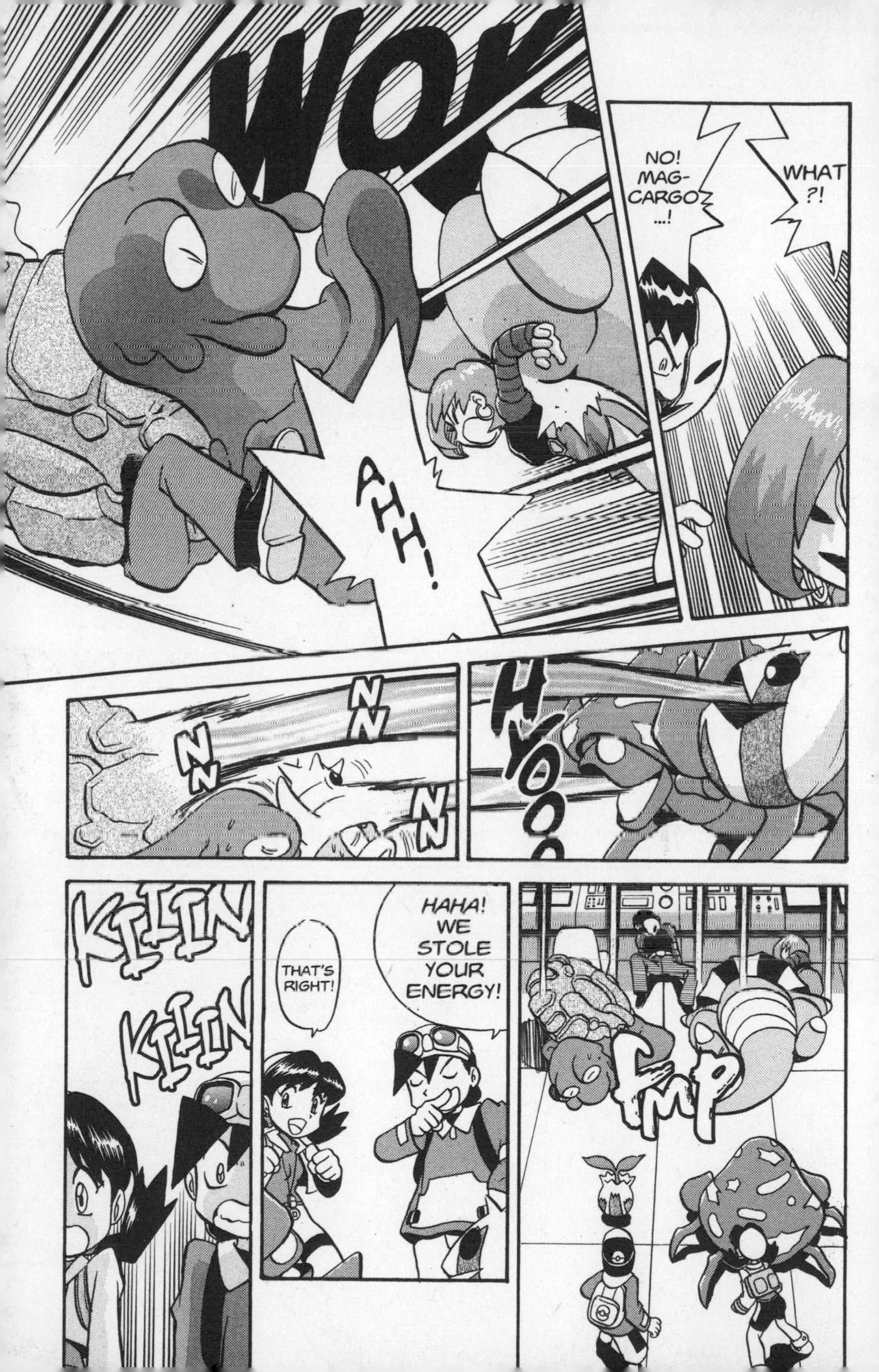
WHAT ?!
NO! MAG-CARGO ...!
AHH!
HAHA! WE STOLE YOUR ENERGY!
THAT'S RIGHT!

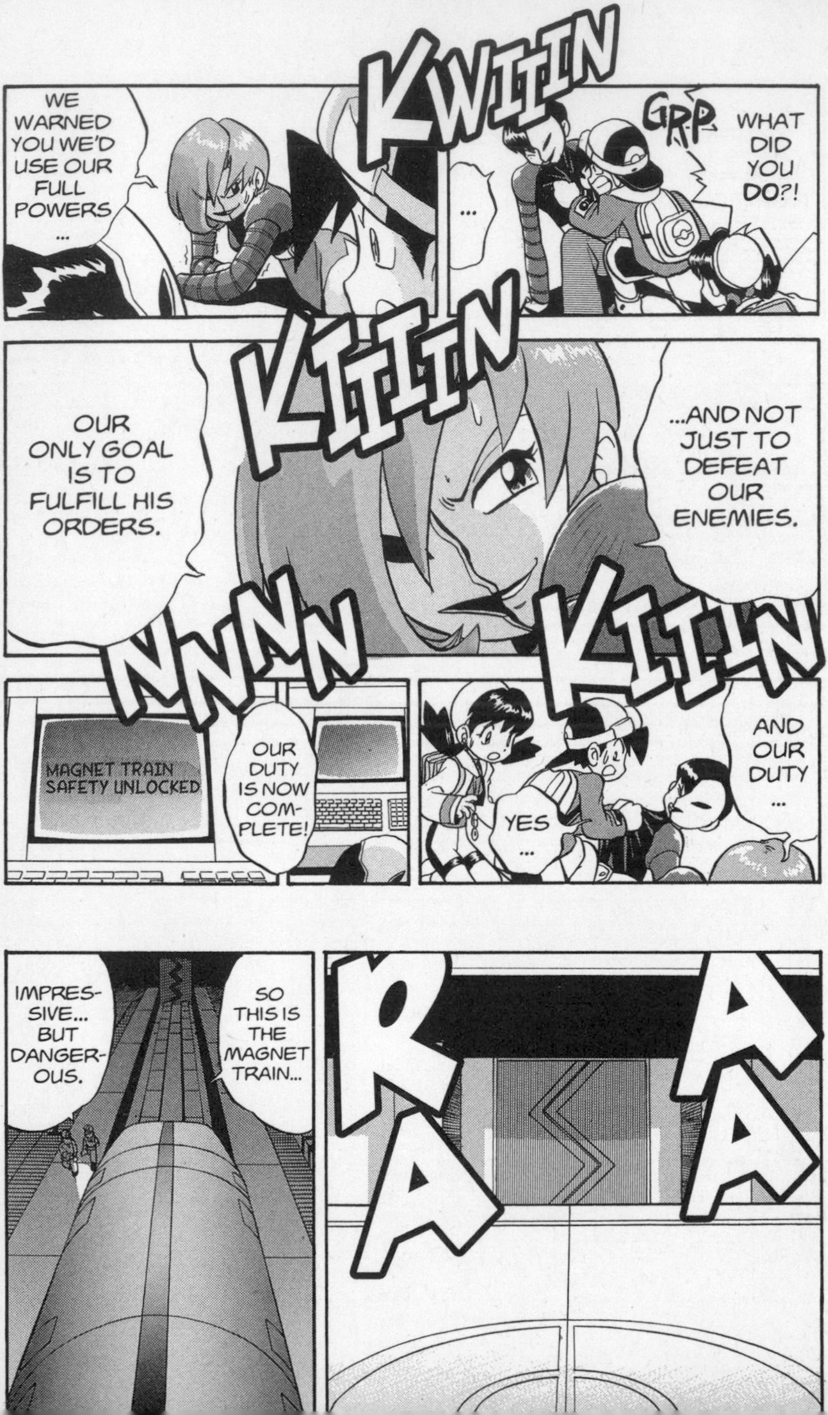
KWIIIN
GRP
WHAT DID YOU DO?!
...
WE WARNED YOU WE'D USE OUR FULL POWERS ...
KIIIIN
...AND NOT JUST TO DEFEAT OUR ENEMIES.
OUR ONLY GOAL IS TO FULFILL HIS ORDERS.
NNNN
KIIIN
AND OUR DUTY ...
YES ...
OUR DUTY IS NOW COM-PLETE!
MAGNET TRAIN SAFETY UNLOCKED
RAAA
SO THIS IS THE MAGNET TRAIN...
IMPRES-SIVE... BUT DANGER-OUS.

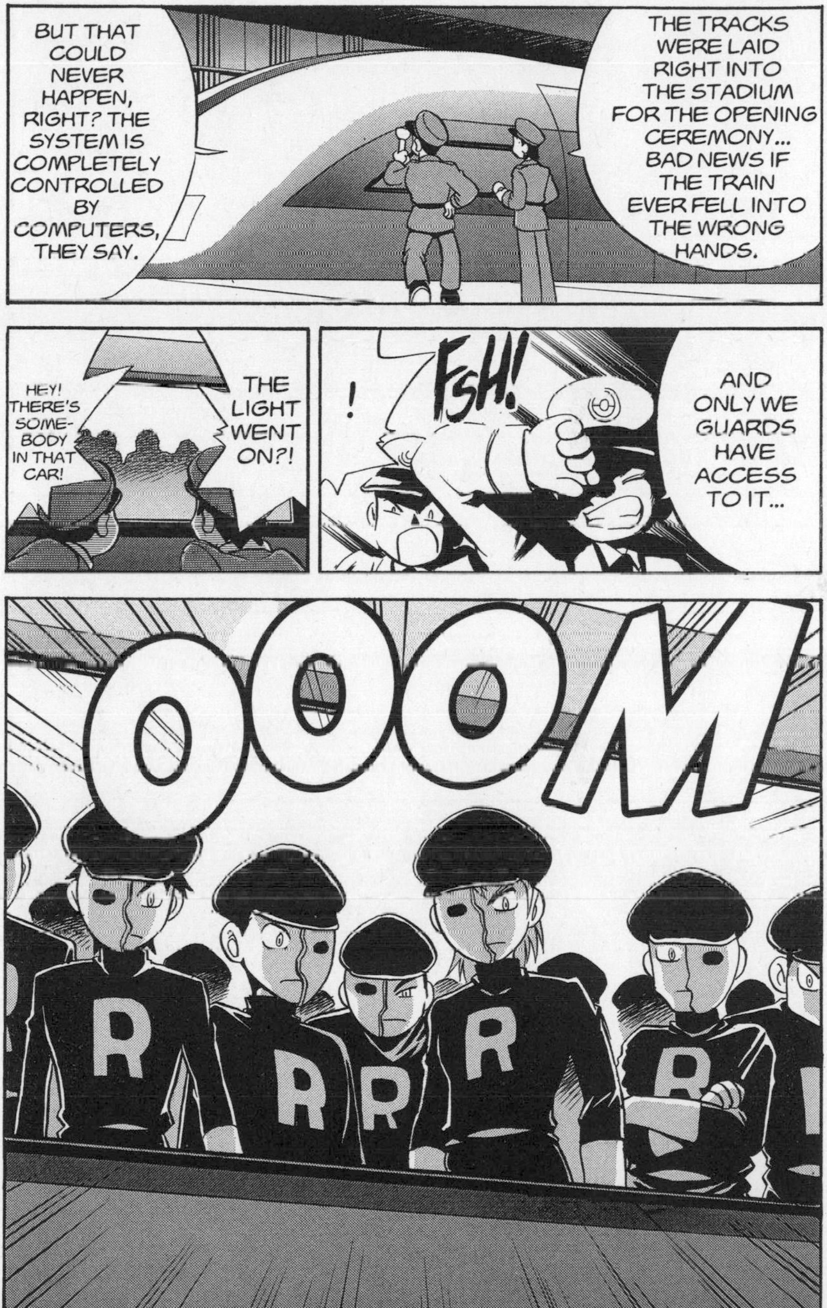
THE TRACKS WERE LAID RIGHT INTO THE STADIUM FOR THE OPENING CEREMONY... BAD NEWS IF THE TRAIN EVER FELL INTO THE WRONG HANDS.
BUT THAT COULD NEVER HAPPEN, RIGHT? THE SYSTEM IS COMPLETELY CONTROLLED BY COMPUTERS, THEY SAY.
AND ONLY WE GUARDS HAVE ACCESS TO IT...
FSH!
!
THE LIGHT WENT ON?!
HEY! THERE'S SOME-BODY IN THAT CAR!
OOOM

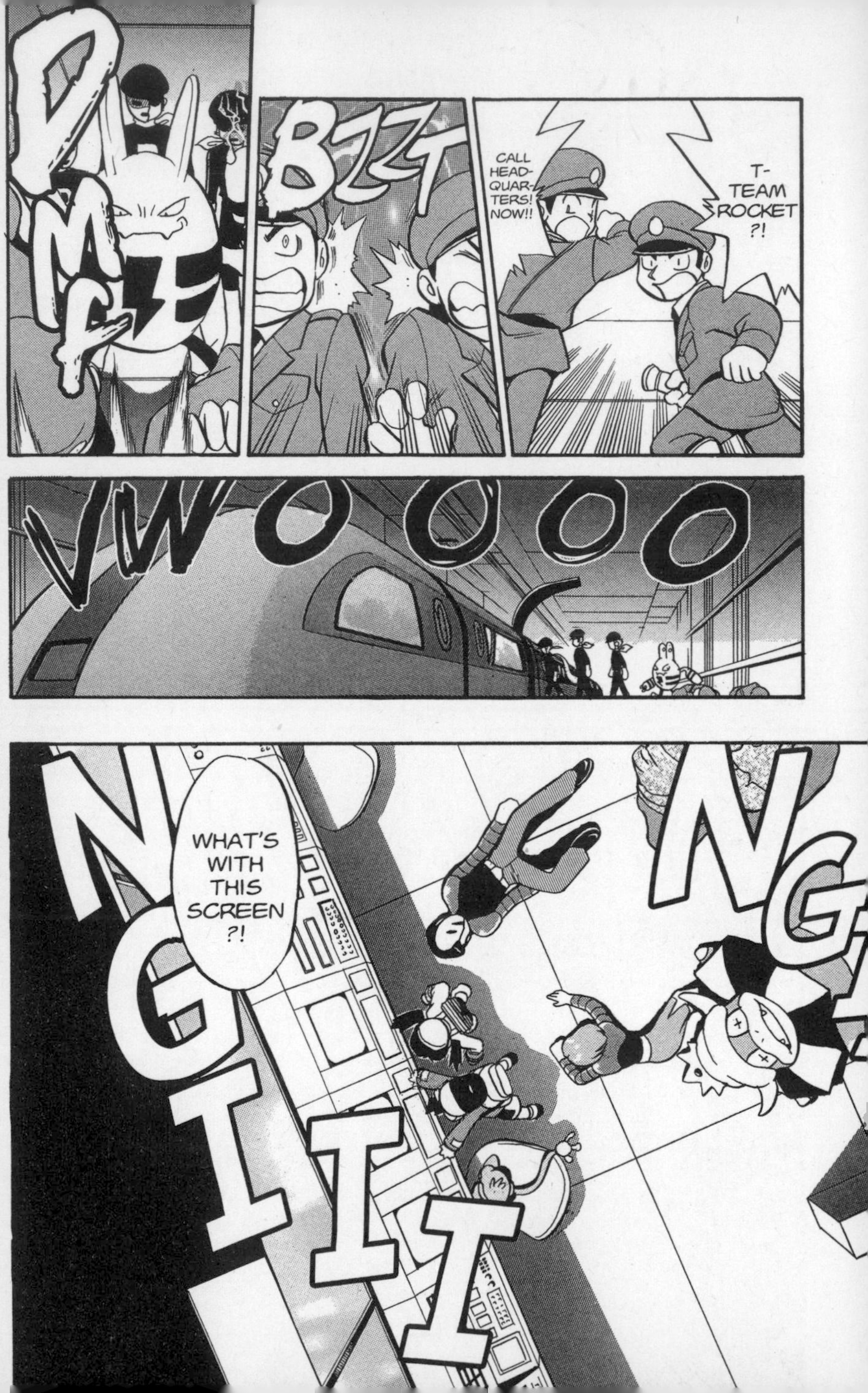
T-TEAM ROCKET ?!
CALL HEAD-QUARTERS! NOW!!
BZZT
VWOOOOO
WHAT'S WITH THIS SCREEN ?!
NGIII

165 Lugia and Ho-Oh on the Loose, Part 1

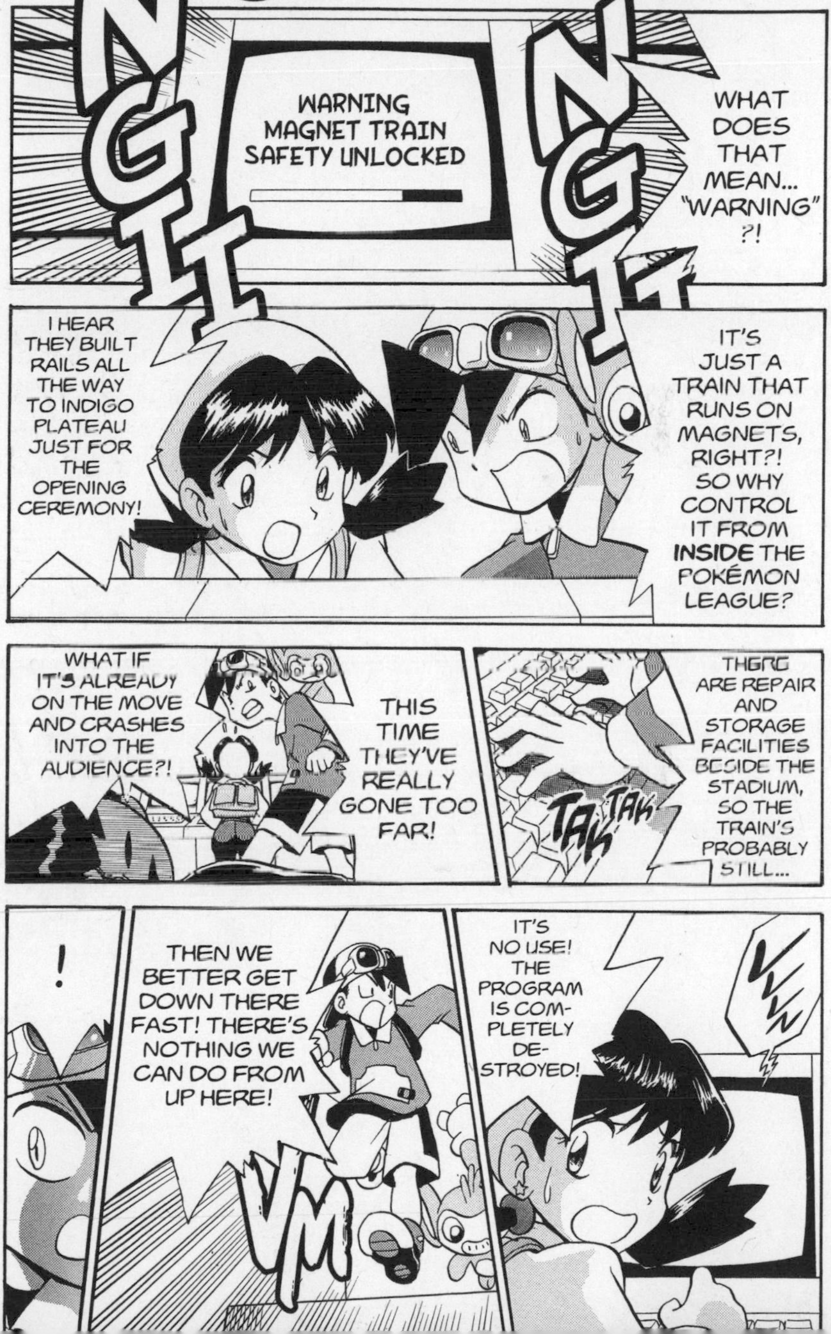
NGIIN
NGIIN
WARNING MAGNET TRAIN SAFETY UNLOCKED
WHAT DOES THAT MEAN... "WARNING"?!
IT'S JUST A TRAIN THAT RUNS ON MAGNETS, RIGHT?! SO WHY CONTROL IT FROM **INSIDE** THE POKÉMON LEAGUE?
I HEAR THEY BUILT RAILS ALL THE WAY TO INDIGO PLATEAU JUST FOR THE OPENING CEREMONY!
THERE ARE REPAIR AND STORAGE FACILITIES BESIDE THE STADIUM, SO THE TRAIN'S PROBABLY STILL...
TAK TAK
THIS TIME THEY'VE REALLY GONE TOO FAR!
WHAT IF IT'S ALREADY ON THE MOVE AND CRASHES INTO THE AUDIENCE?!
VVVN
IT'S NO USE! THE PROGRAM IS COMPLETELY DESTROYED!
THEN WE BETTER GET DOWN THERE FAST! THERE'S NOTHING WE CAN DO FROM UP HERE!
VM
!

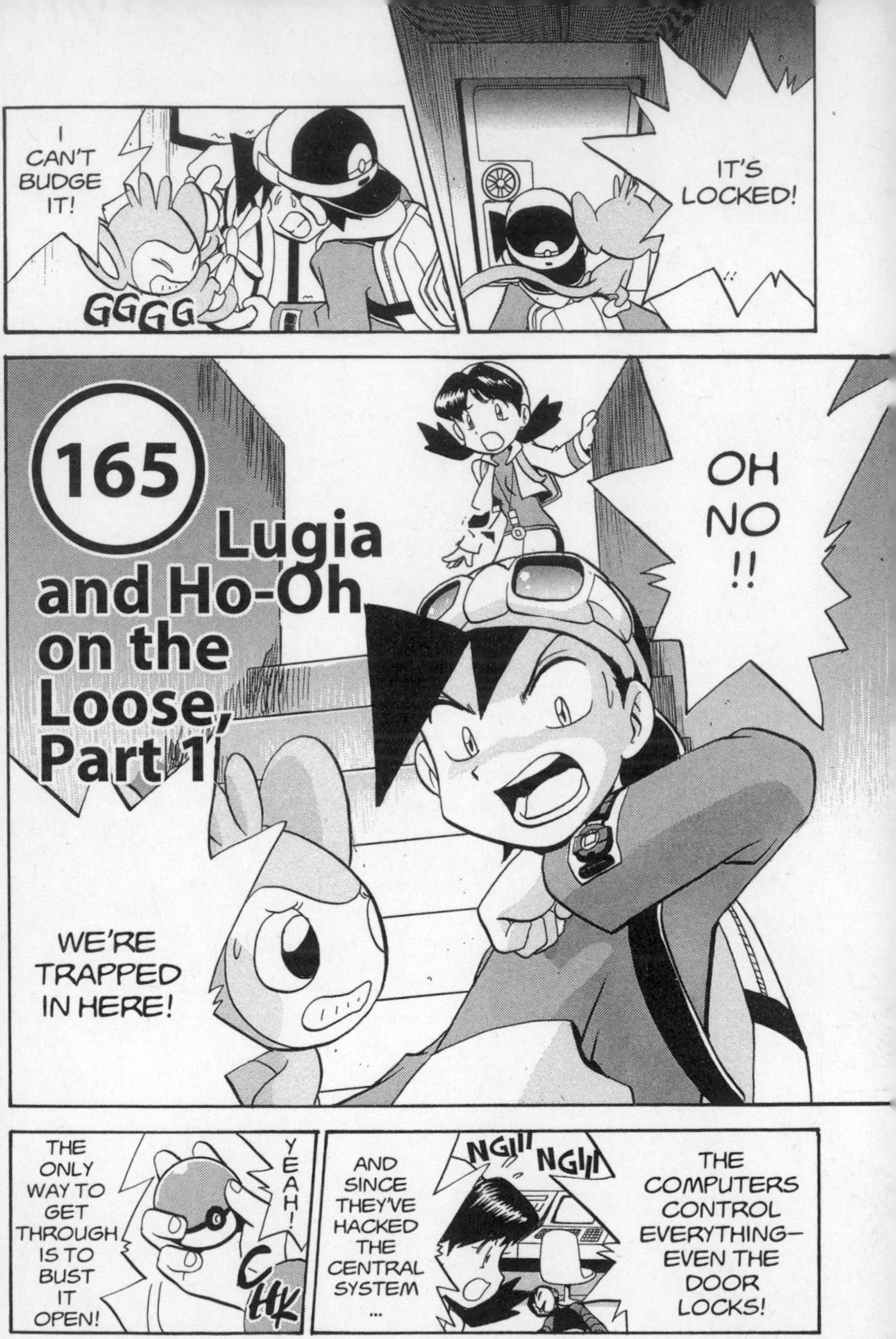
IT'S LOCKED!
I CAN'T BUDGE IT!
GGGG
165
Lugia and Ho-Oh on the Loose, Part 1
OH NO !!
WE'RE TRAPPED IN HERE!
THE COMPUTERS CONTROL EVERYTHING— EVEN THE DOOR LOCKS!
NGH NGH
AND SINCE THEY'VE HACKED THE CENTRAL SYSTEM ...
YEAH!
THE ONLY WAY TO GET THROUGH IS TO BUST IT OPEN!
CHK

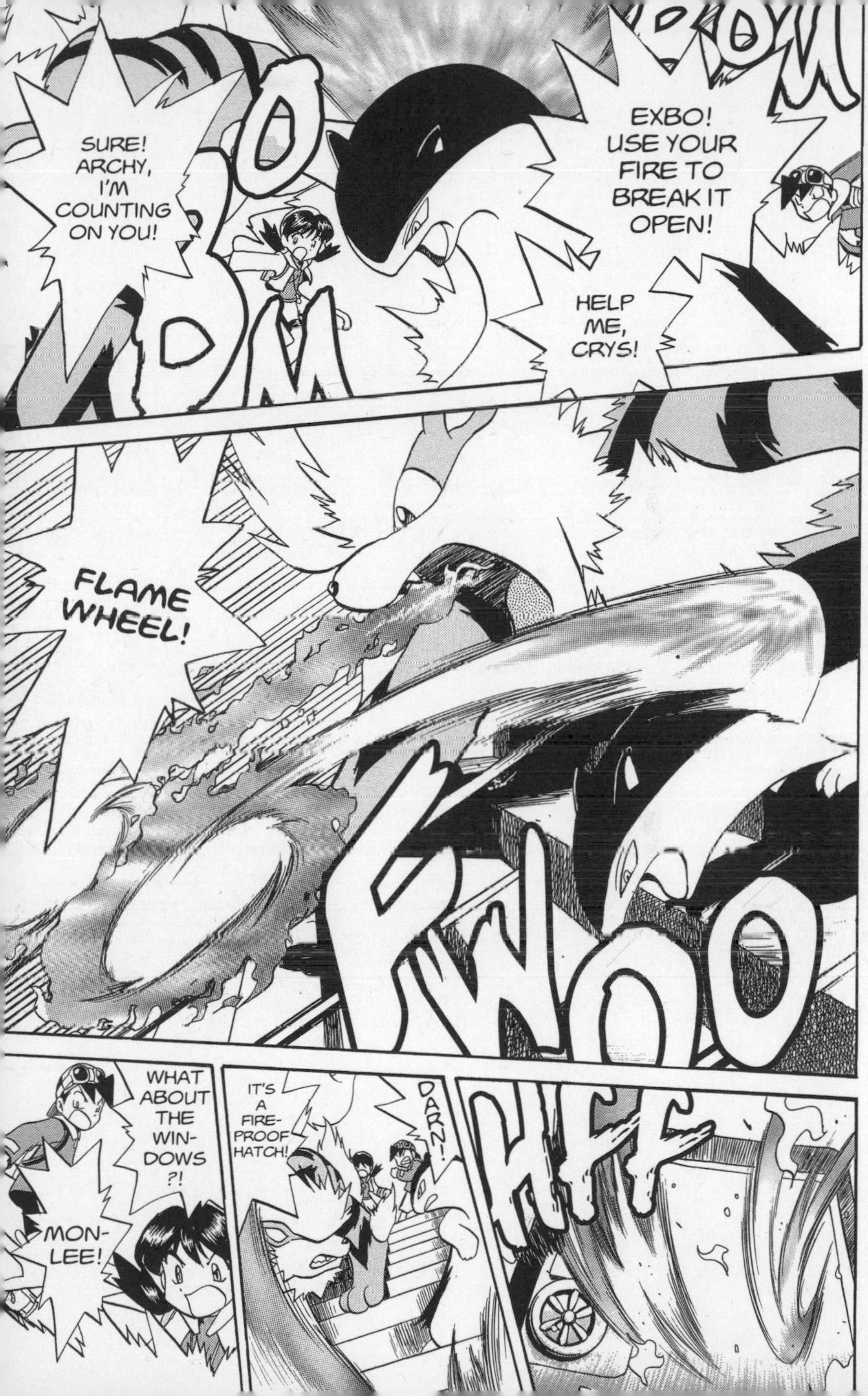
EXBO! USE YOUR FIRE TO BREAK IT OPEN!
HELP ME, CRYS!
SURE! ARCHY, I'M COUNTING ON YOU!
FLAME WHEEL!
FWOO
DARN!
IT'S A FIRE-PROOF HATCH!
WHAT ABOUT THE WIN-DOWS ?!
MON-LEE!

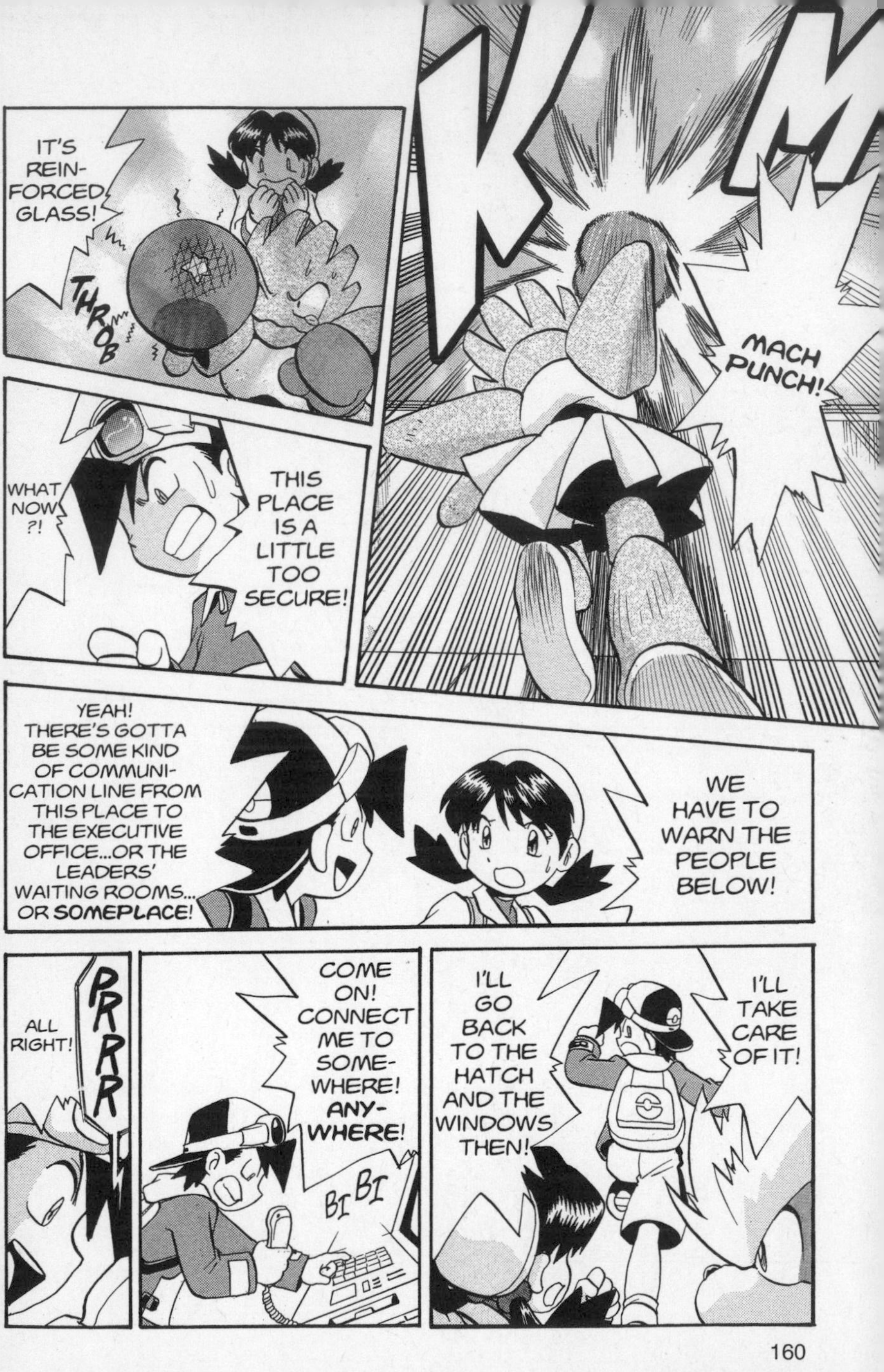
MACH PUNCH!
IT'S REIN-FORCED GLASS!
THROB
THIS PLACE IS A LITTLE TOO SECURE!
WHAT NOW?!
WE HAVE TO WARN THE PEOPLE BELOW!
YEAH! THERE'S GOTTA BE SOME KIND OF COMMUNI-CATION LINE FROM THIS PLACE TO THE EXECUTIVE OFFICE...OR THE LEADERS' WAITING ROOMS... OR **SOMEPLACE**!
I'LL TAKE CARE OF IT!
I'LL GO BACK TO THE HATCH AND THE WINDOWS THEN!
COME ON! CONNECT ME TO SOME-WHERE! **ANY-WHERE**!
BI BI
PRRRR
ALL RIGHT!

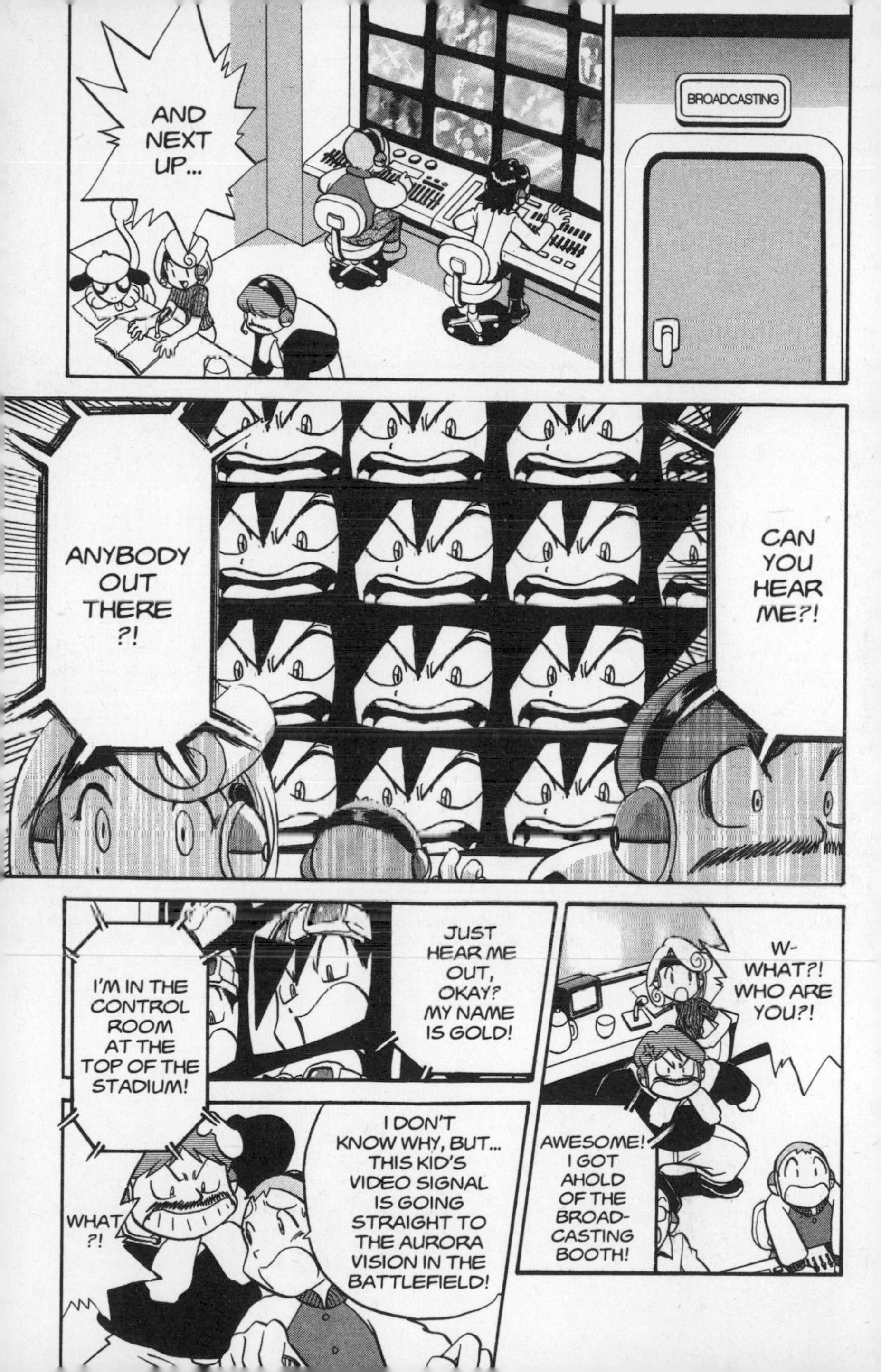
BROADCASTING
AND NEXT UP...
CAN YOU HEAR ME?!
ANYBODY OUT THERE ?!
W-WHAT?! WHO ARE YOU?!
AWESOME! I GOT AHOLD OF THE BROAD-CASTING BOOTH!
JUST HEAR ME OUT, OKAY? MY NAME IS GOLD!
I'M IN THE CONTROL ROOM AT THE TOP OF THE STADIUM!
I DON'T KNOW WHY, BUT... THIS KID'S VIDEO SIGNAL IS GOING STRAIGHT TO THE AURORA VISION IN THE BATTLEFIELD!
WHAT ?!

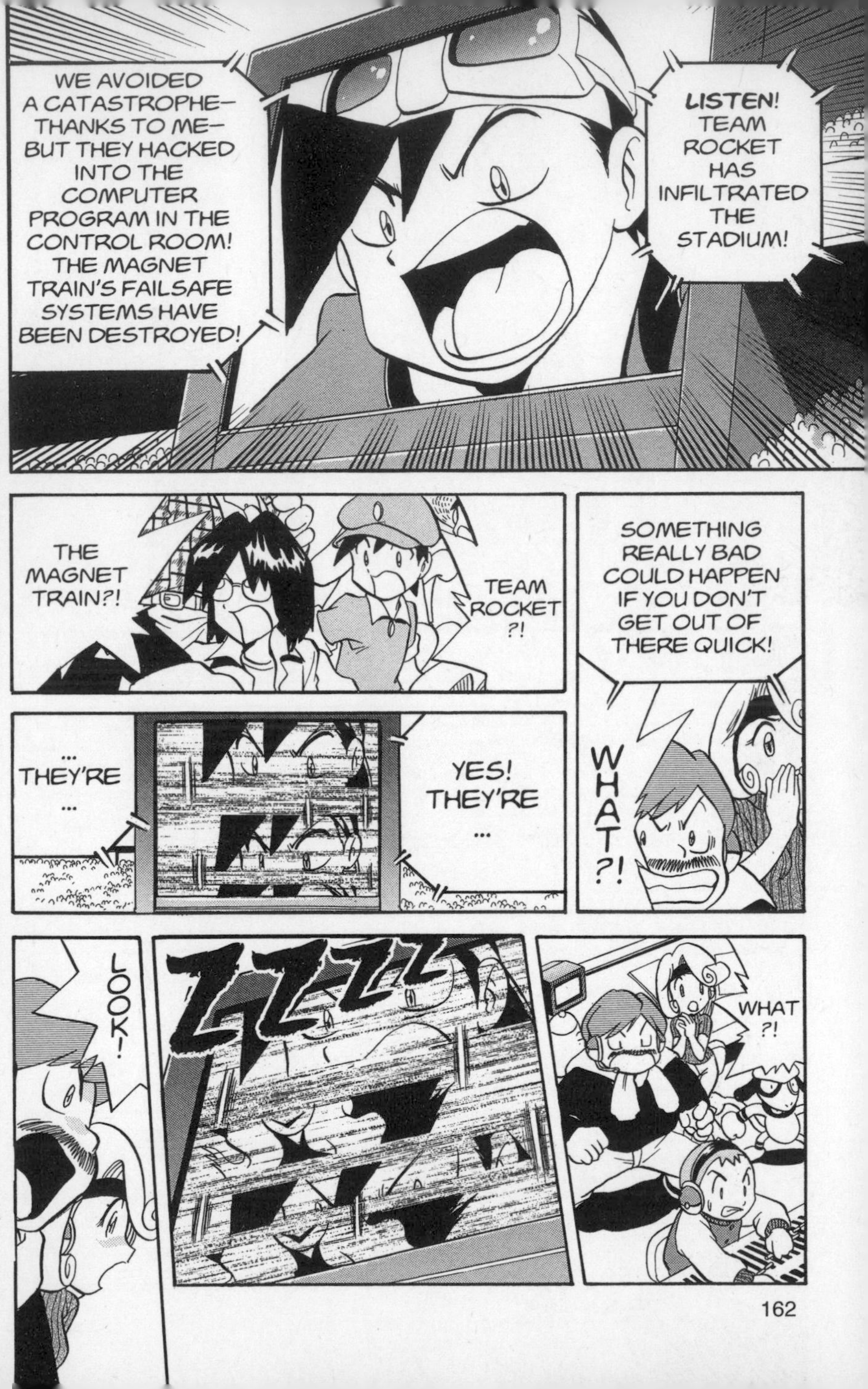
LISTEN! TEAM ROCKET HAS INFILTRATED THE STADIUM!
WE AVOIDED A CATASTROPHE—THANKS TO ME—BUT THEY HACKED INTO THE COMPUTER PROGRAM IN THE CONTROL ROOM! THE MAGNET TRAIN'S FAILSAFE SYSTEMS HAVE BEEN DESTROYED!
SOMETHING REALLY BAD COULD HAPPEN IF YOU DON'T GET OUT OF THERE QUICK!
WHAT?!
TEAM ROCKET ?!
THE MAGNET TRAIN?!
YES! THEY'RE ...
... THEY'RE ...
WHAT ?!
LOOK!

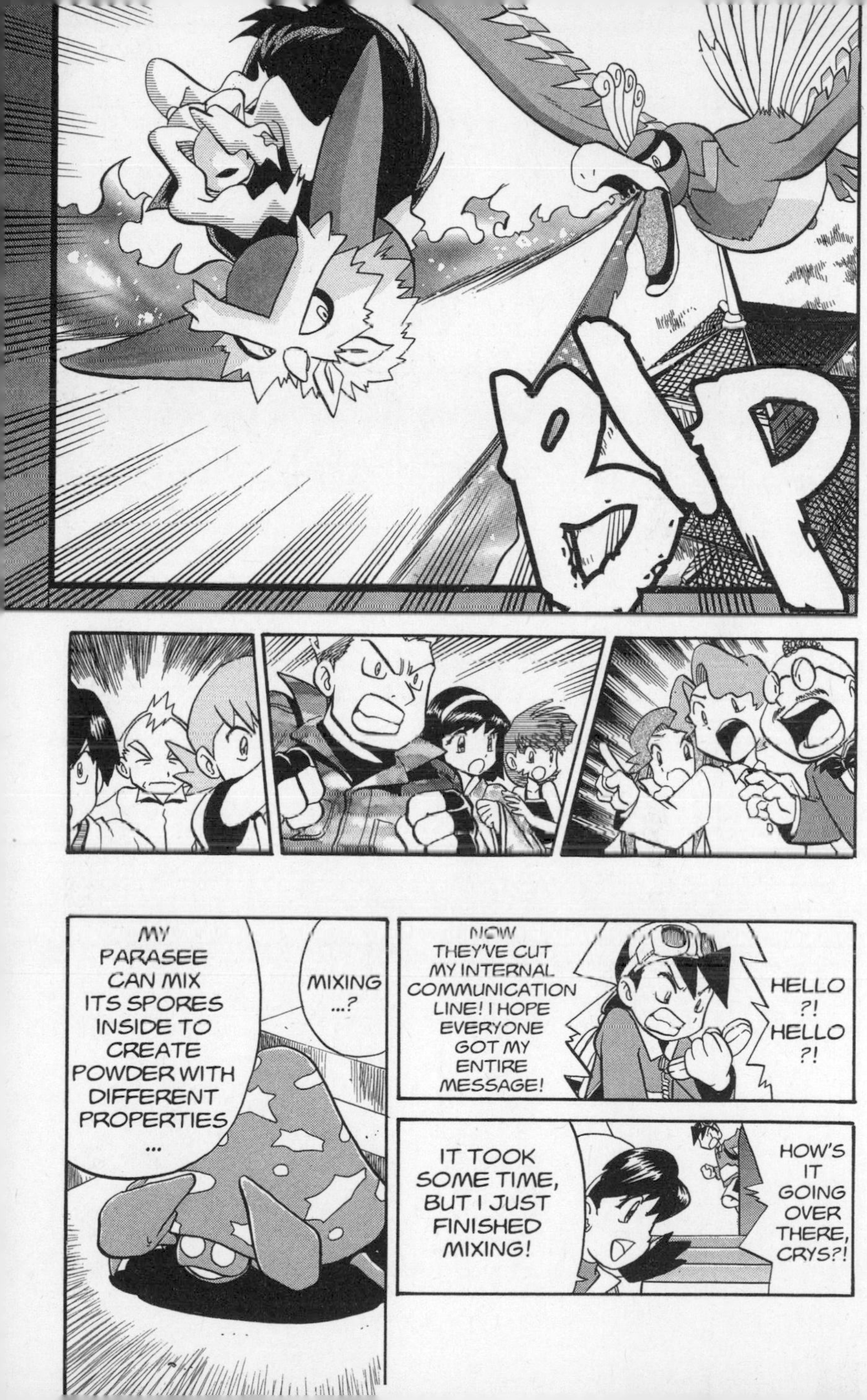
RIP
HELLO ?! HELLO ?!
NOW THEY'VE CUT MY INTERNAL COMMUNICATION LINE! I HOPE EVERYONE GOT MY ENTIRE MESSAGE!
HOW'S IT GOING OVER THERE, CRYS?!
IT TOOK SOME TIME, BUT I JUST FINISHED MIXING!
MIXING ...?
MY PARASEE CAN MIX ITS SPORES INSIDE TO CREATE POWDER WITH DIFFERENT PROPERTIES ...

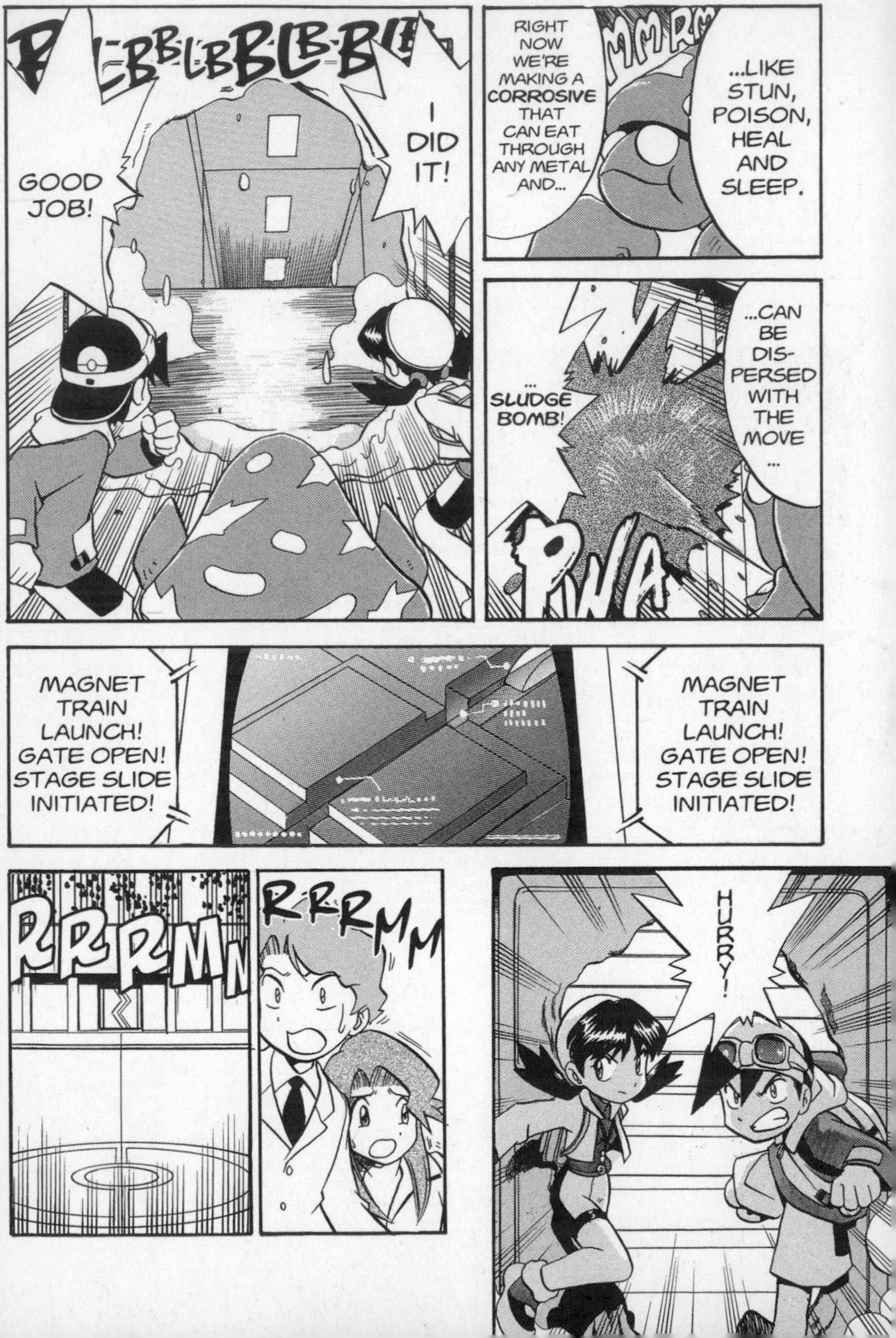
...LIKE STUN, POISON, HEAL AND SLEEP.
MMRM
RIGHT NOW WE'RE MAKING A **CORROSIVE** THAT CAN EAT THROUGH ANY METAL AND...
...CAN BE DIS-PERSED WITH THE MOVE ...
... SLUDGE BOMB!
PWA
I DID IT!
BLBBLBBLBBLB
GOOD JOB!
MAGNET TRAIN LAUNCH! GATE OPEN! STAGE SLIDE INITIATED!
MAGNET TRAIN LAUNCH! GATE OPEN! STAGE SLIDE INITIATED!
HURRY!
R-R-RMM
RRRMM

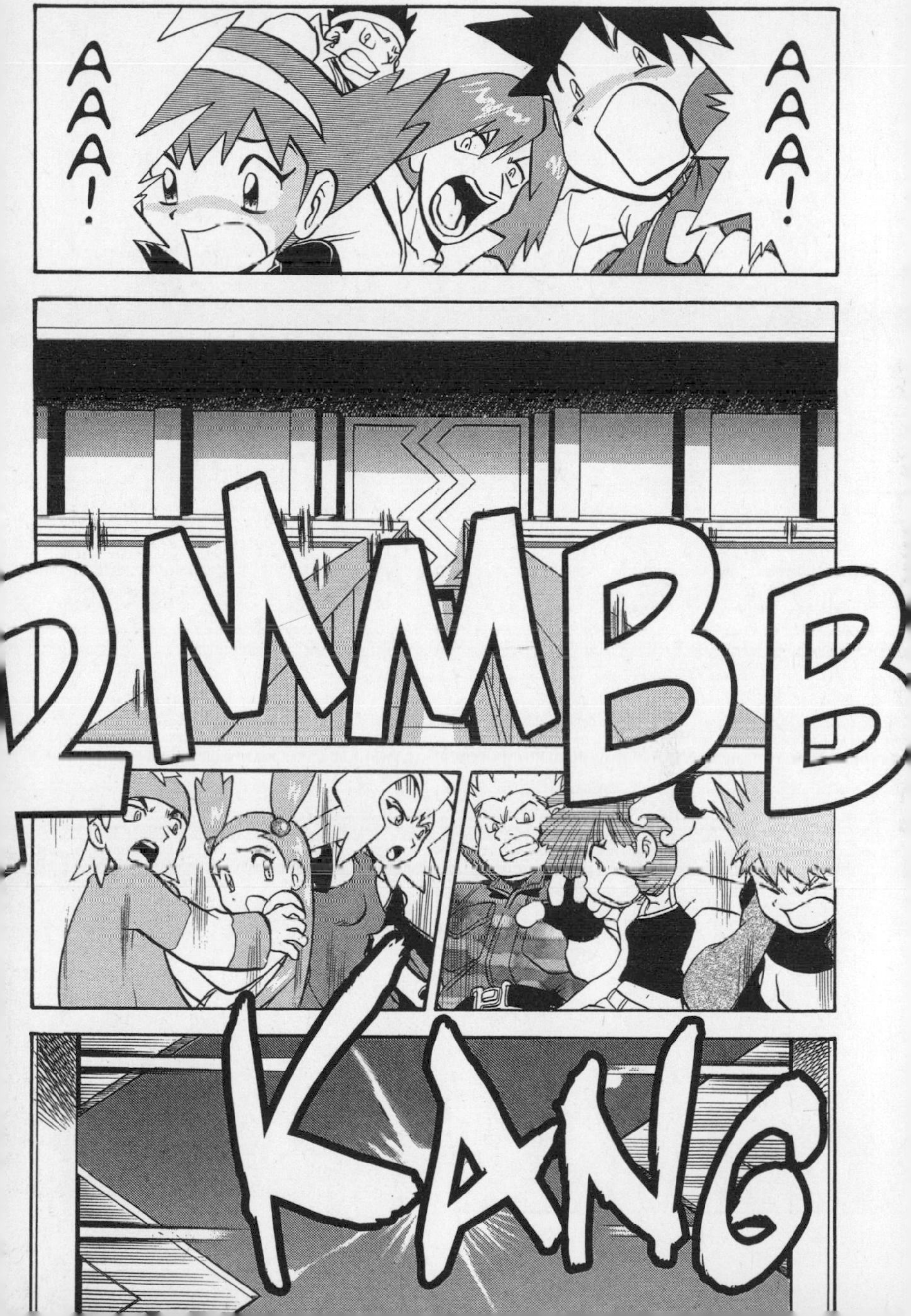
AAA!
AAA!
MMBB
KANG

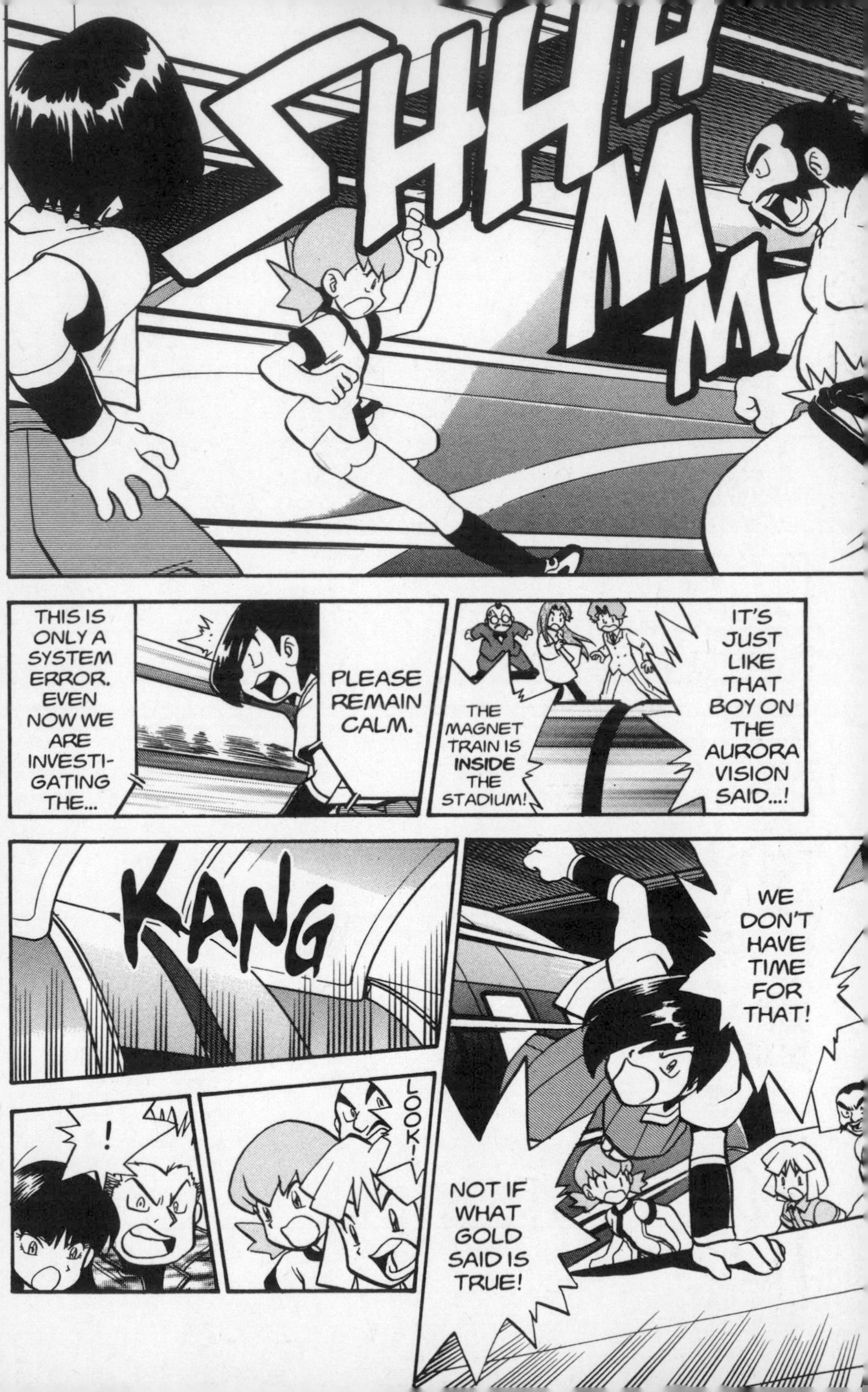
SHHMM
THE MAGNET TRAIN IS INSIDE THE STADIUM!
IT'S JUST LIKE THAT BOY ON THE AURORA VISION SAID...!
PLEASE REMAIN CALM.
THIS IS ONLY A SYSTEM ERROR. EVEN NOW WE ARE INVESTIGATING THE...
WE DON'T HAVE TIME FOR THAT!
NOT IF WHAT GOLD SAID IS TRUE!
KANG
LOOK!
!

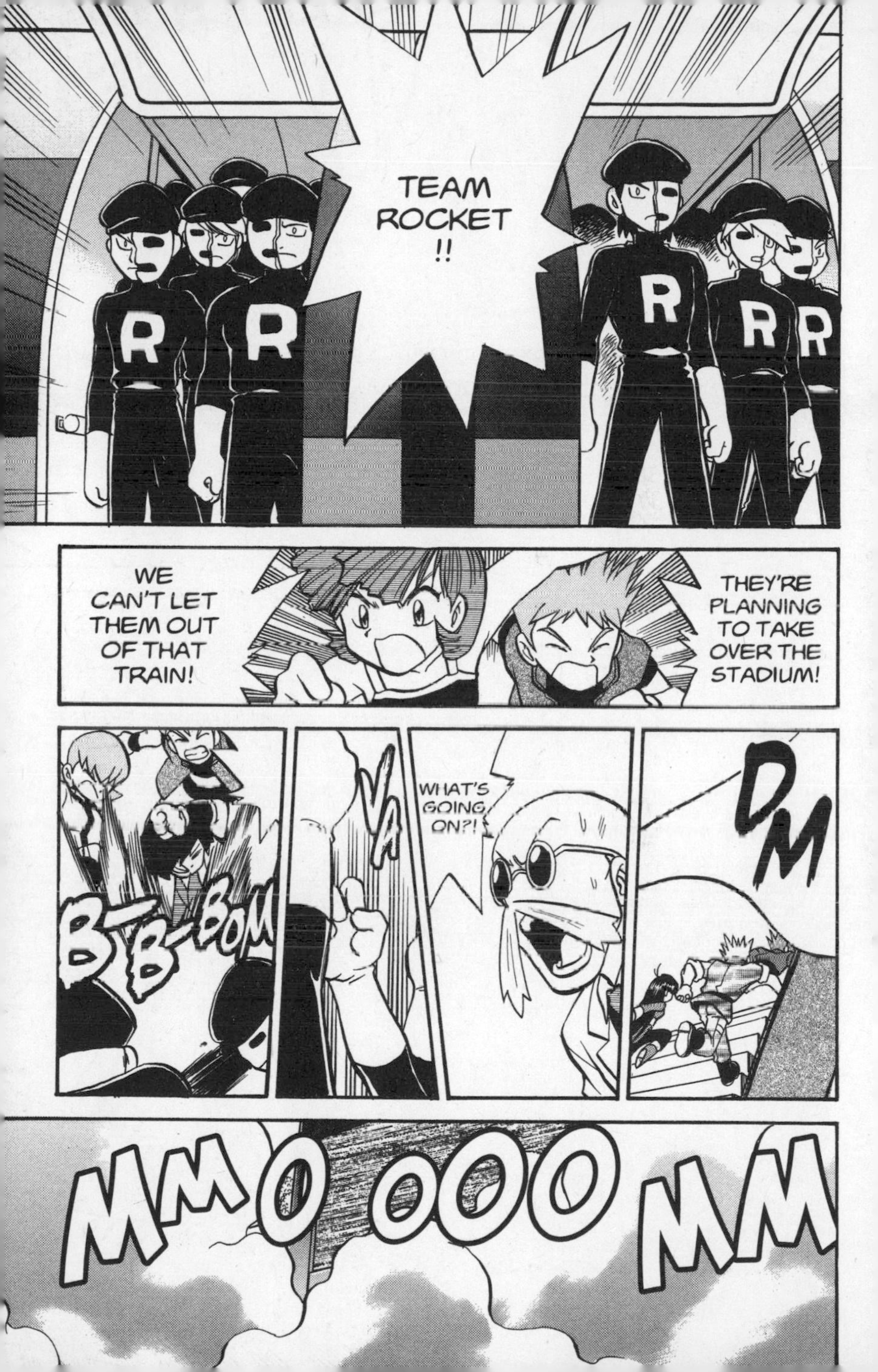
TEAM ROCKET !!
THEY'RE PLANNING TO TAKE OVER THE STADIUM!
WE CAN'T LET THEM OUT OF THAT TRAIN!
DM
WHAT'S GOING ON?!
VA
B-B-BOM
MMOOOOMM

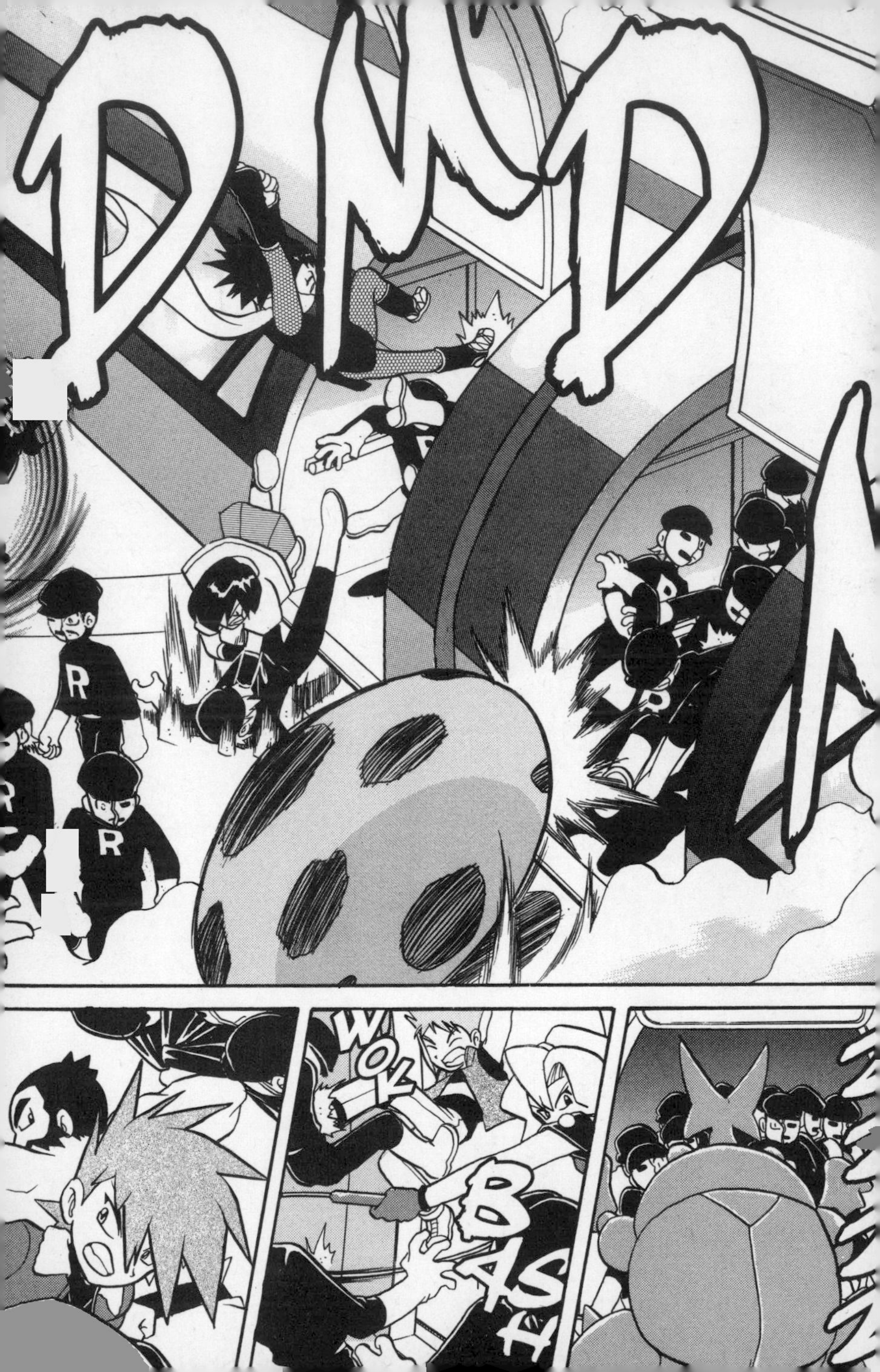
WOK
BASH

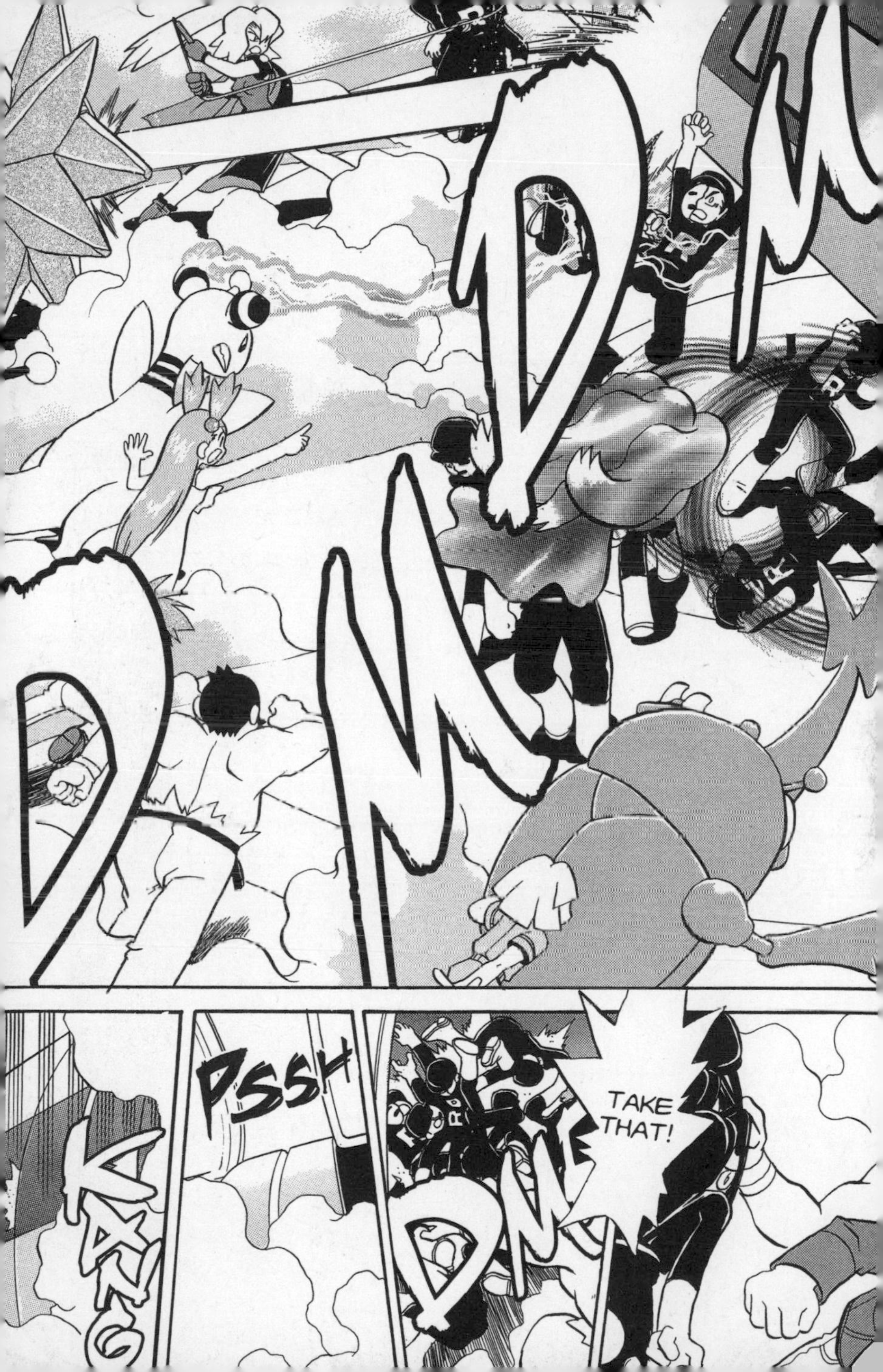
TAKE THAT!
PSSH

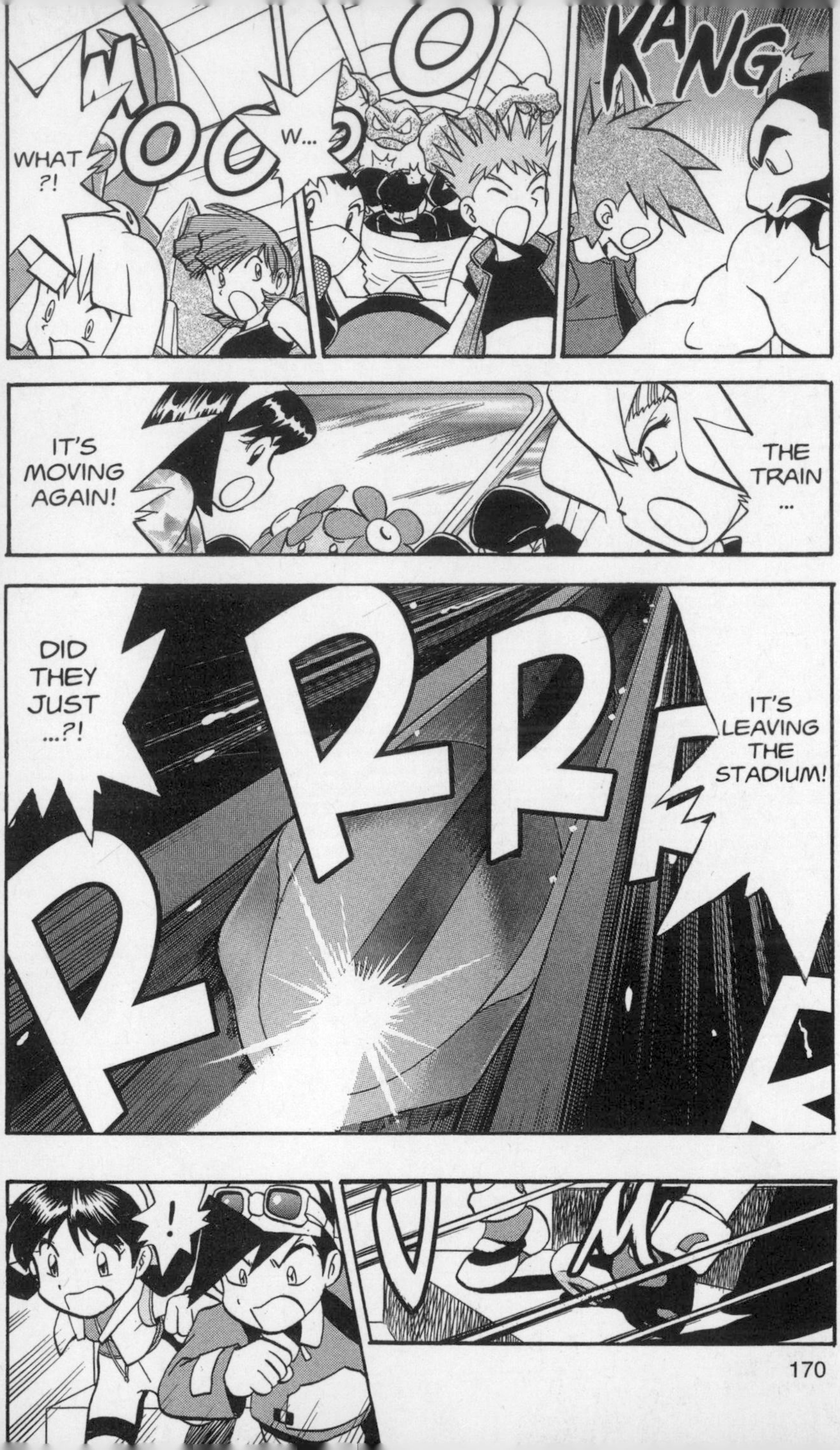
KANG
W...
WHAT ?!
THE TRAIN ...
IT'S MOVING AGAIN!
IT'S LEAVING THE STADIUM!
DID THEY JUST ...?!
!

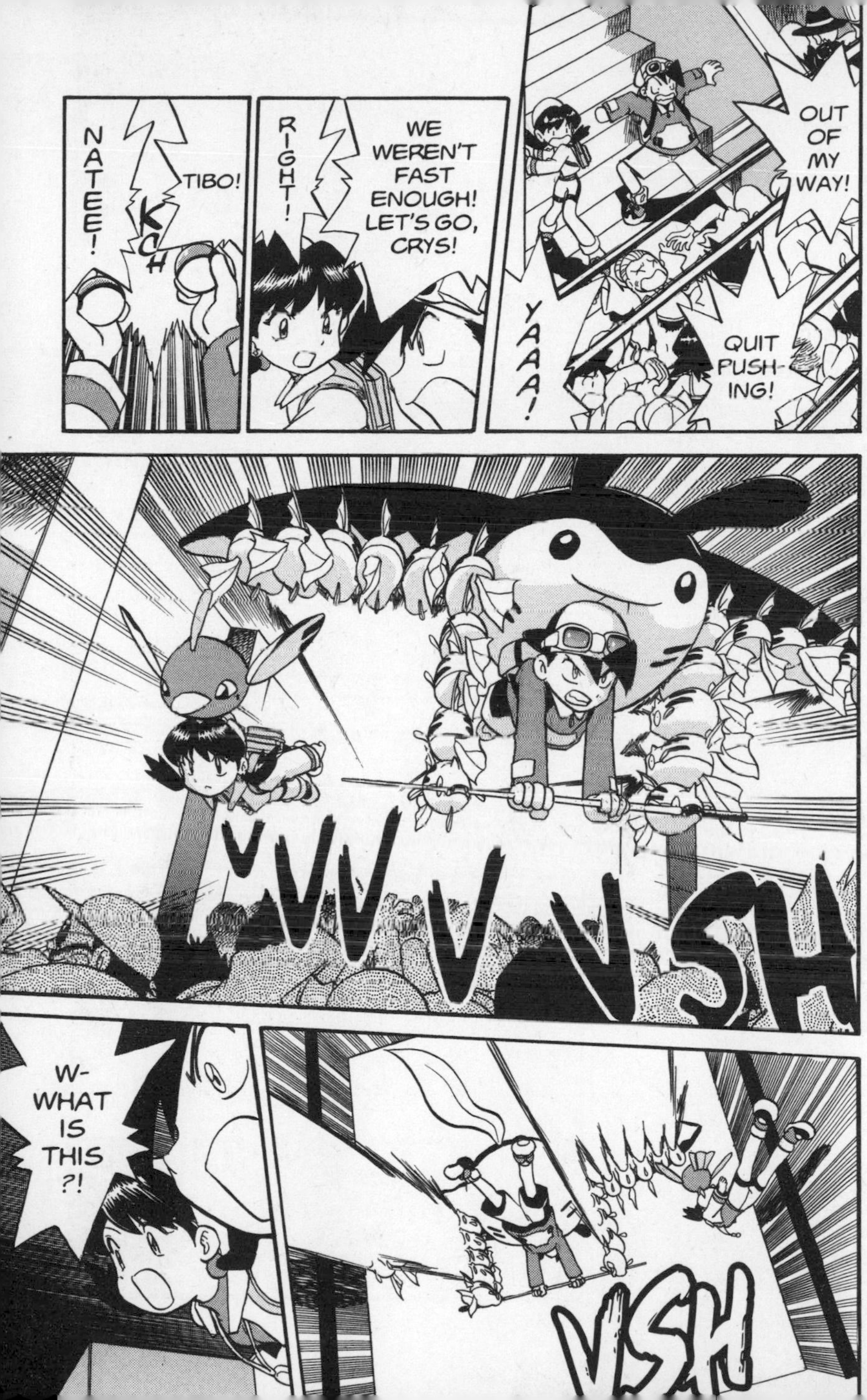
OUT OF MY WAY!
YAAAA!
QUIT PUSHING!
WE WEREN'T FAST ENOUGH! LET'S GO, CRYS!
RIGHT!
TIBO!
KCH
NATEE!
VVVVVSH
VSH
W-WHAT IS THIS?!

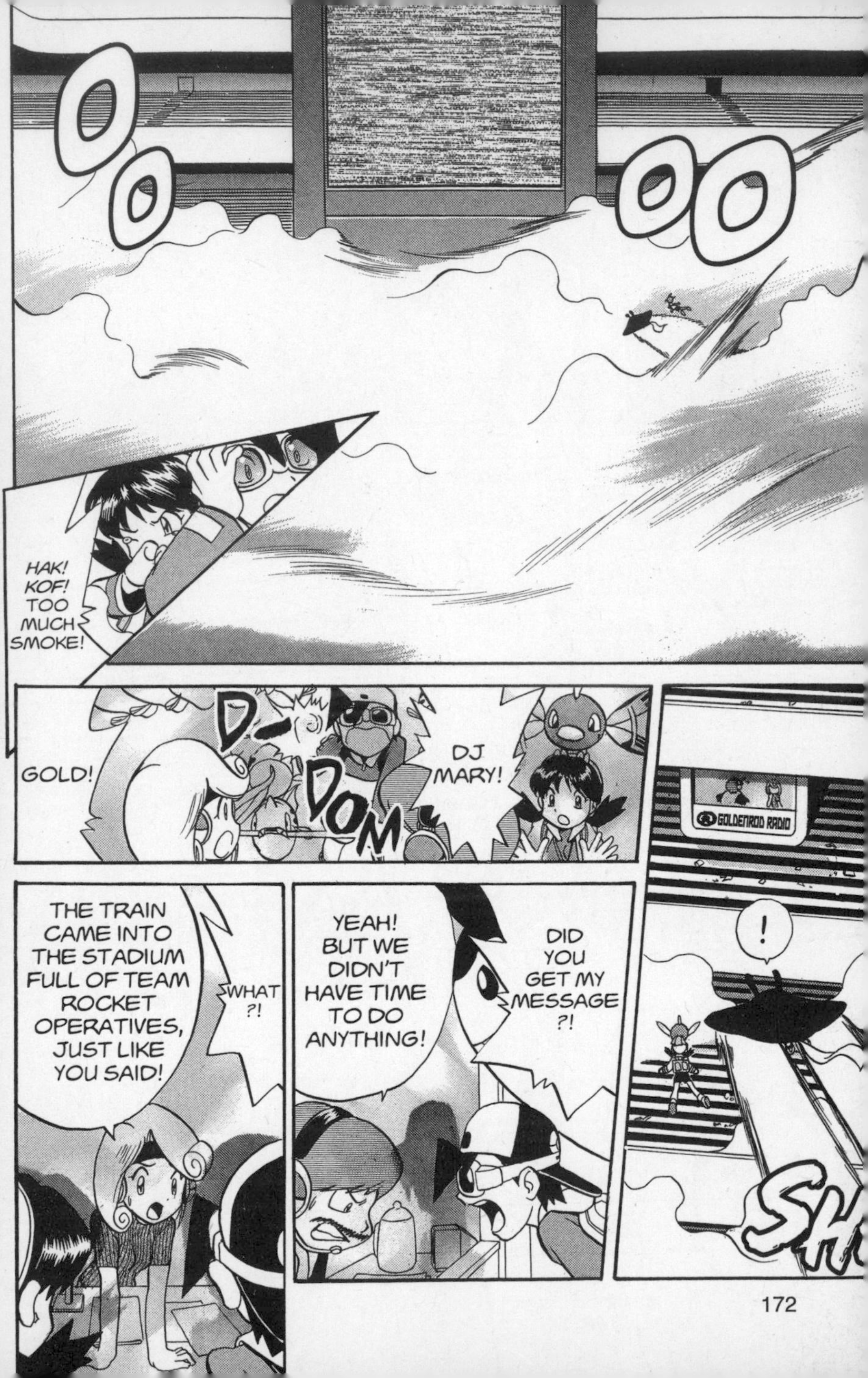
OO
OO
HAK! KOF! TOO MUCH SMOKE!
GOLDENROD RADIO
!
SH
DJ MARY!
D-DOM
GOLD!
DID YOU GET MY MESSAGE?!
YEAH! BUT WE DIDN'T HAVE TIME TO DO ANYTHING!
WHAT?!
THE TRAIN CAME INTO THE STADIUM FULL OF TEAM ROCKET OPERATIVES, JUST LIKE YOU SAID!

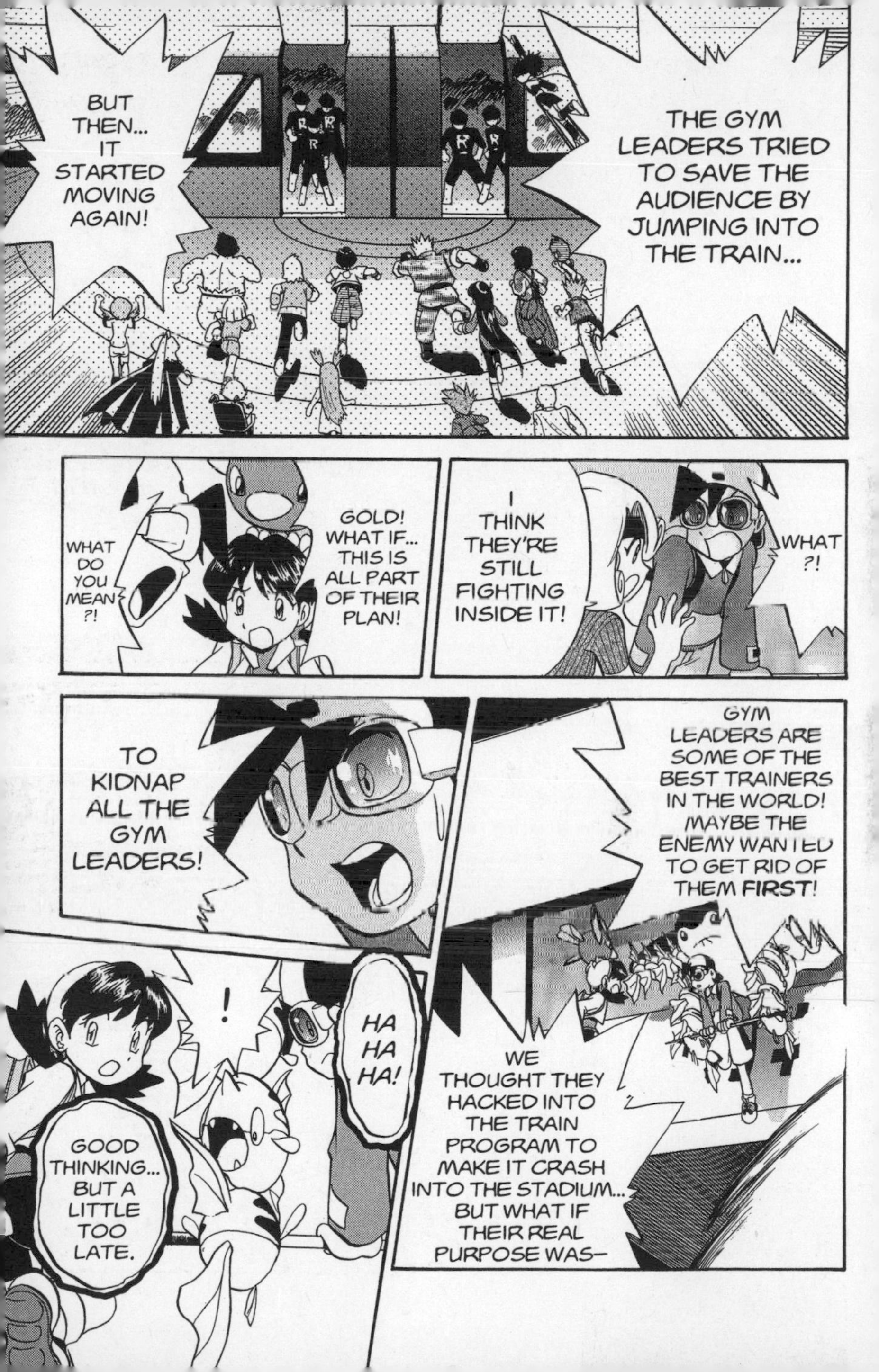
THE GYM LEADERS TRIED TO SAVE THE AUDIENCE BY JUMPING INTO THE TRAIN...
BUT THEN... IT STARTED MOVING AGAIN!
WHAT?!
I THINK THEY'RE STILL FIGHTING INSIDE IT!
GOLD! WHAT IF... THIS IS ALL PART OF THEIR PLAN!
WHAT DO YOU MEAN?!
GYM LEADERS ARE SOME OF THE BEST TRAINERS IN THE WORLD! MAYBE THE ENEMY WANTED TO GET RID OF THEM FIRST!
WE THOUGHT THEY HACKED INTO THE TRAIN PROGRAM TO MAKE IT CRASH INTO THE STADIUM... BUT WHAT IF THEIR REAL PURPOSE WAS—
TO KIDNAP ALL THE GYM LEADERS!
HA HA HA!
!
GOOD THINKING... BUT A LITTLE TOO LATE.

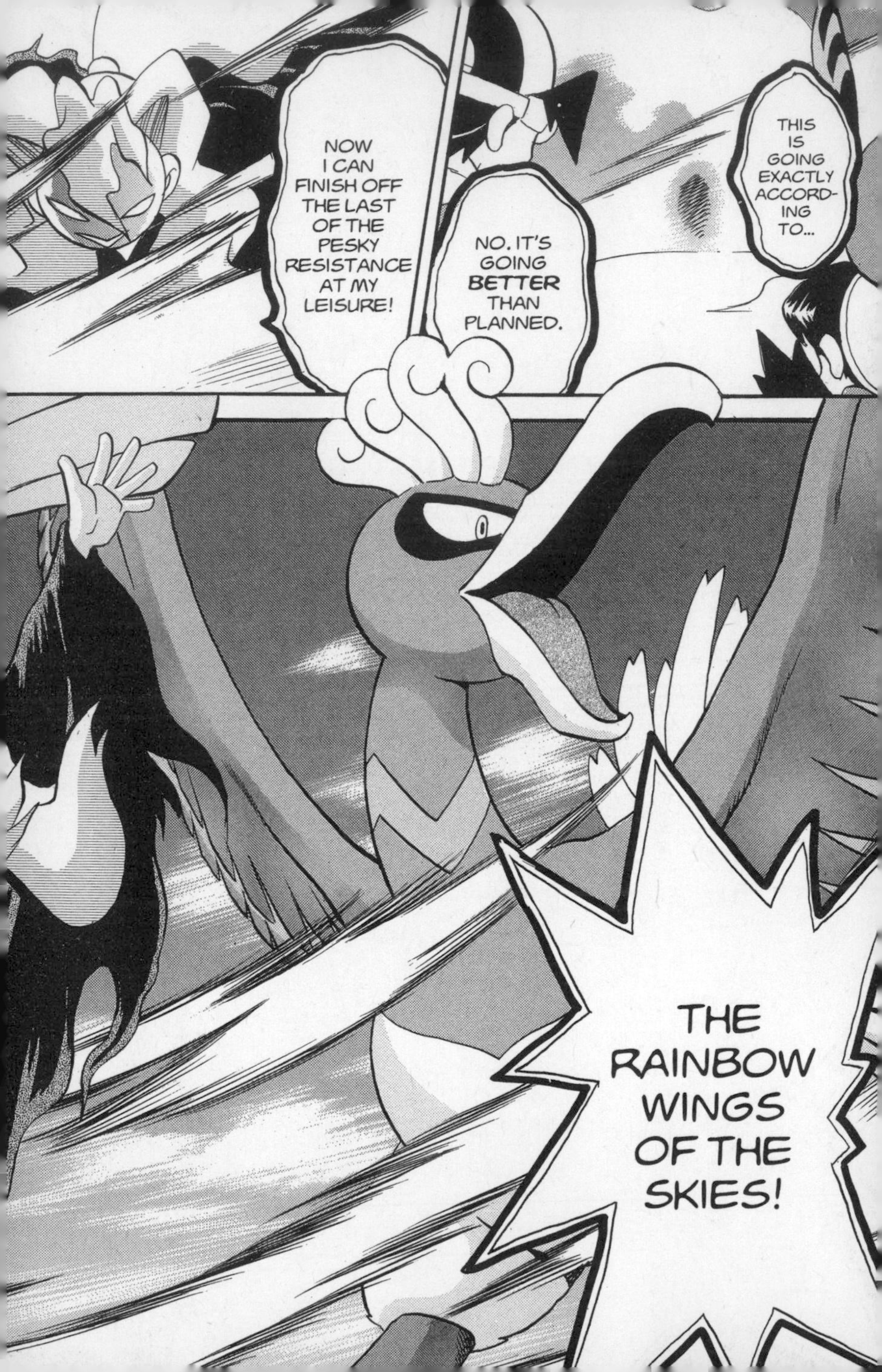
THIS IS GOING EXACTLY ACCORD-ING TO...
NO. IT'S GOING **BETTER** THAN PLANNED.
NOW I CAN FINISH OFF THE LAST OF THE PESKY RESISTANCE AT MY LEISURE!
THE RAINBOW WINGS OF THE SKIES!

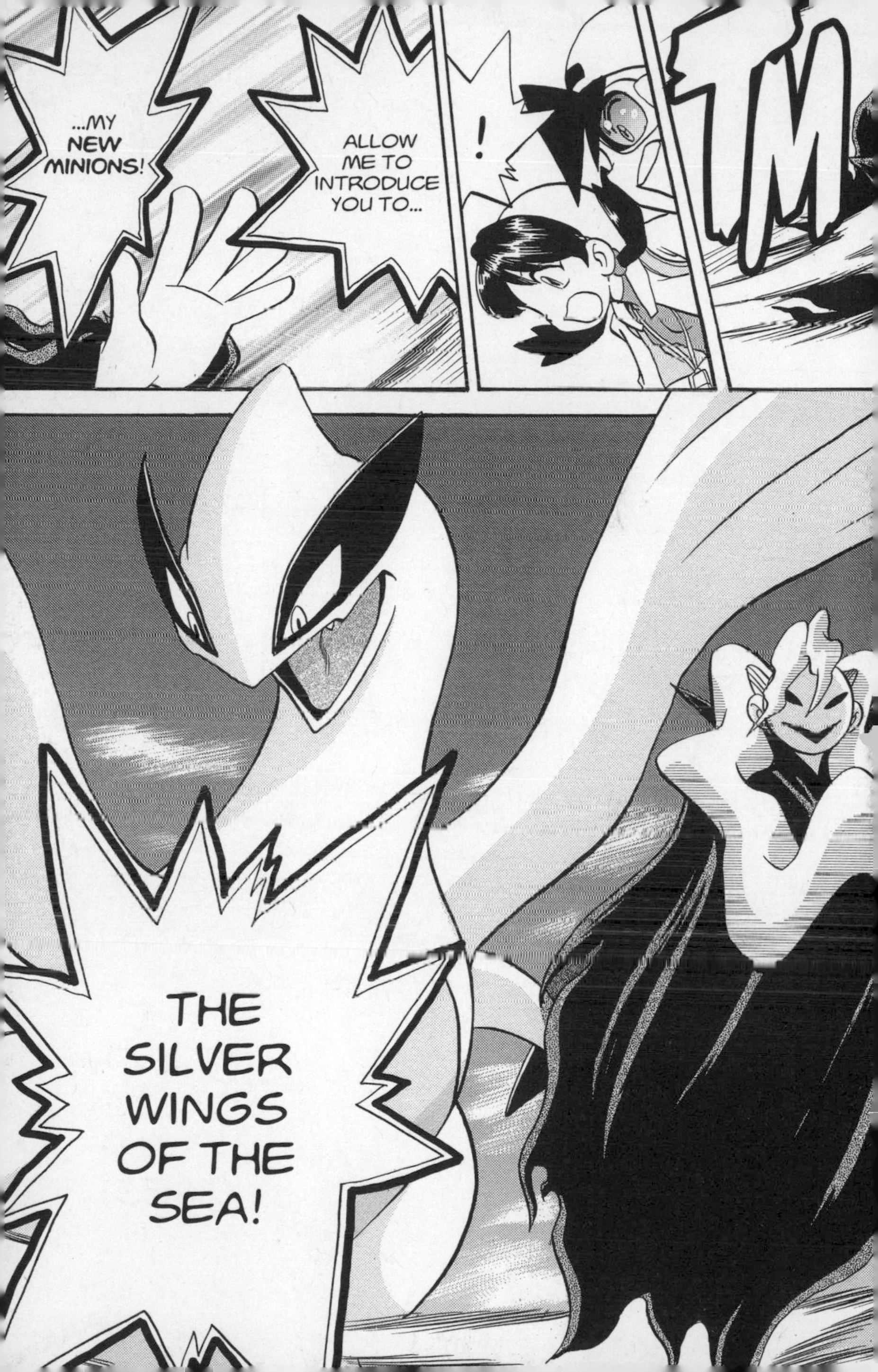
!
ALLOW ME TO INTRODUCE YOU TO...
...MY NEW MINIONS!
THE SILVER WINGS OF THE SEA!

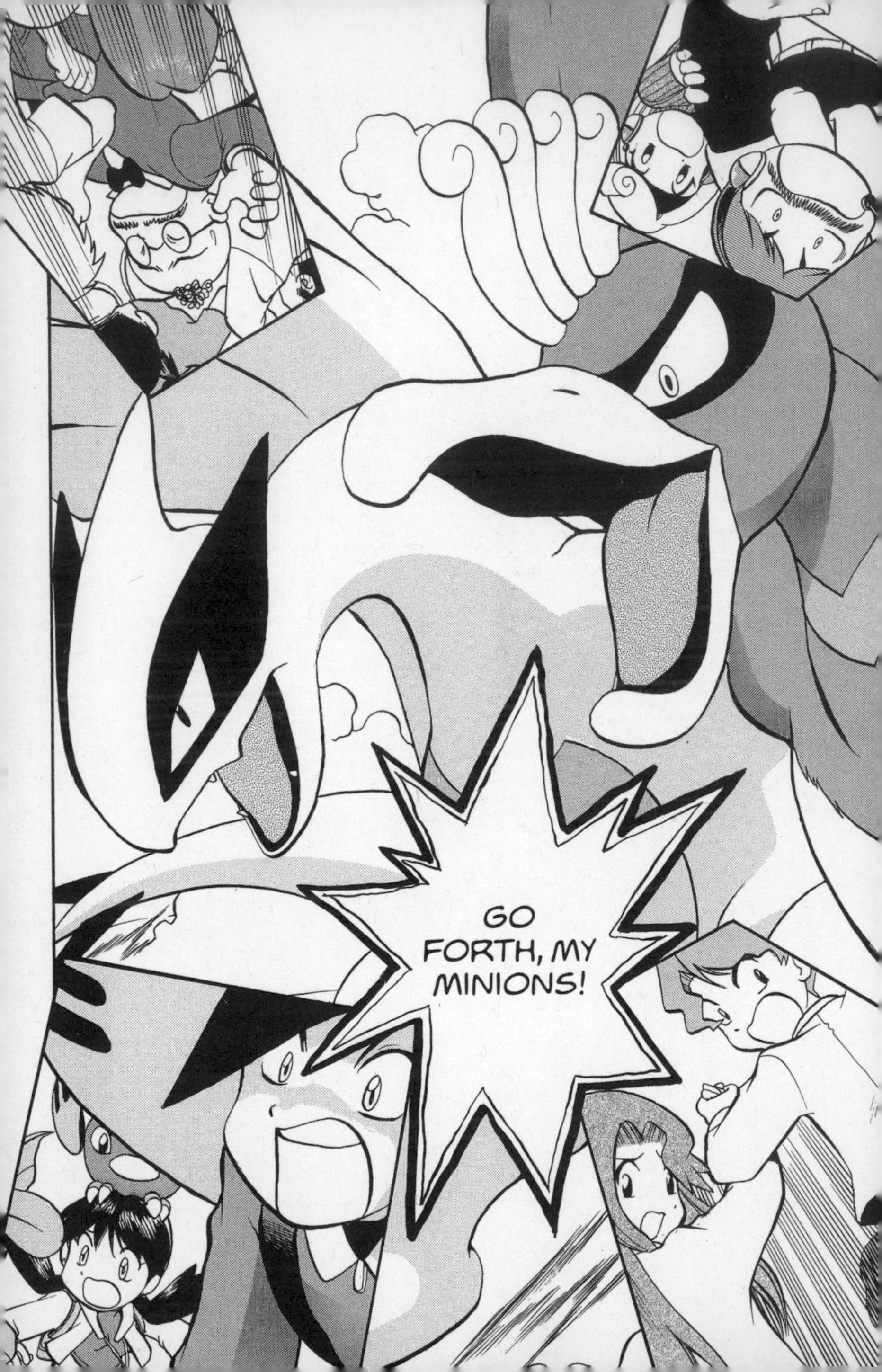
GO FORTH, MY MINIONS!

166 Lugia and Ho-Oh on the Loose, Part 2

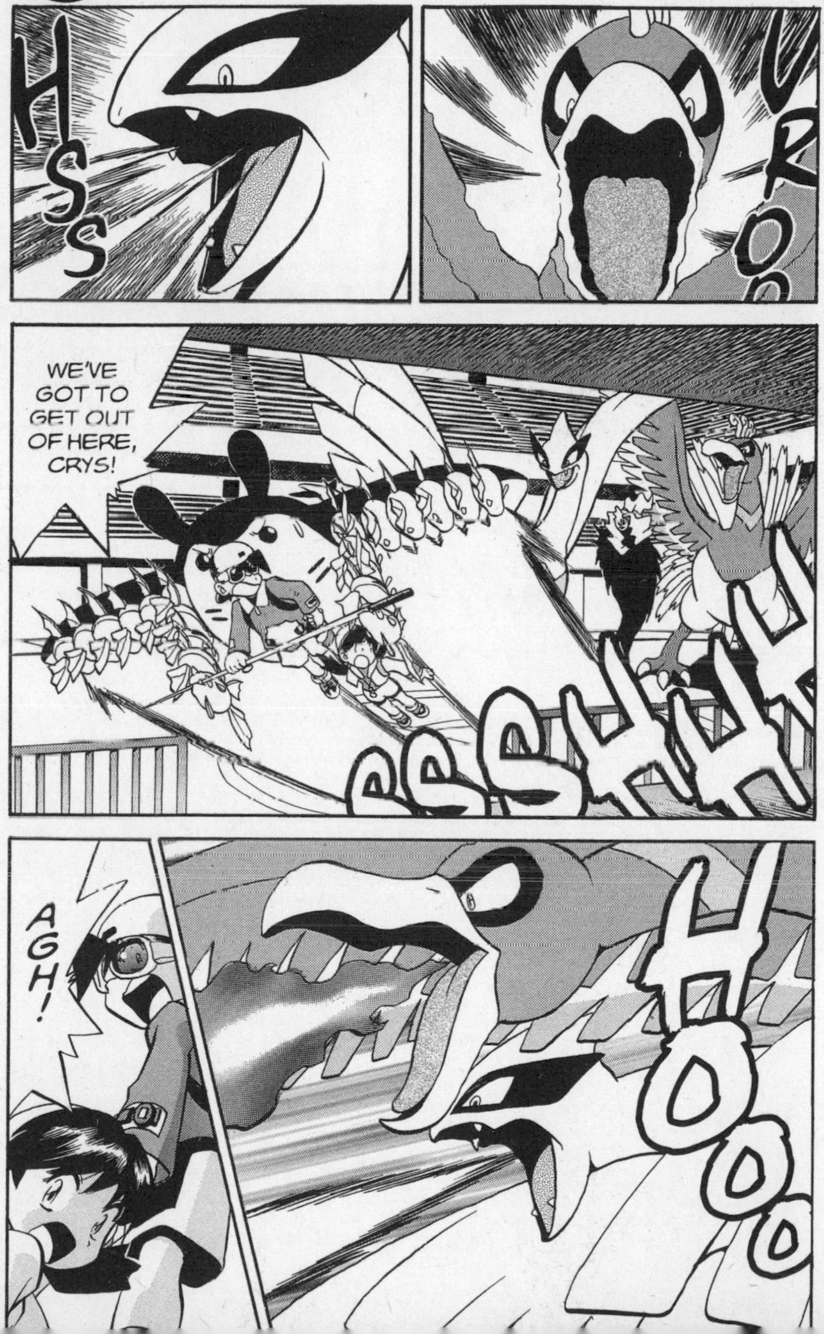
WE'VE GOT TO GET OUT OF HERE, CRYS!
HOOOO
AGH!

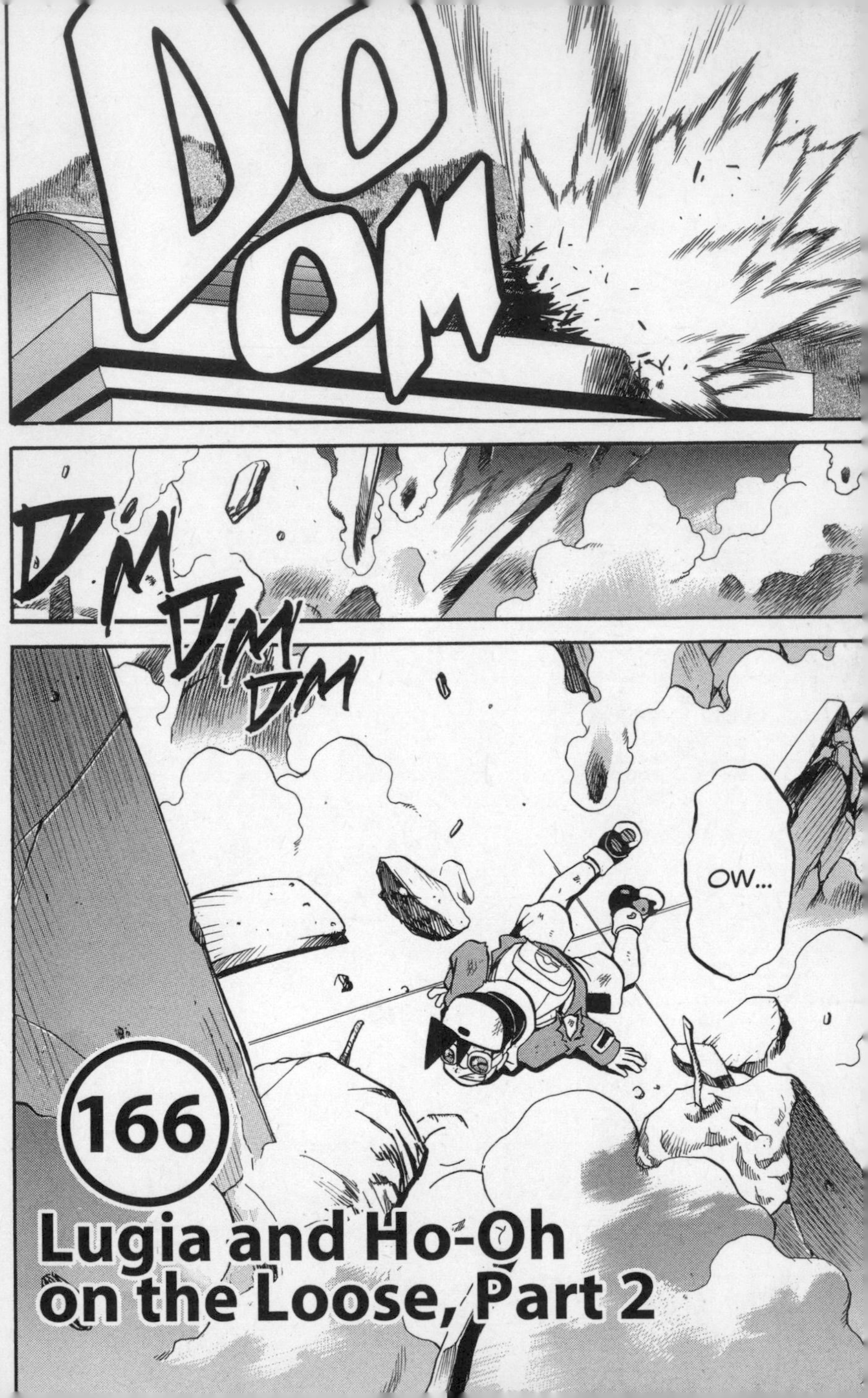
DOOM
DM
DM
DM
OW...
166
Lugia and Ho-Oh on the Loose, Part 2

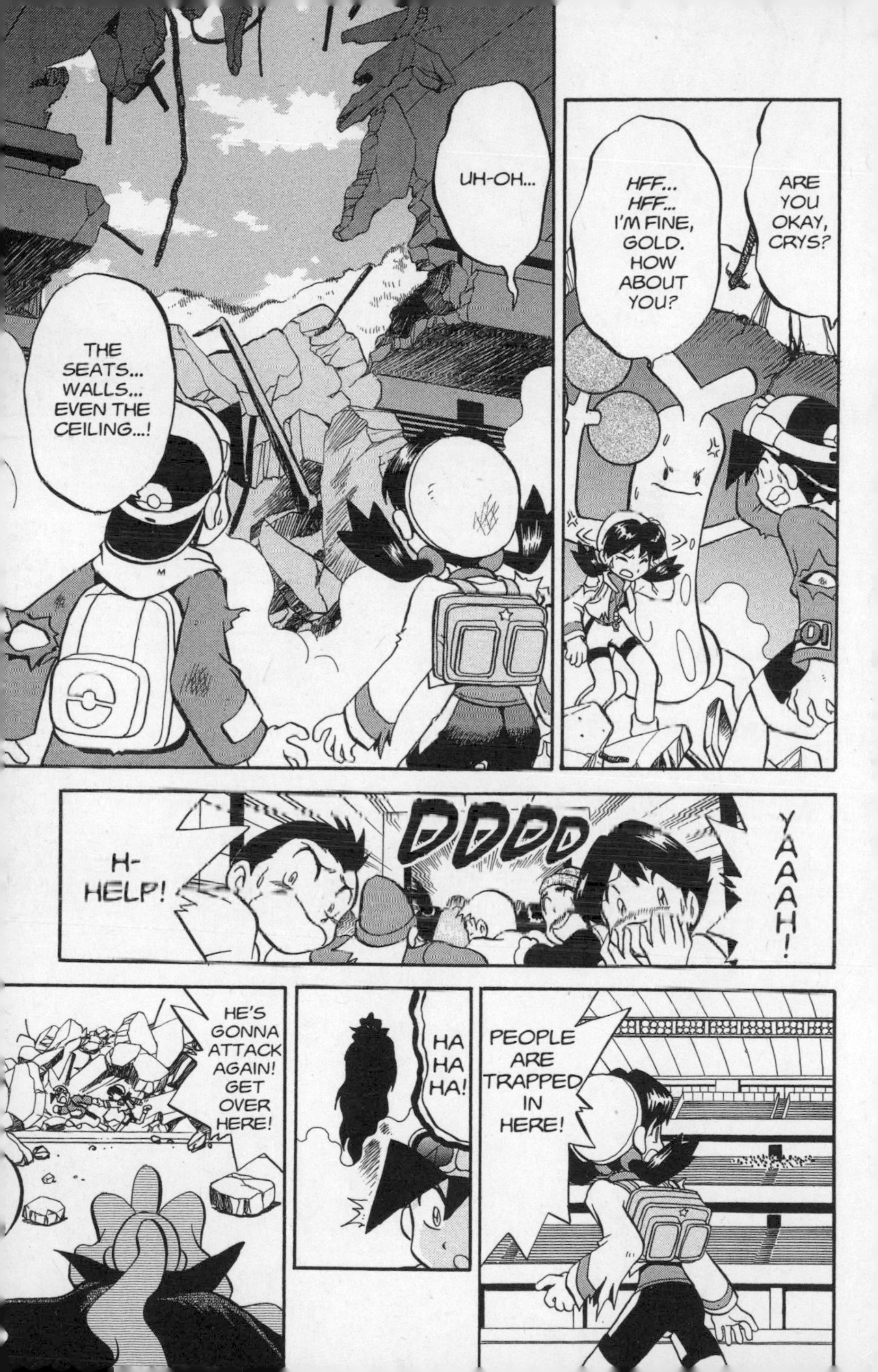

ARE YOU OKAY, CRYS?
HFF... HFF... I'M FINE, GOLD. HOW ABOUT YOU?
UH-OH...
THE SEATS... WALLS... EVEN THE CEILING...!
YAAAH!
DDDD
H-HELP!
PEOPLE ARE TRAPPED IN HERE!
HA HA HA!
HE'S GONNA ATTACK AGAIN! GET OVER HERE!

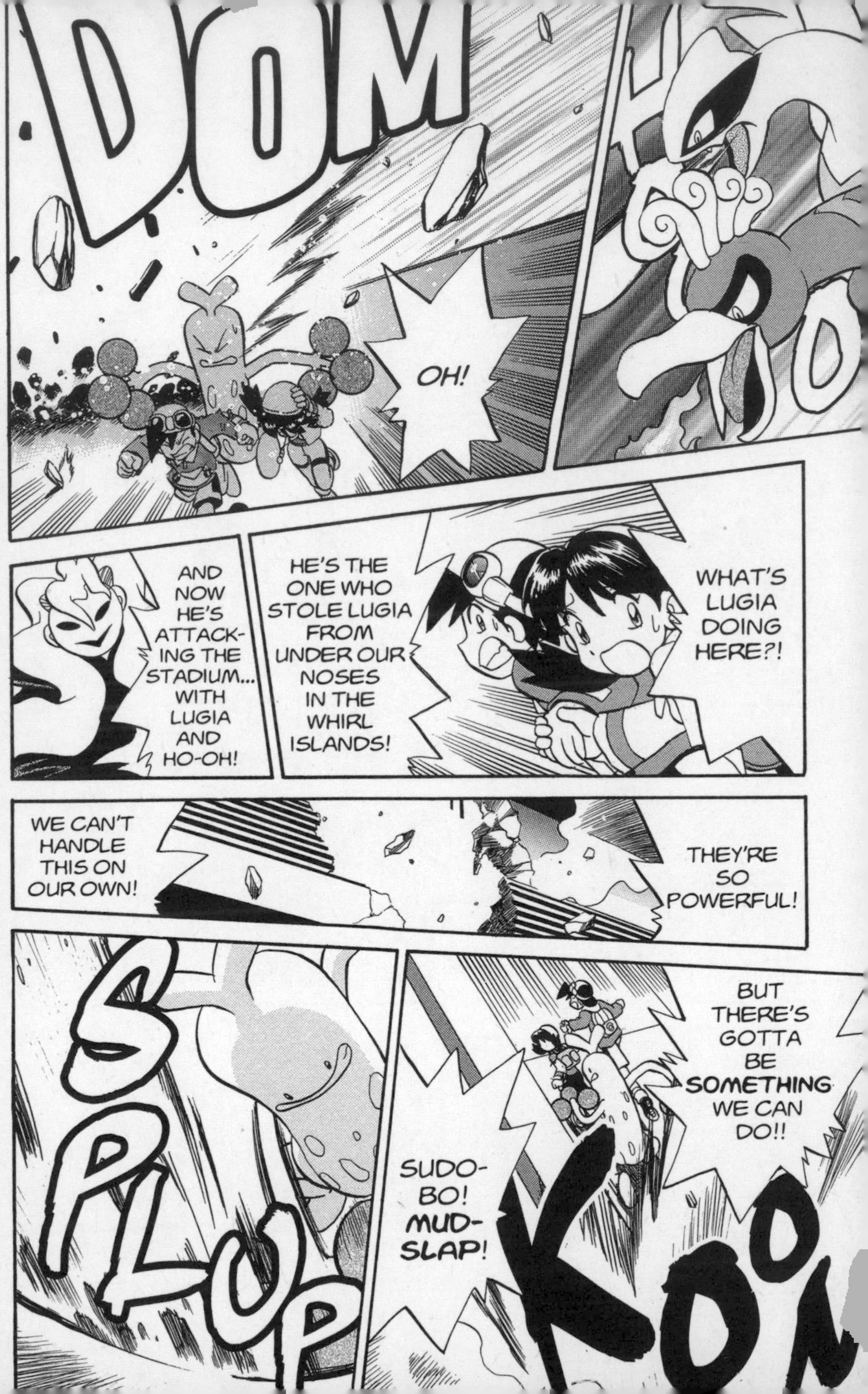
DOM
OH!
WHAT'S LUGIA DOING HERE?!
HE'S THE ONE WHO STOLE LUGIA FROM UNDER OUR NOSES IN THE WHIRL ISLANDS!
AND NOW HE'S ATTACKING THE STADIUM... WITH LUGIA AND HO-OH!
THEY'RE SO POWERFUL!
WE CAN'T HANDLE THIS ON OUR OWN!
BUT THERE'S GOTTA BE **SOMETHING** WE CAN DO!!
SUDOBO! **MUD-SLAP!**
SPLUP

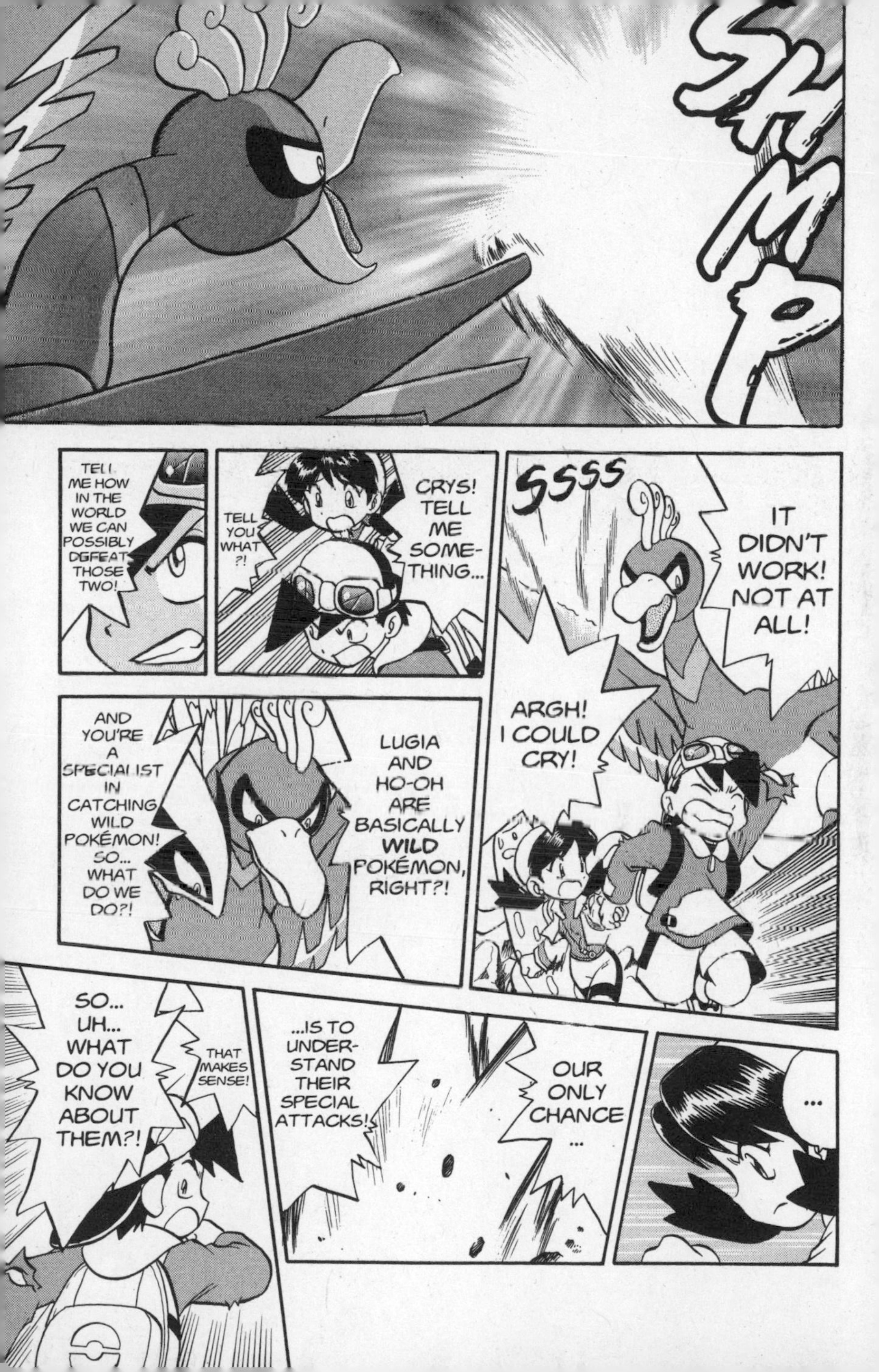
SHMP
SSSS
IT DIDN'T WORK! NOT AT ALL!
ARGH! I COULD CRY!
CRYS! TELL ME SOMETHING...
TELL YOU WHAT?!
TELL ME HOW IN THE WORLD WE CAN POSSIBLY DEFEAT THOSE TWO!
LUGIA AND HO-OH ARE BASICALLY **WILD** POKÉMON, RIGHT?!
AND YOU'RE A SPECIALIST IN CATCHING WILD POKÉMON! SO... WHAT DO WE DO?!
...
OUR ONLY CHANCE ...
...IS TO UNDERSTAND THEIR SPECIAL ATTACKS!
THAT MAKES SENSE!
SO... UH... WHAT DO YOU KNOW ABOUT THEM?!

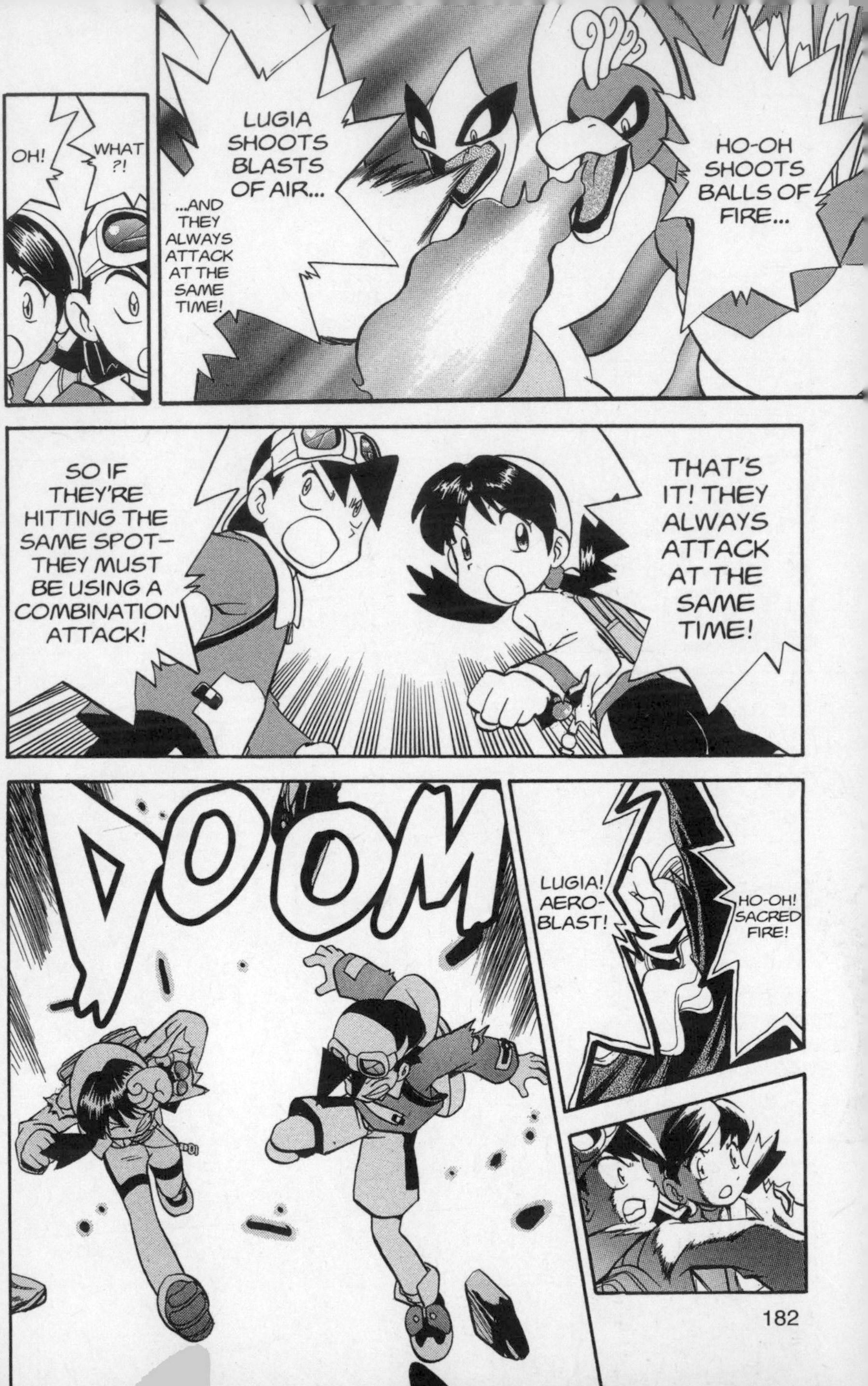
HO-OH SHOOTS BALLS OF FIRE...
LUGIA SHOOTS BLASTS OF AIR...
...AND THEY ALWAYS ATTACK AT THE SAME TIME!
WHAT?!
OH!
THAT'S IT! THEY ALWAYS ATTACK AT THE SAME TIME!
SO IF THEY'RE HITTING THE SAME SPOT—THEY MUST BE USING A COMBINATION ATTACK!
HO-OH! SACRED FIRE!
LUGIA! AERO-BLAST!
DOOM

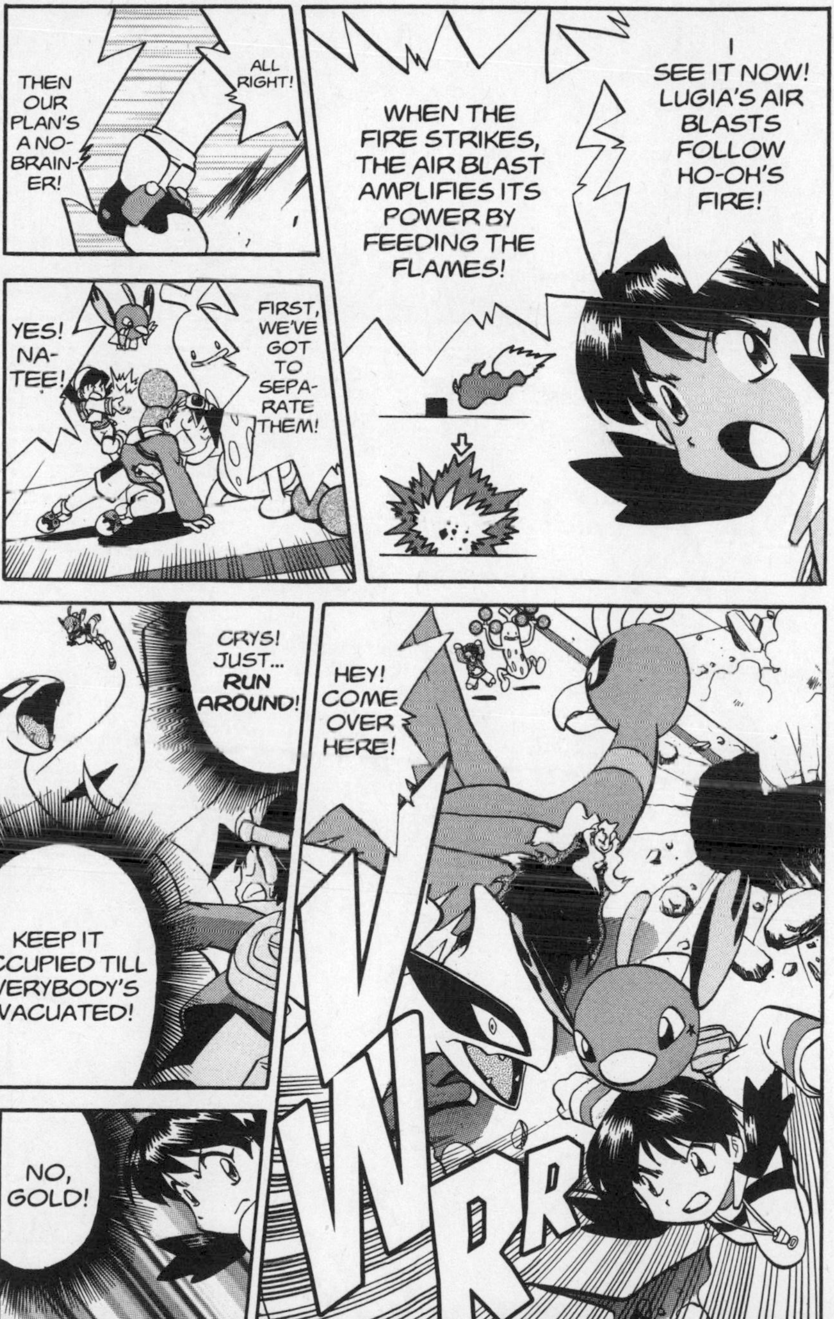
I SEE IT NOW! LUGIA'S AIR BLASTS FOLLOW HO-OH'S FIRE!
WHEN THE FIRE STRIKES, THE AIR BLAST AMPLIFIES ITS POWER BY FEEDING THE FLAMES!
ALL RIGHT!
THEN OUR PLAN'S A NO-BRAINER!
FIRST, WE'VE GOT TO SEPARATE THEM!
YES! NATEE!
HEY! COME OVER HERE!
WRR
CRYS! JUST... RUN AROUND!
KEEP IT OCCUPIED TILL EVERYBODY'S EVACUATED!
NO, GOLD!

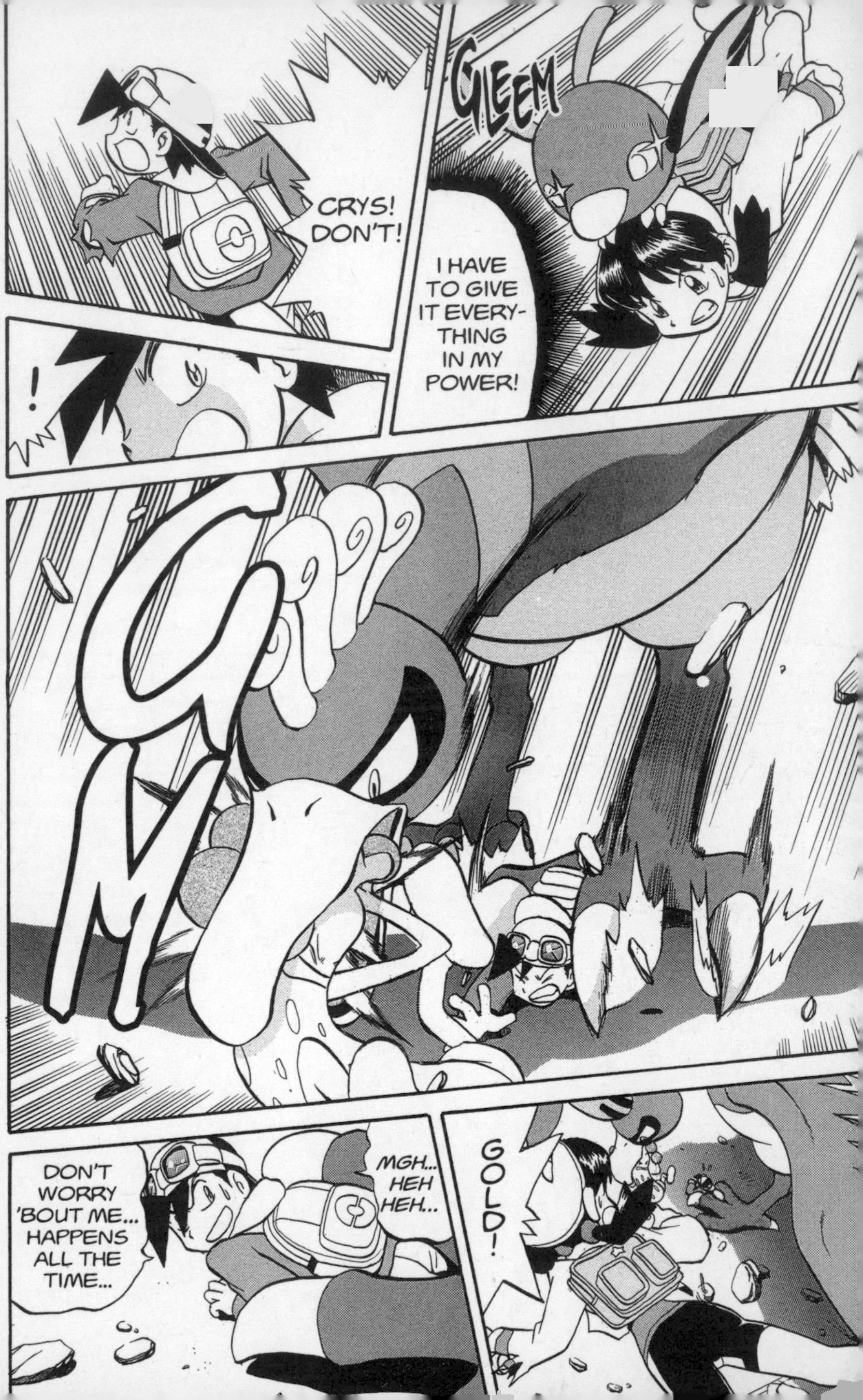
GLEEM
I HAVE TO GIVE IT EVERYTHING IN MY POWER!
CRYS! DON'T!
!
GOLD!
MGH... HEH HEH...
DON'T WORRY 'BOUT ME... HAPPENS ALL THE TIME...

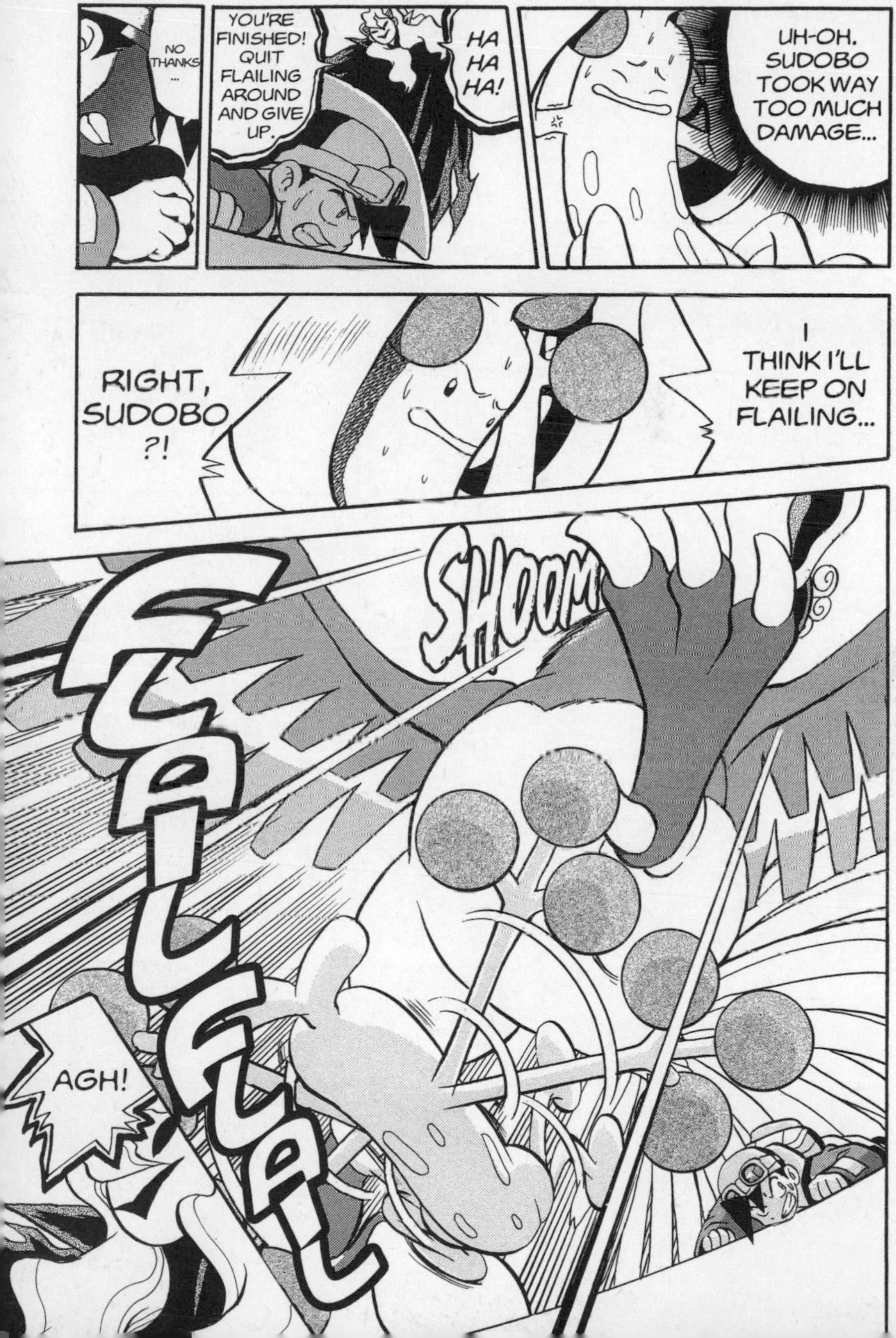
UH-OH. SUDOBO TOOK WAY TOO MUCH DAMAGE...
HA HA HA!
YOU'RE FINISHED! QUIT FLAILING AROUND AND GIVE UP.
NO THANKS ...
I THINK I'LL KEEP ON FLAILING...
RIGHT, SUDOBO ?!
SHOOM
FLAIL FLAIL
AGH!

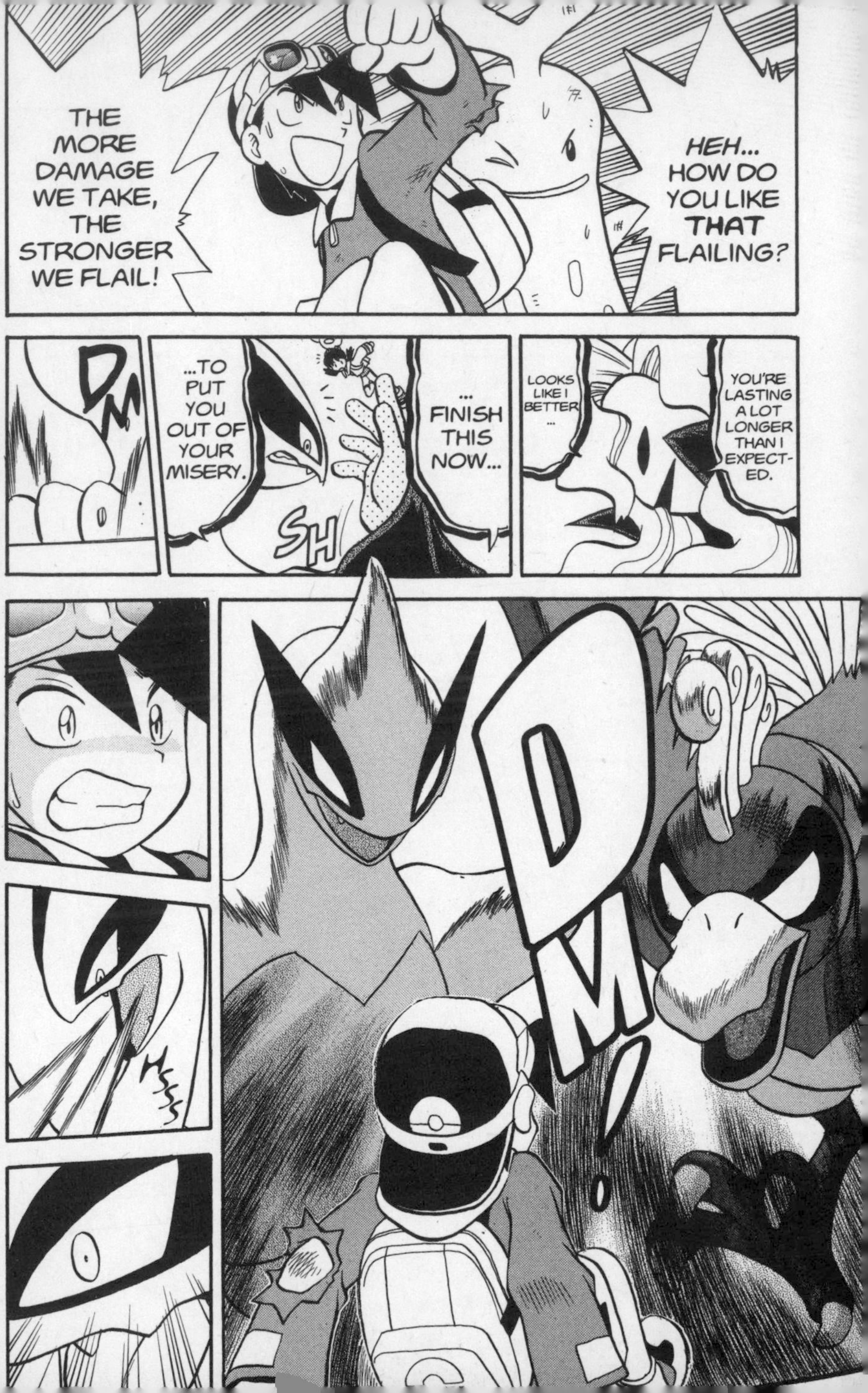
HEH... HOW DO YOU LIKE THAT FLAILING?
THE MORE DAMAGE WE TAKE, THE STRONGER WE FLAIL!
YOU'RE LASTING A LOT LONGER THAN I EXPECTED.
LOOKS LIKE I BETTER ...
... FINISH THIS NOW...
...TO PUT YOU OUT OF YOUR MISERY.
SH
DM
DM!
HSSS

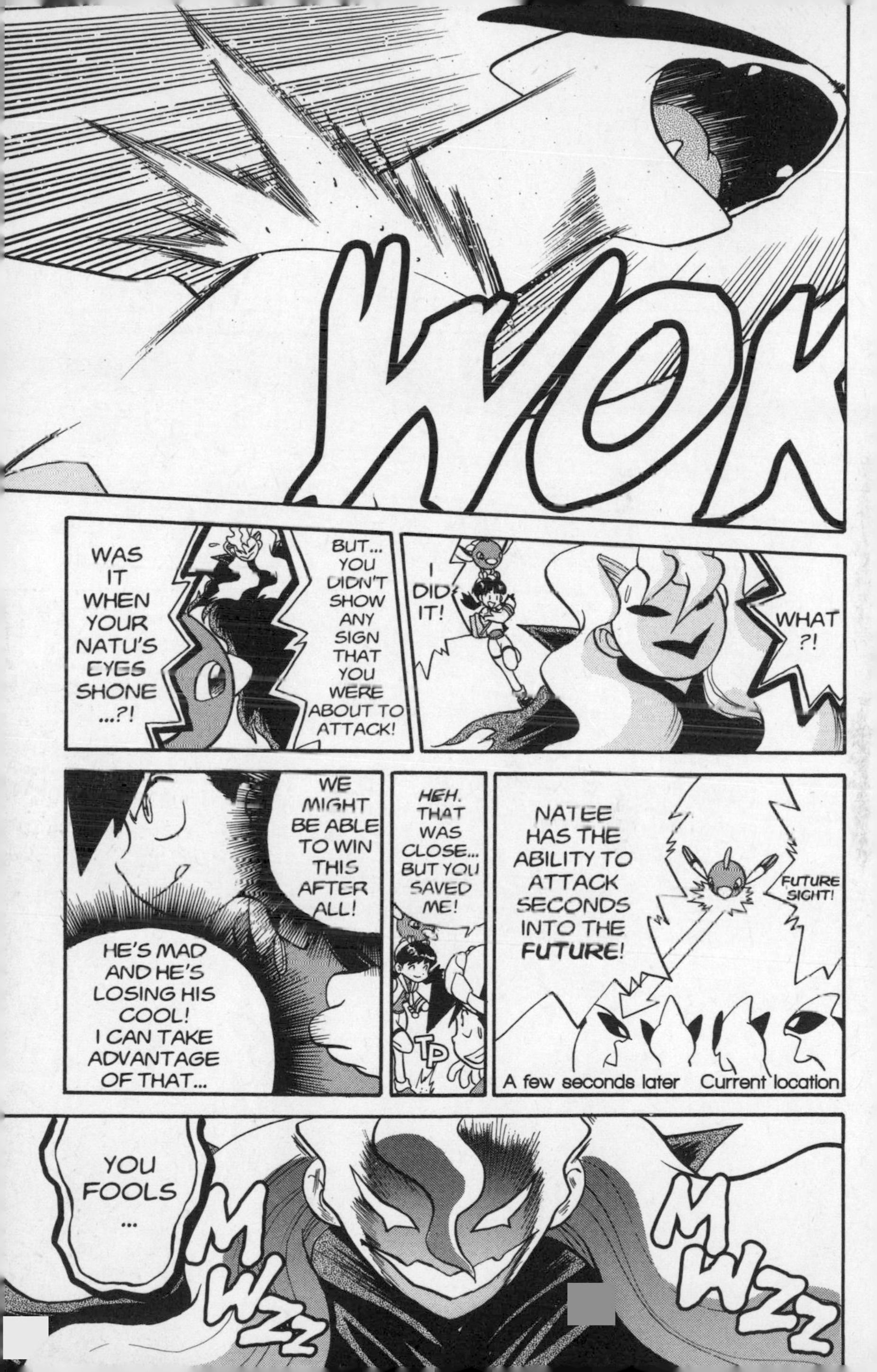
WOK
WHAT?!
I DID IT!
BUT... YOU DIDN'T SHOW ANY SIGN THAT YOU WERE ABOUT TO ATTACK!
WAS IT WHEN YOUR NATU'S EYES SHONE...?!
FUTURE SIGHT!
NATEE HAS THE ABILITY TO ATTACK SECONDS INTO THE FUTURE!
Current location
A few seconds later
HEH. THAT WAS CLOSE... BUT YOU SAVED ME!
TP
WE MIGHT BE ABLE TO WIN THIS AFTER ALL!
HE'S MAD AND HE'S LOSING HIS COOL! I CAN TAKE ADVANTAGE OF THAT...
MWZZ
YOU FOOLS...
MWZZ

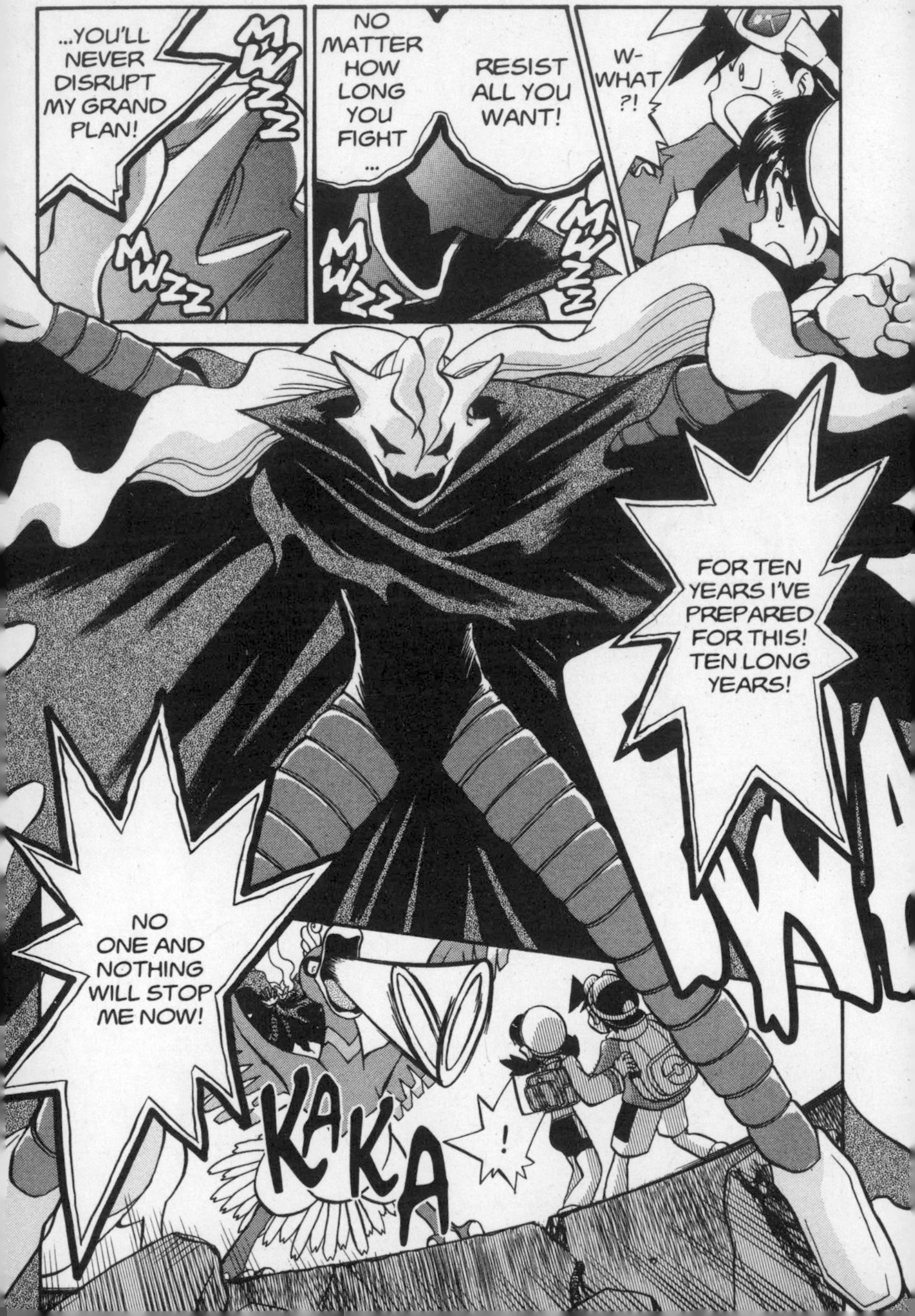
W-WHAT?!
MWZZ
NO MATTER HOW LONG YOU FIGHT...
RESIST ALL YOU WANT!
MWZZ
MWZZ
...YOU'LL NEVER DISRUPT MY GRAND PLAN!
MWZZ
FOR TEN YEARS I'VE PREPARED FOR THIS! TEN LONG YEARS!
NO ONE AND NOTHING WILL STOP ME NOW!
!
KAKAKA

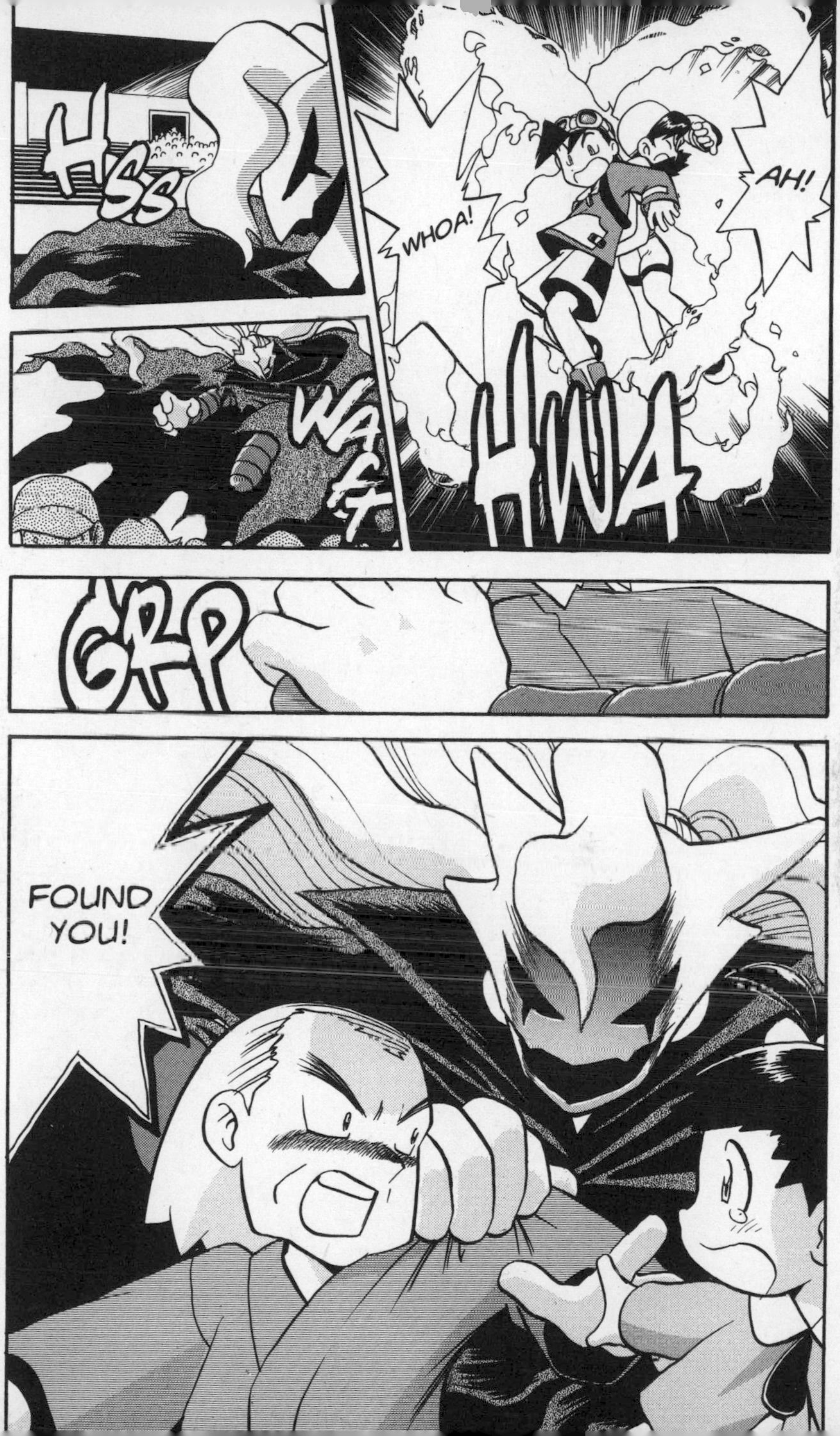
AH!
WHOA!
HWA
HSS
WAKK
GRP
FOUND YOU!

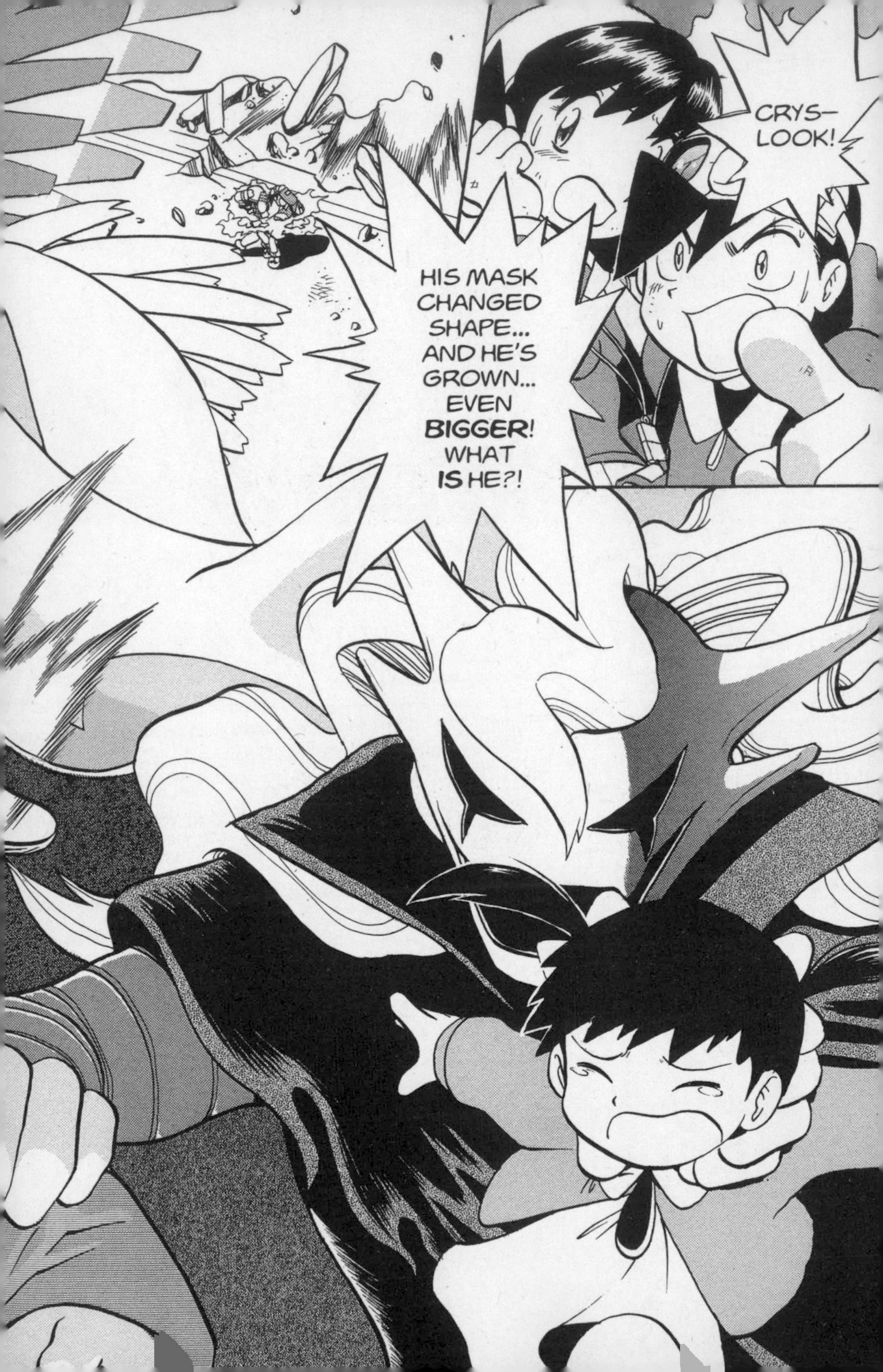
CRYS—LOOK!
HIS MASK CHANGED SHAPE... AND HE'S GROWN... EVEN **BIGGER**! WHAT **IS** HE?!

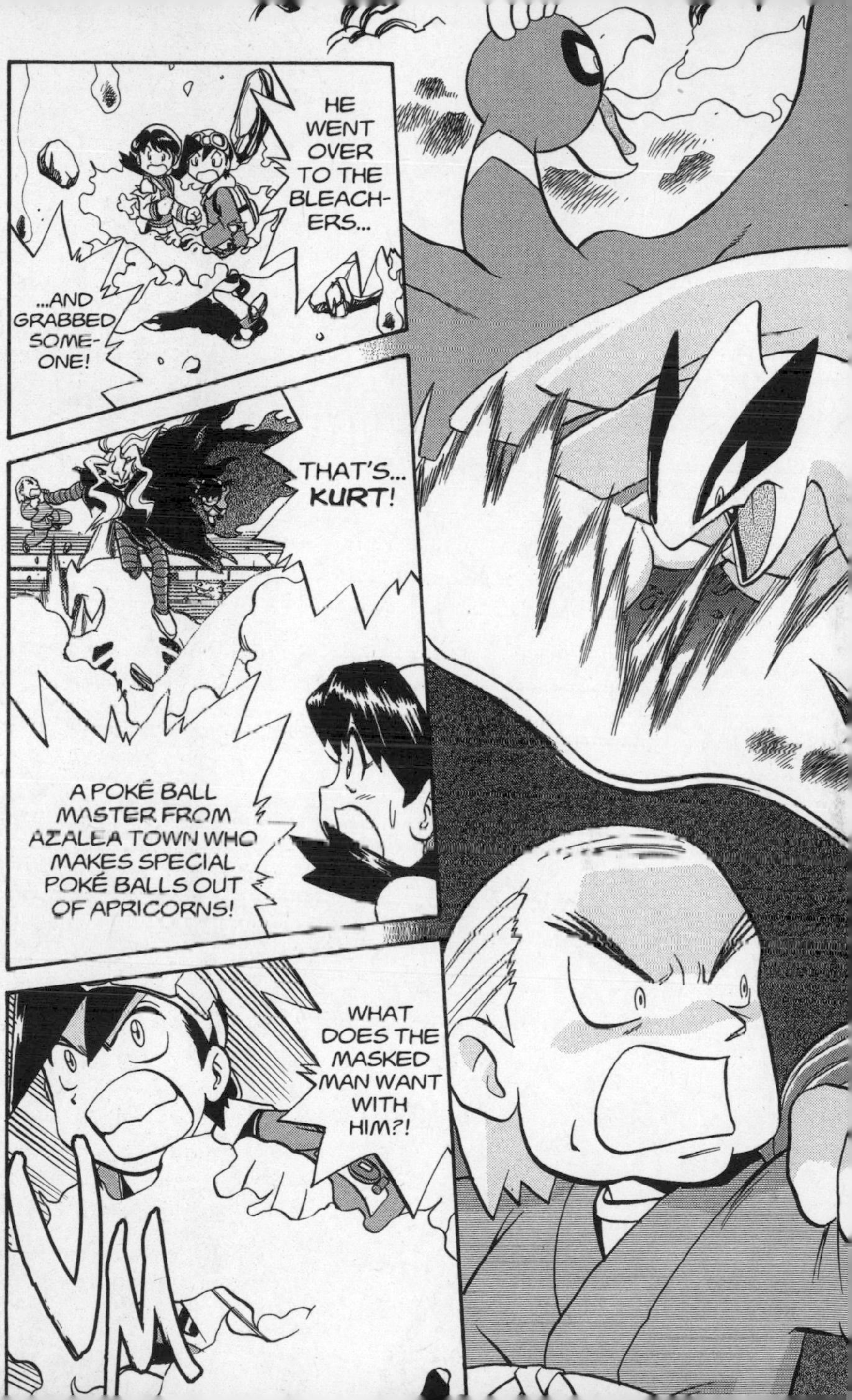
HE WENT OVER TO THE BLEACHERS...
...AND GRABBED SOMEONE!
THAT'S... KURT!
A POKÉ BALL MASTER FROM AZALEA TOWN WHO MAKES SPECIAL POKÉ BALLS OUT OF APRICORNS!
WHAT DOES THE MASKED MAN WANT WITH HIM?!

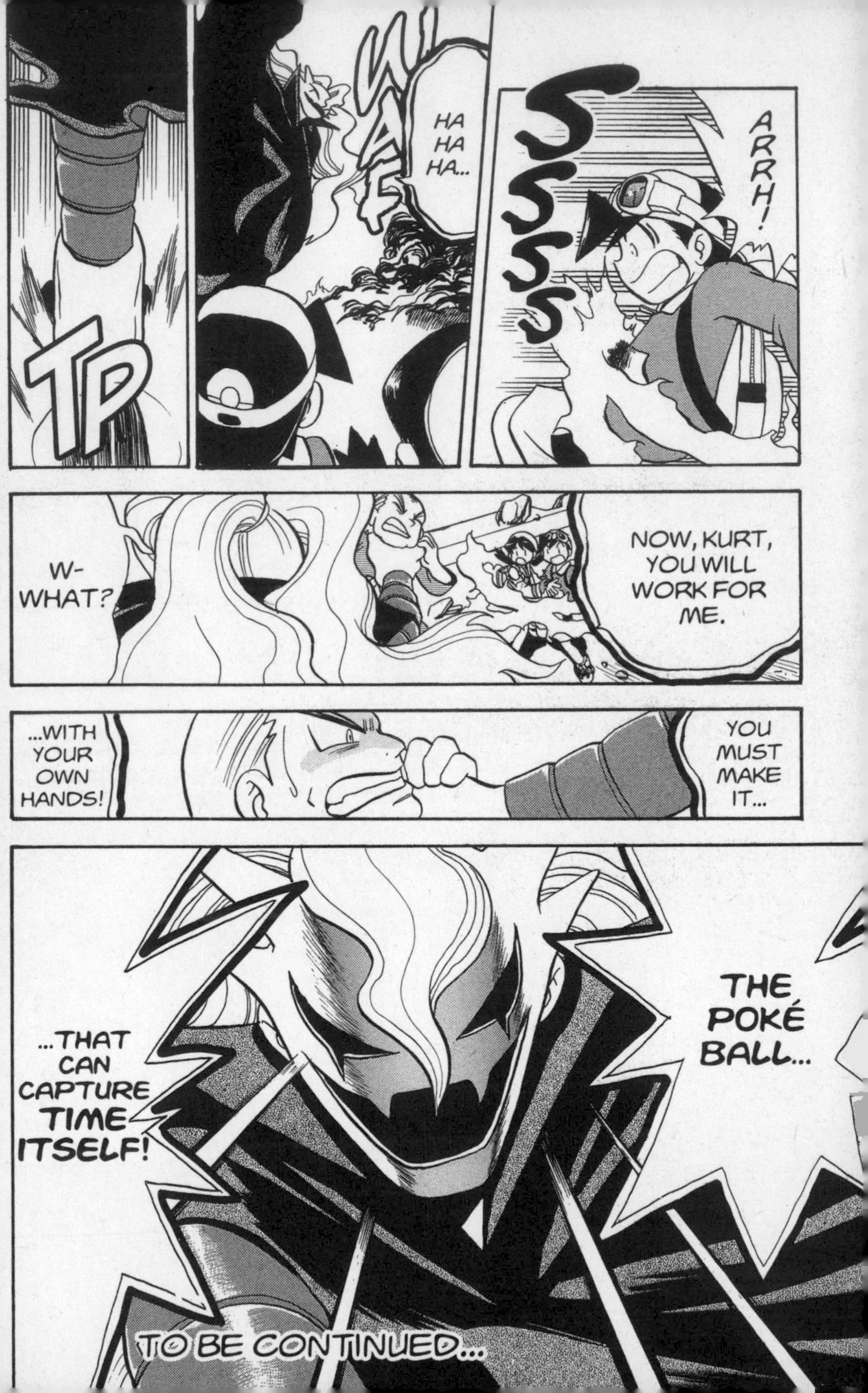
SSSSS
ARRH!
HA HA HA...
TP
NOW, KURT, YOU WILL WORK FOR ME.
W-WHAT?
YOU MUST MAKE IT...
...WITH YOUR OWN HANDS!
THE POKÉ BALL...
...THAT CAN CAPTURE TIME ITSELF!
TO BE CONTINUED...

TO BE CONTINUED

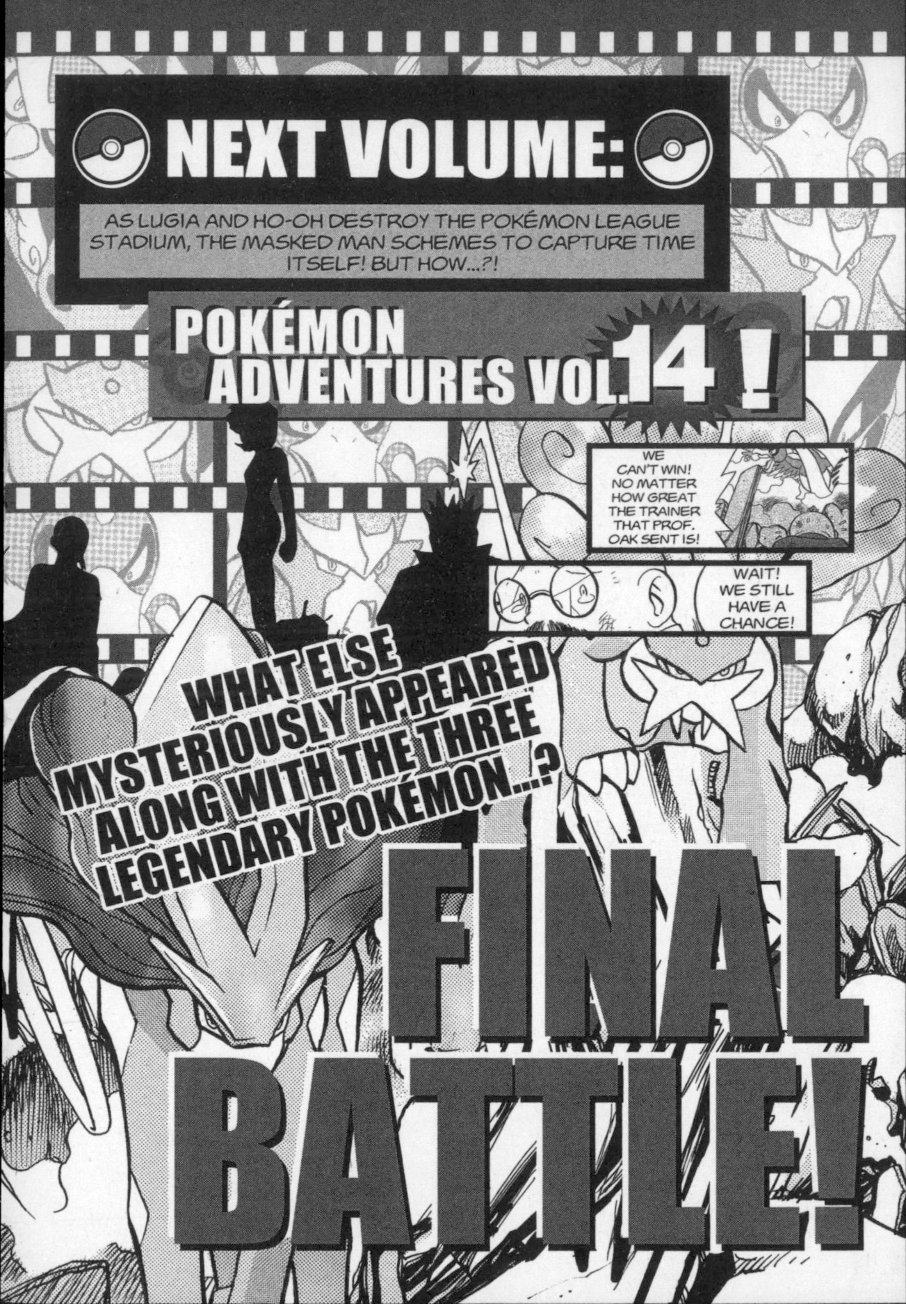
NEXT VOLUME:
AS LUGIA AND HO-OH DESTROY THE POKÉMON LEAGUE STADIUM, THE MASKED MAN SCHEMES TO CAPTURE TIME ITSELF! BUT HOW...?!
POKÉMON ADVENTURES VOL. 14 !
WE CAN'T WIN! NO MATTER HOW GREAT THE TRAINER THAT PROF. OAK SENT IS!
WAIT! WE STILL HAVE A CHANCE!
WHAT ELSE MYSTERIOUSLY APPEARED ALONG WITH THE THREE LEGENDARY POKÉMON...?
FINAL BATTLE!

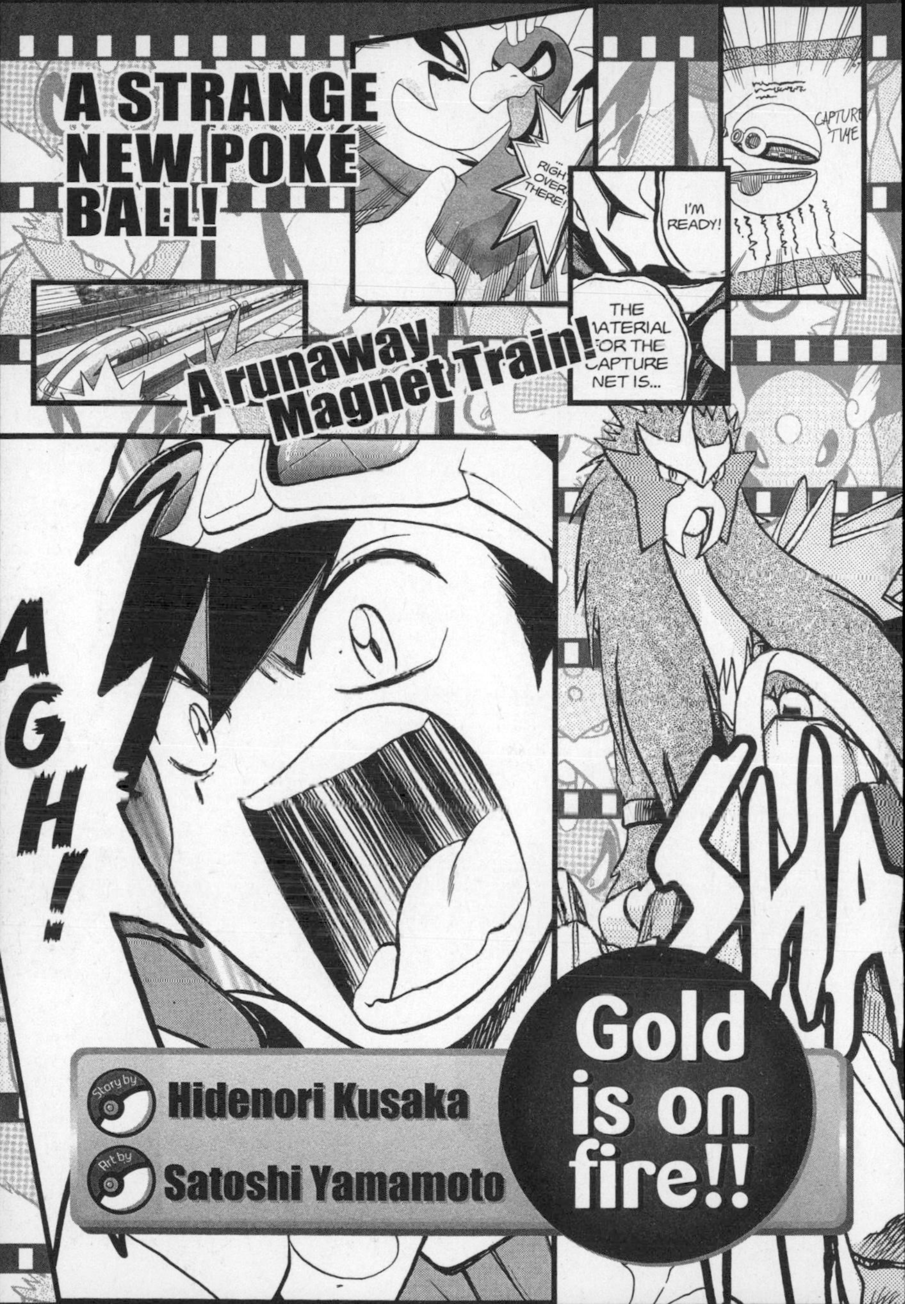

CAPTURE TIME
I'M READY!
...RIGHT OVER THERE!
A STRANGE NEW POKÉ BALL!
THE MATERIAL FOR THE CAPTURE NET IS...
A runaway Magnet Train!
SHA
AGH!
Gold is on fire!!
Story by Hidenori Kusaka
Art by Satoshi Yamamoto

ADVENTURE ROUTE MAP 13

THE BATTLE HAS SHIFTED TO THE POKÉMON LEAGUE STADIUM. HERE IS A DIAGRAM OF THE STADIUM NOTING THE LOCATION OF EACH BATTLE!

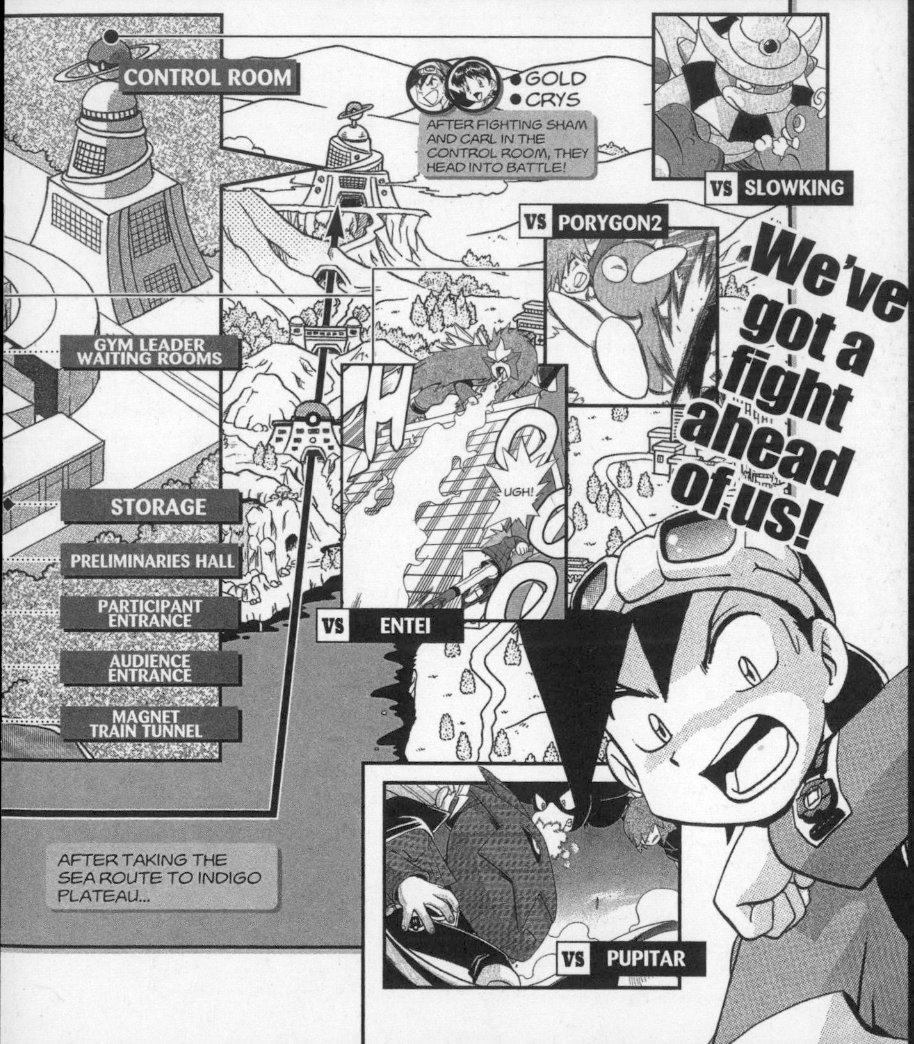
CONTROL ROOM
GOLD
CRYS
AFTER FIGHTING SHAM AND CARL IN THE CONTROL ROOM, THEY HEAD INTO BATTLE!
VS SLOWKING
VS PORYGON2
We've got a fight ahead of us!
GYM LEADER WAITING ROOMS
VS ENTEI
UGH!
STORAGE
PRELIMINARIES HALL
PARTICIPANT ENTRANCE
AUDIENCE ENTRANCE
MAGNET TRAIN TUNNEL
AFTER TAKING THE SEA ROUTE TO INDIGO PLATEAU...
VS PUPITAR

“GOTTA CATCH ’EM ALL!!”

ADVENTURE ROUTE MAP 13

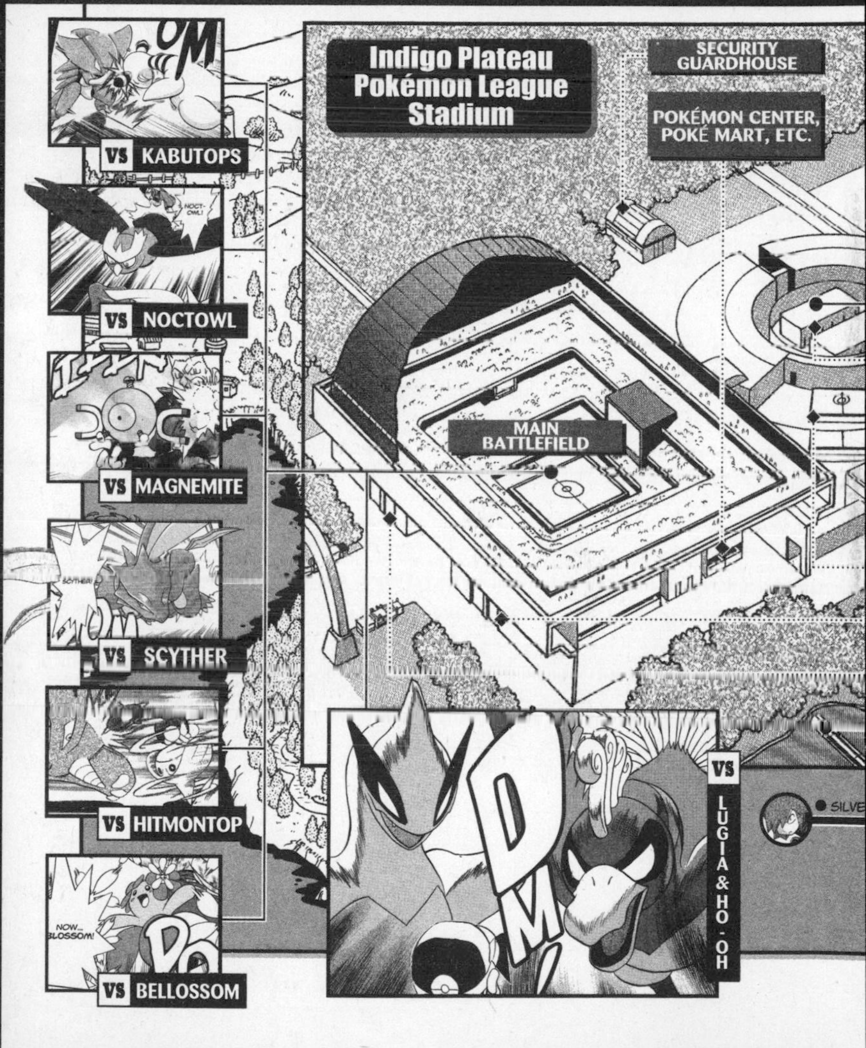
Indigo Plateau
Pokémon League
Stadium
SECURITY
GUARDHOUSE
POKÉMON CENTER,
POKÉ MART, ETC.
MAIN
BATTLEFIELD
VS KABUTOPS
NOCT-
OWL!
VS NOCTOWL
VS MAGNEMITE
SCYTHER!
VS SCYTHER
VS HITMONTOP
NOW...
BLOSSOM!
VS BELLOSSOM
VS LUGIA & HO-OH
SILVE

○ GOLD TEAM ○

POKÉDEX REVEALED!

MAIN CHARACTER: GOLD
BADGES: 0
POKÉDEX: 14

NUMBER SEEN
107
NUMBER CAUGHT
14

He's seen a lot of new Pokémon since he left New Bark Town. (See vol. 8.)

—POKÉDEX—

154	MEGANIUM
155	CYNDAQUIL
156	QUILAVA
▶157	TYPHLOSION
158	TOTODILE
159	CROCONAW
160	FERALIGATR
016	PIDGEY
017	PIDGEOTTO
018	PIDGEOT

GOLD TEAM AS OF ADVENTURE 166

The six Pokémon that Gold trusts implicitly. This will be his team in the final battle!

TOGEPI IS AT PROF. OAK'S LAB!

Gold personally hatched this Pokémon, and the Prof. is keeping a close eye on it!

Prof. Oak's Comment

THIS IS A STRANGE ONE...COMPLETELY DIFFERENT FEATURES FROM OTHERS OF ITS KIND...!

● A real mischief maker...

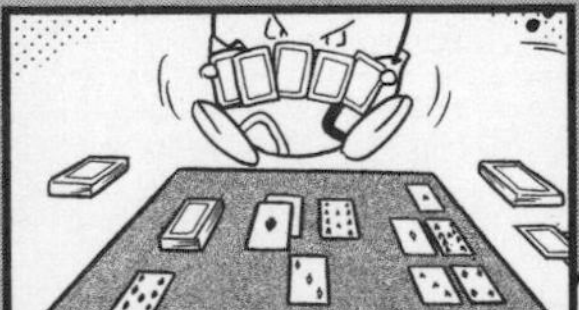

▲MOST TOGEPI ARE SO MILD-MANNERED...

● Tyranitar VS Togepi

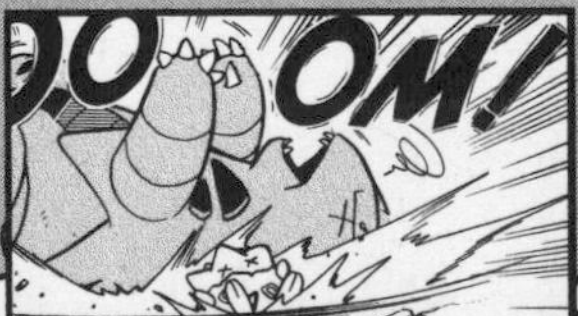

▲WHAT AN UNPRECEDENTED DEFEAT FOR A TYRANITAR!

TYPHLOSION

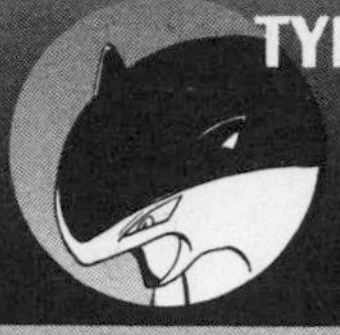

TYPHLOSION: Lv41
TYPE 1/FIRE
TRAINER/GOLD
NO.157

● EXBO GENDER: ♂

CAME FROM PROF. ELM'S LABORATORY TO LEAD THE TEAM WITH POWERFUL FIRE ATTACKS!

AIPOM

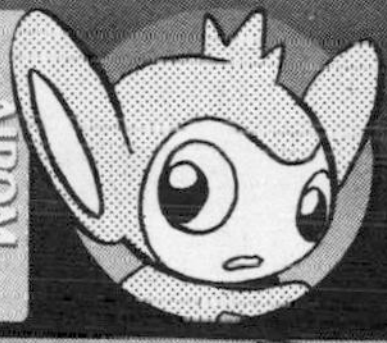

AIPOM: Lv40
TYPE1/NORMAL
TRAINER/GOLD
NO.190

● AIBO GENDER: ♂

A VERSATILE TAIL, WHICH SAVED GOLD IN THE CONTROL ROOM WHEN HE COULDN'T OPEN HIS POKÉ BALLS!

SUNKERN

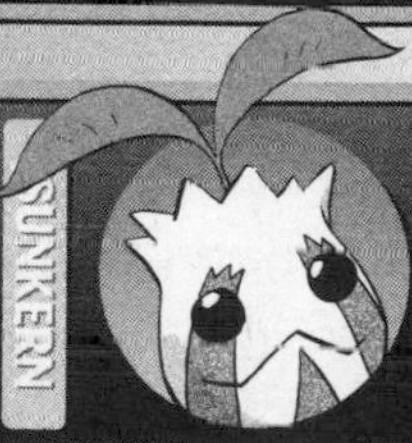

SUNKERN: Lv37
TYPE 1/GRASS
TRAINER/GOLD
NO.191

● SUNBO GENDER: ♀

A FORMIDABLE POKÉMON WITH A POKER FACE AND A GIGA DRAIN THAT ABSORBS THE ENEMY'S ENERGY!

POLITOED

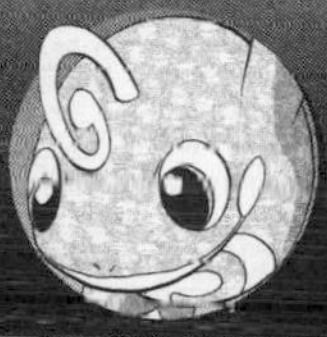

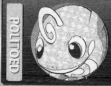

POLITOED: Lv40
TYPE 1/WATER
TRAINER/GOLD
NO.186

● POLIBO GENDER: ♂

BECAME A POLITOED AFTER A "LINK TRADE EVOLUTION"...THANKS TO SILVER'S QUICK THINKING!

SUDOWOODO

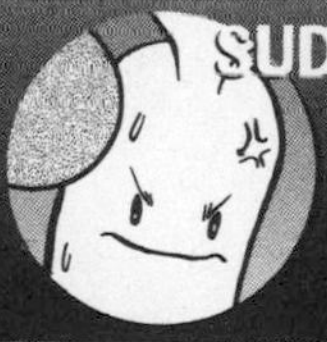

SUDOWOODO: Lv42
TYPE 1/ROCK
TRAINER/GOLD
NO.185

● SUDOBO GENDER: ♂

LOOKS LIKE A GRASS-TYPE BUT IS ACTUALLY A ROCK-TYPE. FOUGHT BACK THE LEGENDARY HO-OH!

MANTINE

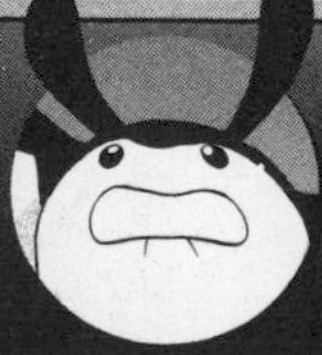

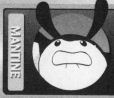

MANTINE: Lv25
TYPE 1/WATER
TYPE 2/FLYING
TRAINER/GOLD
NO.226

● TIBO GENDER: ♂

MOVES IN BOTH WATER AND AIR...WITH TWENTY REMORAID ATTACHED!

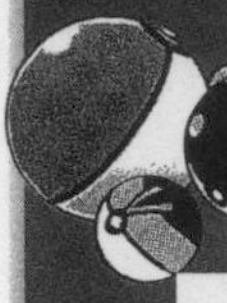

The Poké Ball!

POKÉ BALL PERFECT DATA

A Complete Guide in Seven Parts

HOW DO DIFFERENT POKÉ BALLS AFFECT THE CAPTURE AND POSSESSION OF POKÉMON?

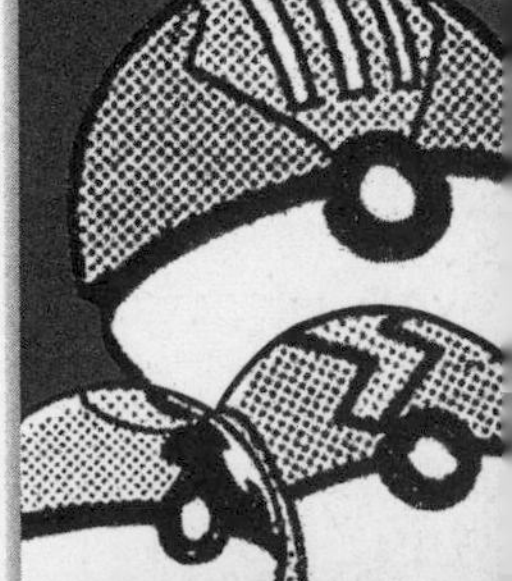

POKÉ BALL PERFECT DATA

Basic Features

01 Portability

Making Pokémon Portable with the Poké Ball

TRAINERS KEEP THEIR POKÉMON IN POKÉ BALLS, WHICH ARE OFTEN STORED IN THEIR POCKETS. THE ESSENCE OF A POKÉ BALL IS PORTABILITY. (SEE CHAPTER 1, ETC.)

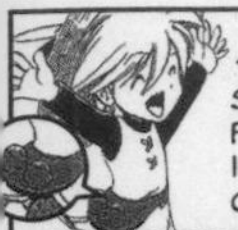

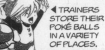

◀ TRAINERS STORE THEIR POKÉ BALLS IN A VARIETY OF PLACES.

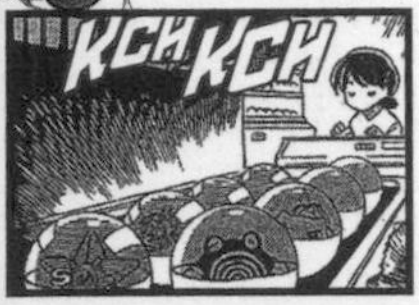
KCH KCH

▲ SOME ACTIONS—SUCH AS ELECTRONIC TRADING AND HEALING THROUGH MACHINES—ARE POSSIBLE ONLY AFTER THE POKÉMON ARE ENCASED IN A POKÉ BALL. (SEE CHAPTER 8, ETC.)

THE NUMBER OF POKÉ BALLS A TRAINER CAN CARRY

ALTHOUGH THE NUMBER OF POKÉ BALLS IS UP TO THE DISCRETION OF THE TRAINER, THE CONSENSUS IS THAT SIX POKÉ BALLS ARE THE MOST EFFECTIVE NUMBER. (SEE CHAPTER 119.)

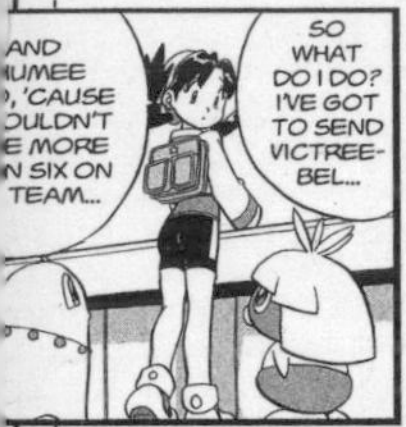
SO WHAT DO I DO? I'VE GOT TO SEND VICTREE-BEL...

02 Catching

Tool to Capture Pokémon

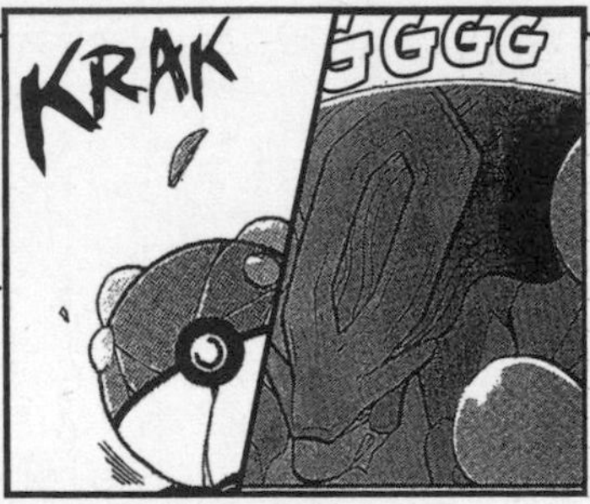
GGGG
KRAK

USUALLY ▶ A TRAINER MUST WEAKEN A POKÉMON FIRST TO BE ABLE TO CAPTURE IT. (SEE CHAPTER 131.)

OBVIOUSLY AN ESSENTIAL FUNCTION OF THE POKÉ BALL IS TO CAPTURE POKÉMON. WHEN A POKÉ BALL IS THROWN AT A WILD POKÉMON AFTER A BATTLE, THE POKÉMON IS PULLED INTO IT.

◀ SOME POKÉMON MUST BE HIT AT PARTICULAR POINTS TO BE CAPTURED. (SEE CHAPTER 148.)

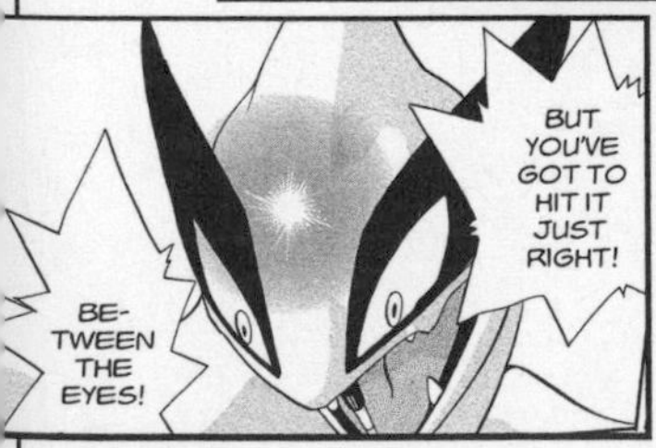
BUT YOU'VE GOT TO HIT IT JUST RIGHT!
BE-TWEEN THE EYES!

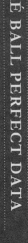

03 Types — Poké Ball Usage

DESIGN	NAME & FUNCTION	APRICORN
	Heavy Ball EFFECTIVE AGAINST HEAVY POKÉMON	BLACK
	Lure Ball EFFECTIVE AGAINST POKÉMON HOOKED BY A FISHING ROD	BLUE
	Fast Ball EFFECTIVE AGAINST POKÉMON WHO ARE QUICK TO FLEE	WHITE
	Moon Ball EFFECTIVE AGAINST POKÉMON WHO EVOLVE USING THE MOON STONE	YELLOW
	Love Ball EFFECTIVE IF YOUR POKÉMON IS A DIFFERENT GENDER FROM ITS OPPONENT	PINK
	Level Ball EFFECTIVE IF YOUR OPPONENT'S LEVEL IS LOWER THAN YOUR OWN POKÉMON'S	RED
	Friend Ball DEEPENS THE FRIENDSHIP WITH THE CAPTURED POKÉMON	GREEN

DESIGN	NAME & FUNCTION
	Poké Ball CATCHES WILD POKÉMON
	Great Ball MORE POWERFUL THAN A POKÉ BALL
	Ultra Ball MORE POWERFUL THAN A GREAT BALL
	Master Ball CAN CAPTURE ANY KIND OF POKÉMON
	Safari Ball FOR USE IN THE SAFARI ZONE
	Park Ball ONLY FOR THE NATIONAL PARK BUG-CATCHING CONTEST

YOU CAN PURCHASE DIFFERENT KINDS OF POKÉ BALLS MADE BY DIFFERENT PEOPLE FOR DIFFERENT USES.

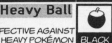

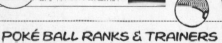

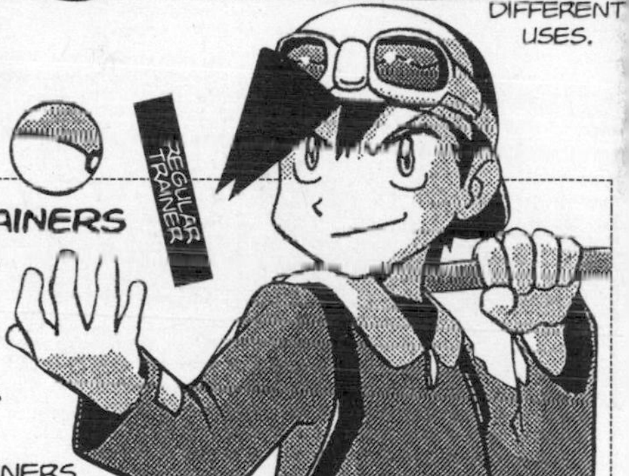

REGULAR TRAINER

POKÉ BALL RANKS & TRAINERS

POWERFUL POKÉ BALLS ARE USED TO CAPTURE ESPECIALLY STRONG WILD POKÉMON. BECAUSE POKÉMON ARE USUALLY STORED IN THE SAME POKÉ BALL AFTER CAPTURE, THE RANK OF THE POKÉ BALL GENERALLY MATCHES THE SKILL LEVEL OF THE TRAINER.

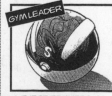

▶ MOST TRAINERS SIMPLY USE REGULAR POKÉ BALLS.

GYM LEADER

▲THESE TRAINERS ALL USE GREAT BALLS ISSUED BY THE POKÉMON ASSOCIATION.

▼MATCHING THEIR SKILL LEVEL, SOME USE ULTRA BALLS.

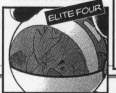

ELITE FOUR

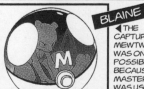

BLAINE

◀THE CAPTURE OF MEWTWO WAS ONLY POSSIBLE BECAUSE A MASTER BALL WAS USED.

04

Modification

Different Usage Depending on the Trainer

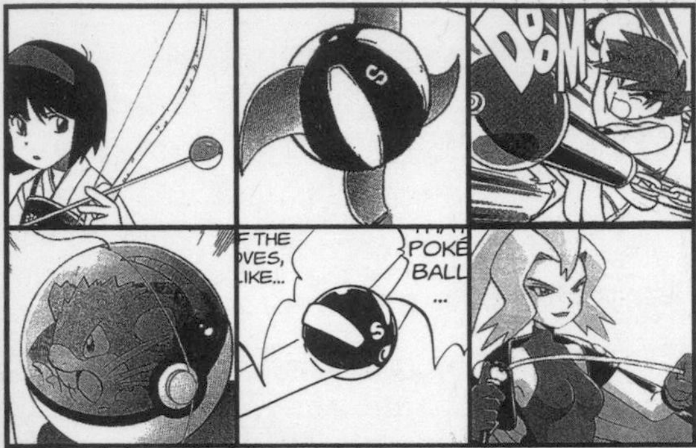
DOOM
POKÉ BALL ...

SKILLED TRAINERS OFTEN APPLY THEIR OWN SKILLS WHEN USING THEIR POKÉ BALLS. SOMETIMES, POKÉ BALLS ARE MODIFIED TO MATCH THE SKILLS OF THE TRAINER WHO USES THEM, GIVING THEM AN ADVANTAGE IN BATTLE. (SEE CHAPTER 66, ETC.)

SOME ▲ TRAINERS CUSTOMIZE THEIR POKÉ BALLS FOR RANGE, OTHERS FOR PRECISION, TIMING, OR TO MAKE THE POKÉ BALL MOVE IN AN UNPREDICTABLE WAY. THE OPTIONS ARE ENDLESS.

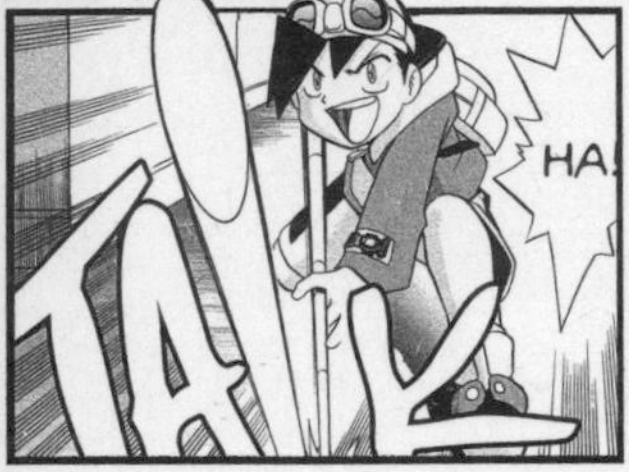
HA!
TAK

THIS ISN'T ◀ A MODIFICATION, BUT THE "BILLIARDS METHOD" CAPITALIZES ON THE SPHERICAL FORM OF THE POKÉ BALL.

05

Opening & Closing

Use of Poké Balls by Other Trainers

UNDER NORMAL CIRCUMSTANCES, TRAINERS CANNOT OPEN POKÉ BALLS THAT BELONG TO OTHERS. THIS IS BECAUSE THE OPENING AND CLOSING OF THE POKÉ BALL IS A RECIPROCAL ACT REQUIRING BOTH THE WILL OF THE TRAINER AND THE POKÉMON INSIDE. BECAUSE POKÉMON TRUST THEIR TRAINERS, THEY ONLY ANSWER THEIR TRAINER'S CALL TO COME OUT. (SEE CHAPTER 10, ETC.)

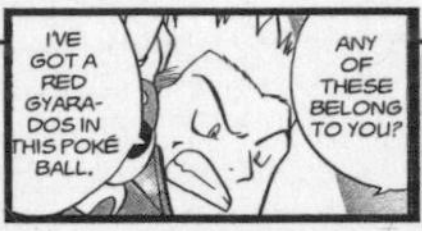
ANY OF THESE BELONG TO YOU?
I'VE GOT A RED GYARADOS IN THIS POKÉ BALL.

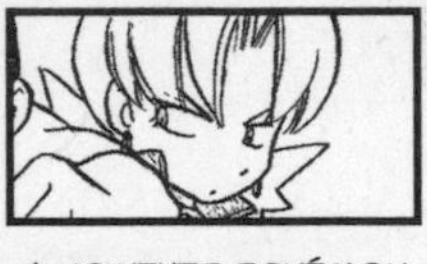

▲ HOWEVER, POKÉMON WHO ARE SEVERELY WEAKENED CAN BE FORCED TO OPEN UP TO OTHERS BESIDES THEIR TRAINER. (SEE CHAPTER 145.) SOME RESEARCHERS HAVE FOUND A METHOD TO OPEN ANOTHER TRAINER'S POKÉ BALLS. (SEE CHAPTER 85.)

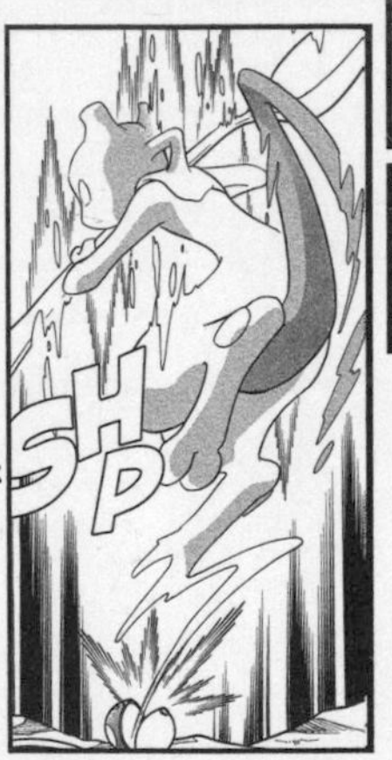
SHP

POKÉMON ▶ WITH HIGH INTELLIGENCE CAN ENTER OR EXIT THEIR POKÉ BALLS AT WILL. (SEE CHAPTER 81.)

OPEN/CLOSE SWITCH

THIS IS THE SWITCH THAT TRIGGERS THE POKÉ BALL TO OPEN OR CLOSE. SOME HAVE EMPLOYED A STRATEGY OF DESTROYING THIS SWITCH TO PREVENT THEIR OPPONENT FROM BRINGING OUT ANOTHER POKÉMON IN BATTLE. (SEE CHAPTER 80, 135, ETC.)

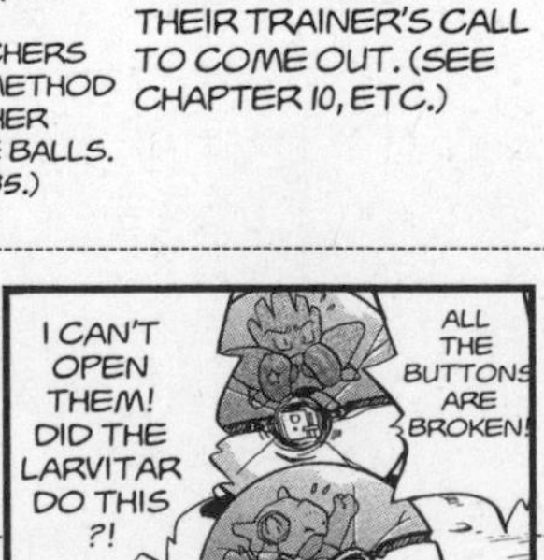
ALL THE BUTTONS ARE BROKEN!
I CAN'T OPEN THEM! DID THE LARVITAR DO THIS ?!

06 Internal Structure

Capture Net

INSIDE THE POKÉ BALL IS AN INVISIBLE NETTING CALLED THE "CAPTURE NET." THIS IS WHAT EJECTS FROM THE POKÉ BALL AND PULLS A POKÉMON INSIDE. ONE GYM LEADER USES A SPECIAL POKÉ BALL WITH ITS CAPTURE NET ON THE OUTSIDE. (SEE CHAPTER 134, 158.)

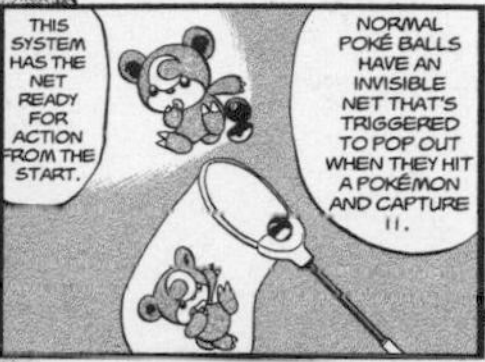
NORMAL POKÉ BALLS HAVE AN INVISIBLE NET THAT'S TRIGGERED TO POP OUT WHEN THEY HIT A POKÉMON AND CAPTURE IT.
THIS SYSTEM HAS THE NET READY FOR ACTION FROM THE START.

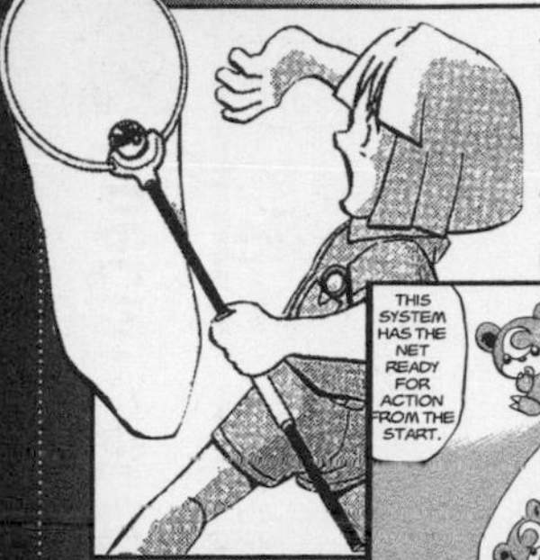

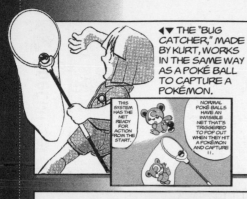

◀▼ THE "BUG CATCHER," MADE BY KURT, WORKS IN THE SAME WAY AS A POKÉ BALL TO CAPTURE A POKÉMON.

07 Time ...?!

The Poké Ball That Capture Time

THE MAN CALLED THE **MASK OF ICE** ASKED KURT ABOUT THIS WHEN HE ATTACKED THE POKÉMON LEAGUE STADIUM. BUT WHAT DID HE MEAN? IS THERE A COMPLETELY NEW TYPE OF POKÉ BALL THAT WE DON'T KNOW ABOUT?! (SEE CHAPTER 166.)

DOES KURT KNOW WHAT IT IS?

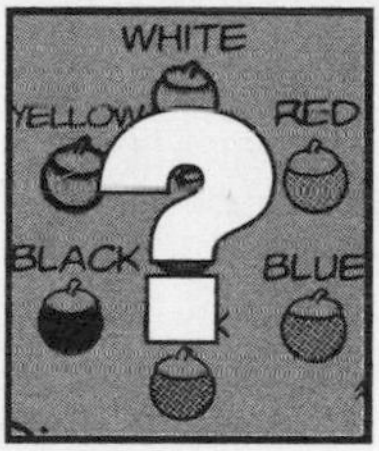
WHITE
YELLOW
RED
BLACK
BLUE

◀ HIS OPPONENT THINKS HE KNOWS HOW TO MAKE IT!

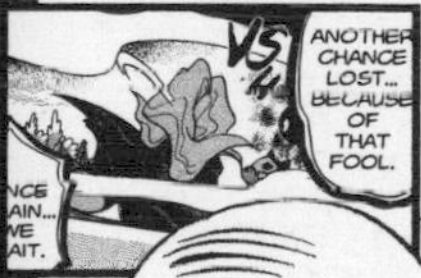
VS
ANOTHER CHANCE LOST... BECAUSE OF THAT FOOL.

▼ THE MASK OF ICE SAID HE DOESN'T HAVE ANY TIME LEFT... DOES THAT SHED ANY LIGHT ON THIS MYSTERIOUS POKÉ BALL?

KURT, A POKÉ BALL MAKER FROM AZALEA TOWN...

◀ ...CREATES SPECIAL POKÉ BALLS USING APRICORNS. WHY DOES THE MASK OF ICE THINK HE KNOWS HOW TO MAKE THIS SPECIAL POKÉ BALL?!

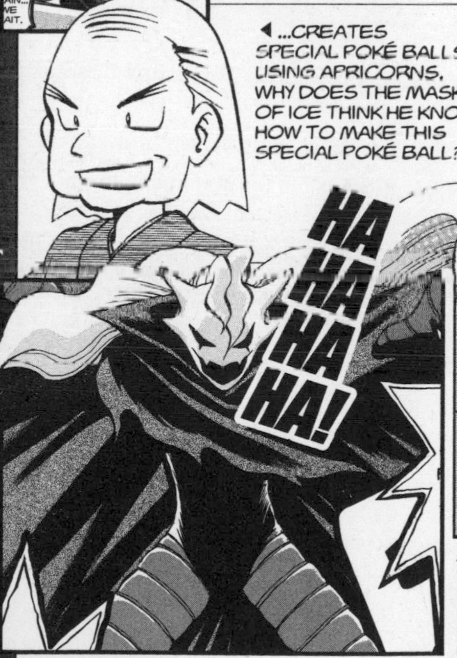
HA HA HA HA HA!

WHERE AND WHY IS IT USED?

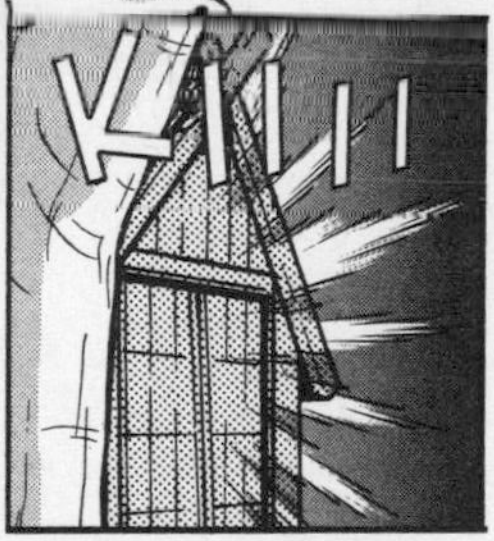
KIII

▲ THE MASK OF ICE WARDED OFF PEOPLE WHO CAME TO THE ILEX FOREST! IS THAT WHERE THE POKÉ BALL WILL BE DEPLOYED?!

Message from
Hidenori Kusaka

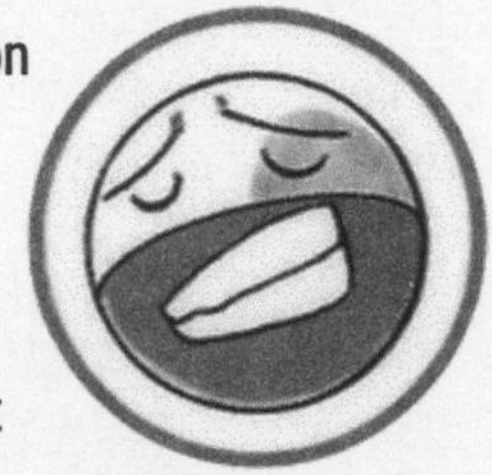

Lugia and Ho-Oh are the two Pokémon who appear on the covers of the *Pokémon HeartGold* and *SoulSilver* games. How powerful would they be if they attacked together? How would the heroes fight back and meet this challenge? That's what inspired me as I created volume 13. English-speaking readers, please enjoy this volume! Gold, Silver and Crys are about to face their destinies!

Message from
Satoshi Yamamoto

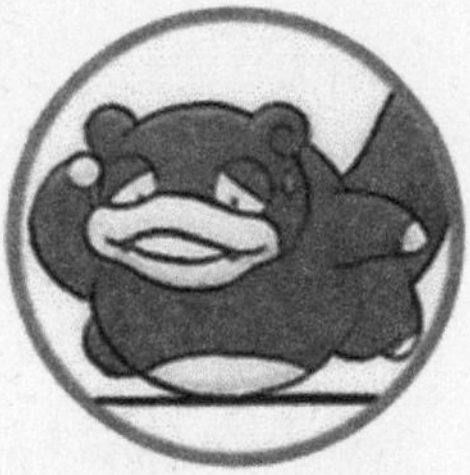

The Gym Leader battles are about to start! Not to mention the battle between the Masked Man and the main characters. In volume 13, we head toward the climax of the story by leaps and bounds! This story arc features the greatest Pokémon Trainers of all time. You'll view them in a whole new light after this... Also, prepare yourself for the spectacle of giant Pokémon destroying the battle arena! Did I go too far (LOL)? Perhaps I have, but in my defense... at least I gave it my all! Hope you enjoy the results!

The Final Volume of the Gold and Silver series!

Gold discovers what Silver's mission is and uncovers the secret identity of the Masked Man. A massive battle is about to begin in the Ilex Forest, and the Legendary Pokémon and the Pokédex holders will all be there.

In the midst of chaos, what will Gold do?!

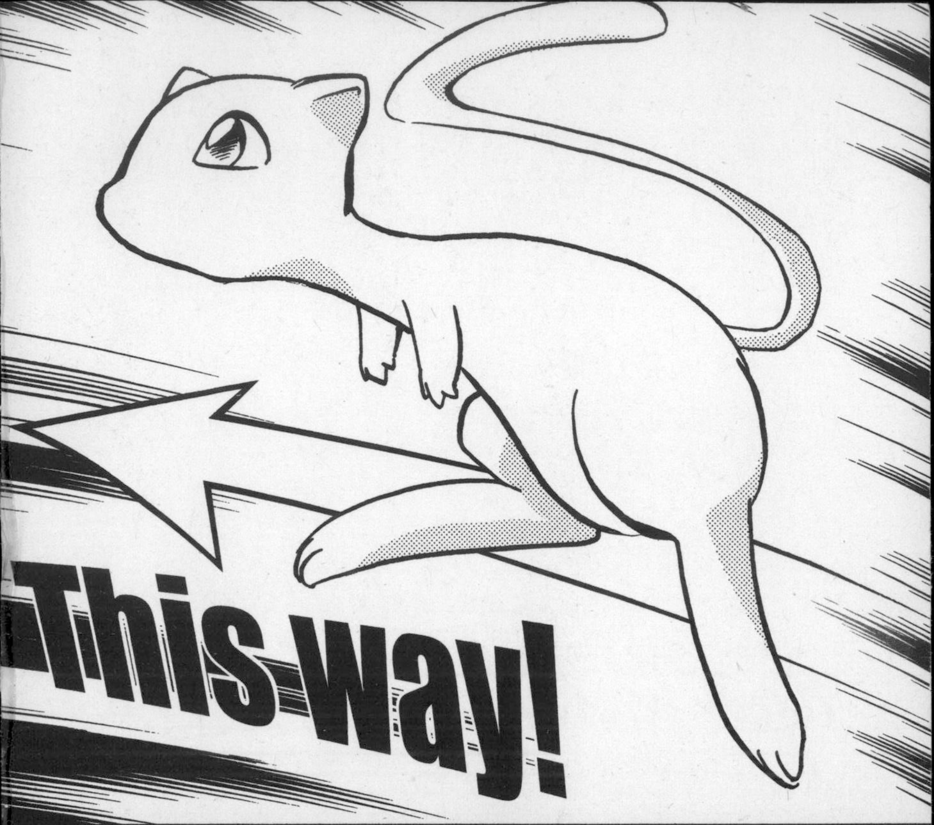
This way!

THIS IS THE END OF THIS GRAPHIC NOVEL!

To properly enjoy this VIZ Media graphic novel, please turn it around and begin reading from right to left.

This book has been printed in the original Japanese format in order to preserve the orientation of the original artwork. Have fun with it!

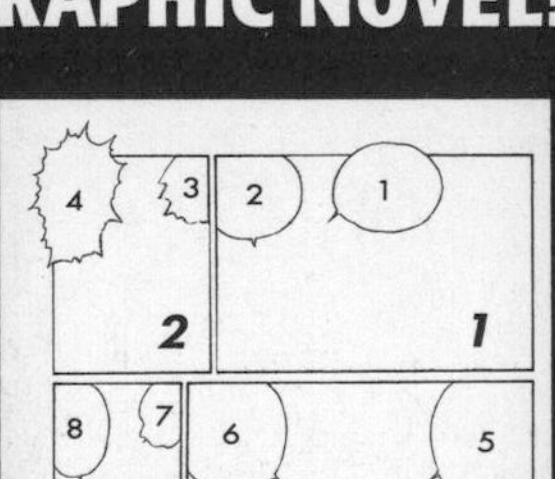
1
2
3
4
1
2
5
6
7
8
3
4
9
5
142
FOLLOW THE ACTION THIS WAY.

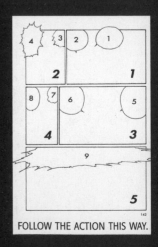